DEATH OF A CENTURY

DEATH OF A CENTURY

A Novel of the Lost Generation

Daniel Robinson

Arcade Publishing • New York

Arcade Publishing books may be purchased in bulk at special discounts for sales promotion, corporate gifts, fund-raising, or educational purposes. Special editions can also be created to specifications. For details, contact the Special Sales Department, Arcade Publishing, 307 West 36th Street, 11th Floor, New York, NY 10018 or arcade@skyhorsepublishing.com.

Arcade Publishing® is a registered trademark of Skyhorse Publishing, Inc.®, a Delaware corporation.

Visit our website at www.arcadepub.com.

10 9 8 7 6 5 4 3 2 1

Library of Congress Cataloging-in-Publication Data is available on file.

Print ISBN: 978-1-62872-755-5
Ebook ISBN: 978-1-62872-550-6

Printed in the United States of America

Acknowledgments

WHILE I CHANGED MANY FACTS CONCERNING THE SECOND Battle of the Champagne in 1915, I tried to remain true to the effects of that bloody battle on those who participated in it. World War I was an amazingly destructive war, with nearly 22,000 people dying every day during its prosecution, and my intent in this novel was to explore the effects of the war on the men in the trenches and not necessarily to present a history of its battles.

This novel could not have been written without the aid of many. Much of the research material that I used is included as chapter epigraphs. Other works include William Wiser's *The Crazy Years,* Barbara Tuchman's *The Guns of August,* John Keegan's *The First World War,* and G. J. Meyer's *A World Undone.*

I am extremely grateful to a number of people who helped in seeing this novel to print, especially my agent, Sarah Warner, and my editors at Arcade, Lilly Golden and Alexandra Hess. Much of what is good on these pages are because of their wonderful advice; all that is not so good is my fault alone. I also wish to thank all at Arcade who assisted in the creation of this book: Sara Kitchen, Catherine Kovach, and Brian Peterson. And I owe a great deal of gratitude to Ron McFarland for his expert eye.

Thanks as always to Sandra Lea and Caitlyn, who provide hope in my life, and to those whose assistance and inspiration has helped in all of my writing: Bub, Joad, Otto, Kenzie, Lucy, and eddieB.

To Glenn Robinson & Bill Prator,
who placed their lives in harm's way in service to our country.

And yesterday's *Tribune* is lost
Along with youth.

—Ernest Hemingway

Into the destructive elements immerse!

—Joseph Conrad

I

"America's present need is not heroics, but healing; not nostrums, but normalcy; not revolution, but restoration; not agitation, but adjustment; not surgery, but serenity; not the dramatic, but the dispassionate; not experiment, but equipoise; not submergence in internationality, but sustainment in triumphant nationality.... Speak it plainly, no people ever recovered from the distressing waste of war except through work and denial. . . . Let's get out of the fevered delirium of war."
—Warren G. Harding, May 14, 1920

JOE HENRY STEPPED FROM HIS HUDSON SEDAN AND PULLED UP the collar of his overcoat to protect against the evening rain mixed with icy snow and coming down in pellets. It had been snowing on the cold days and raining on the warmish days every day for two weeks, creating pools in town large enough to drown lap dogs and toddlers. Raining hard enough to send rats running for the cover of warehouse basements and alley cats scurrying after them. Keeping bums inside their canvas tents and timid children under the cover of protective awnings. Keeping smart men inside their homes with a glass of bootleg to warm them. Which is where Joe should have been instead of wandering into the night's skein of rain.

Around the back of the restaurant, Joe knocked twice on the alley door. The door to Willie's had a Judas hole the size and shape of a mail slot at about eye level. It opened. Shadowed eyes peered through the grate at Joe followed by the sounds of chains and bars being removed from the door. When it had swung fully open, Joe walked in, thanking the mute man who sat on the stool and guarded the door. He shook off his rain slicker as he walked into the room's circle of dim light. He knew Gresham would not show. Why should a man drive into town on an angry night just to talk about a book he had written? *Still,* Joe thought as he waved to Willie, *it would be bad form to not at least wait just in case.* So he sat and asked the big man behind the stick for a whiskey.

Willie, the speakeasy's owner and bartender, had arms the size of rough-hewn timbers and a thin scar a few inches up and out from his mouth that provided the appearance of a constant smile. He looked as though he would be more comfortable under the hood of an automobile or in a fighter's corner than dressed in a starched white shirt and striped tie serving illegal drinks from behind polished oak.

Willie poured a shot for Joe and placed it on the counter. "You take up drinking alone, Joe?" he asked as he leaned against the bar, a slight brogue rolling his words.

Joe smiled in return. "Looks like it. I was set to have dinner with Gresham and talk about some book of his on the war." He tilted his glass in silent toast and drank. "But the rain, you know." He nodded toward the door.

"Gresham not like to get wet?" Willie asked, smiling.

"Not especially. The rain. Memories."

"The war?" Willie's smile dissolved.

"Yes."

"He ain't the only one."

Joe nodded. Like Gresham and Willie and others who had fought in the Great War, Joe carried both an abiding sense of loss and an overwhelming memory of the climate of death.

"He in the trenches?" Willie asked as he cleaned a glass with his rag.

"Yes," Joe said.

"Where?"

"Western Front."

"Where?"

"The Somme, Passchendaele, the Champagne." Joe took another drink. "With the Brits."

Willie sighed, "Bad."

Of the several speakeasies in town, Joe preferred Willie's. Willie had been in Donovan's Irish 69th. He had been over there from Rouge Bouquet through the Argonne. He knew the stories and the lies, and he knew enough truths to not pretend to know any more.

Willie pushed himself from the bar, tossed his rag over a shoulder, and went to wait on a couple of college kids fresh from the rain. Joe watched them shake out their coats and giggle at the drops wetting the wood floor. The young man, his hair black and slick from cream, wanted to look like an Oxford man but fell several levels short. The woman's laugh sounded like cheap change. Joe watched them for a few minutes then turned his attention back to the last of his whiskey. He paused, picked up his glass, and drank all but a single mouthful, then raised the glass to inspect the amber liquid in the light.

Finishing his first whiskey in silence, Joe watched in the mirror the few people who had braved the rain to come in for a drink. None was Gresham. Pulling from his shirt pocket a notebook and fountain pen, he wrote a short note to Gresham in case the man arrived later in the night, after Joe had slid himself between cold sheets.

"His book about the war?" Willie asked as he placed a second whiskey in front of Joe.

Joe took the whiskey and tilted it. "To the Lost," he said this time and closed his eyes for a moment, then drank. "I think so," he said, answering Willie's question. "He never told me, but I think it's about the Champagne."

Willie shook his head. "Bad," he muttered again.

"Worse than most," Joe agreed, "and most were bad enough."

Willie did not at first reply, but following a breath he asked, "It going to be one of those with maps and arrows, a lot of numbers? Those are the ones I like, the ones with maps. I never knew where the hell I was over there until I got me a book about the war that had maps and arrows. Them writers don't know a damn thing about what it was like over there, I already know that, but at least they can show me where I was. They set everything down in black and white, clear as gin. That I like." To emphasize his point, Willie tapped his finger against the top of the oak bar illustrating the importance to him of seeing things in some material and tangible form. Then he strolled down the bar, a man in control of his universe, no matter how small it may be.

A woman as alone as Joe and wearing a dress the green of pool table felt slid over a seat to be next to Joe. "You looking for company tonight?" she asked, her voice husky from drink and smoke.

He looked at her and saw that at one time she had been beautiful. However, like any rose at end of season, what was left of her beauty was remnant. She had dark circles under her eyes. Her lips were poorly painted and her dye job was new. Her skin was dry and wrinkled from a life lived on the lip of a bottle.

Joe smiled and said, "No. Not tonight."

She nodded, almost a shrug. She knew. She said, "I don't have what you're looking for."

"I didn't say that."

"You don't have to. I know."

Joe took a sip of his whiskey and let it slide down warm and comforting. "What do you know?"

She lit her own cigarette, blowing a breath of smoke toward the ceiling to join the decades-old haze of cigarette smoke already there. "I know you need something you lost a long time ago." Another drag. "Love maybe. That I don't know."

"What makes—"

She cut him off, "Because that's what I need. Only I'll settle for a lot less."

He nodded and she winked at him. "See you around sometime, maybe?" she asked.

"Maybe," Joe nodded.

She slid back over a seat and looked down at her drink on the bar between her elbows like a seer reading leaves. Only she couldn't see any futures. She saw what any lonely person sees when they look into a half-empty glass of whiskey. . . . She saw the ruins of her life and heard only the inaudible voice of the past.

Like so many other young men who had gone to the trenches of the world war, Joe knew well those same sights and sounds of loss.

He stood and tossed silver coins on the bar. He nodded toward the fallen woman for Willie to bring her another round. Willie understood.

Holding the note outstretched toward Willie, he said, "Give this to Gresham if he comes in tonight."

Willie nodded and put the note in his shirt pocket.

"I'm heading home for a good night's sleep," Joe added as a pleasantry, for he never got a good night's sleep. Not since the war.

"I could use one of them myself." Willie reached to retrieve the silver then raised his hand for Joe to listen, "Matter of fact, there were these Frenchies in last night looking for Gresham. Said they were friends of his."

"How'd they know to come here?"

"Beats the hell out of me." He rubbed the stubble of his chin. "They said they had a present for him from a friend in France, a book by some Joyce woman. I told'm I didn't know where he lived and they left. Said they'd check at the newspaper later."

Someone called from down the bar and Willie walked away to draw a beer for another customer. Joe pushed himself from the counter. He might just drive out to where Gresham lived outside of town. The short drive in the sleet was better than staring at plaster cracks in his bedroom ceiling.

The young collegiates were leaned into each other ignoring the rest of the world. Joe remembered once being something like that. That time seemed long in his past, before everything went all to hell in his life. A lot can be lost in the span of a handful of years.

As he walked past their table, he could hear the man singing into the woman's ear, "*I am the Sheik of Araby / Your love belongs to me / At night when you're asleep / into your tent I'll creep.*"

The woman giggled her giggle and leaned her breast into the man's arm.

"Take care, Joe," Willie called from behind the counter.

"Will do," Joe said, waving. "You do the same."

Willie tilted his head as to say, "What else?" Willie had once told Joe that he had never gotten over the war but he had gotten past it by concentrating on simple things—properly brewing a pot of strong coffee, pouring a drink just right, tying a fly that catches a good fish. That helped, he said, because it was immediate and allowed nothing else and there was a right and a wrong and nothing else. And nothing hidden.

Joe drove his Hudson toward Gresham's home south of town, moving through the night with the sky and darkness pressing around him. He drove into the slanting rain, his headlights pinching shallow holes in the night, and felt as though he had been transported back in time. The sleeted rain beat against the roof of his automobile, thrumming a devil's tattoo causing him to miss the turn to Gresham's home.

Joe cursed himself when he realized his mistake and drove on to find the next available place to turn around. He knew, though, that roads engineered in the previous century for horse and wagon traffic were lucky to be paved, much less wide enough for a turnabout.

A dozen miles down the road, he spotted a number of car lights. Drawing closer, he saw the spotlights of police and ambulance pointing into the brush alongside the road like the jacklights of poaching hunters. He pulled in behind them and parked. Keeping his coat collar up and his fedora low over his ears, he walked to the first policeman he saw, a tall man in yellow rain slicker.

"What happened?" he asked the officer huddled into himself under the long slicker.

The officer lifted his head just enough to look through a curtain of water drops. "Who're you?"

"Joe Henry." When that brought nothing more than a blank stare, Joe added, "Reporter at the *Beacon*."

The officer ignored Joe and turned into the wind-driven rain, cupped his hands and yelled, "Hey, Sheriff, you got a reporter here. Henry something."

"Joe Henry."

"What?"

"Joe. Joe Henry."

"Yeah." The officer turned his back on Joe and walked away, cupping his hands around a cigarette to light it but the rain kept drowning the match. He unrolled the paper and dropped the tobacco between his lower lip and gum.

Joe looked in at the wreck. The car had come to rest on its side after rolling once, the top tilted like a man's hat tilted over one eye, and a couple of bodies on the ground with a gaggle of people walking around the scene. Wet snow had accumulated in patches on bushes, but everywhere else, where the car had rolled and where the sheriff's people had walked was a muddy mire.

A short man made even shorter by his heavy yellow slicker approached Joe on the shoulder of the road. The man wiped his face with his wet hands and spat fully on the ground. He worked a chew over in his mouth like a masticating bull, spat again, then said, "Hello, Joe. What brings you out here? Can't be this. We ain't had time to report it yet, so's nobody could have told you."

"I was driving out to see Wynton Gresham."

Sheriff Jackson stepped one pace closer and looked over Joe's shoulder, down the long dark road in the direction of the turn off to Gresham's home that Joe had driven past.

Joe read his mind. "Missed the road," he said. "I was looking for a place to turn around. What happened here?"

The sheriff looked over his shoulder at the yellow-lit scene. "Accident," he said. Turning back to Joe, he asked, "Why do you smell like whiskey?"

Joe shrugged. "Throat lozenge."

"Throat lozenge." Sheriff Jackson nodded.

Joe nodded toward the wreck spread along the borrow ditch. "What's the story?"

"The story is just what I told you, an accident. People driving like bats out of hell on slick road top."

"That's it? No names?"

The sheriff smiled and spat again. He rubbed the brown spittle into the rain soaked dirt with the sole of his boot. "A couple of Frogs couldn't keep to the road and killed themselves in a car accident."

"Frogs?"

"Frenchies. Frenchmen. Hell, Joe, didn't you learn nothing when you were over there?" He paused to scratch the back of his neck. "Don't know why they'd be driving around here in the middle of the night though."

"You sure they're French?"

"Wee-wee, moan amee. French as fries. They have papers and boat tickets and letters, all in French, and they have French passports. I haven't checked all their pockets, but I'd say that about makes them Frenchmen, wouldn't you?"

Through a curtain of water dripping off the lip of his hat, Joe looked at the sheriff who looked back at Joe through dark and thin eyeslits that showed Joe just how displeased the sheriff was at having to venture out that night from the comfort of his home. He'd probably already kicked off his boots and had sat in front of his fireplace, sleepy from dinner and holding a glass of confiscated hooch in his hand, when the call had come in about a road accident. He had to leave that hearthstone, don his slicker and overboots, and return to the slush and rain of the night.

Joe retrieved his notebook and fountain pen from his shirt pocket and wrote down the specifics of the accident. He huddled over the notebook like a hunchback as he wrote, asking a question and writing the sheriff's answer before asking another. The sheriff waited patiently between questions, sometimes watching his men clear the accident area and sometimes spitting and watching Joe write.

At night, Joe dreamed too much for restful sleep. And the images he dreamed, the memories conjured, were as etched by acid to the point where he sometimes woke wondering whether the world was his. Writing this story would give him purpose while he held off sleep. Better than walking the walls.

After visiting Gresham he would drive home and spend a while with his bottle of bathtub as he drafted the story. In the morning he could call in about the accident, tell Fleming, his city editor, that he would write the story before coming in to the office. Then he could relax for an extra hour over another cup of coffee. Around noon, he'd just waltz into the day room with the completed copy. Simple stuff, he thought, like living life as though it were mapped— fill a white page with black letters, tell the facts. Like watching the world go by from an upstairs window.

He scribbled what he learned from the sheriff—who the victims were, the approximate time of day, the make of the vehicle. He added a few quick notes from what he could see in the dark and hollow night. He considered walking through the mud and wet grass to where the dead men lay but he knew enough of how men looked when they died violently that he could write that himself. It was a memory that visited him with the regularity of a wound clock.

The ambulance drivers hauled two filled gurneys to the road, humped and swaddled bodies of the dead. Under those rainwet blankets, they no longer looked like the shapes of men. Covered with gray blankets, they became something else, bags of sand. He would not write that in his story, he thought as he turned to leave.

The rain, steady and loud, feathered rivulets of water down his windshield as he sat in his automobile. With eyes closed, he pressed hard on the bridge of his nose with the palm of his hand. That was what his life had become—questions and answers. Reporter's questions that elicited the facts but few of the truths. They were easy to ask. No abstracts, no complications, no immersions. Since his return from the war, he had become an observer of life. That was safe.

His stories answered the five questions with the dispassion of an atomist, viewing the particles of life with scientific reserve. Never truly opening that Pandora's Box of "Why?" Never delving deep into the visceral reasons behind beatings and murders or slit throats or rapes or suicides. Oftentimes not even using those words, using instead euphemisms—"Unlawful Familiarity" instead of "Rape" in order not to offend the readers while in the comfort of their Morris chairs. But, he sometimes thought, deep in the night when he turned his jaded eye upon himself, that lack of emotional honesty helped keep him from having to venture back into the sight of the world's destructions, kept him from venturing into those lightless corners of life. Still, every soulless story left him increasingly more unable to sleep at night, more unable even to breathe—as though a hemp rope were being drawn ever more taut around his chest.

Sometimes he felt lost in the America he had returned to. An America that valued normalcy and serenity at the expense of ideals and passions. America had even elected a president in Harding who had campaigned on the bland promises of blindness and forgetfulness.

Joe watched the sheriff carry a shoebox into the rain-washed light of a car. The contents spilled when he pulled open the box and hundreds of pages of unbound paper dropped to the mud to be caught by the rain and turned into mulch. The sheriff tossed the empty box into his car and stooped to pick up a few pages, wet and limp. He looked at them and then he looked toward Joe in his car. He opened his slicker to pocket the pages then turned to the gurneyed men, not yet slid into the ambulance, to rummage through their pockets. Joe started his car, got it turned around, and drove off. In his rearview mirror, he could see the sheriff, backlit and silhouetted, step into the road to again watch him. Joe was not a paranoid man but he did not like the receding look of that attention.

Joe had not been afraid of the dark as a child when, in those young years, the sable darkness meant adventure and mystery in the hills and arroyos near his family's ranch near Terceo, Colorado, along the New Mexico border. Since then, however, the mysteries of night had pitched into a hard and fearful darkness. His father had died as a purple twilight deepened into night in what was called an accident. His mother died bedridden in convulsed sorrows ten years later, although her life had ended with her husband's. Joe had then lost the last of his remaining youth in the trenches of the Great War where even daytime lacked light.

Joe turned onto Gresham's driveway and followed inside another set of tire tracks, sliding within their miry ruts. The two-story brick house sat tucked a hundred yards off the road and hidden by a copse. The darkness cast from rain and night and overhanging trees was palpable. Joe felt himself push on the accelerator to drive a little faster until he saw the dirty brick bungalow, weather-beaten and not much larger than the outbuilding Gresham called his garage. The bungalow was dark other than a muted light behind the curtains of the front room window, and Joe thought that Gresham might be reading.

He pictured his friend sitting under the yellow light of an electric floor lamp with a whiskey in one hand and a book held open by the other, a robe loose around his pajamas and a pipe dying in the ash tray.

He parked in front of the house and ran up the steps to the porch. Slapping rain from his fedora, he knocked on the front door.

No answer. He knocked again. He tried the doorknob and opened the unlocked door.

"Gresham?" he called.

No answer except for the drumming of a mantel clock.

He stepped into the entryway, its floor planks stained dark and wet from others who had stood there earlier in the night and not all that long ago. He called for Gresham again, louder. Again there was no response. A sober pencil of light bored into the darkness of the hallway from the front room.

Joe smiled. More than once, he had found Gresham slack-mouthed and snoring off a drunk.

The hallway runner had been pushed aside and left rumpled, not at all like Joe knew Gresham to keep his home. Gresham had kept his corners of the world ordered, his kitchen clean. Joe felt his body tighten and considered leaving the house to retrieve the sheriff. A childish thought. He called up the stairs toward Gresham's bedroom. No response. He stepped into the lighted front room and found Gresham lying on the sofa, an arm hanging leisurely to the floor and another up over his head. Gresham wore his shirt and tie, still knotted from work, with his suit coat slung over the back of the desk chair. Two blackened circles of blood stained the man's white shirt.

He was used to finding Gresham passed-out dead drunk, but this time Gresham was just dead.

Joe stifled a cough and stood silently for a half-dozen seconds which filled with an increasing roar. He felt a spectator in Gresham's life just as he had felt following his own wounding during the war when he had felt a spectator to his own life.

He knew there was no use in it but he checked for breath and the distant beat of the man's heart. He knelt close to Gresham's body and listened. The remnants of the rain that had ceased continued to tap a code as it dripped from the roof of the house, knocking against a pail or something else metallic and empty. The mantel clock sounded its steady rhythm before tolling the hour with nine hollow peals. Nothing else.

He stood on unsteady legs and went to the front door to look through the window into the dark night. Voltaic wires of lightning illuminated gray processionals of rain-laden clouds. He remembered the double set of tire tracks he had driven inside of to get to the house. He thought for a moment to have a look at the tracks but realized that they would have been destroyed by the rain and by his own tires sloughing through the mud.

Back in the front room, he glanced again at his friend lying on the sofa. Except for the two black holes in the man's chest, he might have been sleeping. Joe touched the blood. It had stopped flowing and had begun to dry blackened and viscid. He wiped his bloodied fingers on his trousers and touched his friend's forehead. A trace of warmth remained but that little heat was remnant and draining from the body to join whatever else had already left it.

He looked around the room. Nothing was terribly disturbed, no tables up-ended or desk drawers spilled, although one had been left open. All of the electric floor lamps had been left upright, two turned off. The light above the sofa where Gresham lay tossed a yellow oval across the room. The cushions of chairs were left untouched. A whiskey glass was on the desk, mostly full with ice remnants drifting in the amber liquid. Another glass of whiskey, nearly emptied, sat on the end table near Gresham's head. Joe considered numbing himself with the contents of the full tumbler but then thought better of it.

Also on the end table were a notepad and pen. Gresham was a devoted taker of notes, keeping paper and notepads in pockets and on tables for moments of need or desire as some people keep Bibles. The top page of the pad showed the ghosted indentations of the previous page's notes, but there were no pencil scribblings.

A copy of Joyce's *Ulysses*, which Gresham had told Joe he was expecting from a friend in France, lay on the table next to the whiskey glass. A brown paper wrapping from a bookstore in Paris lay crumpled on the floor near the cupped fingers of Gresham's empty hand.

Not a thing in the room appeared wrong. Except the dead man.

Joe looked at the novel, remembering that Gresham had mentioned that because of its questionable, even pornographic, nature, the book needed to be delivered by hand and not posted through the mail. A friend of a friend happened to be passing through town with a copy smuggled and well-wrapped.

Joe walked down the hall and into the kitchen. Nothing but an empty table and uncluttered counters and shelves. One set of unwashed dishes neatly stacked in the sink. The yellowed remains of eggs mixed with toast crumbs on the plate. The pulp from orange juice clung to the sides of a glass.

Joe went upstairs to the bedrooms there, musty and dark. In an extra room were ordered and random piles of books and wooden boxes and magazines and old furniture with broken legs or fallen-through cane seats. All carried a thin film of dust and cobwebs.

He scanned the titles. Unlike the downstairs bookcases, which Joe had thumbed across at times while Gresham poured second and third tumblers of drink, the books in the upstairs room were from another age. Those downstairs were decidedly more modern, an uncertain term that Joe had recently been introduced to as the world had become "thoroughly modern," works by Eliot and Lewis and Tarkington and Dos Passos and Millay. Gresham also kept a number of histories of the war in his study, the compendious volumes by Colliers and the *London Times* and works by Hayes and Benedict and Vast and others.

But in that upstairs room, as though castoffs, were older books by older authors from a different century. From what often felt like a completely different world. He looked at the faded spines of Dickens and Coleridge and Wordsworth and Cooper and Hawthorne.

Down the hall, he paused for a moment outside Gresham's bedroom, feeling somehow immoral about entering and looking over a dead man's most personal property. He opened the door and, still holding the doorknob, leaned slowly into the room. He flicked on the light switch. The room unfolded its lack of secrets. A made bed, a pressed shirt and suit lying atop the coverlet, an empty glass on the side table, a worn chair. A place for everything and everything in its place.

He heard a car come to a stop outside in the muddy driveway, thought of turning off the light but left it on, and descended the stairs in time to greet the opening door. Even though the rain outside had stopped, rainwater dripped from the sheriff's slicker onto the wood floor of the entry and his breath plumed like that of a sailor in from the tempest.

Joe opened his mouth to speak, but before he could utter a word, the sheriff said, "Found this in one of the dead frog's coat pockets." He reached an opened hand toward Joe. Folded in the man's palm was a single piece of paper. Joe unfolded the paper. At the top was Gresham's name, below that the name of the newspaper with its address and telephone, and below that, in different ink but the same script, the address and phone number of Gresham's home. The ink was black. The script was ornate and masculine, long sweeping letters like the calligraphic penmanship of a monk and not at all like his own quill driving.

The sheriff took the paper from Joe's fingers. "Now why would he have this?" he asked slowly. He stared pointedly at Joe and flexed his brows.

"No idea," Joe said. He found himself on the answering end of the questions of fact; however, the questions carried an undercurrent of distrust in the sheriff's tone.

"You upstairs?" the sheriff asked.

"Yes."

"I see, and where is the owner of the house? Upstairs also?"

Joe looked toward the front room entry and said, "No." He paused, his mouth foul and warm. "He's in the next room. Dead."

The sheriff blinked but did not move. His eyebrows tightened further as he studied Joe, then he stepped forward and closed the door behind him. "How long before you were going to tell me this, Joe?"

"I just did, Sheriff."

"I see. Only it took you a good while to get around to this bit of news."

"What're you getting at, Sheriff?" The sheriff had suspicions. Joe didn't know what they were, but he knew Jackson wasn't showing his hole card.

"I'm not getting at nothing, Joe," Jackson said slowly, his voice thick. "You just happened to mention it like it wasn't nothin' too important or it was somethin' you'd just as soon I didn't know."

Joe shook his head. "Nothing like that."

"Maybe not, but right this minute I think I'll have a see to this dead man." He stepped past Joe, took two steps toward the front room before turning and speaking to Joe over his shoulder, "You stay right there."

"Like you'd let me go," Joe said.

The sheriff let it ride and walked on into the front room.

Joe leaned against the banister and closed his eyes. With the meat of his palms, he pushed against his closed eyes making himself see white flashes like Very flares on the inside of his eyelids. He heard as through cotton wadding. The air in the room smelled sharp and electric.

He heard dead men and saw dead men. Flayed breathing just before death. Wailed expirations of life. Eyes curled back into their heads and mouths wide, exposing tongues grotesque and huge. A fog of poisoned gas wrapping around the dying body like a winding-sheet until only soft eddies in the chemical fog remained from the body's last convulsive movements.

He remembered something Gresham had once said about the dead, that years don't remove them from place or memory, that hard rains can't wash them away. Like the stories old men tell of war and of slaughter, the memories of death have no end. They become as part of a man's being, etched upon his soul. Those memories of dead men remain. As do sometimes the dead men themselves.

From the front room, Joe heard the sheriff exhale loudly, "He's dead, all right."

"No shit," Joe whispered just loud enough for himself to hear.

The sheriff walked back to stand in front of Joe, rubbed his hands vigorously and pushed them deep inside the pockets of his slicker. He looked at Joe and nodded back toward the front room. "Damn, Joe, but dead bodies are beginning to pile up tonight. Only this one's been murdered."

Joe straightened and frowned at the sheriff. In his tunnel vision he saw only his friend's body lain out in the next room.

The sheriff continued, speaking in a monotone, "Funny that you should arrive at the other accident scene and now I find you here with a murdered friend. Even funnier that those Frenchies had your friend's name and address on their person." He sighed and spoke loudly and specifically to Joe. "If I believed in coincidences, which I definitely do not, I'd think you were just unlucky. But like I said, I don't believe in coincidences."

Joe sighed into his hands. "I can only tell you what I know."

"What is it you know, Joe?"

"Not much," he said. "I got here just a couple of minutes before you. You see what I saw."

"I see. Where's the telephone in this house," said the sheriff as he looked around the entry.

"Front room." Joe pointed without looking. "On the desk across from the sofa."

"You mean across from the sofa on which lies your friend who just happens to be a dead man?"

"Yes," Joe nodded still looking down at the floor. He didn't like the flow the conversation had taken.

The sheriff opened the door to call in his deputy and told him to look around the front room. Like an afterthought, he said to Joe, "You seem to know this house pretty good."

"He was my friend."

"I see. You and him were partners, huh? Good friends?"

"Yes." Joe did not feel like elaborating. He wasn't kidding when he added, "Like brothers," for they had been brothers in blood spilled on distant fields. Neither he nor Gresham had any remaining family, so their friendship had deepened when each had discovered someone whose experiences were similar enough that they could talk about them to each other. It was a shared bond in a fraternity that few belonged, one forged in the foundry of the Great War.

The sheriff nodded. He pushed the tobacco wad from right cheek to left, but said nothing. He sighed and walked back to where Gresham was.

Joe watched the sheriff's back lit by the electric light in the ceiling and wondered what had taken place. Murder, he knew. The Frenchmen in the accident were probably the murderers. That left a litany of questions. One of which was typeset in capital letters:

"WHY?" Following close on that question were how he had the bad luck to find himself embroiled in the mess and then how to convince the sheriff that he had nothing to do either with the Frenchmen's or with Gresham's deaths.

"Damn," he said, rubbing his eyes with the palms of his hands. He tried remembering the Hail Mary, but could not finish, for he was certain that since the war such prayers were no longer answered. He could hear the sounds of furniture being roughly pushed aside and drawers opened and papers shuffled. The sounds of unwelcome men rifling through the life of a lost soul.

After his telephone call, the sheriff returned. He said, his voice flat, "Okay, Joe, tell me everything. Take it from the top. The whole night."

Joe told the sheriff what little he knew, about the tire tracks in the driveway and about finding the door closed but unlocked. He told the sheriff about missing dinner with Gresham and about driving out to talk with him, about how he thought Gresham had simply decided against driving into town in the rain for their dinner meeting. He told the sheriff about passing the driveway and coming onto the accident.

He talked in flat and unexaggerated tones befitting the reliance of facts.

The sheriff listened without interrupting and without taking notes. He stood across from Joe with rain water continuing to drip from his slicker as he rocked from foot to foot, the wad of tobacco rolling inside his left cheek. His hands remained on his hips.

After Joe finished, the sheriff asked, "How come you were upstairs after you found Gresham dead down here? Looking for something?"

Joe shook his head and said, "I thought whoever had killed Gresham might still be in the house. I checked the rooms."

The sheriff nodded, but his nod lacked conviction. "Why didn't you call my office and report this? They didn't hear nothing from you."

"I wanted to be certain that I was alone. I didn't want somebody drilling me as well."

"I see."

"I wasn't here that long before you arrived—"

"No," the sheriff said and paused as he moved the tobacco to his other cheek. "That's true, but. . . ." He left his thought hanging.

Joe could hear the indictment that flowed through the sheriff's pause. He could envision the noose of that hanging silence strung around his neck.

Within the hour, three more of the sheriff's deputies arrived, yawning and scratching their bellies and not at all pleased at having been called from a warm bed into a rainy night. They searched Joe's car and the house while the sheriff and Joe remained in the silent entryway. He again heard the slide of desk drawers and the scoot of furniture across bare wood. Each deputy eventually reported that he could find nothing extraordinary other than a dead man and a rumpled rug. The opened desk drawer had not been ransacked. The whisky in the glasses was Scotch, real Scotch, good Scotch whisky from the spirit stills of Macallan. Nothing bathtub about it.

The sheriff kept his eyes turned on Joe as the last officer explained about the drawer and whiskey glasses. Joe recognized the sheriff's understanding that Gresham had quite obviously known his killers.

"Two glasses of Scotch?"

"Yessir," answered the same officer Joe had talked with at the accident scene.

"Two?"

"Yessir. One drunk by the dead guy in there." He pointed over his shoulder toward the front room. "And the killer or one of the killers drunk part of the other." Both the sheriff and his underling looked at Joe.

Joe shook his head. It's one thing to dig your own damn hole; it's quite another to just stumble into an already excavated pit.

The sheriff stepped closer, uncomfortably close. Slowly leaning in toward Joe and looking him hard in the eyes.

"Where you been tonight before you came here, before I saw you at that accident?" he asked.

"At home. Then at the restaurant where I was meeting Gresham."

"You been drinking?"

"What do you think?"

"I think your breath smells like Scotch, or something like it. Same as in them glasses on the desk."

Joe said nothing. The sheriff was tossing a bone with a string attached. Any bite from Joe and the sheriff would yank. With nothing to hide, anything he said seemed to incriminate him, so he stood straight and met the sheriff's stare.

The sheriff sucked a breath through his teeth then said to Joe, "I like you, Joe, and I really hope you've got nothing to do with all this." He nodded toward the room where Gresham lay, but he also meant the Frenchmen. He sighed before continuing, "I've never had any trouble with you other than your drinking down at Willie's. I suppose that's where you were?"

Joe nodded. "That's where I was."

The sheriff nodded. The movement of his head was long and slow. All the while he kept his eyes on Joe as though he were in a debate with himself. He finished nodding and said, "You keep in touch."

"I'll be around," Joe said as he backed a step away from the sheriff.

He walked from the house. Squinting into the darkness ahead of him, he looked to the starless and moonless ceiling of night. Hard on his back, he felt the sheriff's eyes as he rounded the car. He felt as though a crosshairs had been laid upon him. He forced himself to walk slowly.

Driving back to his apartment, he first thought through the circumstances of the night, a night that had left him unsteady and uncertain. Slowly, however, he came to the realization of loss. A man, a man who might have been his best friend, had died. A man who was certainly the only person with whom Joe had ever discussed the war and a man who had shared memories of the world turned wrong. All warmth had been lost in the night and the rain had fully turned to snow, a wet snow that came down in flakes the size of quarters. The hard snow on the hood and windshield of his automobile and the car's whisk on the wet road fused in a background dirge to his lonely drive home.

In his apartment, Joe stripped and showered. He soaped and scrubbed himself vigorously as though the act of washing himself would cleanse him of both mud and memory. He brushed his teeth and stood naked in front of the mirror watching his hands shake with that involuntary palsy of an old man. He was not an old man. But he had seen what only old men should see, and he would never be young again.

Four years earlier, lying wounded in the mud of the Argonne Forest in Eastern France, Joe had fully understood both fear and mortality. Having woken from the morning roar of a mortar attack, he had been certain of his own death in the way a man is certain of little else. He was certain that he would die or that he had already died, for he felt no pain. With the return of his senses and the onset of his pain, however, he knew that he was alive, bleeding, and covered in the blood and body parts of other men. After that day, he would taste his own fear and sense his own mortality many times, returning time and again to the lessons of his lost youth as he woke from his dream in the middle of a barren sleep. The death of Gresham replayed his own wounding as well as deaths he had seen and even caused.

After hanging his wet clothes from the rod for the shower curtain, he poured himself a tumbler of bathtub whiskey in the kitchen and walked to his bedroom. He sat on the bed and cut the evening with a heavy drink and watched the rainwet snow on his window.

He finished the whiskey and fell into restless sleep. His dreams cowled the night, never allowing him that comfort of rest. He had dreams of dead men rising from a muddy barrens and he woke at three in the morning with the rain tapping a hard rhythm against his window.

II

"Hell holds no horrors for one who has seen that battlefield. Could Dante have walked beside me across that dreadful place, which had been transformed by human agency from a peaceful countryside to a garbage heap, a cesspool, and a charnel-house combined, he would never have written his Inferno, because the hell of his imagination would have seemed colourless and tame. The difficulty in writing about it is that people will not believe me. I shall be accused of imagination and exaggeration, whereas the truth is that no one could imagine, much less exaggerate, the horrors that I saw upon those rolling, chalky plains."
—E. Alexander Powell, *Vive la France*, 1916
★Describing the First Battle of the Champagne★

HE LAY WITHOUT SLEEP. WELL BEFORE THE SUN WOULD RISE, HE continued to trace the cracks and shadows of his ceiling, intermittent light cast from the neon sign of an all-night diner across the street. After an hour of searching for the cool spots in his bed, he got up and walked the walls of his apartment. Another hour later, he poured his third cup of coffee. At ten minutes past six, the telephone rang.

"Joe." It was Fleming, his editor at the *Beacon*, a man with a loud and gravelly voice much larger than his actual stature.

"Yes." Joe leaned forward, his cup of coffee on the kitchen table between his elbows. He waited for Fleming to continue. While he waited he rubbed his finger into the old cigarette burns on the table's Formica top. He knew what Fleming wanted. He knew what Fleming would probably ask and what Fleming would not ask.

Joe pressed the first two fingers of his free hand into his temple and rubbed, lightly at first and then harder as he listened to the protracted silence fill with his and Fleming's breathing. He had

21

hoped that with the new day, some revelation would present itself, some discovery of the sheriff's that would solve Gresham's murder. From the rigid tone of Fleming's voice, however, Joe knew that his own innocence may have been further drawn into question.

"I just talked with Sheriff Jackson," rasped Fleming's cigarette-stained voice. "What's this about Gresham?"

"He's dead," Joe sighed.

"Murdered, the sheriff told me."

"Murdered." Joe nodded his head.

"What about it?"

"I don't know any more than you do."

"The sheriff said you were there. That maybe you even had something to do with it."

Joe felt his anger rise and he spoke with heat. "What do you want me to say? Gresham was shot, killed. That's what I know, all I know."

"Ee-zee," said Fleming, and Joe had the image of Fleming raising his hands, palms outward, as though calming a young boy.

"Damn, man, I found the body," Joe said. "That's all." He continued to knead his temple, even though the pain in his head was much deeper and darker. His short outburst left him vaguely nauseous.

"So he said," Fleming said and coughed, then held a hand over the mike of his telephone and said something to another person. He spoke back into the telephone, "Jackson also asked a lot of questions, about you and Gresham. Mostly about you. He seems to think that you are involved in this somehow. You and some Frenchmen from an automobile wreck. How about that?"

"The sheriff's wrong." Joe let that sit for a moment before adding, "I have the information on the wreck, and I'll type that up this morning before coming in later."

"First thing," Fleming snapped, "and I mean first thing. As in an hour. Seven-thirty at the latest. And I'll want something on Gresham for this afternoon. You give me what you know from last night, and I'll have someone else begin working on any new angles."

Covering me, Joe thought. He hung up and read through his notes.

Nothing. Just notes. They told what had happened. As to the meanings of the events, they might as well have been written in an ancient language. He decided, then, to follow the simple patterns of his life, the patterns that he had adopted since the war. Walk a straight path, write the articles, cover the stories, hope the loose ends of his life did not hitch around his neck like a bowknot.

Joe found his notebook and pen on the dresser, a Mont Blanc, green with his initials on the side. Rolling the capped pen between thumb and fingers, he thought momentarily of the woman, still almost a girl, who had given it to him. Alice Bright, freckled nose and light brown hair always pulled back but always some having escaped to flutter in the wind. They were high school sweethearts and had promised to each other in the way that kids do. Only a few months before he was set to return from France, he had received the letter from her. She had fallen in love, deep and real love, and was marrying and she hoped that he understood and she would always remember him with fondness.

He had received the letter while on R&R in some nameless French town, and with a few days before returning to the front he slipped past the guards and went into town. His sergeant, seeing him leave, called out, "Remember, Joe, an hour with Venus brings a month with Mercury," but he did not stop Joe. Neither did Joe stop for the Padre who called to him. Religion had never been much in his life and following the deaths of his parents and the slaughterland of the war, he could not see a reason to talk with a God that allowed such things to happen. He found a French woman who could speak no English but could do other things.

As he sailed back from the war, he had come to realize how little was left for him in Terceo. His memories had become like smoke in a cracked jar, eventually emptying to nothing. He felt no pull to return to that high desert along the New Mexico border. He would one day, he knew, for there did remain a distant tug of a truth unknown.

He uncapped the pen and sat with his third cup of coffee to compose his stories, two brief articles that answered all of the questions he knew, but it was the questions he did not know that haunted him. As he wrote, he could feel himself slip into that comfortable world of absolutes that excluded any complications of life. It was a world as numbing as any drug.

Joe checked his clothes drying in the bathroom. After finding them still too wet to wear, he put on his other suit. Once the suit finally dried, he'd take it to the cleaners and get the blood off the pants. He finished his coffee. Then he rolled his copy and stuck it in the inside pocket of his overcoat and left for the *Beacon's* offices downtown.

He drove the same streets he had driven for the past three years, wet with streams of rainwater in the gutters and dark under a hovering fog. Dark buildings, wetted by the previous night's rain and snow, frowned on either side of the wet road as he drove through Greenwich. The buildings slumped together as though huddling for warmth, dark and ominous in the clouded day. He drove through the streets as though he drove through a shadowed valley.

The *Beacon* was housed in a tile building covering an entire city block and rising a half-dozen stories above the street and two below. The white tile had long ago faded gray from years of sun and rain and pigeon droppings. One corner tile, four-foot square, had broken in half sometime before Joe had first seen the building. The dark hole left after its falling looked like a vacant eye. Eleven soiled steps mounted from the sidewalk to the large double doors. The clamorous music of the streets, automobiles and streetcars and vendors, slowly faded behind those wood and glass doors as they swung closed behind Joe.

He walked up two flights of stairs to the newsroom, stopping just outside the doors to catch his breath. He could hear the steady clack of typewriters broken by loud talk and laughter. Footsteps danced across the fatigued and timeworn oak floor.

Joe opened the door and walked in. A pall fell over the room like a black curtain. Typewriters skipped a beat, loud talk muffled, laughter stopped, the dancing feet slid back against the outer walls of the room.

Nobody looked at him. That was what Joe noticed first. Some people looked his way while some waved their hands in imitation of a greeting. Even those few who waved quickly averted their eyes as though even looking at this leper might infect them. He walked through the room to the desk he had shared with Gresham and felt the blind scrutiny from everyone he passed. Heads turned and whispers swirled in his wake, rippling murmurs that placed him in the tension of having become a story. News travels fast.

He and Gresham had sat facing each other at the large double-sided desk. Gresham sat on the south with Joe the northsider. The side of the desk hugged the wall for both to pin ideas onto the bare wood. Pen lines bisected the wooden desktop at odd angles and a particularly deep line broke the plain until it fell in suicide over the desk's edge. Joe trailed the tip of his finger along its ruinous course. He hung his overcoat on the rack and stood over the desk, fingering the piles of papers and opening the drawers with the feeling that he was at someone else's desk. Everything remained not quite neat but also not messy, almost like he kept things. The stacks, however, were just off, the drawers a little more disorganized.

The door opened and the room's muted noise fell off even further. Fleming's unsteady gait approached. The man kept his office upstairs, one flight above the newsroom. Fleming likened himself as a bird of prey soaring above his hacks, but Joe had always thought of Fleming as a pigeon on the roof, ready to shit upon any writer with whom he was displeased.

Fleming would walk into the newsroom three times a day, the clockwork of a neurotic, seldom speaking during his tours but often pausing to look at individual reporters long enough to make the person nervous. That was his form of supervising, a nervous worker was a hungry worker, a hungry worker was a productive and compliant worker. Gresham was the only reporter who could not be intimidated by Fleming. Everyone knew it, especially Fleming, who avoided the desk whenever Gresham was working.

"Joe," Fleming said.

Joe turned and looked up from his seat. Fleming wore the same white shirt he may have worn the day before or the week or decade before that. Heavy suspenders held up the man's pants and made his shirt bulge like a tattered flag. He had a ruddy face and veined nose, eyes bloodshot and a cigarette hanging from the corner of his mouth with a perpetual half-inch of ash.

Joe nodded.

"You got the copy?" he asked, standing near Joe, attempting to loom over Joe.

Joe pointed to the papers he had placed on the desk.

"Mind if I take a look?" He did not wait for Joe's answer but reached over Joe's shoulder, picked up the papers and rounded the desk to sit in Gresham's chair to read while Joe watched.

Dust motes floated in the muted light that came through the window above them. Joe stood and looked out the window at the morning fog that had been trapped in the shadows of the buildings across the street and at the small birds huddled on the glazed branches of empty trees, which stood like stick-figured prisoners in sidewalk planters.

He sat again and tapped his fingers on the arms of his chair as he watched Fleming read, comforted in being able to watch someone else. That was the life he knew and had become familiar with. He watched other people. He recorded their actions and asked for their thoughts. He witnessed the remains of people's lives as though they were projected upon a screen. He preferred that, the distance and the reconstruction of the lost days and ways of other people's lives.

Fleming nodded as he read. "Good," he said. "Good. A dozen inches each? Good. I'll take 'em right down and have 'em set for this afternoon's edition."

Joe nodded.

"You okay?" Fleming asked.

"Fine as silk," Joe lied.

"Why don't you work on something else after you finish with the piece on Gresham. Maybe that road project Gresham started last week."

"Yes. Maybe that," Joe said, looking hard at Fleming and feeling himself close to losing his temper.

"Easy, Joe. I didn't mean anything by it."

Joe could see in the man's eyes all of the questions he wanted to ask, but he met Fleming's inquisitive stare with as flat a gaze as he could offer.

"No," he said. "Nobody means shit about anything. I know that."

Fleming blinked and said, "Check Gresham's desk for notes. You know him, he always kept a stack of notes."

Joe nodded. He looked at the piles on his desk and asked, "Did the police come by today?"

"Not unless they came by in the middle of the night, but I think Sheriff Jackson would have mentioned it when he called this morning. Why?"

"No reason. You don't think the sheriff'd be too upset if I went through the desk and took work notes?"

"Don't see why," Fleming answered and winked. "Work goes on after all."

For a moment, Joe thought to attack Fleming, kick his bloody ass and slap his winking face. Not for any specific reason. Just to hit someone.

Fleming walked away. While his footsteps receded into the din of hushed voices, Joe once again surveyed his desk. He could see that someone had looked through his papers. Piles had been rifled, drawers emptied and replaced. Had nothing happened to alter the flow of his day, he probably wouldn't have noticed the disturbances. He would have sat down to lay out his copy for correction or began making calls or jotting notes. But the day had been disturbed, and the disturbance had caused him to notice things not quite right.

He rounded the desk to sit in Gresham's chair. All that populated the top of that side was a black Corona #3 typewriter with a clean sheet of white paper rolled in along with carbons between three sheets of paper. Everything in triplicate for Gresham.

He pulled open the center drawer. Cheap newspaper pens and worn down number two pencils stuffed the bottom of an old cigar box, old clippings yellowed in the drawer's back, opened envelopes and read letters and undefined notes from past stories littered the drawer.

He pushed aside the cigar box of spent writing utensils. Underneath it was a sealed envelope. He looked up to see if anyone was watching. Nobody was. He turned the envelope over to find a scrap of paper gem-clipped to the envelope. On the paper was a list in Gresham's handwriting.

He bobbed his eyes once again to check the room, but those in the room looked to have filled their curiosities and to have found a rhythm in their own work. Hunched over Coronas or Remingtons or huddled in small groups discussing racing forms or how long it would take Tunney to dispose of Charlie Weinert next week in New York, laying bets in either case on a hunch or an overheard tip.

Joe slipped the paper from its clip and read the handwritten list:

Champagne—25 Sep 15
Paul Dillard
Paris—Pl St Andre d Arts

Joe took the unopened envelope out of the drawer and slid it across the desk. He read the list again. He stared at it. He knew the Champagne as one of the bloody battles that Gresham had been a part of, one that had killed twenty thousand English and French soldiers in a single morning and several hundred thousand men over a matter of weeks. That he knew, but anyone who had been in the war or had read about the war knew about the Champagne. It was discussed in London and Paris in the same hushed tones that Texans reserved for the Alamo or veterans of the Civil War reserved for Antietam or Pickett's Charge. Along with Verdun and the Somme and a dozen others from Belgium to Gallipoli, the Champagne had lived on in Europe as an example of the utter waste that was the Great War. It seemed as though every Brit knew someone whose life was shattered by the battle; the stain of blood left an etched image on the landscape of France. The death and the stench that rose from its muddy no-man's land and the supposed treachery that initiated the slaughter had inscribed that September morning in the world's unconscious.

The name and address on the paper, however, meant nothing to Joe. His next thought was that the list might extradite him from the sheriff's hard glare. Give it to Sheriff Jackson and turn from under the microscopic eye of Greenwich's constabulary. He smiled.

"Okay," he muttered as he pocketed the list. A weight lifted, he closed the middle drawer and foraged through the side drawers. No manuscript. In the bottom drawer he found an address book, which he also slid across the desk to his side.

Joe walked through the tracers of clouded light from the window above, welcoming the slight stab of warmth as he rounded his chair. Before he could sit, however, he caught the cold stare of Sheriff Jackson. The sheriff, hunched a little more than the last time Joe had seen him, was followed into the room by Bernie, the day janitor, and a uniformed police officer Joe recognized from the night before, a tall and thin man who walked as though he could fill out his undersized uniform but not his oversized self-perception.

Joe felt the sheriff's eyes lock on him and could not shake the sensation of having once again ended up at the intersection of the man's crosshairs. However, he did have the list and the address book and that might ease Jackson's concerns, so he reached to pull the list from his shirt pocket.

Driven by his own intentions, the sheriff turned and said something to Bernie, and Bernie, walking quickly to keep pace, nodded his head and said something back.

"Joe," Sheriff Jackson said in a terse and monotone voice as he stepped near. Bernie stood at the sheriff's shoulder. The uniform stepped to the side of the desk, effectively sealing in Joe. Once again, the newsroom buzz dropped off and Joe again felt the spotlight of sudden notoriety.

"Sheriff." Neither man offered a hand to the other. Sitting on the edge of his desk, Joe met the sheriff's eyes on the level. They each took a moment to gauge the other. He ran a finger along the list's paper edge.

"I'm glad you stopped by, Sheriff. I have something for you," he said and handed the piece of paper to Sheriff Jackson. "This as well," he said, lifting the address book from the desktop.

Jackson looked at them and handed them to the uniform standing next to him. The uniform huffed and handed them back to the sheriff, who pocketed the address book without a second, or even first, look.

"What is this, Joe?" the sheriff asked flashing the paper.

"I'm not sure, but it might have something to do with what happened last night." Joe had the feeling that what he saw on the piece of paper as important, the sheriff saw in a completely different light and would be more than happy to ignore it.

Joe watched Jackson finger the paper as though it were glue-paper populated with flies, and realized, not for the first time, that the sheriff was no Sherlock Holmes deducing a solution to the crime. No, Jackson was working in the opposite direction. He had his theory and only needed to fashion whatever facts necessary in order to come to his preordained answer. If he were to run across a square peg, he just needed a bigger hammer to fit it into that round hole.

"I see." The sheriff folded and pocketed the list and rubbed his eyes. He stood close to Joe, close enough for Joe to smell the man's pomade and see the tiny nick on his jawline from the morning's shave. "This the desk you shared with Gresham?" he asked, changing the subject.

Joe looked down, said, "Yes."

The sheriff nodded.

"That paper," Joe said.

"We'll get to that," Jackson said.

"For damn-sake, Sheriff," Joe said. "Look at the paper."

Jackson pursed his lips but said nothing. He pulled the paper from his pocket, unfolded it, and looked at it again. The plug of tobacco worked inside his cheek. He looked back at Joe. "What d'you want me to see?"

Joe thought to reach out and slap the man twice, palm then backhand, and say, "Open your damned eyes." But he just sighed. *The blindest of men are those who don't look,* he thought.

"The date there. That's the Champagne," Joe said, his finger pointing toward the piece of paper in the sheriff's hand. "Look in the library and read on it. And there's an address in Paris and a name. I don't know who it is, but that's the name I'd begin with."

Jackson studied the paper. He looked at the uniform standing next to him and Joe thought he might have actually winked. The uniform smirked. Jackson nodded and said, "You think I should take a visit to Paris—"

"Maybe take the missus with you," the uniform added.

Jackson's smile dissolved. "The murder happened here, and here I am." He paused, then, as though starting over, repeated, "Now, this the desk you shared with Gresham."

Joe muttered, "Two-by-fours." As in dumb as. . . .

"What?" Jackson asked. "I didn't catch your meaning."

"Nothing," Joe said. "Not a damn thing." He paused, adjusted his weight. "Yes. It's the desk we shared."

Bernie nodded his head enthusiastically. Joe liked Bernie. He was a good man, always did his job, never bothered anyone while they did theirs. Joe could not help but notice, however, how Bernie enjoyed having his presence elevated. "That's theirs," he agreed.

"Another coincidence," the sheriff said as though talking to himself, making mental notes. "Which side was his?"

"The other side," said Bernie. "He's sittin' on his. A right neat worker, that Mr. Gresham is. For all the notes and writin' he does, he don't leave a big mess like most of the rest of the room. He keeps his place clean. I always 'preciated that."

Joe smiled at Bernie offering his observations of the newsroom. He wondered what bits the man had to offer about him and the others while at home with his wife over the dinner table or at some Northside speakeasy on Saturday night.

"You been here long?" the sheriff asked Joe.

"Today or in this job?"

"Both," Jackson said, then added, "and can the sarcasm."

Joe smiled. "I've worked for the *Beacon* about three years, since I returned from France. Gresham let me have this side of his desk."

"What do you mean, 'He let you'?"

Joe shrugged. "He wasn't an easy man to get next to."

Bernie nodded as though in agreement. "Ain't that the damn truth."

"So why'd he favor you?"

"I didn't ask. He read a piece I had written on men returning from the war and he liked it, or maybe he liked the fact that I was the only other person in this room who had any notion of what he saw in the trenches. I didn't have to ask him about it, I already knew well enough. He liked that."

The uniform snorted. Joe looked the uniform up and down and shook his head. He had seen the type plenty since his return, someone who had wanted the glory of war but had been turned down for one reason or another, maybe a bad eye or maybe a boil on his butt or maybe his testicles had yet to drop, and now the uniform had to prove his manhood in another way, including the mockery of a war vet.

"You had no troubles with him?" Sheriff Jackson asked.

"Me? No. Everybody argued with Gresham, me no more than anyone else."

"What did you argue about?"

"Copy mostly. Gresham was a perfectionist. He would comment on my previous day's work. I appreciated his interest, if not always his honesty, but I learned a lot from him."

"I see," the sheriff said. Joe felt like saying that the sheriff saw a lot for a blind man.

The sheriff took a moment to look around at the faces trying hard not to look back at him.

The uniform stepped around the sheriff and removed a framed photograph from the wall as though it were his. After glance at the image, he placed it face up on the desk. He stepped back to keep the symmetry of the odd circle complete, blocking any escape attempt.

The sheriff sighed. "Back to my question. You been here long . . . today?"

Joe put his chin to his chest and smiled and shook his head. He raised his head and said, "Not long. Less than an hour, I'd say. Why?"

"Just asking." The sheriff took a leather pouch from his back pocket, opened it and added a two-fingered pinch of tobacco to the masticated wad already stretching his cheek.

Joe asked, "Did you already go through my desk?"

The sheriff stopped his action and looked at Joe from the corner of his eye, a furrowed line across his forehead. "Why?"

"Just asking."

"No," Bernie interrupted. He stepped closer. "It weren't the sheriff. Least not according to Francis." He looked at the sheriff. "That's the night janitor. He said some guy come 'round early last night askin' for Mr. Gresham's desk but he coun't hardly understan' the fella'. Francis said this guy said he was a cop, policeman, and he just pointed him over here and the guy comes over and picks around for a few minutes in Mr. Henry's desk here but din't take nothin'."

"Probably one of the Frenchmen you found in the accident," Joe added.

The other three men looked at Joe as though he were speaking some foreign tongue unknown in their world.

"I see," said the sheriff to Bernie, wiping a piece of tobacco from his lip.

Jackson scratched his head and suppressed a yawn and looked at Joe. "You haven't been picking around in Gresham's desk this morning, have you, Joe?"

Joe said, "Yes, and I found the list—"

Before he could finish, Sheriff Jackson waved him off and said, "So you've been rutting around. And you just happen to find this paper."

"Listen, Sheriff—"

"No," Jackson said, cutting Joe short. He pointed a finger at Joe's face. "You listen here. I just talked with Gresham's lawyer today and had me a look at Gresham's will. You know what it said?"

Joe said nothing.

The sheriff drew a breath. "He left his worldly goods to you. Now why is that?"

Joe closed his mouth. "I don't know, Sheriff. He didn't have any family and—"

The sheriff cut him off once again, "And ain't it just another coincidence. Those coincidences just keep building up around you, don't they?"

"Like a high gallows," the uniformed offered.

"Maybe he knew his life was in danger and—"

"Maybe shit," the uniform laughed. "His life was most definitely in danger." He laughed again.

The four men waited through a silence, an uncomfortable silence like that which follows a single bullet shot. The uniform lifted the photograph he had taken from the wall. "This you?" he asked.

Joe looked at the photograph held loosely in the man's stubby fingers, a photograph of Joe standing alone amid a rubble of stones. Silhouetting Joe in the photograph were the skeletal remains of a church's empty and ruined windows held within a blackened and truncated wall. The sky behind was hazy and indistinct. Joe remembered that the photograph did not capture the tears that had welled over in his eyes.

"Yes," Joe said. "That's me."

"Pretty." The uniform placed the photograph on the desk and smiled down at Joe. All Joe could think of was that here stood a man whose only importance in life was inside the confines of his own small brain.

The uniform held a crooked smile on his face and asked, "You guys have a lot of time to take pretty pictures *over there*?" He stressed the last two words with heavy sarcasm.

Joe looked at him long enough to force him to divert his eyes. Joe said, "Yes. It was like a festival over there. Everyday a holiday; every meal a picnic."

He looked at the photograph with its fold marks and creases and torn edges. He remembered how the war was brought home through camera work; mostly, though, and especially in the beginnings, the camera had lied, telling the story only politicians and generals wanted told and mothers wanted to hear. The French and English had been first to use photography as propaganda. Early on in 1914, they had dedicated photography units to chronicle life in the trenches. Let those back home see that their loved ones in the front lines were well off. When the American doughboys arrived, special units of the Signal Corps accompanied them, clicking their cameras to record haircuts, hot meals, clothes-washing days, and mail delivery.

Very soon, though, the photographers saw that the real picture of war was elsewhere and turned their lenses on the felon scenes of death and destruction. The photographs might never be published, but they could not ignore what was right in front of them. A photographer accompanying Joe's unit had wandered upon Joe standing in the rubble of the ruined church and asked to take a picture. He sent Joe a copy, which Joe had kept wrapped and tucked inside his war bag until his return from Europe.

The sheriff returned to his game of cat-and-mouse and said, "If you're wondering whether we're ready to make any arrests, the answer is 'No,' but you'll be the first to know."

The uniform snorted a laugh and had to wipe his nose on the inside of his shirt sleeve. "We got our suspects," he said. The man talked as though he held a secret that he wanted badly to let loose from behind his smothered smile. The secret wasn't difficult to decipher.

Joe looked at the floor, at the hardwood both scarred and polished by decades of scuffing shoe leather. He couldn't blame the sheriff for suspecting him. The coincidences were close enough to damning that an ungenerous man with a minimum of imagination might easily add them up on his tally sheet. And Jackson was as ungenerous and unimaginative as a broken fencepost.

The sheriff continued, "I stopped by your apartment this morning to talk with you."

"Must have just missed you," the uniform added.

"I was probably here."

Bernie looked at his pocket watch and nodded his head.

"Most likely you was," the sheriff said. "But I let myself in to make sure you weren't hurt or nothing."

"You broke into my apartment?"

"No, hell-no." He held out his hands defensively. "Your land-lord—nice fellow—let me in. After I explained that I was concerned for your safety, he was more than happy to help."

Joe shook his head. "He's a saint."

The sheriff smiled and nodded in agreement. "While I was relieving my concerns over your safety—"

"Concerns for my safety?"

"Yes. While I was relieving my concerns," he smiled again, "I found your clothes hanging in the bathroom."

"They were wet," Joe said. "I only have two suits. When one gets wet, I hang it up to dry."

"Yes. I figured so." He nodded and added as though they were buddies talking about the weather, "I've had to change my clothes every day for the past few weeks, it's been so wet. You too?"

"Yes," Joe said, uncomfortable with the false intimacy.

"I see. So you changed since yesterday. Those were your clothes you wore last night?"

"Yes," Joe said, hesitantly.

"I see." He nodded. "Well Snyder, here," he motioned toward the uniform standing next to Joe. "Snyder notices this dark spot on your pants. He and I looked at it pretty damn close and, by God, it sure looked like blood. Now where did you happen to get blood on you last night?"

Joe felt tired and small, small and tired enough to hang his feet over the side of a thin dime. He scratched his chin and frowned as though he did not understand how a collection of trifles could build into something important. The whole becoming greater than the sum of its parts.

The sheriff did not wait for Joe's answer. He stepped closer to Joe and said, "You keep showing up in my sights, Joe. I don't like it, but there you are. I don't know why you might have killed Gresham. His inheritance?" He shrugged. "The oldest motive in the world. Where the Frenchies might fit in, I don't know that either. That relationship is what I need, and maybe this here list will help provide that. I still hope that what I'm thinking is bunk, but I keep inching closer to charging you. I need all them ducks in a row before I pull the trigger. So to speak."

"So to speak," Joe echoed.

The pit Joe had fallen into kept collapsing around him. His mind flashed suddenly on an English trench he had waded through during one of his first days on the Western Front. The mud and excrement had clung to his pants and shoes. As he had felt then, he again felt wrapped inside the paranoia of having wandered into his own grave.

"Why would I kill my best friend?"

The deputy, Snyder, snorted sarcastically.

"Why does anyone kill anyone?" asked Jackson.

Joe sighed. He couldn't argue with that. "You're looking in the wrong bucket. You should look a little more closely at the Frenchmen in that accident and the names on that list." However, he could not shake the feeling that all he was doing was circling the drain.

The sheriff nodded his head and moved the wad of tobacco from cheek to cheek. "I didn't say they weren't involved. They were. In their automobile, I found a box that held a bunch of papers."

"They had Gresham's manuscript?"

Joe saw the sudden flash in the sheriff's eyes, the wattage turn up as he put two and two together and came up with MOTIVE— another piece Jackson thought he needed to complete his puzzle. Joe watched those eyes move and brighten. There are times in one's life when you just want to knock your head against the wall, hard. This was one of those times.

"What about this manuscript?" the sheriff asked, leaning forward toward Joe. "What I found might be something Gresham was writing, but it got all wet and muddy. I only got me a few pages with good writing on them."

And Joe remembered Jackson spilling the paper contents of a box in the snow and rain and mud. That would be at the top of his stir list.

The uniform said, "That's what he went back to the house for, to find that manuscript." He stabbed at Joe with his finger.

"What about it, Joe?" Jackson asked.

Joe wiped his brow. "I don't know that much about it," he said, his words flat. "Gresham had mentioned it to me but never really talked about it. I believe it was about a battle that he was in, the Champagne."

He looked at the sheriff and then at Snyder, the uniform, and met blank stares from each. The empty eyes of the ignorant. Anyone who was there, even if not in the battle itself, would know. Anyone in western Europe would know. Separated by four thousand miles of water from France, however, Americans didn't have the visceral attachment to the war that those in Europe had, especially with a president whose campaign had rested on a plank of forgetting—putting the war in the past, forgetting it like it was just a child's bad dream.

He continued, "If the Frenchmen had taken it, it must have been important. Whatever's in it might tell you who killed him."

"I think we know that already," Snyder said under his breath.

"Maybe I can make something of those pages you saved, and maybe we should go back and see if any of the other pages are still readable."

The sheriff rocked back on his heels as though he might actually consider Joe's idea. He pulled a loose piece of tobacco from his upper lip and rolled it between finger and thumb, and he squinted at Joe, his jaw working at the wad in his cheek and greasing the rusty wheels of his mind to make all the cogs mesh.

After a moment of silence filled with the whispers of others in the room, the surrounding gallery of newsmen, Snyder offered his views, stretching over the sheriff's shoulder to look down on Joe. He spoke quickly, as though he feared he might lose the words before they reached his lips. "Is that why you was driving out to meet the Frenchies after they killed Gresham? You hired them to murder him because you couldn't do it yourself, and they were supposed to meet you out on the road and exchange the papers for money? Them being Frenchies, though, they don't drive so good and your whole plan goes to hell."

Joe withheld the impulse to show Snyder exactly how shallow violence remained beneath his surface and said to the sheriff, "I told you that I never saw the manuscript. I don't know what was in it, but those Frenchmen obviously did."

"I see," said the sheriff, "and how do I know you never saw this manuscript?"

"Because I'm telling the truth."

Another snort from Snyder.

"I see," the sheriff said, nodding and pulling at his chin. He cocked an eyebrow and smiled. "Only thing, though, a man who'd kill someone certainly wouldn't shy from a little lie, now would he?"

"Shit," said Snyder with a grunt. "You as much as did it yourself."

Joe ignored him, a big man with a little-man problem.

"We talked with Willie," the sheriff added, working himself into Snyder's groove. "He said that when you left, you said you were headed home to sleep."

"I changed my mind."

"Shit," said Snyder again. "He changed his mind. I think you was laying down an alibi." He added derisively, "Gee, Sheriff, I was home asleep. Just go ask Willie and he'll tell ya'." He offered a staccato laugh.

The sheriff waved his hand for Snyder to calm down. "Like I said, Joe, when I do finally figure this whole mess out, I hope it's not what it looks like. Either way, though, you and I will talk more. Until then, I don't want to see your vehicle heading out of town. Understand?"

Joe did not respond.

The sheriff walked away, followed closely by his small entourage. In their wake a void quickly filled with the tale-bearing babble of men whose lives were spent observing other people's worlds.

After the door closed behind them and the sound of their heels faded, Joe continued to listen. The room felt as though it had turned alien to him. He remained sitting on the edge of the desk, his nerves risen with the room's noise and his ears shaking from the unforgotten din of distant cannonades. He felt as though he had once again been let down in a wasteland. He had not felt that way in years, not since the war, but the feeling was as raw as the previous night.

He pushed himself from the desk onto unsteady legs. Under his coat, the back of his shirt felt cold and damp. He flexed his muscles involuntarily. How good a whiskey would taste, how good any liquid would taste but especially a double whiskey, flashed through his brain. His mouth had dried completely. He could not work any moisture into it and he considered going to Willie's for a snort or ten. He decided to postpone that surrender until the evening.

He stood in the light from the window but the light no longer held any warmth. Clouds had veiled the sun, dropping a flat gray through the room, the reflected gray like that of water-filled shell holes echoing a bleak and hollow sky, the gray of empty and pitted helmets lost in the avid mud, the gray of a dead man's face.

He sat in his chair with his back to the hum of the newsroom. The envelope lay on his desk. He fingered it open. A first-class ticket on a Cunard liner to Cherbourg leaving New York on Monday, the next day. Joe rubbed the ticket between his fingers as though testing its validity. He again checked the date against a wall calendar and exhaled a long breath as he sat heavily in the wooden chair.

Gresham had planned a trip to France. Joe's first thought was to open the window, to call down to the sheriff, ask him to come back up, and then show him the ticket. Joe's second thought, however, was that the sheriff was peering through blinders. Anything that did not point toward Joe in a noose would be bent in such a way that it would. He sat back, his finger rubbing a trail along the ticket as though divining truths. He wondered why Gresham would so suddenly want to explore his past, a past that for Joe, at least, was still raw in its wounds.

Gresham's trip may have been a simple return to the land where he and Joe and so many other young men had lost their innocence and youth. Joe had read of others returning to France's growing expatriate population, American soldiers whose lives had been formed in the furnal fires of the war and who had returned to find what had been removed from them in that dark time. Like him, they had gone to war in support of the hollow words of the last century only to find an obscenity in those words. Now they returned in search of something to fill their resulting voids—jazz and drink and sex. However, Joe doubted any such thing in Gresham's visit, for Gresham had been a man who held concrete reasons for the things he did. Joe knew that Gresham would not have returned to France on an errant desire for recapturing a lost youth.

Holding the ticket in the fingertips of both hands, rubbing the coarse and heavy paper, he could not shake the feeling that Gresham had planned his trip for a very specific reason and that reason had gotten him killed.

The man's secrets may have killed him and Joe wondered whether the intended dinner the night before, had it occurred, would have pulled Joe into the swirl of murder, a swirl he had been pulled into anyway. Gresham had wanted to talk about his manuscript, a book about the war, and Joe had supposed that it was another in a long line of journalist rehashes of what had been gained and what had been lost in a war that meant nothing other than a great deal of death. Sitting across from Gresham's empty chair, Joe knew he had been wrong.

He wondered where copies of the manuscript might have ended up. The dead Frenchmen had one copy, which left at least one more and probably two for Gresham would have carboned copies somewhere. He knew two things for certain: If he had the manuscript he might be able to find the real killer, and, second, he had only guesses as to where another copy might exist.

Joe closed his eyes and conjured the piece of paper that had been clipped to the envelope. Champagne and the date. A name—Paul something. He concentrated. Something like Dullard. Dillard. A place, maybe an address. Paris. Place André des Arts No numbers, no address numbers. He wrote it all down on the envelope.

Before leaving the newsroom, Joe pocketed the enveloped ticket safe inside its folds. It was his now.

If I am to be a fool, he thought, *I am to be my own fool.*

A small puddle from the morning's rain had formed around the base of the coat rack, having fallen in drips from his overcoat. He stepped to avoid the water as he lifted his coat from the rack to walk swiftly from the room.

Just before the door, he turned to look once more at the desk with the sense that he had overlooked something telling. As though a broken light shined on it, he saw the typewriter with its triple pages rolled and waiting for the next beat of metal keys.

Early in Gresham's mentoring of him, Gresham had told him always to carbon his pages, always make a copy of everything he wrote. He closed his eyes. Joe could think of only three places Gresham might have left a copy of his manuscript—in his desk at home, in his desk at work, in his box at the bank. That left two places for Joe to look.

He pulled the watch from his pocket and checked the time—9:56. Noon would be the best time to search Gresham's bank box, for only the newest and least experienced bank workers would be at their desks. That, at least, would provide two hours to find the appropriate keys. Those would be somewhere in Gresham's home.

The gray day became a cold drizzle of snow as Joe pulled his Hudson across lanes and headed out of town. He checked his mirror and watched as another vehicle, a black Ford like every other black Ford in America, fell in behind him, keeping a discreet distance but turning when he turned and slowing when he slowed.

Joe changed his plans.

At the next intersection, he turned north, away from Gresham's house and parked in front of the National Bank, a brick building three stories high with sandstone framing the windows and a large double door.

Even though he knew the answer, Joe asked the receptionist for directions to the bank's box vault, setting the hook for when his tails asked. She pointed him to the stairs at the rear of the building. Instead of walking down the stairs to the basement, however, he went up one flight and waited for two policemen, Snyder and another uniform, to follow his lead. He watched from the railing above as they descended before he walked back down and back through the bank's lobby and out the front.

He drove past their black Ford, which was parked a block down the street and had the city's insignia painted on its doors in white paint. He double parked in the road. Ignoring the horns of others on their way to or from work, he used his pocket knife to loosen the valve stem in one of the front Firestones before driving off, watching his mirrors the entire distance but seeing no other cars following him.

A wet and heavy snow began to fall in earnest, coming down in sheets and again sending alley cats inside to chase basement rats. Joe wondered whether he was the chasing cat or the fleeing rat.

Gresham's home was drenched in a pall. The morning had been pulled down around the house to lay soggy on the structures and ground. Water dripped from the corners of the roof. The driveway was still muddy from the previous rains and was beginning to be layered in white. The air was colder than in town, offering a promise of a full winter's snow.

Joe saw no new tracks in the mud of the long driveway and parked out of sight behind the brick garage, hoping the snow would turn full enough to erase his own tire tracks. With his overcoat wrapped around his shoulders, he pulled his fedora down tight and ran from the garage to the overhang of the front porch.

The front door was closed but not locked. Joe felt the unpleasantly familiar feeling of having been there before. Not just the previous night. The sudden vision of death the night before mixed in kaleidoscope quickness with deaths from a further past.

The first step into Gresham's foyer echoed in the silence of the house as well as memory. The hush of death. The rain dripping outside, the mantel clock ticking down, the haunted sounds of emptiness. Joe listened to the absence of life sounds, his ears warm as though from a low-grade fever, until he felt certain that he was alone. He walked through the foyer and into the room where Gresham had been killed, draping his wet overcoat on the back of a chair.

A faint light of day from behind drawn curtains was all that lit the room. Joe stood for a moment before he pushed the wall button to turn on the ceiling light. The room appeared much as he had last seen it. Small stains of blood had dried on the sofa and wood floor. The sofa, however, had been pulled farther from the wall as the sheriff's deputies had been searching for something behind it. An imprint of death remained in the cushions of the sofa as though a ghost still lay there. Everything else in order. Joe thought that there should be something, some marker, some monument to signal the death of a good man. But the room was empty and it left him feeling hollow.

The desk drawer which had been open the night before had been closed. He opened it and found a lidless cigar box of pencils, stacks of writing paper and carbon paper. Beneath that was a single letter with a French postmark. He pocketed the letter without opening or reading it. An empty space in the drawer the size of a ream of paper signaled the absence of something. Gresham's manuscript. The original had been taken from there, that he was certain of. The Frenchmen had lifted the manuscript from the desk drawer and left without closing it.

Joe rubbed his mouth, thinking how he had become so familiar with death that he would even notice whether an assassin should stop to close a desk drawer after murdering a man. During the war, he had known men who ate meals in between sniper shots, killing a man then having a spoonful of weak stew, and he knew one man who had sung lullabies during the pitch of battle, killing other men while he sang "The Land of Nod." The infinities and incongruities of violence had cauterized the world's emotions.

The other drawers held books from the public library in Greenwich about the Great War, a war fought to end all wars except those still fought in the spectral memories of young men.

Folded pieces of paper marked pages in several of the books, all noted pages concerned with the same battle in Northern France at the Champagne in which Gresham had participated. That was where Gresham had watched as so many of his comrades charged to their death in a day that had netted no land. Joe had heard rumors of incompetence and of treason surrounding that battle, but he had heard that about many battles, along with the tales of angels in the trenches and ghost spies and cannibal traitors and vampires who populated the cratered no-man's land between the trench lines. Since the war, he had paid little attention to any of the rumors, knowing that the true cannibals were the old men in politician's suits who had sent young men to their deaths.

Mostly, though, he preferred to think of anything other than France. He was often unsuccessful in that.

He closed the books back inside their drawers and turned to walk out before remembering the engravings on Gresham's notepad, the indented lettering left from the previous page's words. The notepad was still on the end table near where Gresham's head had fallen on the sofa, and Joe tilted the paper in the light to expose the phantomic outline of pressed words. Other than recognizing the page as a list of names, however, he could not read what had been written.

He turned on the electric lamp next the sofa and tore the page from the pad and held it closer against the light, turning it in every direction and angle to the light of the floor lamp, but he could read little more than before. From the desk, he took a page of carbon paper and placed it over the note page, rubbing lightly over the imprint. He felt like a young boy discovering the mystery map to a long lost treasure as the list of names with simple marks next to each formed in relief, white against black. He read them out loud, as though the act of speaking the names would reveal their identities. Then he placed the page on the table and looked at it.

> *Rene Marcel*
> *Jean Marcel* ★★
> *Thomas Wilde* ★★
> *Frederick Gadwa*
> *Paul Dillard—*

None of the names meant anything to him, no Churchills or Hydes or Pershings among them, except that of Dillard which he recognized from the paper he had given to the sheriff. He copied the names into his own notepad, folded the original, and put them both into his shirt pocket. He looked again at the desk. There was nothing to explain what the names meant nor why Gresham had written them.

He wondered if Gresham might have kept another copy of his manuscript in the house. Not in the desk, but maybe upstairs in his dresser or boxed in the spare room. He took the stairs to the second floor singly and slowly, feeling the presence of death hovering in the house like Banquo's ghost.

All he found in the spare room were traces of the Great War— worn uniforms, a mess kit and bed roll, tarnished medals, a pitted and rusted helmet, other helmets and knives and a Lugar pistol stolen from dead or captured Germans, an Austro-Hungarian flag. He pocketed the Lugar for no better reason than he had no gun and its weight felt reassuring. Searching through the boxes was like returning to the trenches, for as he searched the things of war he could hear the distant terrors of injured or blinded men, the shrieks of dying horses, the necrotic hum of circling flies.

He walked to the bedroom, turned on the floor lamps, opened drawers in the night stand and dresser, searched the closet and under the bed. He opened a packed steamer trunk left in the middle of the room filled with clothes ready for the trip. On top of the trunk was Gresham's passport and a safe deposit key, which he might be able to use if given time and opportunity. Before he could search the trunk, however, he heard another automobile in the drive outside.

An engine stopped. Two car doors slammed shut.

Joe looked through a crack in the window shades, knowing while he looked that whoever it was could see all of the lights on in the house as well as his silhouetted figure in the upstairs window. Two uniformed policeman jogged through the increasing snow and mud from the garage to the house, their heads down and shoulders hunched inside yellow slickers, their hands tight on their hips holding holstered weapons from bouncing. Neither seemed to notice the rear bumper of Joe's Hudson beyond the back wall of the garage. For once Joe was happy about the rain and snow, for it kept the two officers' eyes looking down at their feet and the muddy driveway.

Joe took the stairs two and three at a time, then started toward the kitchen door in the rear of the house before remembering his overcoat draped over a chair, leaving a wet spot on the front room floor. As the front door opened to send a flare of light across the entry, Joe lifted his overcoat from the chair. He had few choices and only one that he had time to try. In those wet winter months of Connecticut, people kept furniture eight to ten inches from the wall to allow for air circulation and keep mold and mildew from growing along the baseboards. The previous night someone had pulled the sofa an extra couple of inches out, looking for some clue. He slid behind it, feeling much like a man crawling into his trench.

Two sets of footsteps stopped in the entry before continuing into the lighted front room.

"And look here, Will." Joe recognized the voice of the tall uniform, Snyder. Joe listened as Snyder's disembodied voice trailed into a whisper.

"I see it," said Will, the other uniform, his voice graveled and low. "He was here for sure. Lights on, wet floor. Gone upstairs, you think?"

"Maybe. Most likely he's already gone, though, else we'd have seen his car."

"Probably right."

"Damn but I was wishing he was here. After that little stunt in town, I was looking forward to taking a little air out of his tires."

"I'll check upstairs anyway."

"Okay. You have a look-see and I'll check around down here."

Joe heard the sound of snaps unlocking and the rub of something against leather, the sounds of a pistol being drawn. He pulled closer into himself, compressing into his small trench as much as he could. He listened to both sets of footsteps, hearing them in a parallax of sound, one ear following the feet of those that ascended the stairs and with the other ear those of Snyder's shuffling from front room to hallway to kitchen and back.

Echoing from the second floor landing came Will's voice, "Nothing up here 'cept a few drips of water."

"Nothing down here either."

A silence followed in which Joe felt each second pass, listening to the shuffles and movements of the two men and hearing the loud beat of his own pulse. He knew they had found him and that they were training their pistols on the sofa, ready to kiss it and him with a flurry of bullets. He readied himself against the wall in order to push the sofa into the two men and dash for the door.

He heard Will speak, "There was some boxes open upstairs."

"They weren't open last night. Let's go back up and see if we can find anything missing."

Another silence filled with the rush of blood through Joe's ears.

"First, though, let me call the sheriff and let him know what's what."

One set of boots walked to and up the stairs. The other crossed the room to the desk. A phone lifted from its hook and four numbers dialed on the rotary.

"Sheriff Jackson."

A desk drawer opened. Some papers were crumpled and others shuffled. Something was lifted from the wall and after a moment was placed on the desk. Snyder mumbled, "Damn if those doughboys sure liked to photograph themselves. Like they was on a world tour or—" His words stopped short and Joe held his breath.

"Sheriff? Snyder. Me and Will are out here at Gresham's house. . . . Yes, he was, but he must have left just before we arrived. Lights were on and there's puddles of water on the floor and a wet spot on the back of a chair. . . . Probably from his coat. . . . Yes. Some opened boxes up there. Will's looking through them now. . . . Yes. . . . No. I'll go have a look with him. . . . Yes . . . Like I told you, this guy's the one. We should have. . . . Yes, I know. Sorry, sheriff. . . . We parked in the garage, so if he comes back he won't see us. . . . Okay. We'll wait, and if he comes back we got him. If he runs, I'll just have to shoot his sorry ass. . . . Yessir."

The phone slapped down.

"Stupid son-of-a-bitch," Snyder said and walked off to join Will upstairs.

Joe poked his head from behind the sofa, ready to recoil if he saw Snyder looking back like some sniper in the woods. He was alone but he knew not for long and crawled from his spider hole. Out of a pen box on the desk, Joe took scissors with which he clipped the phone line.

He took the copy of Joyce's novel and a framed photograph of five men standing in a muddy trench, the object he had heard Snyder remove from the wall and place on the desk. He walked quickly into the kitchen, conscious of the pad of his heavy-soled shoes on the old wood floor. He slipped out the back door, and without looking back, he ran first into the garage to pull loose the spark plug wires from Snyder's car. Then he rounded the garage on the opposite side from the house, started his car's engine, and jumped the Hudson through the mud and down the driveway. He caught a mirrored glimpse of Snyder raising his weapon before Snyder and the house disappeared behind a line of trees. A shot rang out, but the noise—like the bullet and the house and the shooter—was lost in the woods.

Nobody lived within three miles of Gresham, so Joe figured he had at least forty minutes before Snyder could slosh through the mud and find a telephone to call the sheriff. He hoped the sheriff would first drive to Gresham's home. That would give him another thirty minutes to get to his apartment and grab a few things and leave. If the sheriff went to his apartment first, Joe figured he might have only five extra minutes. Forty-five total, and half those taken up driving to town. He pressed on the accelerator, wheels sliding a little before taking purchase.

The clouds had settled even more fully since Joe had left town. With the snow falling hard and heavy, the day was settling into darkness. He turned on the small box heater in his automobile, but he was still cold, shivering. The trees lining the road passed like brief shadows.

He parked in an alley a block away from his apartment building and ran to the building, not at all concerned that someone might take notice. He hoped that people would think he was running to get out of the snow and would not see the unstable look in his eyes. So he ran, his fedora pulled tight on his forehead, overcoat open and flapping wildly in the wind and snow. He did not bother jumping slush puddles or looking at traffic and barely slowed at the building's door. He bounded the stairs, taking two and three in a stride, and stopped once inside only for a quick breath after closing and locking the door behind him.

He spared no time taking note of his up-turned apartment, the product of the sheriff's intense curiosity. With his breath coming in gasps, he pulled clothes and shoes from the bedroom dresser and closet to stuff into a tattered canvas duffel bag. On top of those clothes he spilled toiletries from his bathroom and the suit he had hung to dry, its incriminating blood stain still marking the pant leg.

He started from the bathroom back into the front room when he heard a key tickling the front door lock to his apartment. He stepped back against the bathroom wall, pressing himself as tight as possible against the wainscoting.

"Thank you," the sheriff told someone, probably the building manager. "No need to worry. I'll just wait here until he returns." The door closed. Joe again listened to the sound of someone walking.

The sound of the steps grew then receded into the bedroom.

Joe's jaw tightened. He found it difficult to swallow. He wished that the water falling from his overcoat would stop hitting the floor with such loud drips, drips loud enough to eclipse the sounds of his breathing and heart pulsing through his ears.

He looked around the bathroom for a place to hide. Nowhere and no chance of making it to the front door without being caught or shot. The window was too small for him to shimmy through, so he pushed himself tighter into the cracks of the wainscoting.

The sheriff's steps returned from the bedroom, moving with quickened and tightened spacing. The sheriff had found the emptied drawers and the emptied closet.

"Shit-almighty," the sheriff swore beneath his breath as he stepped into the bathroom.

Joe punched the sheriff in the temple, a cold-cocked sucker punch that sent the little man straight down quick and hard and face first on the tile floor.

Joe turned him over and sat him against the bathtub like a stringless marionette and stopped the bleeding from his nose, then tied his arms and legs tight with a telephone cord from the front room. He thought of gagging him, but worried that, with his nose probably broken, he may need his mouth to breath.

"Sorry, Sheriff," he said.

He took the sheriff's gun, a Smith & Wesson .45 revolver with a short barrel, balanced it in his hand for a moment, thinking how he was accumulating a nice arsenal of small guns. Lifting his bag of clothes through the bedroom window and out onto the fire escape, he took one last look at his home before slipping out and down the metal staircase and then the alley to his car.

The bank was on his way out of town. He stopped long enough to close out his own bank account. He knew the police would have already placed a stop on Gresham's accounts after the morning's escapade. The teller hesitated giving him so much cash. Following an okay from a manager, Joe pocketed nearly $500 in large bills.

He drove out of Greenwich with his lights on and not a single look in the mirror until he had almost reached the limits of the small city. Pointing the Hudson toward New York City meant passing Gresham's house one more time and possibly meeting Snyder driving back into town. His luck had held through the day, either by a cable or by a thread but held nonetheless. He just hoped that there was enough elasticity to it that it would hold a while longer.

He passed a Ford truck coming into town. Through the driving rain, he could just make out Will sitting between the driver and

Snyder. The two men were engaged in a heated argument and the driver was watching the road. Joe slid back far enough in the shadows of his car to not be seen. He watched as the three faces in the farmer's truck passed. None of them paid notice to the traffic leaving the city; the deputies' faces turned in anger to one another and the driver having a hard enough time in the snow and looking through discordant windshield wipers and distorted glass. Joe held his breath and watched the truck disappear into the veil of snow behind him. Neither their Ford nor his Hudson slowed or wavered.

Joe pulled quickly into Gresham's driveway to take the steamer trunk with him. He could easily do without Gresham's clothes, even if they might fit, but he did not want to draw attention to himself checking into a first class cabin on a Cunard liner with no major luggage in tow. As he left, he offered one last salute to his friend, "To the Lost, brother."

As he neared the wreckage of last night's crash, he slowed and stopped on the road's narrow shoulder. He wandered for a few minutes through the mired and snow-covered ground. The only papers he found not already turning to mulch in the snow and mud were sodden, with the inked words running together as though speaking an ancient rune. With no help there, he left.

Driving to New York, through the intermittent changes of snow and rain, he stopped once in Mamaroneck to fill his gas tank. The rain there had stopped and the air smelled heavily of wet grass and sulfur. The clouds were marbled, gray and black, and threatening another storm. A pair of large oak trees near the garage were thick with birds clinging to the skeletal frame of branches. Stripped of his overcoat and coat, Joe's shirt clung to his back wet from sweat. The air was electric. He knew that the storm was not yet over.

He took a hotel room a few blocks from the Fourteenth Street dock before driving back up to the Bronx, leaving the car parked near the new Yankee Stadium, the keys swinging in the driver's door. He then rode the subway back downtown to his hotel.

The next morning he woke early, well before the sun had risen. With the reflections of the city's lights, the sky was a blue-black, the color of singed steel. A dream of his father had woken him fully from his sleep. The sudden crack. His father's slow roll into death and the absolute lack of anything he could do except watch, which he did in his dream, though he had not in his youth. No bells, no tears, no priest, no church.

Joe blinked and sighed. A shiver went through his body. He rose and dressed, preparing to return to the place where his generation and the last century had died.

III

"One must have lived through such moments to realize their tragic and passionate beauty. Hundreds and thousands of men in the vigor of their youth are massed together awaiting the shock."
—"Captain X," *Scribner's Magazine*, May, 1916
★Describing the Second Battle of the Champagne★

WHEN THE SUN CAME UP, IT WAS TO A HARD, SHARP WETNESS THAT sliced to the bone. Joe took a clean suit and wool overcoat from Gresham's steamer trunk before sending the trunk to the ship ahead of him. Gresham had been slightly less than an inch taller and only a bit wider in girth than Joe, so the suit fit Joe with the looseness of someone who had recently lost weight, or who had just recovered from an illness, or returned from war. He left the hotel and began his walk to the docks, steam rising from the gutters as he stepped across them outside his hotel's entrance. The day was cold enough that he considered wearing Gresham's rough buffalo robe but decided that the short walk would keep him warm inside the heavy weave of his overcoat.

The *Berengaria*, a twenty-year-old prize of war, would return him to France. The only other times he had sailed on a ship of that size was going to and returning from the war. The large and stout ship with its three black funnels scraping the heavy sky rested like a steel monolith in its berth. Ropes and boarding planks tethered the ship to the old wooden dock.

Waiting until a crowd arrived, he fell in with a group of college men as they boarded. He was the only sober one of the bunch. Gresham's passport was looked at and the ticket was stamped. A young officer with red hair and more freckles than whiskers welcomed him to the *Berengaria*. After finding his cabin, Joe returned to the deck for the embarkation. Once underway, the ship's broad beam would cut a wide and steady line through the ocean, leaving his past in its wake.

Standing near the stern of the big ship as it pulled away, he watched New York and America slip to the horizon and then drown into the line of the sea. In so many ways, his life had been formed in the crucible of that European war, and now, on that large and three-stacked ship, he was returning to the maw of the furnace that had forged him.

He spent the remainder of that day and most of the next three in his cabin, taking his meals there and venturing out early in the morning or late at night, avoiding others and hoping nobody recognized either him or the name he sailed under. He exhausted the hours inside his cabin in unsuccessful attempts to not think about the last few days. He tried reading *Ulysses,* the book that had been delivered to Gresham, but found it required more attention than he could muster. He played solitaire with a deck of cards found among the clothes in Gresham's trunk, disassembled and cleaned the Smith & Wesson taken from the sheriff and the Lugar taken from Gresham's home, twice read the *Scribner's* magazine and a copy of Mencken's *Black Mask* he had bought at the pier terminal before boarding, slept unsoundly for short periods of time.

In the middle of the third night at sea, he woke with the realization that he had become a fugitive from more than the police and the near past. His flight from prosecution formed something of a pattern. Since returning from the war, Joe had sensed that he had slipped to the leeward side of his life. Before the war he may have thought in terms of tomorrows and the molding of the possible. Since returning, however, he thought mostly in terms of the past and of what he no longer was.

In increments his world and then his future had been removed from him. Alice Bright's letter had not been a complete surprise— too many men in his unit had received their own versions for it to be so—but, still, it had removed what he thought was his last tie to the land around Terceo, Colorado. With his family dead and his father's ranchland foreclosed on, he had no place to return to. With Alice Bright married to another man, he had nobody to return to.

With nothing else, he stayed in the first place he woke up sober after leaving the Army in New York. It was not his past nor was it a future. It was barely a present. It was more like an escape.

Even so, like the rim of a turning wheel, the world was rolling forward. He felt that he was being dragged along as well, and that possibly he would find in Paris some purchase on firm ground and be able to chart a course for himself. Maybe, he thought, once he had extricated himself from the slough in which he had found himself, he would finally return to Southern Colorado.

He did not have a suite, but the cabin Gresham had reserved was spacious with bed, end tables, matching sitting chairs and round maple table, desk and high-back chair, and maple dresser in a deco style. The room held a tattered luxury that spoke to its magnificent past in the decades before the war when she was a grand lady of the sea. Like so much else that had entered the war's crimson insanity, the *Berengaria* had finished the war almost a shell. The ship's renovation returned only a degree of its previous stature, a façade of the past. Joe examined the contents of Gresham's trunk. He could wear his own suits during the day and use Gresham's dinner jackets and tuxedo coat in the evening. Joe had never worn knickers as a child and saw no reason why a man would ever willingly allow himself to don the clothes of a painted Willie, so he refolded the pairs of plus-fours Gresham had packed and returned them to the steamer trunk. The rest of the clothes he transferred from the trunk to the cabin's dresser.

Joe felt certain that if he was not recognized or recognized as not being Wynton Gresham, that he would not stand out on the ship. The very last thing he needed was to be discovered as a stowaway, arrested, and detained in Europe for American authorities who would soon find a warrant for his arrest, so for those days he had become a dead man, Wynton Gresham, a prospect that did not disturb Joe nearly to the degree as the idea of being arrested as the murderer of that same dead man.

Inside the steamer trunk's sock drawer, he found another envelope and whistled a long and low note when he opened it and found

$800 in cash. That plus his own bank cash meant he could live quite well in Paris for at least a year. Long enough, he hoped, for Sheriff Jackson to discover who had actually killed Gresham or long enough, if need be, to establish a new identity in that old city.

When Joe took his lunch in his cabin on the voyage's fourth day, the waiter mentioned that cabined meals were something of a custom. Many travelers needed a day or two in which to acclimate their legs as well as their stomachs to the gentle rolling of even a large ship like the *Berengaria*. Brought to him with his meal that afternoon was a simple note that was being sent to all passengers. A turbine had been damaged on the previous west-bound journey, "battling against high seas at a high rate of speed." Thus, the note continued, the *Berengaria* would "omit calling at Plymouth and proceed directly to Cherbourg then Southampton for repairs."

With a whiskey in hand, he toasted the smiles of fortune, "Thank you, Neptune, you old man of the sea."

He ate fully, for not docking at Plymouth meant one less customs agent he might have to encounter, and unlike the French, who were notorious for their laxity in such matters, the British were their stodgy and anal selves. While he felt claustrophobic in his cabin, he was pleased with the prospect of leaving Britain on the northern horizon as the ship continued on to France.

After his lunch, he studied what little he knew about the mystery that had landed him on the ship. He unfolded his papers and placed them side-by-side on the round table, turning the sheet with its written list next to the list of names he had copied from Gresham's notepad. Above them, he set the photograph he had taken during his escape from Gresham's house.

For hours and through the afternoon, with his fingers tracing the outline of his face, he studied the items. He knew a relationship existed between the notes and the photograph but did not know what that relationship might be nor its extent. He translated his thoughts to paper, in notes and outlines and complete sentences, then crossed each out as each proceeded blindly to a dead end. The associations extended no further than the obvious—Gresham had begun a manuscript exploring the disastrous Battle of the Champagne, a manuscript for which he had probably been murdered.

Bending over the table to examine the photograph more closely in the looseness of the cabin's ceiling light, he searched the grainy images of six men staring back at the camera from the duck board of a muddy trench, one man standing and the other five kneeling or sitting against the thatched and reinforced side. All six had dressed against the weather, wearing long wool coats with collars turned up. Their helmet rims cast straight shadows across their foreheads. The man standing, Gresham, turned partially to the side, looked across his shoulder at the camera and stood compacted against a cold wind with only the side of his face fully available to the light. A mist of steam rose transiently from the cup he held in his right hand as the others ate from their mess kits. The men who offered a smile offered only beige smiles. Their expressions were distant, except one, a stoop-shouldered Englishman whose face was partially hidden inside the shadow of his helmet. Across the bottom of the photograph, in the loose, sprawling hand Joe associated with the French, a caption had been written in white ink: "Champagne, 20 September 1915." Beneath that, in smaller script as though an afterthought another date and a quotation: "25 September 1915—The feast of vultures, and the waste of life." The later date was the date of the destruction that was the Champagne.

"The feast of vultures," Joe said aloud. "I know that banquet well." His words did not echo in the empty cabin although they might as well have.

Down the trench from the six men pictured, Joe could make out the hunched figures of a mass of men standing behind short ladders with a hand raised to the withy sticks. Joe recognized, even in the grainy photograph that he held in his fingers, the repose of men readying themselves for sudden death. A photograph of men who had gone to war with the optimism of youth and courage and had met a force much larger than them. There, in the Champagne as in Ypres and Gallipoli and Belleau Wood, the abstracts of nationalism had been defeated by the gross realities of violence.

Joe assumed the five men in the foreground of the photograph with Gresham were those on the list, one of whom would be Paul Dillard, the name on the envelope he had found in the desk, but Joe could not tell whose face might belong to which name. The name, Dillard, sounded English, but that helped little. He felt as though he was putting together a puzzle without the benefit of a guiding picture on the pieces. The hours of studying the papers and the photograph left Joe with little more than the certainty of their importance, the same sense he had when he had first laid them out on the maple table. Finally he pushed himself from the table and dressed for dinner.

It was time to join the living.

He was not surprised but impressed at seeing the ship at sail in the open ocean as he walked along the promenade deck toward the dining room. The sea was calm and black, the weather mild. Joe stopped a moment to view the Atlantic, its blackness spreading out from the ship until reaching the equal blackness of the night sky. The only noises he could hear came from the ship's steady movement through the water. He bent over the railing to view the wake but could not. He could only imagine its white-topped curl snaking into the night.

He stopped for a moment to smoke a cigarette and taste the salt air. Three women, young enough not to have been affected by the war, stood nearby. They glanced at him and huddled for a talk, and Joe looked at them and felt nothing, no stirring of animal desire. They were children, not in age maybe but in experience. He envied their careless lives of innocence, of ignorance, but he wanted nothing to do with them. If he were to tell them what he had seen, they would run from him as they might run from a carnival freak show. His world was no longer the world they inhabited. Anymore, if he wanted a woman, he'd buy her. Just like in Paris when he was on leave during the war—he didn't need to talk and he didn't need to listen.

They walked past him as they left the railing like a line of dancing girls, and each looked the echo of the others—tall, thin, coquettish smile, cloche hat, oversized shoes that flapped noisily as they walked. Each carried a copy of *Town Tattle*, as if it were a real newspaper.

The first winked at Joe as she passed and said, "Wasn't it nice?"

The second added, "Wasn't it sweet?"

The third finished with "Wasn't it good?"

Joe felt vaguely nauseated.

He walked along the empty deck with a continued feeling of unease at the luxurious and ostentatious beauty of the floating city. The floating mountain of light on which he walked seemed transitory in the night and in certain unformed ways he preferred the heavy-laden rocking and cramped quarters of the ships he had sailed in before and following the war. Like the world he knew, they had been stripped of their disguises. The *Berengaria*, however, had re-established its disguise as easily as having had its name changed from the German *Imperator*, which it had been for the first part of its life before the English had appropriated it as a war reparation.

He entered the dining room and stood implanted in its entry. A Louis XIV dining room spread out before him complete with an oak-beamed ceiling and paintings on the walls between floor-to-ceiling windows looking out on the blackness. He looked upon this grand beauty but could not shake the feeling that all he saw was the façade of a past century, one that had been lost. The people seated at their tables wearing tuxedos and evening gowns were the last ghosts to be exorcised.

A steward stepped toward Joe and asked as though he did not necessarily care, "Your name, sir?"

"Joe—" Joe began without thinking, then added, "Gresham."

"Joe Gresham?" The steward looked him up and down, surveying the loose fit of his tuxedo and passing judgment, mentally assigning Joe to an appropriate table, one far from the Captain's table.

"Wynton, actually," Joe said.

The steward huffed and consulted his list, taking his time, looking up twice to study a table and shaking his head, then looking back at his list then glancing again at Joe's ill fit and again at a table and finally saying, with a wave of his hand, "This way, sir."

They rounded the room until arriving at a table for six already serving five.

"Mr. Joe Winston," the steward announced as he pulled out a chair, removed a white flag on the table marking the seat as vacant, and left.

"Gresham, actually," Joe said to blank stares, forks of food held between open mouths and the table. "Wynton Gresham."

Introductions at the table were made with difficulty as Joe found himself at a table of Swedes who spoke as much English as he did Swedish. They stumbled through the civilities, mirroring each other's courtesy. The Swedes had eaten early and were finishing their entrées as Joe joined them. While Joe ordered his aperitif of Gendarme Herring, they began their ices. Debating for some time in their language that sounded like gargling to Joe, they finally decided to take their coffees elsewhere, maybe their state-room, and left Joe alone at the table following apologies and bows and handshakes.

Joe watched them leave, as relieved as they obviously were at not having to fake niceties to someone they did not understand. When he looked around the room, he saw no suggestion of a ship at sea. The room, with miniature potted trees bordering the entrance and panels and paintings lining the walls, resembled more a large hotel's dining area than that of a ship. The room could easily seat three hundred. Each table was covered with white linen. Lighting the room were honey-colored domes hung from the ceiling and brass torch-ieres along the walls. One entire wall of glass looked out over the water with tall windows veiled at the top in frostwork and curtained with patterned silk. Small tables for two lined those windows and in the interior of the room were tables of varying sizes, but none larger than for a seating of twenty. Joe felt in awe at what money could purchase—if not happiness then at least a big boat in which to cruise right up next to happiness.

He finished his aperitif and ordered Atlantic salmon for his entrée. Throughout his dinner, he listened in on the conversations at the tables near him, the games of circles each couple or group played. At the table behind his, an Englishman had been captured in conversation by an American couple from Oklahoma. The couple had taken a liking to a painting hanging in the bedroom of their suite and described it in some detail to the Englishman.

"That," the Englishman said, "is a reproduction of 'Flower Girl,' George Frederick Watts's famous painting. I served with his great-grandson at Passchendaele, a topping man."

"It's famous then?" the woman said more than asked.

"Oh, yes, absolutely."

"I told you it was famous."

"Yes, I heard him," the husband said, his voice fat and jowly. "A copy, you say? Tell me, Huntington, where is the original?"

Huntington, the Englishman, said with obvious pride in a voice that bordered on but did not fully slip over to arrogance, "It belongs to the Duke of Marlboro and hangs in Grosvenor House, London. I have seen it often on my visits there."

"How much is it?"

"'How much,' sir?"

Joe closed his eyes and pictured the trio. Huntington in his sporting tweed and pencil-thin moustache, long and aquiline nose, dashing in the country gentleman way. The American husband, a pig packer from the Panhandle who had followed Hormel's lead in creating a disassembly plant and had become rich from selling pounds of bacon and ham and roasts. The wife, a woman larger even than her fat husband. She had never been as thin as she thought she was and would never be anywhere near as urbane as she wanted. *But, then again,* Joe thought, *in Oklahoma, who would notice?*

"Yes. The price. How much?"

"I doubt that it is for sale . . . at any price." His words carried the warmth of a London fog.

The husband huffed. "It's a famous painting?"

"Very famous and a great work by one of England's finest artists. I recall—" and he was cut off by the husband.

"We will be in London in January. Grosvenor House? Watts? Enough money should buy any painting, don't you think?"

Joe quit listening. In the past few years he had too often heard the same exchange, not about a painting but about an ideal, a standard reduced. Another intrinsic element lost. As when the newel post is removed from a staircase, the staircase loses strength and tumbles, the removal of what Joe and his generation had been taught were the cores of civilization had resulted in a generation destroyed by war.

The next afternoon, heavily bundled inside Gresham's buffalo robe, Joe left his cabin for the men's smoking room. A room with the rough, stretched leather elegance of a men's club, it offered liquor and beer and conversation to those who wanted them, liquor and beer and privacy to those who wanted them. Joe considered the liquor, decided on the beer, and sought out the privacy.

Dozens of men loitered about the room, sitting together under the smoky lights, talking too loudly as men almost drunk often do. They fit into their booths, behind their whiskey and beers, surrounded by the haze of floating cigar smoke to debate the world's problems.

"What about this upstart—Hitler?" one man asked another as they held their brandies in one hand, their cigars in the other. Neither really looked at the other, and they both spoke as though scripted. "Do you think he's a communist?"

"No. Old Henry Ford wouldn't be his best friend if he were."

They nodded their heads and moved on to the next subject, pleased that they had at least settled that little bit.

Another table kept a livelier discussion running on how to approach Clemenceau's call for America's return to Europe to police the German stockpiling of weapons. Another table wagered on Dempsey's wrestling match with "Strangler" Lewis to see whose sport was tougher, a debate that ended with two at the table taking things outside. A couple of other men talked like reporters on their way to the conference in Lausanne about the shipping problems along the Dardanelles. Joe kept away from them all. None of their words seemed to strike very deep for him, but the noise, the ambient buzz of all those conversations, settled around him, allowing him to relax for a few moments in his anonymity.

The room held a rustic comfort in its feel and smell of worn leather and rubbed wood, whiskey and cigar smoke. A few men had tipped their heads in Joe's direction when he had entered, but neither they nor he offered to share a conversation. He sat in a large corner chair, leather and well worn, and eased himself behind a five-day-old copy of the *New York Times*, not the international edition but the New York morning edition from the day of the ship's launch. He searched the paper for any mention of Gresham and found none. By the time his third stout arrived, he was rereading past news from before the departure, enjoying a comfortable detachment from the place and actions that he had left four days and a thousand miles behind him.

When the cabin boy first walked through the smoking room, Joe did not even notice his call. Eventually, though, the boy's words penetrated his trance, "Cable for Mr. Gresham. Mr. Wynton Gresham. Cable for Mr. Gresham."

Joe folded his paper on his lap and called over the boy, tipping him before settling back in the chair. His intrusion into Gresham's life, while never a game, took a ghostly turn as he fingered the cable's envelope. He rested his head on the back of the chair and scanned the wood ceiling, finding only shadows and darkened wood.

The feeling of communing so closely with the dead had never rested well with Joe. It bored a hollowness through him, a white vacancy that emptied him, and he closed his eyes and steadied his breathing. He traced the seams of the envelope as though they were scars, lightly leveling his fingertips across the paper.

"Bad news, Mr. Gresham?"

Joe opened his eyes. The Englishman Huntington from the previous night's conversation at the nearby table stood over him, well dressed in buttoned suit and knotted Oxford tie, hair slicked, and eyes steeled. On the surface, Huntington looked like too many officers Joe had seen in the war, men who cared less about other men's lives than about their own polish. Joe never felt comfortable around men so quick to glorify themselves.

Huntington was a tall man, tall and thin and perfectly groomed. A man well bred. He had a half-inch scar at the bridge of his nose and his nose had shifted slightly to the left. That and another scar, slightly longer and razor thin, along his right cheekbone gave him the dashing look of a soldier of fortune. That look was made more so by the cock of the man's eyebrow and slant of his smile.

Huntington wore a red and blue lapel pin that Joe recognized as from the British Fourth Army, Rawlinson's group that had lost so many men during the Somme offensive. This man, Huntington, had been an officer. And from the scar on his nose and the sadness in his eyes, Joe could see that Huntington had been at the front of his men when they went over the top. He had received his pin honestly, along with his scars—for combat and not for drawing a general's bath.

It was an earned sadness drawn with a deep sense of something ruined that Joe saw in the man's eyes. The look of someone who had been there. It was a look that only another member of that club might understand. Others might recognize the sloe slant and comment on how that man seemed lost in some way; those of the brotherhood, regardless of allegiance or class, however, realized the cause.

"James Huntington," he said, extending his hand for Joe to shake then sitting across from him. He removed a silver cigarette case from his inside pocket, opened and removed one, and tapped the cigarette against the case a few times, returned the case to its pocket and lit the cigarette. A drift of smoke made him squint at Joe.

"I could not help but overhear your name," he said, leaning back and crossing his legs.

"Do we know each other?" Joe asked.

"No, no," he said with a rakish flick of his hand. "My cousin, though, served with you. Thomas Wilde. You and he were together at the Champagne." He breathed in and exhaled another plume of smoke. "Nasty battle, that Champagne. Worse, I think, than the Somme. At least we had a bloody chance, nobody selling us out before the scrape began."

Joe nodded. He remembered the name from Gresham's list, but with nothing more he couldn't talk about Thomas Wilde. He said nothing, nodding in a way that he hoped sent a message of acceptance.

"Expecting a problem?" Huntington asked, nodding toward the cable.

"No." He glanced at the cable and shook his head.

"I just thought by how you were avoiding the wire that you might have trepidations as to its contents, old man."

"No. Nothing like that. I was just enjoying being at sea and away from any business." Joe smiled. "Prolonging the eventual."

"I see." He slid back the cuff of his shirt to look at his watch. "Well, I was on my way to a dinner engagement when I heard your name. I do wish to talk with you, however, at a later time."

Huntington stood, nodded in that English way of almost bowing, and walked slowly from the room. In the wake of Huntington's cigarette, Joe was left wondering whether that had been a coincidence. Not likely, echoing the sheriff's words. While Joe believed in coincidences in general, he did not trust them when they actually happened. And here, with Huntington, was more grist for his mental mill to grind away on. Huntington knew that Gresham was on the *Berengaria*, but Huntington did not know Gresham personally.

Joe didn't like posing so publicly as Gresham with someone who might be able to identify his impersonation. He had little choice. He breathed heavily and slipped the edge of his pocket knife under the envelope's fold and opened it to study the message on the yellow paper:

GRESHAM—
WILL BE PLEASED TO SEE YOU—STOP—AGREE W PREMISE—
WILL TALK PARIS—STOP—DILLARD

He held it open in front of him, looking over the words, searching for meaning. Dillard's premise was most likely associated with Gresham's manuscript, and Joe had an idea of what it might entail, although nothing more than a vaguely formed notion, no specifics. He imagined this Dillard having a copy of the manuscript or at least a detailed summary. He had read and agreed with something Gresham had written, something both men had known about and had possibly shared in experience. Joe folded the paper back into the envelope and tucked it safely in his coat pocket. The matter of clearing his name with the police in Greenwich might come in course, if Dillard did have a copy of the manuscript or could at least explain that premise he agreed upon.

Joe removed the wire and reread it before returning it to his pocket, and he filled in a scenario for the night when Gresham was killed. The men had come as representatives of Dillard, pretending to be friends of a friend, bringing a copy of Joyce's book as well as news about Gresham's former comrade. A little lie told at Gresham's front door and the men were welcomed inside, offered a drink.

He considered what happened next. They offered to return to Paris with the manuscript, and Gresham would have informed them that it was unnecessary since he had already booked passage. They killed him, they probably would have anyway, and took the boxed manuscript.

Joe was startled by the sound of a bell. He looked around quickly, not quite certain where he was before he saw the room's movement. The dinner call roused the roomful of men to the dining room like the Angelus calling the Catholic faithful. Joe fell in behind the other men moving slowly from their comfort to join wives and family. As the room emptied, Joe noticed two men near the door who did not leave their seats and who watched him. He met their stares long enough to know that they held an interest in him. He looked over his shoulder to see if they followed him from the room but they did not.

Joe checked his buffalo robe and was again escorted to join the Swedes. Again their conversation was polite but limited, and again the Swedes left quickly and Joe sat alone to finish his dinner. A five-piece string orchestra played Edwardian music, orchestral songs by Wood and Beecham that Joe remembered from his short time in a British convalescence hospital in Calais. Following a meal of tournedos and morels on a bed of braised cabbage, Joe drank a cup of weak coffee. Before leaving, he ordered a bottle of Bushmills to be sent to his cabin. He took the stairs to the "C" level and walked the deck back to his room, holding the buffalo robe closed tight against the winter cold and stopping once to look out into the dark from the amber-lit ship. He removed the buffalo robe upon entering the hallway and carried it over one arm.

His cabin was quiet and dark and slightly rolling in the calm sea as he entered.

Once the door was shut behind him, a flash of light erupted inside his head as a blow glanced off his temple. He fell to the floor, the room's darkness his only shield from further punishment. Someone kicked out at him, but the kick landed against his shoulder. He rolled away from the kick then quickly back to grab hold of the man's leg. He stood, lifting the leg and driving the man to the floor with the calf held tight against his chest. Joe let loose and fell with his entire weight on the intruder who exhaled a loud groan followed by the sucking sound of a man trying to find his breath. Joe raised up and punched into the darkness, finding the man's chest and again finding the man's neck and again punched at where he thought the man's face to be. Another groan followed and he thought he must have finished his attacker.

He began to stand, but was stopped short by a hard blow between his shoulders. He fell back to the cabin floor, sucking hard for a breath. None came. His breathing, when he did finally regain it, came slow and laborious, as from a worn leather bellows. He could not rise and felt no strength in his arms or his legs, just a series of spasms as he struggled to regain his footing. He panicked and reached to find his gas mask even though his mind told him that he had already been exposed too long, long enough for his skin to blister and his eyes to close shut and allow only permanent darkness. Those actions and those thoughts, however, coming within a second that seemed like a threshold to eternity, faded as quickly as they had appeared.

A hard kick landed against his side as he rose to hands and knees followed by a series of punches. Within the room's darkness, few of the punches landed with exacting force, but the number that did find the surface of his neck and back and then his face and chest as he fell and rolled away left their imprint. Before he passed out, a glaze of light from the opening door crossed over him. In his blurred state it appeared like the wavering light of a candle. All he saw of his intruders were the silhouetted shapes of two forms leaving the room and shutting the door behind them, shutting him into a double darkness.

He woke some time later to the sound of someone knocking on his door. He tried to speak, but the only sound that came from his mouth was like the gargled cackle of a pullet. The knock continued. He lay back in the dark room and let them knock. He lay on his side with drool crusted in the corner of his mouth, his face raw, his body a tender bruise, his senses battered.

When he realized that the person knocking on his door had probably been a cabin boy with his whiskey, he cursed. There were only a few things he felt he needed at that moment. Bushmills was high on the list.

He pushed himself from the floor and steadied himself against the reading table, found the pull cord and turned on the table's reading lamp. There had been nothing professional about how the room had been searched, no order and no means. Just a matter of having spilled the contents of every drawer in the dresser as well as the steamer trunk, stripping and overturning the bed, piling every piece of clothing in the middle of the room as though readying it for a bonfire.

He sat on the empty bedsprings, one hand rubbing his forehead where it had broken his body's free fall against the carpeted floor and the other wrapped around his chest. Joe knew what the trespassers had wanted for there was little reason to be so thorough if it were only about money, which he kept clipped inside his pockets in case he needed to make a quick bribe. He also knew that they had not found what they wanted, for he did not have it. Had it not hurt so badly to do so, he would have laughed at the irony of it all: He had hoped to become known as Wynton Gresham, and now he had paid a price for that. Someone thought he was Gresham, maybe they were connected to Gresham's killers in Greenwich and thought that they had failed, now they may try finishing things during the cross-Atlantic.

IV

"The officers scrambled out of the advance parallels with a last shout of 'En Avant, mes Enfants' to the men and the wave of 'invisible blue' tipped the parapet with foam. The great offensive of 1915 had begun, and all those who took part in it are agreed that no moment of the battle was so thrilling, so soul-stirring and impressive as that which saw the first wave of Frenchmen in blue uniforms, blue steel Adrian Casques, with drums of grenades hanging at their waists, burst from the trench in which they had hidden for so many months and strike across the intervening No Man's Land for the enemy's line."
—The [London] Times History of the War, vol VI, 1916

JOE SAT IN A HEAP ON THE FLOOR AND TOOK INVENTORY OF WHAT hurt. It wasn't difficult except in discerning where one pain left off and another began. His head hurt, his neck hurt, his back and sides and chest hurt, his hands hurt. His legs did not hurt, but he figured that was because they were farthest from his brain and had to wait until closer body parts registered their complaints before they could get an open line.

He had been in fights before and had been beaten worse, but any beating left its legacy. His breathing was heavy and his heavy breathing ached inside his chest, but he felt nothing loose or broken. That was good news. He could see, he could breathe through his nose, and he could walk. Everything worked more or less as it had been originally designed. Over the night, however, he knew that he would tighten like dried leather.

He pushed his hair off his forehead and sat back against the over-turned mattress of his bed. He was not seeing double, he felt no blood on his head and just a trickle from his nose, his ribs still attached, his hands not too swollen to make a fist. Not too bad after all.

When he stood, though, he felt the years of an arthritic man four times his age as the blood coursed through his wounds and bruises, and he had to sit again. The second time, he stood more slowly and used a chair for balance.

Weak and dizzy, he was like a man suffering through the blue devils of the DTs. He took his time walking to the light switch, a couple of stumbling steps then a pause to regain control then a couple more stumbling steps, until his body and brain began to register in approximately the same time and order. He turned on the wall switch. His eyes and head immediately rebelled against the light. Covering his eyes, he braced himself against the wall like an old drunk come from the pub to find the morning sun. Once he regained a semblance of control, he crossed the room to the porthole window, opening it to let in a draft of fresh air. He inhaled as deeply as his chest would allow, which was considerably less than a full breath, but he felt better for the air's salty freshness.

From a side wall, he lifted off a framed picture, a landscape print by Cezanne, a single tree in front of a stand of trees on a Provence ridge. With his pocket knife, he removed the pins holding the paperboard backing. Inside the backing were the envelopes of names, the lists, and the photograph of the men in a trench, along with his few speculative notes. He replaced the paperboard, taking care to keep from leaving markings that would signal the backing had been removed.

He checked the bathroom and found his Luger missing. He had taped it to the back of the commode and all that was left was the tape. Back in the main room, he checked the desk's trashcan for the .45. It was there beneath a pile of crumpled papers, cold and hard, a Smith & Wesson .45 1917 revolver with a short barrel the metallic color of a tempest sky. He smiled. The best place to hide something, he thought, was in plain sight. He glanced back at where Gresham's photograph was hidden and thought momentarily of what his manuscript might involve—something hidden in plain sight.

His head hurt too much for such thoughts, so he went over the .45, something concrete with nothing hidden about it. After opening the cylinder to check the bullets and sighting through the foresight to gauge his unsteady hand, he lay the revolver on his washstand.

His mind flashed quickly and unexpectedly on a warm scene from his youth with his father sitting on the edge of a leather chair to work on the pieces of a revolver laid out on a trivet table pulled from in front of the fireplace. Joe kneeled across from his father to watch the man's large hands disassemble and clean and reassemble the gun, which in his youth appeared enormous to Joe. After arranging the separate pieces across the metal table, Joe's father would tap down the tobacco in his pipe before commenting on each piece, describing its fitting and its purpose. He wiped and oiled the revolver, its function and its placement and its mechanism, like a tuner at his Steinway.

In front of a banking fire with the revolver spread on the table in front of him and the night-sounds of the high desert outside their ranch house, Joe came to know his father's .45 as well as he knew the sandy arroyos he rode each day. Not a Smith & Wesson but a Colt that waited, along with his father's tooled Western saddle and a cache of family heirlooms, in his uncle's basement for his return to the Purgatory River at the base of the Sangre de Cristos in Southern Colorado.

Joe shook away the reverie. He stripped down to undershirt and pants, suspenders hanging slack to his sides. He pushed the pile of clothes to the wall before replacing the mattress so that he could just fall into bed when the time arrived.

Because the water pitcher had been placed on the floor beside the washstand and not broken against the floor, whoever had searched his room had done so with some care against noise. He put it back on the table and looked into the oval mirror above the table and wondered if Lazarus emerging from the dark had looked as bad as he did. He poured water into the bowl to clean his face then spoke to himself in the mirror. "You can't run, buddy, and you can't hide."

He considered sliding into bed but knew that he should take a little exercise first. He had learned years earlier that after a fight, win or lose, the best thing to do was keep moving. If not, he would stove up tight as a chimney pipe and not even be able to rise from bed in the morning.

Dressed and wearing the buffalo robe, the .45 in one of its deep pockets, he set out for a couple of walking laps around the deck. He knew that he could expect a return visit from his intruders looking for what he did not have, but he did not want to be surprised again. After he closed and locked his door, he broke a toothpick between frame and door. Anyone opening the door would let it loose and not know where it belonged even if they saw it fall. If he could not keep them from entering his cabin, at least he could be prepared for them when he returned.

He walked a trail once around the ship with the air cold and wet and fresh, freezing in his nostrils as he breathed. He stepped to the railing and stood in the cold darkness to enjoy the sea air.

Around him lay a suspension of silence, with the ship's turbines a continual dull thrum of sound. He looked out again at where the blackness of the sky met the blackness of the sea, the liquid traces of moonlight on the dark water. Above, the night's stars shined like distant diamonds shook out on a velvet sheet. Closing his eyes, he listened to the deep churn of the turbines. Only with concentration could he feel the easy movement of the big ship in the water. Joe opened his eyes and stared into the dark, unblinking with his head raised as though smelling the salt in the air

"You don't look so bad off, old man." Huntington's polished voice came out of the darkness from behind him. Joe turned and watched the man approach along the railing, walking with a quiet and steady gate. One of the Englishman's hands stayed in his coat pocket, as did one of Joe's. He wore a properly pressed English smile across his face, his black hair slicked back. His eyebrows were cocked and he still wore his rakish smile, which made him look like a man who enjoyed an occasional adventure or even a good scrape.

"Pardon me?" Joe said.

"The way you were standing," Huntington said, nodding toward the railing. "I've seen plenty of sick men lean against the rail like that." He paused. "You don't look all that ill. *Mal de mer*, the French call it. They have such a way of making even unpleasant things sound romantic."

Joe made a half turn to face Huntington. "You're not looking hard enough."

Huntington looked at him again and smiled. "Yes," he said. "I suppose not. You appear to be wearing a few rather new bruises."

"I slipped," Joe said.

Huntington nodded as though absorbing Joe's words, then said, "You slipped?" He punctuated his words with a half-laugh. "You must take proper care."

"I lack the necessary sea legs for ocean voyaging."

Joe looked as closely as he could into Huntington's eyes, searching for any sign that Huntington had been involved in the beating. He saw none, but that meant little.

Huntington smiled a pleasant smile. He looked out toward the sea. "You must be anticipating our arrival with eagerness."

Joe did not answer. One more day on the ship, then clearing customs at Cherbourg, and after that he could choose his person— himself, Gresham, or someone else entirely, someone with no past. He could hide himself in with the thousands of other American men traveling to France. In plain sight.

"Are you going to Paris?" Huntington asked, watching Joe with steady eyes.

"Undecided," Joe said, his words tinged with a growing distrust. "Why do you ask?"

Huntington turned his back to the railing and leaned against it. While the man had the unmistakable air of superiority bred deeply into an English gentleman, Huntington did not have that aura of disdain and smugness. He removed his cigarette case, silver on top with a college line traversing one corner and his monogram in the middle. Holding the case in the palm of his hand, he opened it with his thumb and held it out toward Joe. A dozen short, white cigarettes perfectly lined the inside of the metallic box.

Joe shook his head and turned so that he also leaned back against the rail. "No thanks," he said.

"They're American. Chesterfield's."

"No," Joe said and began to add more but just stopped.

"A Yank who doesn't smoke. Something of a rarity, I suppose," Huntington mused and took a cigarette from his case.

"Never had the urge, except maybe once during the war when I was wounded."

"Ah," Huntington said, nodding, "necessity's sharp pinch. I know that need quite well."

Joe wondered whether they were playing a game, how much Huntington knew of Gresham, whether he was really a cousin to one of the men in the photograph, whether Huntington had anything to do with the searching of his room.

Huntington tapped the cigarette twice on the closed lid of his case and put it unlit in the corner of his mouth. He then opened his overcoat, loosened his tie and collar, and pulled his shirt open enough for Joe to see the purple remains of a round scar just inches from the base of his neck. "Got it during the Somme. Lucky bastard potted me just as I stepped from the trench ladder."

He retightened his collar and added, "Another . . . to the arm . . . in the mud, Passchendaele. I suppose I didn't learn my lesson the first time."

Joe nodded. "Mine aren't as easily exposed," he said.

"Funny thing, though," Huntington said. "I turned out the lucky one at the Somme. I was wounded right off and right in front of a medical lad." He blinked and added, "Not one in four of my men survived that morning. A bloody waste."

They said nothing for a moment while Huntington lit his cigarette from a silver lighter and took a deep drag. Joe began to like Huntington. The man was a bit arrogant, to be sure, but the arrogance was a bred arrogance that had been softened by a life lived outside of manors and manners.

Looking at the orange glow of the cigarette between his fingers, Huntington asked, "What is your name, sir?"

Joe felt his face darken. "You know my name. Wynton—"

"I mean your real name." He leaned closer.

Joe could smell the man's expensive cologne as though he had been set for a good night, dressed in black and detailed like a prince.

"You ever heard what happened to the curious cat?" Joe asked.

"You mean the one who lied about his name, was found to be a stowaway, and turned over to the authorities? That curious cat?"

Huntington looked at Joe, eyebrows raised, a non-committal grin on his face.

Joe fingered the revolver in his pocket. "What's your point?" he asked and felt his body tense and his eyes press.

"No point, old man. Just asking for your name, your real name." He continued to study his cigarette some more, holding it a foot from his face and tilting it so that the smoke curled in its own gray column against the black backdrop of the ship's walkway. He held it that way and gazed at it in a posture that seemed to Joe as something Huntington might have learned at Eton or choreographed from a duke or a prince.

Joe breathed heavily but did not say anything, his breath pluming in the night's cold air.

Without looking at Joe, Huntington said, "I'm sorry, old man, did you say something? Your name?"

Through a plume of cigarette smoke, he added, "And please don't tell me that you are Wynton Gresham. Wynton Gresham is dead. I know that." He looked around and scratched at his cheek before continuing. "Against my better judgment, I like you, old man. Don't make me call a ship's mate to assist us."

Had Joe not been so tired and sore and stiff and addled, he probably would have felt a panic rush through his body. As it was, though, he just felt tired.

Huntington breathed in a long drag on his cigarette and exhaled softly, tilting his head slightly and letting the cloud dissipate before he spoke, "Still fingering the gun in your pocket?" He smiled and added, "Something of a crude joke, wouldn't you say, had a woman said the same thing to you?"

Huntington leveled his gaze and continued, "What I want to know, sir, is who you are and why you are impersonating Wynton Gresham."

Joe took a minute to consider his options—tell the truth, tell another lie, or toss Huntington to the sharks. The last option sounded most appealing to Joe, but he might as easily end up swimming with the fishes himself. He flipped a mental coin and it came up tails.

"My name is Joe Henry," Joe said with a sigh, his words forming through a cloud of steam from his breath. "I'm a friend of Gresham. A week ago, he wired me in New York and said that he had reservations on this ship and could not come—I don't know why—and asked if I wanted the ticket. I said yes and he wired it to me."

Huntington looked at Joe through eyes that studied and weighed and gauged him without any hint either of acceptance or disbelief. Joe did not smile nor did he allow his eyes to break from Huntington's stare. It was a simple lie. He hoped that its simplicity would carry it, even under the scrutiny of the Englishman's hard gaze.

Huntington remained leaning against the rail until it appeared that he had sifted through the conjured story and had come to some sanction. He flicked his cigarette into the ocean. Joe could see the orange glow disappear into the drift. He stepped away and turned to face Joe head on as though forming one pole of dueling opposites. "It is probably a lie, but it might not be. If it is another lie . . . well, at the least, you will be detained in Cherbourg. Maybe, I will simply kill you."

Joe met Huntington's gaze. "Killing me would not be that easy," he said.

"Possibly," and he shrugged.

"Now let me ask you something," Joe said, hoping to deflect the conversation from him. "Did you search my room earlier?"

Huntington coughed a laugh. "No," he answered, "I am not the only person interested in Gresham."

"Who else is?" Joe asked.

Huntington laughed again, not unpleasant. "What an interesting irony life can become." Huntington smiled and pushed himself from the rail. He removed and lit another cigarette, inhaling a drag before taking a step toward the entrance to the deck.

"Wait a minute," Joe said.

Huntington turned back. "Yes?"

"I talked with you. You talk with me. Give and take."

Huntington laughed. "You told me enough lies to fill a Scottish maun. Do you want me to tell you a lie as well?"

In his mind, Joe worked around the rough edges of the truth. He nodded. "Okay," he said. "You're right. Gresham is dead. Shot. By whom, I don't know. I found him and the police think I killed him, but I didn't. I needed a quick exit. His ticket on this ship provided that for me."

"And your name?"

"Joe Henry, as I said."

Huntington nodded. "That sounds closer to the truth. With Gresham's death, what makes you think I won't now turn you over to the ship's officers?"

"You may, but you may have anyways," Joe said, regaining some balance. "You need something, or you want something from me, else you would not have searched me out. You came to me hoping to find Gresham. You didn't, and now you have more questions. Maybe I can help."

After a full-beat pause, Huntington stepped closer. "Maybe."

Joe said slowly, "And maybe you can also help me."

Huntington nodded. "Quid pro quo."

Joe said, "You scratch mine, I scratch yours."

Huntington nodded.

"Who searched my room?" Joe asked.

Huntington took a drag on his cigarette, holding it in for an extra second before tilting his head to exhale. He watched the gray smoke disappear as though he was searching its depths.

"There are others," he said, "besides myself, who are interested in the manuscript Gresham was writing about Champagne. I had been doing some research into the battle myself when I found the address of a man in Paris who had been there with Gresham and my cousin. He told me about the manuscript and I reserved passage as soon as I could. Unfortunately, I was unable to locate Gresham before his murder. My . . . friend in Paris told me that Gresham was sailing for France on this charter. I had already booked it for myself in case I could not connect with Gresham in the States, and then I read about his murder and thought that the entire trip had been a waste. Imagine my surprise when I find that a dead man is a sailing mate."

Joe shrugged.

"Who's your friend in Paris?" Joe asked. "Your friend's name?"

Huntington smiled and shrugged. "Not yet," he said.

Joe looked out at the sea then back at Gresham. "What do you have against Gresham?"

"Until recently, I had believed, as did others, that Gresham was the one who sold out the advance."

"I don't believe that."

"Neither do I; not anymore," Huntington said. He held out his cigarette, studying the half-inch of ashes on the end before flicking the cigarette out and over the railing. "If you give me a copy of the manuscript to read tonight, tomorrow I will tell you everything you want to know."

Joe shook his head. "I don't have a copy." He added. "Not with me." He watched Huntington arc a single eyebrow.

"Ah, well then—"

"Who else is on board?"

Huntington smiled. "I'll contact you in the morning."

"Why was Gresham killed? What had he written that would get him killed?"

"That should be obvious." Huntington held a finger up as though silencing a school boy. "Tomorrow we shall speak more." He waved his hand in the air and walked toward the doorway, trailing a wake of breath steam behind him.

Huntington disappeared into the white light of the ship's vestibule. Joe watched him until the swinging doors shut, then turned toward the bow of the ship and let the wind wash his face with a cold and steady breeze. He wondered, looking at the charcoal outline of the ship receding into the darkness ahead of it, where he would have been had he just stayed in Greenwich and let himself be arrested. He wondered also where he would be in a week from that moment, where a smart man would be if he himself were a smart man. He had not liked the idea of someone pulling his strings when he was in the army, and the closer he sailed to France the more that uncomfortable feeling returned.

Joe walked through the empty hallways to his cabin and found the toothpick still tight where he had left it. He unlocked and opened the door and let the toothpick fall to the carpet. He lay down on the bed and fell asleep with his clothes still on, the buffalo robe as a covering.

In a dream he studied himself naked, eyes closed and mouth shut tight in a strained line as though he were clenching it against the pain. Blood stained his left cheek from a wound to his shoulder which had already crusted and blackened. His torso was streaked with sweat and mud. Another wound blackened on his left hip and pinpricks of shrapnel had turned his legs into mosaics of blood and bruises and mud. He dreamed of a morning, but his dreams were felon and uncertain. He dreamed things that could not have happened. Men and parts of men flying in slow motion through the smoke-hazed morning to land in small and large splashes within the muddy and water-filled hollows from old bomb shells. Holes opened inside the middle of men's bodies as they ran and some fell as though tripping when they suddenly lost the lower portion of a leg. A man, his jaw shot off, walked dumbly across the pockmarked landscape, arms limp and useless, his eyes speaking a horrible language. He tripped over men who lay with their bodies opened and entrails spilling out and giving off a purplish vapor like whiskey lit with a match. He saw a no-man's land in his dream. Within that no-man's land there was nothing alive. Every tree truncated and left to stand with jagged tops, no bushes or grasses to hold water in the ground, only mud stained red. Every man not dead felt dead and felt as though he would never again be alive. In his dream, the morning became afternoon. He lay in his own blood and filth through the rest of the eventide and through that night. The next morning he listened to flies and to the moans of men who prayed to die. He heard rats feed on men, some of whom not yet dead. He watched a bloody and muddy mongrel dog pick its way through the broken rubble of bodies until finding one it wanted and then begin to eat pieces of a dead man's exposed and opened stomach.

V

"Those were soul-thrilling days. We who lived through them, knew that
they marked a dividing line in our experience, and that henceforth all we
did and were would gravitate about that central moment of our lives."
— "Captain X," *Scribner's Magazine*, October, 1915

WAKING IN SWEAT AND WAKING SUDDENLY TO THE DARKNESS OF his room, he felt a panic from rising in a dark place and not knowing where he was. Slowly he recalled where and who he was and who he was not. He lay back down and sighed. For most of the rest of that night he lay mostly awake but fell asleep again near sunrise. Hours later the light from the morning sun through the porthole window woke him for good.

His head and his body ached in companion, two bloody chaps at the bar rail besting the other in the consumption of pain. Joe wished he had a couple of pints with which to drown them both. In the mirror above the washstand he again looked into the face of Lazarus, although not as healthy.

"Bloody fool," he said to his reflection and waited for an answer that did not come.

Joe imagined the coroner's jowly face in Greenwich hanging above his as he lay stretched on a table like that etherized patient he had once read about. The coroner would look up from his notes to announce the results of his inquest. Joe said out loud into the clear liquid of the mirror, "Cause of death—gross ignorance and stupidity," and he smiled, which hurt.

Near noon, Joe found the focus for his eyes. He sat on the rumpled blankets of his unmade bed, wondering what new ignorance he would suffer that day. He wrote his quick list for that day:

Wash & Shave
Pick-Up Clothes
Exercise
Stay out of Damn Trouble
Dammit

He sat for a moment, fountain pen in hand, thinking of nothing else for his list, so he began to rearrange the mess of his room, returning his clothes to their hangars or to the chest of drawers. He washed and shaved and set himself for the day and wondered why Huntington had not yet contacted him. By mid-afternoon, he was again leaning on the ship's railing, dressed in Gresham's tweed suit, standing on the promenade deck to inhale the salt air that was almost cold. Its brisk bite made him feel more alive than he had felt for days.

He looked up at the ship's three large funnels, and erupting from each came columns of black smoke that drifted behind the ship like a cloud-trail in the sky.

Stiff and slow, he walked toward the ship's bow and felt the tightness of his muscles, a heavy pain like a gnawing hangover afflicting his entire body. He stepped to the railing for a moment to rest, and he watched the ocean's shroud roll around the ship.

A large man pulled to the railing a dozen paces behind him. When Joe took two steps, stopped and looked out over the ocean again, the large man did the same. The man was bull necked, with dark skin and thick black eyebrows like pieces of coal and short-cropped black hair. He wore a black overcoat and kept his hands in his pockets.

Joe's fingers felt for the grip of his revolver. He held it loosely, resuming his walk and feeling the man trail behind him like a dog on a leash. It was something he could deal with, no obscure playing with words and no darkness, except he wondered about the large man's intent.

Joe's shoulders hunched instinctively, as though he were walking down a duckboard trench in the morning light. The first rule his sergeant had told him at the front was to never walk around during the day. The second rule was that if he did walk around in the daylight to never let his head bob above the top of the trench. As he strolled the deck, it took some effort for him to straighten his shoulders and look ahead instead of pulling into himself. He walked casually until he neared a set of closed glass doors entering the ship.

Another man, shorter and slightly stoop-shouldered, hurried past Joe, pushed open the door and walked quickly down the hall. That man's quick stride had caught Joe's attention. Joe followed the short man's path through the doors, seeking the safety of numbers.

The inchoate sense of the prey stopped him short, and Joe turned to see if the large man would follow him inside. Instead the man had leaned back against the railing to light a cigarette in his cupped hands, tossed the spent match over his shoulder, took a long drag, and smiled, staring purposefully at Joe.

He thought back to the list he had written that day and knew that he had accomplished three of his list's elements but had probably failed at the last, the one with the exclamation.

Rounding a corner, he glimpsed the man ahead of him rounding another corner. He felt as though he was being herded, so instead of following him, Joe turned the opposite direction and walked toward the men's smoking room, the room that felt of comfort and smelled of rubbed wood and leather and weathered whiskey. Once there, Joe inhaled its air like a curative and felt at ease in its embrace. Most of the tables in the room were empty, chairs pushed out and at angles to tables from the flux of patrons having enjoyed a constitutional. A few men sat reading wire dispatches as they would the Sunday morning newspaper. One table was surrounded by a handful of men playing an early game of cards and a second table seated another group arguing about the riots in Germany and who should be blamed.

He realized as he warmed with the ship's inner heat how tense his body had become, either from the cold air on the deck or from the sensation of being followed. His body began to loosen and he closed his eyes and breathed purposefully.

Joe ignored the few men there. He sat in a booth by himself and ordered a pint of stout to steady his nerves. He read the wire dispatches to see if there was any word about him, or Gresham. When one man returned a sheaf of dispatches to the reading table, Joe retrieved it and sat at his booth table facing the room's entrance. He drank from his stout and read only the first few lines of each dispatch.

Joe raised his eyes to study everyone who entered the room, watching to see if they took any note of him. Before long, the large man walked in and took a seat by the door and was soon joined by the smaller, slightly stoop-shouldered, and more smartly dressed man. The two were not in the least discreet in their attention to Joe.

The two huddled together to exchange words, then leaned back and looked at Joe like partners in a chess game they alone recognized. The first man, whom Joe named the Turk for his hulking size and dark olive skin, pointed a steady finger at Joe. The other, Dapper for his better clothes, nodded and smiled. Dapper rubbed the side of his chest and winced, and Joe thought that Dapper was the one in his room he had landed a few punches against.

The Turk rubbed his knuckles lightly as though in confirmation of Joe's thoughts. The man's knuckles looked like marbles. His smile was more like a sneer and his eyes were black and lifeless. It was the Turk he studied more closely. A large and swarthy man with heavy eyebrows and coarse black hair cut close and poorly as though he had cut it himself with scissors in front of a mirror. He could have been twenty-five or fifty, Joe could not tell, and his eyes were deep and spaced wide and his five-o'clock shadow had arrived early, the full and continually potential beard of a Mediterranean.

Joe did not like the idea that he was caught in some still-hunt with him as the quarry. He pushed the dispatches onto the table and began to rise, his eyes fixed on the two men. They tensed noticeably, not expecting the action being taken to them.

Joe's movement was arrested by a hand on his shoulder.

"Do you mind?" Huntington asked. He sat across from Joe and took up the dispatches.

Joe looked again at the two men before he eased himself back into his booth. "You need to wear a bell," he said and took a long and slow pull on his stout.

Huntington laughed. "Or you need to be more observant."

Joe wondered what other things, things maybe as equally obvious as a man sitting alone in a half-empty room, he had been missing.

Huntington fingered the dispatches. "Looking for something, are we?"

"Just reading the news and enjoying a pint."

"Why not enjoy another?" Huntington asked and called for a waiter to bring them a round. "Two Scotch, if you please," he said to the waiter, who bowed and left.

Huntington smiled at Joe, "I served with some officers from a Texas division early in your involvement, jolly good men you colonials are."

"We try."

Joe looked again at Dapper and the Turk. They had rested back in their chairs now that Joe was fully seated in his booth. They each drank from a whiskey glass and watched Joe and Huntington like a bored audience at a bad stage play.

Huntington leaned to the side and reached into his coat pocket. He pulled a folded piece of yellow paper from it and pushed the paper across the table between them.

Joe looked at Huntington, who nodded and said, "Interesting reading."

He removed a cigarette from his silver case and lit it while Joe unfolded the paper.

It was a dispatch dated early that morning that had come over the wire from New York. Joe read it carefully, but after the first line he knew what the dispatch said.

"Was that what you were looking for?" Huntington asked.

Joe refolded the dispatch and handed it back to Huntington.

"No. Keep it, old man," Huntington said with a dismissive wave. "Our secret," he smiled. "Lucky for you, though, that I have insomnia and can't sleep into the morning. I didn't before, but I do now. I found it first thing today. The ship's crew is too busy to check these things and would not find out unless someone bothered to inform them. Had another passenger found it and not I, say those two behind me at the door who seem to have taken a great interest in you, well, then, you might presently be in a bit of a boil. Anyway, a sea of troubles, you might say." He smiled at his own pun.

They sat in silence as the waiter placed their drinks on the table, then each tasted his.

"What do you want?" Joe asked, holding the folded dispatch in the cup of his hand like a weight.

Huntington deadened his cigarette in the glass ashtray and said, "More than you gave me last night."

Joe glanced toward Dapper and the Turk, thinking that they were with Huntington and had been posted in case of emergency. Huntington followed Joe's gaze over his shoulder to the men by the door.

"Don't worry about them, old man," Huntington said.

"They your watchdogs?" Joe asked.

"My watchdogs?" He laughed. "No. They're probably the men who attacked you last night. I suppose they work for the Frenchman, Rene Marcel."

Joe looked at Huntington. "Marcel?"

"You know him?"

"The name."

"From Gresham, no doubt."

"Yes, but I don't know who Marcel is."

Huntington sat for a moment, his eyes leveled on Joe and his jaw muscles twitching as though he were working over some algebraic formula in his head.

Joe knew what the formula was and offered an answer. "Like you said last night, 'Tit for tat.'"

"'I scratch yours and you scratch mine'?"

"That's right. I answered your questions then; now you can fill in some blanks for me."

"I suppose it's fair, but I don't know how useful it is."

"We won't know until you tell me."

Huntington scratched the scar on his cheek, then began. "My cousin—"

"Thomas Wilde."

"Yes. Thomas was a business associate with the Marcel family before the war. Import-Export out of Normandy. That may be how Thomas ended up with them in a mixed unit during the war. Two important families integrated by business, then integrated to watch over the other. I don't know; I'm just speculating. What I know is that they were involved in quite lucrative investments prior to the war, that they were together during the war and together on the 25th of September in Champagne, that my cousin died and that Rene Marcel lived."

Huntington paused to drink, and even though Joe had questions to ask he remained silent. Huntington was giving voice to the back-story that Joe needed and Joe did not want to break the thin line that Huntington was drawing.

Huntington scratched at his eyelid before continuing. "Marcel was wounded badly enough that he was sent to convalesce and lucky enough not to be returned to the front. Maybe wealthy enough as well. He returned to his business, his patriotic duty fulfilled, and with the war and the necessity for war materials, he increased his wealth."

Huntington took a lingering sip of his whiskey before continuing his story. "You see," he said to Joe. "I have spent some time studying him. I have my own money and am comfortable enough that I can spend the necessary time and funds to discover the truth as to what took place that morning near Lausanne."

"So you've talked with Marcel," Joe asked.

"No," Huntington said. "That's an interesting part of the story. Marcel never seems to have returned to Normandy. He established his business empire in Paris, even though the workings were being done in Normandy. Now he has auxiliaries throughout France and Germany, Poland, Switzerland, Austria. An amazing expansion of his business empire in such a short time. But," he said, leaning forward and pointing his finger. "And here's the rub. Few have seen him since the war. It seems that everyone who worked for the family before the war were either too old to serve during the war and have since been replaced in the business or died during the war. It seems that nobody who was in service to the Marcel family has remained."

"And Marcel?"

Huntington huffed. "He has secluded himself in various villas and homes—Paris, Berlin, Marseilles, maybe others. He refuses all contact, and he has the money to ensure his seclusion."

"Claiming that his war wounds—"

"Yes," Huntington said before Joe had completed his thought. "He uses his wounds as an excuse to remain far from the public eye, and people can communicate with him only through a maze of intermediaries. As something of a war hero, he is allowed his eccentricities."

"And now?"

"My guess," Huntington said, holding his glass in the air peering into the amber liquid. "My guess is that Marcel had Gresham killed. We can speculate as to why. Now I will have to talk with Marcel," he said with introspection.

"You think Marcel was the traitor?"

Huntington sipped at his drink, savoring the taste of whiskey as the ice began to reveal its flavor. He put the glass down and folded his hands together, fingers entwined, on the table. He looked at Joe, but his eyes were vacant. "Someone sold out the advance. Probably Marcel, I don't know but I suspect, but someone betrayed them and Gresham found out who. Now that traitor is looking to silence Gresham—You."

Joe leaned forward. "What do you know about the battle?"

Huntington nodded his head but took a long time to answer. His face darkened. His jaw muscles moved as though he were in debate with himself. He licked his lips and said, "Good men were fed full to the many guns of that war, but in Champagne the triggers were readied by a traitorous act. My cousin—Thomas Wilde—was with Gresham and Marcel, as I said, and some others—an Englishman named Gadwa and Rene's brother, Jean—in a combined detachment of French and English. They were reconnaissance—spies and spotters. One of them, maybe more, was also in the employ of the Huns. Gadwa is dead as well as my cousin and Jean Marcel. Until recently, I thought that Gresham had also died that day."

Huntington paused and unlaced his fingers. He traced a circle on the wood of the table. He tilted his head, "They are Marcel's men."

Joe sat back and took a moment to weigh the information. There was another name on the list: Dillard. He was about to ask Huntington what he knew about him when Dapper and the Turk stood. His finger reached into the pocket of his coat folded on the bench next to him, finding the revolver. The two men left the room, walking nonchalantly, just two chums enjoying a drink and a smoke in the company of other gentlemen. The Turk smiled at Joe as he turned to walk out, not a congenial smile at all.

Huntington stood. He was not a large man, but well-built and cut an impressive presence if someone were impressed with that sort of man—spit-and-polish, ribboned, titled. Joe was not.

Joe was, however, impressed with the fact that Huntington was more than the façade. The man was not a counterfeit. Joe saw it in Huntington's eyes and in his movements. He was impressed with Huntington's service in the trenches as well as with Huntington's allegiance to his fallen cousin. The man had earned his honors. Joe thought that with time, the two of them might become friends.

Huntington took a step away, but before he could leave, Joe asked, "How can I meet Marcel?"

Huntington scratched the scar across his nose and smiled. "I doubt if that will be a problem, old man. The question is 'When?'"

"Okay," Joe said, "When?"

"When he wants you to."

Before Joe could respond, a steward approached their table. "Colonel Huntington?" The steward stood erect, his right hand loose at his side and his left arm cocked at a right angle, fingers holding a folded piece of white paper for Huntington.

"Yes," Huntington replied, looking first at the steward and then at the piece of paper as the steward handed it to him.

"Begging your pardon, Colonel," the steward said. "This is for you."

"From whom?"

"He did not say, sir."

Huntington cocked an eyebrow and took the paper. The steward nodded and left, a man who knew his position.

Huntington opened and read the note and excused himself, "A meeting. We shall talk again."

Huntington left without offering his hand or waiting for Joe's reply, and Joe ordered another whiskey to drink in the comfortable absence of the prying. He could not see the arrangement yet, but he could see that pieces to his puzzle were falling as though on a plank table. All he needed to do was place them in order. The blank spots still outnumbered those filled and he remained lost in another man's fog, but for the first time he began to see the possibility for understanding his dilemma. With luck he might be able to offer someone as the murderer of Gresham to the police in France. That would pose some problems concerning the legality of his trip, but he would deal with that when it came. Proving his innocence would be worth deportation.

He finished his whiskey while studying the wire that Huntington had given him, but there was nothing in it that he did not already know. The police in Greenwich wanted him for the murder of Wynton Gresham. The police believed that he had acted in union with two Frenchmen, the two from the automobile wreck, for they had a pistol matching the caliber of bullets found in Gresham's body. No motive was known, but one officer suggested that Joe's flight was certain proof of his guilt. Joe could guess which police officer had suggested that. The sheriff had spent a night in the hospital from a struggle with Joe in his apartment. Joe smiled at the description of his single sucker punch being characterized as a struggle.

The wire did not mention Joe's Hudson in New York, and the police speculated that he had left for Colorado where he had grown up. That thought pleased him. The police had no reason to search abroad for him. If that held for another day, he would be lost in Paris, just another American expat wandering the City of Light.

He considered ordering another but decided not. He asked a steward to send his dinner to his cabin as well as take a message to Huntington's cabin asking to meet that evening. Huntington might answer some of Joe's lingering questions, shed light on some of the dark spots in the events that led to the murder of Gresham.

He looked at his watch, a pocket Seth Thomas that was the only thing of his father's that he had kept with him following his father's death and then through the war and then the years since. The time was nearing three in the afternoon. The ship was set to dock in Cherbourg the next day, almost twenty-four hours to the minute from then. Joe wanted to work through a few things before that time.

After washing his face and hands in his cabin, Joe placed the photograph and list of names on the room's writing table and sat back, crossed his arms and looked at the men almost grammured in the shadow-like image. He compared the list of men with the photograph of men in a trench, men who knew for certain they would soon die. Gresham he knew and recognized, even though the Gresham in the photograph was leaner and stooped like a beggar on a city street. He stood farthest from the camera, not smiling, eyes shaded by a pitted and dirty helmet, the strap worn loose under his chin, a weather-worn and ragged overcoat with torn cuffs, left hand outstretched and holding the top row of withy branches used to shore up the trench, the other hand holding a canteen cup, a wisp of steam above the cup marking its contents as either coffee or tea, binoculars hung around his neck and unboxed against his chest, a satchel strung across his chest to rest on his right hip facing the camera, legs and feet in the morning shadow of the trench. There might be a look of concern on his face, but every morning in the trench had begun as though one had hoped to wake from a nightmare instead of waking into a nightmare.

During one of their late-night talks when neither could find rest, they had exchanged stories of the trenches. With whiskey in one hand and brier in the other, Gresham had told Joe that he had been part of a reconnaissance unit at Champagne. He had joined the English army soon after hostilities broke out with Germany. His mother was English, lower nobility but still nobility, and he had been in London visiting cousins when he became caught up in the fervor—that old lie, *Dulce et decorum est*. Because of his family's name, he joined as an officer. Since the oncoming battle in the Champagne was to be a joint affair between the British and the French, the recon unit was also joint. They went out every night to scout the advance, mapping the wires and trails to the German trenches. They worked in pairs and every morning would compare notes. The evening of the attack, they were told to remain in the trench and go out the next morning to watch and record the event. "That was the day," Gresham had said, "when we all went to hell."

Joe studied the photograph, the manner of their bodies, their faces and their uniforms. The three Frenchmen and two Englishmen between Gresham and the camera sat or knelt against the side of the trench, their feet braced on the trench's wooden duck walk. One Englishman held a spoon to his mouth and smiled wearily at the camera. Two Frenchmen next to him appeared to be smiling as well, looking at something across from them in the trench, a rat that had slipped in the mud maybe. They had narrow faces and the same slant to their smiles and could have been brothers and maybe were the two Marcels. Joe drew a quick sketch of the scene with stick figures representing each man. He drew lines from the two stick-figured men who looked like brothers and wrote *Marcels* and a line from the standing stick figure and wrote *Gresham*. That left three others to identify.

Next to the brothers Marcel was an Englishman, as though hovering truncated and silhouetted, fully shaded with only the dark outline of his head visible under his English helmet, his shoulders rounded, his back slightly hunched like that of any man who had spent even a single day below the surface. Another Frenchman looked with stern eyes directly at the camera as though daring this to be his last image of life. He stood closest to the camera. His mouth was opened slightly to show an irregular line of white teeth between full lips.

Joe knew their names but not which face belonged to every name. At least one of them was a traitor. At least three of them were dead. He tried to figure the traitor from the images, what he could conjure behind the two-dimensional faces, but he could not. He studied the list of names and the marks Gresham had put next to each name. Check's behind *Wilde* and *Jean Marcel* and a dash following

Paul Dillard's name, whom Joe had first thought was English but then decided must be the third Frenchman and probably alive and probably the one who had told Huntington about Gresham and the manuscript. Nothing was noted after the names of Rene Marcel and Gadwa.

Wilde and Jean Marcel had checks behind their names and were both dead and were thus linked. Dillard was alive and had a dash behind his name and was alone. Gadwa and Rene Marcel had no marks and in Joe's mind were thus linked together. He had no reason why that might be nor any reason to believe that they were linked. But somehow they were.

"Goddamn nothing," Joe said louder than he expected, leaning back in his chair and rubbing his eyes.

He leaned forward again to look at the photograph, conjuring the image in his mind, bringing it alive as through the divinations of a necromantic shaman, bringing it forth from what he witnessed in his months spent in the trenches of eastern France. What came into view for him were not the images of the photograph but his own memories laid bare as an open wound. One man still snoring as the last of the bombardment sounded with the false dawn rising and then that man fully awake to the increasing sound of nothing. A quiet so dense that Joe remembered believing he could hear the earth move. The collected breath of thousands of young men about to become too old to live any longer. A wren lit in the sunlight and perched along the withy at the top of the trench. A man vomited violently and then another. Someone cursed. Another man whispered softly as though praying his own prophetic supplication, "I'm dead, I'm dead," and answered by another man who cussed an imprecation of damnation upon the man. Slowly Joe had made out the music of a gramophone floating softly from the German lines. He had listened carefully. The song had been in English. Several men near Joe began to hum; some sang along to the music. "*Sing me love's lullaby. Sing me the song of dreams—Dearie, where you and I wander in love-land, where love-light beams. So hold me.*" Then it began. A whistle and a yell. A confusion of feet and bodies climbing and falling. A swirled haze of smoke and dust and fog. The first man over the top and already to the lane in the wire, a lieutenant from Yale shot through the neck and arrested in his fall to the ground by the wire and left moving spastically from the bullets continuing to thrum his dead body. Then Joe was more afraid than he had ever been. Too afraid not to follow the others as they climbed the trench ladders and ran through the lanes in the wire. He had run blindly into the morning fog and toward other young men who were equally afraid but still wanting to kill him.

VI

"BERENGARIA PROPELLER DAMAGED BY
WRECKAGE
Big Cunard Liner Delayed in Reaching Cherbourg,
but All on Board Are Well.
The great former German liner Berengaria, the largest of the Cunard
Company's transatlantic ships, struck part of a submerged wreckage. . . .
She was due at Southampton yesterday, but will not reach Cherbourg,
her first port of call, until some time today."
—The New York Times

A SERIES OF KNOCKS ON THE CABIN DOOR STARTLED JOE FROM HIS restless sleep. His own memories had whipped his dreams and his heart raced with the sudden interruption. He sat on the side of his bed, head in hands, his mind still half a decade away. He looked quickly around the room before again remembering where he was and who he was or who he was supposed to be. The sudden, nervous sweat cooled on his brow. His heart slowed, but he did not reach to answer the door. He gathered the notes and photograph that covered the table in front of him and with no time to properly hide them, slid them inside the pages of his copy of *Scribner's* magazine. Hidden in plain sight.

Above the chest of drawers, the portal window showed darkness.

Once again, he had fallen asleep with his clothes on. He felt as though he were apprenticing for bumdom and tucked in his shirt and straightened his pants. He held the pistol in his right hand, covering his arm with an overcoat.

Another series of knocks measured his door, sounding more like a fight on the wood than friendly raps.

He called out, "Just a moment," breathed deeply and opened the door.

Facing him in a semicircle at the door were five ship's officers, their uniforms pressed to the point of death and as rigid as their postures. At the front of the cluster stood a man of girth carrying a chest full of ribbons above his large stomach. The Captain, Joe decided, looking into the gray eyes of an Englishman who approved of his own of glory, probably earned in the comfort of a state room.

He could see each of the men as they immediately measured him, taking stock of his disheveled state, his day-old beard, his irregular hair, the probable redness of his eyes. He knew that he must have appeared like a stumbled drunk. Whatever they were there for, he was not making a good first impression.

Even with that, however, Joe felt no panic. He had been discovered. He could not run. There was no place to run to on a ship at sea even if he could fight his way out of the room. He loosened his grip on the pistol, allowing his index finger to break from the trigger.

"Yes?" Joe asked, blinking and wiping his mouth with the back of his free hand.

"May we enter?" the Captain asked in response. It was not a question at all, just a polite demand, not even meant to be answered.

Joe stepped aside and waved them in. The Captain nodded and entered, followed by the others. Together, the six of them took up almost the entire floor space of the room.

"Can I help you?" Joe asked, turning his body to hide the movements of his hand as he slid the pistol into a pocket of his overcoat, placing the coat on his bed.

"We are here about August Huntington," the Captain said.

"Huntington?" Having expected them to arrest him, or at the very least to question him about being Wynton Gresham, he felt a certain release along with his confusion. That they had asked about Huntington might have meant that he had dodged another bullet. Had he been superstitious, he might have begun to taste invulnerability, but he was more experienced, if not smarter, than that.

"Colonel Huntington, yes" the Captain said, his voice a deep baritone. Fitting, Joe thought, for a captain of the ship.

"What about him?"

"He is dead."

"What?" At that moment, had he been superstitious, he would have wondered whether he was a curse. That pendulum of fortune that he had been swinging on for the past week, swung with swift speed.

"He was murdered in the hallway outside of his cabin," said one of the other officers, a thin man with a thin voice.

Joe sat on the bed next to his coat, hands on his knees and feet even on the floor in front of him.

He watched the other ship's officers as they coldly fingered through the things in his cabin. At least they were more careful than the last sets of inquiring eyes. They also had the time and sanction to search more closely and slowly. Joe didn't know what they were looking for but could guess that it was something to incriminate him. He had read that script before.

The Captain continued, "A passenger found him last night and reported to our steward. He was dead before our medical officer even arrived."

He nodded to his underlings and they began their search, opening drawers and patting the pockets of hangered suits and fingering inside shoes. The Captain, watching as his men looked for anything of use, picked up Joe's loaded copy of *Scribner's*, and Joe questioned the wisdom of his hiding place.

In plain sight, he silently chided himself.

The captain began leafing through it as he talked. "After we attended to him, we searched his room for any indication of who might have killed him."

"And that's why you're here?" Joe could hear the Captain's assumptions hum through the room and thought with a flatness that too many people assumed too much about too many things.

The Captain looked at Joe, returned the magazine to the side table, pulled from his pocket Joe's written request to meet with Huntington. He opened it and held it out for Joe to read. "From you?" he asked.

"Yes."

"Why did you wish to meet with him?"

"We were in a battle during the war. Same time, same place." He felt himself slide once again into the spiraling necessity of lies.

"You knew him from the war?"

"No" Joe said, shaking his head and keeping his lie simple. "We didn't know each other. We just happened to discover during dinner the other night that we had fought in the same battle."

"And which battle was that, may I ask?"

"The Champagne."

The Captain measured Joe with leveled eyes. "That was a bad day," he said with solemnity. Joe could see the man practicing his visage in front of a mirror, memorizing the proper look for the proper occasion for the man had to perform throughout the sea-voyage.

"In more ways than one," Joe said. *In more ways than you could ever know*, he thought but did not say.

"A black spot on the integrity of the Crown," said the Captain, puffing his chest with self-righteous patriotism.

Chicken-shitting bastard, flashed through Joe's mind.

He gritted his teeth. He wanted to say that the integrity of the Crown during that war had been blackened well before the Battle of the Champagne, that it had been blackened by bastard officers carrying chests filled with medals who never saw the mud and rats of a trench, whose exposure to mustard gas was limited to what they read in the pages of the *London Times*. Those men, old and rich men who sent the young and poor to war, turned Joe's stomach, like the former president and his Western vice-president whose jingoistic ballyhooing had killed thousands of Joe's generation. Joe referred to them as "Chicken-hawks," too cowardly to fight when they were young but more than eager to damn another generation. At other moments, even less-forgiving moments, he called them "Chicken-shitting bastards."

To the Captain, however, did not say anything.

One of the underlings leaned across between Joe and the Captain, taking the magazine from its table and let it flip open to Joe's insertions. He held them for the Captain to see and Joe watched as the Captain studied the photograph.

"Are you or Huntington in this photograph?" the Captain asked, looking from the photograph to Joe.

"No," Joe said, then began to mill his story with counterfeit truths: "I took the photograph. Those are others who were there. I'm going to France to visit some of them." At least that last part was not a lie. He felt his body and mind clear to regain a sense of solid particularity, the sloughing off of another death in a world in which life had become cheap. He pushed thoughts of Huntington to the background and again concentrated on his own survival.

"And you had the photograph out for . . . ?"

"I thought Huntington might know some of them." Joe was becoming accustomed to lying. He had become pretty good at it, easily slipping between truths and lies like a serpent in tall grass.

Another officer, pointing to the list of names, leaned close and whispered something in the Captain's ear. While the man was whispering, the Captain raised his thick eyebrows and turned his eyes toward Joe. Joe had the falling feeling of having suddenly been placed under a microscope, once again pinned beneath the fixed stare of a focused eye.

The Captain looked at Joe but spoke to the officer next to him. "Go and see," he ordered. "Let me know as soon as you know something. And take Montgomery with you." He nodded his head toward a lower-grade officer standing near the door but never allowed his eyes to waver from Joe sitting on the bed.

After the two officers left the room, the Captain said to Joe, "Interesting coincidences."

"What are?" Joe had begun to hate the word in the way a child hates the slap of a strap against an open palm.

The Captain paused before answering. He pulled a chair from the round table and sat with a long and audible sigh, as though relieving himself of a physical burden. With his hands on his knees and facing Joe straight on, he said, "Just that you would meet a man who had been with you during such a disastrous battle, a debacle and treason really, or so the stories say, and then you arrange for a meeting and he is murdered outside his cabin door the same night as your meeting." He sighed again and sat back, thrumming the fingers of one hand on the table. "Interesting coincidences."

"You already said that," Joe said quietly, shaking his head and wishing he had a whiskey.

"Yes, I did," said the Captain, his eyes not smiling at all. "Wouldn't you agree, though?"

Joe's mind flashed on the series of coincidences that had originally interwoven him in the web he felt caught in, a moth having wandered in flight onto the blue leaf of a columbine only to touch to the viscid gossamer of the spider's web. His life had become fixed within that web of contradictions and lies and false assumptions. He wondered how long before he was mummified in silken threads or killed. He answered flatly, "I'm not such a fancier of coincidences."

"Neither am I, sir," answered the Captain.

Joe shrugged. He would have guessed as much, could have said the line for the Captain had he been asked.

The Captain stood, folded his arms across the extent of his barrel chest and pursed his lips. He said, "You do not seem overly concerned about Colonel Huntington's death."

"We weren't friends," Joe said. "We just met. On the ship. We were little more than acquaintances." It wasn't really a lie, but it was also far from the truth. He had liked Huntington, and in the few days that he had known the Brit had come to feel trust for the man. They shared membership in a select group: They had fought and survived the Western Front. He disliked having dismissed Huntington with such an off-handed remark, and he notched another event that would need redemption.

He had once read about the Viking belief in Valhalla, where warriors would meet in the afterlife. He didn't believe in that, but he thought that there must be a special club in heaven for those who served with honor. He hoped that if he made it past St. Peter at the Pearly Gates, that Huntington would welcome him and forgive his callous remark and the two could sit over a pint or ten and share war stories.

"Yes." The Captain nodded and paused as though scripted and practiced in front of a mirror. "We will arrive in Cherbourg late this afternoon and proceed to Southampton in the morning. The police may wish to speak with you, so my first mate will accompany you ashore in Southampton when we arrive there." He paused as for effect and leaned toward Joe. "You will not disembark today. Your trunk is in the hallway. Apologies for the broken hasp, it was not preventable. I have asked for a steward to return later this morning to retrieve the trunk for transport tomorrow." He waited a moment and added, "Do not attempt to disembark in Cherbourg."

Joe did not answer. Each person's world turns on its own axis, and his axis had once again been knocked from its plane. He sat and watched the officers depart in their descending order following in the Captain's wake. They took nothing with them, leaving the photograph and note on the table and not asking for his passport. Gresham's passport.

He remembered the note informing the ship's passengers that Cherbourg would be the initial docking, that the ship would not dock in Plymouth as originally scheduled. Once more he thanked the heavy and rough seas and the broken turbine for that bit of fortune. Joe knew enough to know that there was always a bit of a push once the ship docked for disembarkation. In that rush of movement he hoped for another quiver of fortunate possibility.

After they had all left the room and the room had returned to its silence, Joe retrieved the trunk, stripped, and cleaned himself with the water on the washstand. He felt his jaw tighten as his mind mulled the situation. He felt like a lesser Theseus having muddled his way deep into a maze not of his making, only he lacked his Ariadne with her length of saving thread.

Huntington's murder further muddled things for Joe. He knew who had killed Gresham—the Frenchmen from the accident—and he knew why. That incomplete knowledge traced a slight frown across his face. The two Frenchmen who had died on the rain-slick road outside of Greenwich were not alone and had been working for someone else, the someone who had since killed Huntington. Joe knew the shape of that man, but not the man himself.

He dried himself and set aside a clean gray wool suit, packed the rest of his clothes in the steamer trunk, locking it as best he could with its one broken hasp. He piled all of his money, the photograph and notes, revolver, and passports, his and Gresham's, on the bed next to his overcoat. Standing next to the bed, he looked over the things he had arranged. With them, he might make it. If he could get off the ship all right, then he could make it. He could leave everything else behind if he needed to.

He sat for a moment but felt claustrophobic and decided to leave, for fresh air on the deck. He wished he could keep his trunk of clothes once he left the ship, for if he did get to Paris after landing at Cherbourg, the clothes would be nice to have. He patted his pockets. He had the necessities, money and a gun.

When he opened the door of his cabin, he saw an opportunity. Standing like silenced sentinels outside the cabin doors to two other rooms in the wide hallway were steamer trunks. He pulled his own trunk out into the corridor, leaving it outside his cabin and walking across the hall to knock on the first door.

A woman answered, her face hidden behind a heavy layer of makeup that made her age difficult to guess. Somewhere between seventy-five and dead, Joe thought, and probably closer to the latter.

"Well, can I help you?" the woman demanded in a burnished New England accent.

"I'm sorry ma'am. I must have the wrong room. I was looking for the Blaines, Amory and his wife."

She looked him up and down and curled her upper lip. She did not like what she saw. "You *do* have the wrong room."

"I do. I apologize." He bowed and motioned as though to tip his hat had he been wearing one and apologized again. The woman shut her door without responding. She would not do. He needed someone who might not be as suspicious or as aware. While she had not recognized his *faux nom*, she was too quick to her skepticism.

The next cabin had two trunks outside its door. He knocked and another woman answered. She looked to be dressed more for an opera than for leaving the ship. She even raised her lorgnette glasses to her face in order to study Joe.

Joe repeated his lie, "I'm sorry, ma'am. I must have the wrong room. I was looking for Amory Blaine and his wife."

"Sorry," the woman said. "We are the McKees."

"Who is it, dear?" her husband asked from inside the room.

"Just someone looking for the Blaines, darling."

"The who?"

"Blaines—Amory and his wife. You remember them."

After a pause, the husband answered, "Oh, yes-yes. Good fellow. Drinks a bit much, but still a good chap. Don't know their cabin number, though."

The wife turned to Joe. "I'm sorry. We can't help you, but when you find them, please give them our regards."

"I will do that, Mrs. McKee," Joe said, bowing and thinking how people are easily fooled when played to their vanity.

He went back to his room, leaving the door open, and waited. He waited for the count of one hundred after the McKees left their cabin before pulling his steamer trunk across the hallway to exchange with one of theirs. He left his tags attached and pulled their trunk into his room, cutting their tag with his penknife and sitting back to wait for the steward.

Joe lay back on the bed and closed his eyes and felt the movement of the ship. After a knock on the door woke him from his past, Joe drew in a long breath as in silent prayer. He opened the door to find a small, almost fragile old man standing next to a hand dolly. The man wore an ill-fitting uniform, too long in the sleeves and too large in the waist, and a rigid hat tilted back on his head with tufts of graying hair shooting out at angles.

The man looked at a piece of paper in his hand. "Mr. Gresham?" he asked, Cockney accent winking out the words.

"Yes," Joe answered, standing to the side and motioning for the steward to enter. "Come in. It's all packed and ready for you. You will take care of it, won't you?"

Joe knew officers well enough to know that they would never tell a man in the trenches more than was absolutely necessary. That was something Joe was counting on. The ship's officers would have told the steward to pick up Joe's trunk and place it in a special hold. They would not have told him why, and the man would be more prone to think the trunk held a rich man's valuables instead of a supposed murderer's possessions, especially after Joe tipped the man a sawbuck for his troubles. Which Joe did with minimum flourish.

The steward, startled maybe from the size of the tip, hesitated. For a moment Joe thought he had underestimated the ship's officers or that in his confidence he had overplayed his hand.

"Thank you, sir. Thank you very much." The man beamed and his body seemed to inflate.

Joe smiled and felt a loosening in his breathing, a loosening of the noose.

The steward asked, "You spending the Christmas in Paris, sir?"

Joe knew the question was more a mannered response to his tip than anything else, for from his job with the newspaper in Greenwich he had seen the effect that money could have. A few greenbacks could easily open doors as well as open a working intimacy. The rule held true in the middle of the Atlantic as it had in Connecticut.

Joe smiled and answered the steward's question, "No. I'm going across into Germany."

The steward nodded and busied himself with a strap to hold the trunk tight to the dolly. After pulling the slack from the strap, he said, "I been there once, to Heine-land. Right after the war, it was. Them Heines weren't none too nice, neither."

"So I've heard," Joe said.

The steward never bothered to check the trunk for a nametag, and Joe thought, *Why should he?* He was doing as he was ordered and that was all, retrieve the trunk and not ask why. That ingrained European caste system had maddened Joe during the war, watching the Brits or French unable to as much as dig a deeper latrine without an officer telling them, but that mindset would prove his ally in his departure from the ship.

The steward groaned and pulled on the dolly's handle and worked the heavy load into the hallway. Joe followed, glancing at his real trunk in position down the hall. *It might actually work*, he thought. His clothes, Gresham's clothes, might make it into Cherbourg, but he still needed to find his own release from the ship's officers.

The steward lowered the trunk and wiped his brow with a handkerchief. "You don't needs to 'company me, sir," he said, leaning against the handle of the dolly. "I'll see it reaches the Head Steward's office right quick."

Joe smiled, "Thank you." He carried his overcoat, weighted with a pistol in the right hand pocket and stood outside his door.

"He does this on 'cassion," the steward added. "Has someone's trunk put in his office so's he can take it through customs himself. Quick as a flame, that way, especially with as slow as them Frogs can be."

Joe nodded and stepped into the hallway, closing the door behind him. Then, as though he had suddenly thought of it, he stopped and faced the steward. "Would you be so kind as to return for my friends' trunks here? The loading dock is fine." He pointed to the two trunks outside the McKee's cabin.

The steward looked at the trunks with a heaviness. "I'll do my best, sir."

Joe unfolded another sawbuck and handed it to the steward.

"Don't give it another thought, sir," he said, bowing and pocketing the bill in one fluid motion. "Quick as an arrow, I'll be." He hefted his load and pushed it down the hallway.

Joe watched until the man had turned a corner and was gone, then he opened his cabin door again to make one final check through the room before leaving it to spend the remainder of the voyage on deck. With that tip he had given the porter, he knew that his trunk would be among the first off the ship and waiting for him to claim in customs.

The day opened around him as he walked onto the deck, a gray coolness eddying in the wind, crisp and fresh and filled with promise. The horizon blended into the sea with a smooth alchemy as the day lifted easily from its own shadow. His spirits lifted with it. While he could not tell the future, he felt himself within an even chance of leaving behind something of his past.

Joe avoided his deck chair, with its folded wool blanket, and instead stood near the bow of the ship, mentally hastening its progress. He faced into the ship's wind with the day rising cool but not cold, overcast but not threatening. The ocean continued to lay dark blue and silent all about and gulls flew in tightening circles around the ship, noisy harbingers of land. France was just beyond Joe's sight. His stomach tightened at its approach, the approach of a landscape of freedom but also a continent of destruction.

He remembered the similar tightening in his stomach five years earlier when he had sailed into Cherbourg for the glory of war, nervous at the thought of battle but filled with the expectations of youth and honor on the battlefield. Then, eighteen and filled with the romance of youth, dressed in his green wool and carrying a pack on his back and Springfield rifle with twelve clips of .30 caliber bullets in a cloth bandolier over his shoulder, the approach to France had felt like an entrance, an adventure, a coming-into of his life. At the railing of the *Berengaria*, with all those lies of the past century proved so wrong on the battlefields of France, he could not help but wonder what further lies might await him there.

Leaving France following the end of war, he had stood at the stern of the ship to watch the Cotentin Peninsula and the town of Cherbourg disappear into the line of a gray horizon. The French city, as gray as the cloudy day that shrouded it, had then looked like a tombstone sinking into the sea.

He walked the deck several times, had an Irish whiskey in the Gentleman's Reading Room, walked the deck again, sat in another patron's empty deck chair, walked, stood along the rail of the ship at the stern and the bow and on both sides, and walked, all the time feeling as though a clock were running against him. As the day's shadows shortened to noon and then again lengthened, the ship's deck became busier. More people, dressed in overcoats and hats and some even in evening wear with long furs or top hats and shining black canes with silver handles, lined the railing to watch the ship's arrival into Cherbourg.

Joe lost himself in the crowd near the gates to the ship's secondary boarding bridge. In the tightening compression of the growing and moving crowd, Joe kept his hands in his coat pockets to keep hold of the pistol as well as the money split between the pockets. He patted himself once to make sure the photograph and lists were safe within his inner pocket. He returned his hand to his side pocket in time to feel another hand move inside it. He turned to face a man who quickly ducked his way through the crowd, empty of anything of Joe's.

"Bastard," Joe cursed.

Then he smiled. Maybe his running clock had again gained a minute of time or maybe that swift pendulum of fortune had swung back in his favor.

He looked around the crowd, watching the men closer to the gates, several of them already fingering their papers and passports. Seeing his life as something from a Beadle's Dime Novel, he elbowed toward them until he stood close to one who was near him in size and age and face. As the man returned his passport to the pocket of his fur overcoat, Joe lifted it clean and backed away, letting the crowd fill in like a ship's wake. He smiled and breathed deep, feeling as though he were born to a life of petty larceny.

The ship docked. Passengers waved to lovers or family waiting on the pier, some threw streamers and confetti, some drank from champagne glasses and tossed the empty bottles into the water. The atmosphere was near that of a carnival.

Standing near the railing and with their backs to the approaching pier stood Dapper and the Turk. Dapper busied himself with the lapels of his coat. The smile flat across the face of the Turk was imminent and menacing. His eyes were hard and colorless in their darkness, and they fixed solidly on Joe. The Turk moved his mouth and Dapper looked up at him then followed his glassed gaze to Joe. He then also smiled, nothing friendly in his smile as well.

Joe moved with the pulse of the crowd, a jerking compression of people moving toward the main gate. The closer he got to the gate, the more difficult it was for him to move his arms. The chatter of people became deafening, the deck silenced in its own cacophony of sound, the crush claustrophobic, the Turk's hard stare staggering. The humid air filled with the acrid smells of stagnant water and anxious people, body odor and boozed breath. His breathing felt as cramped as his body.

He looked up toward the gate, at the passengers stopped to identify themselves to a ship's officer holding a clipboard, at those disembarking and walking with a bounce down the bridge, at those waiting on the pier with their arms ready to enfold a lover in an embrace, and then back at the threat carried in the blackness of the Turk's eyes.

Dapper and the Turk were not following. They stood away from the crowd of disembarking passengers, their hands in their pockets and talking to one another, watching Joe's movements like birds of prey waiting for their lunch to bolt from his cover.

They were toying with him, letting him attempt an escape and knowing that he, as Wynton Gresham, would not leave at Cherbourg. How they knew that, Joe could not say, but their easy approach revealed their knowledge. Whoever pulled their strings was quite well placed, having the Captain's ear and being privy to the Captain's orders.

What they did not know, however, was what Joe held in the fingers of his left hand.

As he neared the gate, Joe studied the passport that he had lifted, memorizing his new name and where this man came from. A Princeton man, Joe liked that, ivy-walled eating clubs and traditions extending back to Jonathan Edwards. The passport photograph showed a man wearing a pair of wire-rimmed glasses, banker's spectacles, trimmed hair, and a pleasant smile. Other than no glasses and hair let grow, Joe figured his resemblance was close enough to pass a cursory inspection by the customs agent. He knew that with any amount of interested inspection, his thin cover of anonymity would be exposed, but the officers at the gates had little reason to elevate their level of scrutiny. The name of Wynton Gresham was on a special list, and he was no longer Wynton Gresham.

He looked again at his passport. He was, at least for the time being, Harold Braddock of Princeton and every other inch a gentleman.

He turned when he heard a commotion nearby, expecting to find associates of Dapper and the Turk pushing through the crowd in his direction. Instead, he saw the man whom he had just become pushing people away from him and looking around the deck for his papers, yelling about his passport. A few other passengers looked around as well, but most avoided him, probably thinking the man was either drunk or crazy.

Joe smiled, knowing how hard it was to find, and how easy it was to lose, oneself. Since the war, he had met a lot of men in his generation who were lost. He wished it truly were as easy as lifting another man's name to change one's fortunes.

At the boundary between the ship's gate and the bridge, Joe answered the necessary questions about purpose and length of stay, and he complimented the officer on the capitol service once again provided by the Cunard line. Then he smiled at the officer and nodded and tipped his fedora to the Turk, turned and strode comfortably down the bridge to the pier, another American ready for the sights of Paris. He felt alone, and it was a splendid isolation.

Once he reached the pier, Joe turned for one more look. The Turk had pushed himself almost to the gate, pushing aside even the man still searching for his passport, who punched the Turk and ignited a small melee. The Turk outweighed the Princeton man by a good thirty pounds, but the lost Princeton man crouched like a collegiate middleweight and gave the Turk a good turn.

Joe hurried through customs, using the borrowed passport once again. Because the French officers at the customs table seemed more interested in catching a glimpse of the fight aboard the ship, they rushed everyone through with a minimum of delay. They stopped one man who was trying to smuggle tobacco and pushed him into a back room, but Joe and others moved through quickly. He found a porter, handed him a dollar bill and told him to retrieve Gresham's trunk and place it on the train for Paris. The man obliged with a formal bow. Joe felt not a little drunk by the power of money.

He left the Princeton man's passport underneath a newspaper on a bench—It was difficult enough to remember who he was between two people without adding a third to the mix—and he boarded his train and paid for a compartment seat and sat so that he could watch the station doors for Dapper and the Turk and waited for the train's departure. He switched bench seats before anyone else entered the cabin so that he sat facing front and relaxed into the padded comfort to let his body heat warm against the leather seat. He closed his eyes and felt as though he had taken his first full breath in over a week.

The train took its first sudden tug into motion, followed by the slow climb to speed. With a steady pull, the train accelerated and was soon at its cruising speed for the run to Paris. Joe let out an audible breath and sank further into his seat next to the window and watched the increasing evening envelope the Norman countryside, which at first seemed smiling in its presence and then just asleep.

With the train's hissing steam and broken rhythm, the darkening trees became gaunt and the landscape dark and blurred. Soon he saw mostly his own reflection in the window. He looked through himself at the passing scene that seemed a long time in the past, a return and a dislocation. In the fields, rusting iron objects jutted from the mud, prehistoric weapons of war as though ghosts to haunt the country-side. Like the skeletal remains of long dead animals left to waist in a marginal land, the iron pieces were caught in a moonlit silence, and even though he could not hear, he could see dark skies with large and circling birds descending. And mud. And blood. And then it was dark again and he was thankful.

Wrapped in the heavy buffalo coat, he turned his attention inside. He shared the compartment with two couples. One was a middle-aged and middle-class couple, a man who might work at a bank returning with his wife from a vacation to the coast. They had two wicker baskets, lunch in one and in the other a fawn-colored Chinese Pug unaware of anything other than its own regality. They read French newspapers in the insubstantial light of the compart-ment. The other couple also in the compartment, a young couple, ate a dinner of rolls and wine and talked in hushed voices. They offered him a piece of their bread and a glass of wine.

"*Merci*," Joe said and reached across to take the bread and wine. It was the first that he had eaten since the night before. The nourish-ment reminded him of how tired he had become.

With his wine drunk and bread eaten and the compartment lights turned down and with the fluid rocking of the train, he eased into a half-sleep and did not fully wake until the train's brakes first jolted.

As midnight approached, the train arrived in Paris at the Gare Saint-Lazare. After leaving the buffalo coat in a water closet—for it would be too easily identified—Joe hailed a cab and took it across the Seine to the Hotel Le Couer on Place Saint André des Arts the address he had found scribbled on the paper in Gresham's desk at the newspaper office. The driver had to leave his trunk lid ajar to fit in the steamer trunk, but the streets were less than full and there was no rain. They had no difficulty crossing the city.

As the taxi crossed the Seine, Joe could make out the charcoal outline of the Eiffel Tower against a blue-black midnight sky with the top of the tower kissed by the stars. Below, the Seine ran black with wafers of light bouncing upon its surface. A line of tugs had moored along the cement quay, gray smoke rising from the short chimneys above their living areas and yellow windows candle-lit. A pair of lovers embraced in a kiss against the concrete railing of the Pont Neuf, a streetlamp dripping light from above them. A dusky halo was cast along the quay from the soft glow of restaurant and café windows.

In his newspaper articles, Joe had never been good at writing conclusions. He was good with details, with an objective description of the happenings in other people's lives, but every article he wrote seemed to be a beginning with no closing, a breath with no expiration. More than once, as they sat across from each other at their joined desk, Gresham had told Joe that he needed to bring his stories to closure, that they all sounded like they should be followed with "and meanwhile, back at the ranch."

"No closure," Gresham would have said, leaving his hands spread apart and palms upward as though to mime his words.

Joe wondered if, in that old city of abundant light, whether he could find some culmination, some closure of his own.

The old woman at the hotel desk was startled when Joe asked about his room. She rubbed her hands together as though returning warmth to them, and she kept raising and lowering her glasses to see him while she spoke in halting English, "Monsieur Gresham? We were expecting you. It has been a long time since you were here, but you have changed, no?"

Her gray hair was rolled in a bun on top of her head and she smiled and nodded. She wore a flowered dress that had begun to show its age, thin in the shoulders and some threads showing from the cuff of the sleeve. She was tall and thin and beautiful in her age. She had a slight palsy to her hands and eyes that sparkled significantly in the yellow-lit room.

"Yes," Joe said. "I probably have." He signed the hotel registry. "It's been, after all, how long since I was last here?"

"Ohh, maybe four years."

"A lot happens in four years," Joe said. *A lot happens in two weeks*, he thought.

She handed him a room key and told him that his trunk would be brought up as soon as possible. As he stepped away, she waved him back and told him that the hotel now had heating in all of the rooms, that the plumbing had been fixed since his last visit, that her husband would be at the desk soon and was still lazy, that she preferred him working nights since his snoring kept her from sleeping, and again that a helper would deliver the steamer trunk as soon as possible since both she and her husband could no longer handle such heavy work, as if her husband would even attempt something akin to work.

Joe smiled, assaulted by the mere volume of words that she presented.

As soon as he heard her take a breath, he started for the stairs but stopped when she again called him back. "A message," she said, excited. "Oh, I almost forgot. A message was delivered for you today."

She fumbled through a drawer behind the desk. "Let me see. Right here. Yes-yes, here it is."

Her hand shook as she handed the folded piece of paper to Joe. Gresham's name was etched in a fine script across the outside. He placed it in his pocket and thanked her, bowing and backing away at the same time.

His was a single room on the third floor, old-fashioned with a high ceiling and a French window facing the street, a large mirror with a crack traversing its lower left corner over a writing table, a large brass bed that sang when Joe sat on it, two high-back wooden chairs, a washstand, and panel openings in the wallpapered wall into both the closet and the bathroom. There was a single square heating vent in the floor and an electric light in the ceiling and lamps on the table and beside the bed.

At $1.50 a day for the room, Joe figured he could afford to stay as long as necessary, to complete what needed completion. He was tired, but not tired enough to sleep, and he sat on the bed to open the note. He looked first at the signature, Dillard. "I have news," it began. "Everything will change. Come by as soon as possible. The old place—#17 rue De Fleurus."

"Everything will change," Joe repeated. "As soon as possible."

He closed his eyes again and tried to imagine what it could be that Dillard might know, but Joe was not certain what he himself knew, much less what someone else knew.

He considered visiting Dillard that night to put an end to the masquerade. He considered staying in his room, falling asleep on his bed that sang and spending his first night in Paris gathering what thoughts he could. Then he also considered walking into the night and never returning, just losing himself in darkness. He considered walking into the night and finding a café and sitting alone at the bar and drinking a solitary beer. He needed one, maybe a dozen. For that night he would forget about Gresham and the Champagne and Dillard and Gresham's killer, just drink a cold beer delivered from a legal tap.

He looked again at the note. *As soon as possible.* He looked at his watch. 1:34 a.m. He looked again at the note held between the trembling fingers of his hands. *Christ*, he thought, *I need a drink*. He felt a great need for some palliative to settle his mind and to consider his options, and maybe, just maybe, to forget about his world for a moment.

He decided that he should not wake up Dillard in the middle of the night to tell the man that his friend had been murdered and his friend's identity had been stolen. That might be better presented in the light of day. He would visit Dillard first thing in the morning, and he left his room in search of a beer.

Outside the hotel, the sky was dark and the air was moist and filled with the smells of a Paris night, wet cement and old flowers and diesel exhaust. Buildings limited the sky, and clouds hid the stars and moon. Joe pulled up his collar against the damp cold. It would rain soon. It always rained in Paris in December. He could smell the moisture in the air. It would be a shallow rain, enough to wet but not enough to cleanse the city.

He walked toward the Seine along the narrow cobblestone street, uneven from centuries of horse and wagon and then automobile traffic and nearly futile attempts at repair. Once he heard someone behind him and turned to look, but the sidewalk was empty where it was lit from streetlights and too dark between them to see anything. He listened carefully as he walked but heard nothing more that sounded like trailing footsteps. Still, he was happy that he had placed his revolver in a pocket of his overcoat.

At the end of the street, Joe found a café called the Gentilhomme and opened the front door to a roil of warmth and smoke that blew past him as he entered. A haze floated in the café's indistinct light, and the jazz trill of a single trumpet lit from one of the back corners. He looked and saw a black man, eyes closed and trumpet lifted to the sky like Gabriel. He walked to the bar, as crowded as the tables, and took the first empty seat he found.

"Vide?" he asked the man seated in the next chair.

"Yes," he said smiling. "It's empty." An American.

Joe sat and folded his overcoat across his lap.

"Beer," he said when the bartender stood across from him, wearing a white shirt both wrinkled and stained and a frown pressed like a pleat across his face. He paid with an American dollar bill, waved off the change and said *"compliment"* in French. The waiter nodded and arched an eyebrow in gratitude. Joe figured he had made at least one friend in Paris that night. And if not that, he at least guaranteed that he would not want long for another drink.

"Should have ordered a pint," the man next to him said. Midwestern American.

"Why's that?"

"They cost about the same and you get twice as much."

"Point well taken," Joe said, taking the first cold swallow and letting it ride down slowly. The beer tasted good. It cut through the ship's death, the train's diesel, the tight hotel room's enclosure.

"I'm Joe Henry."

"Diamond Dick Quire. I prefer Quire."

They shook hands.

"American." Joe said.

"As apple pie," Quire said. "At least I was the last time I checked."

"When was that?"

"What year is it?"

"Never mind."

From behind them, like a jive note to bring down walls, the trumpet man hit a note so high that it could call up the dead.

Quire lifted his pint in front of him, the beer glass caught in the café's weak light. He said in toast, "May the wings of liberty never lose a feather."

Joe drank with him, both emptying their beers in long swallows. They signaled the bartender for another round of pints and Joe pulled money from his pocket.

"Alsatian," Quire said to the barman, who nodded and drew two pints from the tap and placed them on the bar in front of the two Americans, the beers so dark they were almost black as stout with a caramel froth floating on top like good espresso.

"Le bonne bière," Quire said with a smile.

Joe estimated that Diamond Dick Quire, like himself, was in his late-twenties but, unlike Joe, a square-headed block of a man, and probably shorter than Joe by a good two inches with thick shoulders and a large chest. His arms barely fit inside the sleeves of his shirt and when flexed to draw on his pint, the seams nearly burst. He was clean shaven with hair brown and long, almost to his collar in the back. He could have been a miner or a block of granite.

"Where'd you get your nickname?" Joe asked.

"What nickname?"

"Diamond Dick."

Quire laughed and drank. "That's no nickname, my friend" he said. "That's my Christian name. Diamond Dick." He laughed again. "My mother said that carrying me was one adventure after another, and since then I seem to be a magnet for trouble. I have luck like that."

Joe nodded. "Don't feel like the Lone Star Ranger," he said.

Quire offered a crooked smile. "To trouble," he said and lifted his pint glass in toast. Joe's glass clinked it and they drank again.

"You live here?" Joe asked.

"Seems like it," Quire said.

"I mean Paris. You live in Paris?"

"For now, maybe until I die. And you? You live here also, or are you a reporter looking for a story on the damn expatriate life?"

"Neither. I just got off the boat," he said with a shrug. "May stay a week or a decade. Don't know yet."

"Me neither," Quire said. He laughed and his laugh descended into a rheumy cough. When he was finished coughing he said, "I came for the gas treatments."

Joe nodded and drank and asked, "You were in the war?"

"Yes. You?"

"With the 42nd," Joe said.

"Good group. Never got gassed, though, huh?" Quire asked.

"Not me. Got shot but never gassed."

"I got gassed in Belleau Wood." Quire shook his head. "Nasty shit. By the time I knew I was in it, I was fucking swimming in the shit and already almost dead, or as good as dead, or wishing to hell I'd be dead. Damn nasty shit, that gas."

"To the Lost," Joe said in toast.

"To the Lost."

They drank. "What's this gas treatment you mentioned?"

Quire evaded Joe's question. "How long were you home after the war?"

Joe rubbed his brow. "I haven't gone home yet. I found a job the first place I stopped and stayed there until last week."

Quire leaned forward with his elbows propped on the bar and said, "I went home, Helena, Montana—Hell-on-earth, Montana—but it wasn't like it was when I left it. Everything was still there and looked the same, train station and mills and Woolworth's, but it wasn't the same place. It all looked so goddamn false, like it was hiding something I'd never noticed before. Then people found out I'd been gassed and treated me like I had tuberculosis or something. Old friends would cross to the other side of the road or try not to shake my hand like I was a contagion from a leper colony. I don't know, maybe they were just embarrassed."

Joe nodded. "They all wanted heroes, like their grandfathers."

"There ain't no such thing as a hero, not in a war like that."

"Just tragedies," Joe said.

"Who said that?" Quire asked.

"Me. Just now."

"Well, shit, you said that right, brother." Quire leaned forward against the bar again and looked at Joe, eyes half mast, and raised his glass for another toast. A splash of beer fell to the bar and the bartender was quick to wipe it up.

Joe met Quire's glass with his own, a toast between men who had seen much the same, who had seen things that could not be told to others, that could not be understood by others. The Great War became a brotherhood of decrement for those unlucky enough to have survived it, and Joe and Quire had offered what amounted to the secret cipher.

Quire laughed, "You know one thing, though, that I got from the war? Other than these worthless lungs." He pounded his chest twice, punishing his lungs for having betrayed him.

"Tell me," Joe said.

"I actually got to use a brick shithouse. A six-holer, at that."

"A brick shithouse?"

"And built like a stacked dame."

"Oh hell," Joe said and laughed along with Quire, even though his was no match in volume or tenor for the baritone laugh of Quire. Quire's laugh, however, slid unevenly to a cough that doubled Quire at the bar, one arm holding onto the bar while the other pressed against his forehead.

They talked for another hour, some about the war, mostly working around the subject until they might know each other better, where they had been and when and how much they hated officers. Some about where they had grown up, Joe in Colorado and Quire in Montana as the sired son of a millionaire goldminer who then went on to prep school in St. Paul and even a year in the hallowed halls of Harvard. Quire talked some about Paris, of which he said, "Paris is a museum and it's a circus and it's a whorehouse. Your choice and your poison."

"Right now I'll just take my bed," Joe said, rising to his feet, but the beers he had drunk coupled with the lack of food and sleep put him back on his stool.

"Another one?" Quire laughed. "It'll help you catch your sea legs."

"No," Joe said. "I'll be heading on. What my legs need is what every other part of me needs—rest. Anyway," he said. "I have business in the morning. First thing."

"All right, cowboy. Stop by again tomorrow night and let me know how this city's treating you."

"Will do," Joe said. He struggled through the crowd and the cigarette haze for the door, drunker than he needed to be but not nearly as drunk as he wanted.

The cold air outside the Gentilhomme assaulted him. He leaned against the brick wall to cough out the smoke and catch his bearings. With his overcoat buttoned tight to his neck, he set off for the hotel, his hand finding his revolver. Like a child with his favorite blanket, he wanted the security of something familiar in his fingers. Even with that, he knew how illusory the idea of security had become.

The air he breathed, as exhausted as him, as neutral as the night, had collapsed around him in darkness and winter haze, raw and chilled with steam rising from the wet gutters. A mist lay sodden on the street, and streetlamps provided only a depthless yellow glow. He could not tell which but either he or the city felt old and tired. Maybe both.

From inside a second story hotel window as he passed, he heard a forced and unpleasant laughter. As he walked, he imagined that he could hear in the mist a continuous and slow whispered "*You.*" He felt as though he was entering another space in time, a dimension in which his life would be blank. Neither the new world nor the old world from before the war were his world, not anymore and maybe never again. His life might no longer even be his own.

He was drunk. He hoped that his thoughts were simply the thoughts of a drunk.

He gathered his coat tighter and walked on, stumbling a little more than on his first trip down the road's uneven cobblestones. Fifty feet short of the entrance to his hotel, he stopped short when the feeling of being watched once again grabbed him. He had the sudden sensation of being an animal in a zoo, unable to get away from the eyes that followed him. He could see nobody near him nor hear anyone, not even the fabled lovers of Paris who were supposed to be kissing under each lamppost.

A shaft of yellow light blew from the hotel's entrance as the front door opened and closed within its recess, sending the light out onto the sidewalk and street. Joe looked up. A suspicious light illuminated the curtains of what he thought was his room. His thumb pushed off the pistol's safety. He walked on.

An old man sat behind the front counter, his head resting on a folded blanket. Quick snores erupted from the man like rattling thunder. Joe stepped past without waking him. He took the first flight of stairs two at a time before slowing as he progressed to the third floor, then waiting to catch his breath at the landing before walking down the hall to his room. No light showed from underneath the door. He tried the door and found it unlocked. He opened it and stepped inside, closing the door behind him and stepping against the wall and leaving the room in darkness. He held his pistol in front of him, pointed toward the darkness at the center of the room.

He could hear nothing except the night sounds of the city from outside his inch-opened window, the drone of diesel-engined cargo boats on the Seine and the muffled clap of horses on cobblestones and animal sounds. No sound from inside the room, however. He stretched his arm out to feel along the wall. The metallic click of the light button snapped and the room was flooded with light. No one was there.

He checked the closet and bathroom. Nobody. His steamer stood at the foot of the bed. Except for the single broken hasp, the trunk was still locked shut.

As quickly as the adrenaline had rushed through his body it depleted, leaving him even more tired than before. Either he had been mistaken about the room or his trunk had been delivered by the hotel worker just minutes before. He was too tired to care. He sat on the bed and rubbed his eyes with the palms of his hands, then stripped and washed in the room's washbasin and lay in bed, naked under the sheet and brown wool blankets. He chased dreams around in his head for a long time before finally drifting into sleep.

VII

PARIS CORONER SAYS U.S. GIRL KILLED SELF
PARIS, Nov. 30—Following Thursday's inquest over the body of
pretty Rose Shannessey of Minneapolis, Coroner Vallot gave the
following verdict: "Suicide during temporary insanity brought on by a
quarrel with her lover."
—The Oklahoman, 1 December, 1922

JOE WOKE EARLY, ONLY A FEW HOURS AFTER HAVING FALLEN ASLEEP. He opened his window to sit on the sill, naked in the morning mist. A silvern haze floated above the city. Listening, he heard sounds that he thought typical and right for a Paris morning. A train's whistle low and slow in the distance, an automobile horn and another and the sound of two men arguing, pigeons, the steady pace of people on their way to work, conspiratorial voices passing unseen beneath his window, the raking sound of a broom pushing garbage into the gutter. A church bell rang the hour of the Angelus. The city's morning concert taking place.

He leaned into the winter morning and watched dark smoke from coal stoves drift in the gray sky, visible in blackened waves above the morning roofline. A light mist like a horse's mane fell wild and ragged around the ancient buildings across from him. Up the street, away from the Gentilhomme, he could see an open street market taking shape. Vendors with fruits and vegetables and flowers, some with meats and others with old clothing, still others with live birds inside of wooden cages. Arranging their carts along the cobblestoned lane, they worked like monks—silent and hunched and serious in their morning duty. A waiter in white shirt and black apron sluiced down the sidewalk in front of a café. Joe could smell freshly ground

121

coffee and just-baked pains chocolate. Not just a city's morning concert but a symphony for the senses, and he closed his eyes to breathe deeply and let the city infuse him.

Joe had always been an early riser, following Teddy Roosevelt's instilled declarations of the strenuous life, but in France in 1918 he had, like many in the trenches, become almost an insomniac. In the four years since, he had not regained the comfort that allows sleep, so he rose early even though he was far from rested.

Naked and cold in the frigid and misted air of a Paris dawn, he felt close to how he had felt in his youth. He felt alive. The somber and soiled city he had walked through the previous night had vanished with the sunrise, replaced with one filled with expectations. He stood and looked out through the window of his room across the rooftops of Paris, all gray and white-stained from pigeon droppings, peaked roofs with the ancient spires of many cathedrals in the near and far distances.

He was ravenous. Joe dressed and emerged, intent on holding something of that new morning with him. He enjoyed a breakfast of coffee and rolls in the hotel's salon and read the *Herald Tribune* as he ate, the crisp crust of a croissant sprinkling the front of his shirt. The headlines trumpeted Clemenceau's trip to America, which he ignored. He scanned the other articles. A long article on Parisians rioting because of the possible murders of two Frenchmen in America covered much of the front page. Joe read that article with concern. It said less than he, himself, already knew.

Both names were mentioned in the article, but he only had two passports—his and Gresham's—so his choice of names if he were asked was limited. The police would be on the lookout for Joe Henry, that name would be highlighted on their reports and posted in their stations. Gresham's might not be, for there would be no reason to be looking for a dead man. That made the choice of who he was to be rather easy. He would be Wynton Gresham for at least a while longer.

One story buried at the bottom of the second page stopped him. A woman in Haute-Loire, an American, had hanged herself at the foot of her bed, using for her noose a fourragère won by a man in the war. The article hinted that she may have been ill for some time. Joe thought of how long the shadows of the past are cast.

He had come to Paris because of Gresham's ticket, a free trip anywhere. He had also come to Paris because of Gresham, in part at least for why Gresham had been killed. He came also because of the manuscript. He had to read it. Even if the sheriff in Greenwich found a copy of Gresham's manuscript, he might not read it; even if he took the time to read it, he probably wouldn't understand the significance. Not without some guidance at least. It would molder in some desk drawer or filing cabinet. Joe knew quite well that he and Dillard might be the only two people alive who could, and would want to, bring light to the meanings of Gresham's work. With that, he thought that he might also be able to provide a sense of closure for Gresham as well as to offer himself something settled that might put his own life back in drive. A talk with Paul Dillard might unshroud the mystery of Gresham's death and might clear his own name from the indictment of the Greenwich police. Following that, he thought he might deal with even more distant pasts in southern Colorado. *Everything in its time*, he thought, remembering poorly the words of a priest he had once listened to.

Joe returned to his room for Dillard's note delivered the previous day but could not find it. He looked on the table and on the floor beneath the bed. He also could not remember the exact address but did recall the street sounding like "flowers."

"Rue de Fleurus," the old woman at the desk said.

"Yes, *oui*," Joe said.

"It is not far," she said and turned to point a palsied finger toward the wall behind her. "That way. You can walk down boulevard Saint-Michel or take the Metro to Jardin du Luxembourg, and rue de Fleurus runs through the garden. Where you want . . . a home? Yes, where you want is probably across the garden, on the west side. You walk across the garden, it is still lovely this time of year, even with the wet and cold, and you will find it. If not, anyone can tell you where."

He left the hotel and walked to the Metro station at Saint-Michel. The fluid elaborateness and elongated loops of its art nouveau entrance blinked in the morning's still light. He descended into the catacombs of the Metro, the resolute push of others steadying him along. He hurried for and boarded the underground train, holding tight to a railing, standing the two stops to the Luxembourg Gardens. The other people on the Metro ignored him, old women on their way to the markets, young businessmen with hair black and slicked back and wearing blue suits pressed tight, students looking fashionably sullen in woolen fisherman's sweaters.

Weak sunshine greeted him as he walked back up to street level. The Luxembourg Garden, still wet from dew, was cast in the shades of winter, and with a light haze upon it, the park became a mystical place. A park on which poems are made. He passed through the garden where, even in the coolness of the winter morning, clutches of heavily bundled old men played boules on the lawn while others sat in pairs playing backgammon or talking. The gravel pathway crunched under his feet, and he felt his pace quickening, from anticipation as well as invigoration.

Before the end of the garden path and the beginning of the paved street, he passed within sight of a number of statues and memorials to men from the past century but did not stop to admire them. Three blocks ahead of him on the street, Joe could see a knot of people and fire trucks blocking the road, bells clanging amid the din of noise.

As he neared the clutches of bystanders and firemen amidst fire equipment, he began to distinguish uniformed gendarme waving traffic down other streets so that the firemen could do their jobs. Joe could see no flames, but some of the men ran around like ants, scurrying between trucks and the smoking rubble of the stone townhouse. He worked his way around the crowd and walked another block until he found an open business where he might ask about Paul Dillard's home.

The business, an automobile garage, had its wide front barn-like doors open to the street. Inside a heavy man dressed in a heavy shirt and overalls worked on a small two-seater automobile.

A round mass of a woman with gray hair shorter than Joe's sat in the driver's seat writing in a notebook while the mechanic mumbled to himself and busied himself under the hood. Another woman, thin and dark and vulture-like, stood to the side, silently looking into the engine compartment while the mechanic worked.

The only one of the three of them to look up at Joe when he entered the garage was the thin, dark woman. Her eyes were hard as black stones and cold as the eyes of a crow. Joe avoided her stare and walked closer to the mechanic who was talking, maybe to one of the women or both or neither, while he worked.

"—*comme lui*," the mechanic was saying in French. "*Comme mon fils et les autres. Tous perdu. Une generation perdue.*" He sighed, shaking his head. "*Tous perdue*," he said again.

He bent back under the hood. The thin woman stared mutely at Joe. The large woman looked at the mechanic, then the meaty flesh of her enormous arms jiggled as she quickly wrote something in her notebook.

"*Pardon,*" Joe said.

The mechanic and the large woman in the driver's seat joined the thin woman in looking silently at Joe.

"*Oui?*" asked the mechanic. His eyes were crossed but his face kind. He placed a wrench on the table beside him and wiped his hands on a rag taken from his breast pocket.

Joe struggled with his French, forming with the help of the others in the garage his question, "*Ou est* Paul Dillard?"

"Dillard?" asked the mechanic, struggling over the l's and the hard d.

"*Oui.* Paul Dillard," Joe said again.

The mechanic exhaled long and loudly through his teeth. He tossed his hands in the air then let them drop to his sides. "Duh-yar. Duh-yar. Iz Paul Duh-yar. *J'y ai vécu*," the mechanic said, picking up and pointing his wrench in the direction from where Joe had just walked. "There. *La.* There."

Joe turned and followed the man's point but saw only the wood frame of a wall with tools and tires and automobile parts lining and piled against it.

"Where the fire was," said the mechanic. "He lived there, his family's home for many years."

"Where the fire was?" Joe asked.

"Yes, yes. The fire. A terrible thing. *Ce matin* . . . I hear sirens this morning and follow them to his home. He was under *une couverture*—blanket. Alive, *mais*, but not good." The mechanic shook his head. "*Pauvre*, unlucky, he was, and very sad, *très triste. Je ne savais même pas qu'il était venu à la maison.* Did not know he was back. . . . So unlucky." The man paused as though collecting his breath, then added, "*Juste hier son amant s'est suicidé,* in her apartment, kill herself. So sad. *Quelle histoire. Tres triste.*"

Joe stood fixed in the slanted light of the open garage door not quite certain what his next step would be. The light in his room last night. Someone had been there and read Dillard's note. He felt the responsibility for yet another killing. He had not committed it, but it had come from his presence. Had he not become Gresham, the Englishman Huntington might not have been murdered on the ship and Paul Dillard might not have been burned alive. Like a pebble having been tossed into a pond, his deception had rippled out in unexpected ways and affected people he had never met. He closed his eyes and pushed hard against his eyelids with the tips of his fingers. The air he breathed was distant and distinct and was not an air that smelled of oil and rubber but one that smelled of cordite and death.

"Are you all right?" asked the big woman from her perch in the automobile. She spoke English like an American and in a deep and full-throated voice.

"Yes—" Joe began.

"Is there anything that we can do to help?"

"No," Joe said. "I was meeting him this morning." He remembered the newspaper article that he had read that morning about a woman who had committed suicide in Paris. "His lover died yesterday, you said?"

"*Oui,*" the mechanic said. "Suicide." He made a gesture as though to hang himself. Joe wondered if somehow he was responsible for this too.

"You were close with Mr. Dillard?" the big woman asked.

Joe did not know how to respond, so he nodded his head and let the charade blossom. The eternal autumn in which he had lived since the war would continue.

"*Moi aussi.* I knew him . . . but not well," said the big woman. "Before the war, he shopped for books where I shop for books. I like books so I liked him because he liked books."

Joe heard the past tense and looked at her and then at the mechanic. *"Mort?"* he said.

The mechanic shrugged and answered in French so quickly that Joe didn't understand. The big woman translated. "We don't know if he is dead, but it was not good."

"Was anyone else in the house?"

"No-no," said the woman, still translating for the mechanic. "Just Dillard. Marie, his sister, oh she is so sweet and now also so sad. Marie, she lives near Saint Séverin, near Saint Michel in the Quarter. She is still so young. Now she is so sad as well."

After the mechanic wrote the address for Dillard's sister on a piece of oily paper, Joe left the garage and turned to retrace his steps back toward Dillard's house where people were still gathered to watch the firemen complete their duties. He walked into the mingling crowd. Whatever warmth he had felt that morning upon rising had cooled. Across the street from Dillard's house, he stopped and leaned against a lamppost to watch the last actions of the firemen.

Smoke from the rubble interspersed with the winter mist to form a dark gray haze, a winter's grisaille above the dirty city. The stone house had been scarred by the fire, scorches blackened the stone above each of the building's windows and the front door, the steps were a wash of water and mud and soot and water hoses. Charred wooden beams showed like orphans inside the empty windows. The exterior of the house was dead, but from inside Joe could hear some firemen still at work. He listened to the rasping sounds they made with picks and shovels.

He heard the abrasive sounds of men at work. The smell of steam and fire, the feel of lingering heat, the sight of a house reduced, the taste of another death. He was so absorbed in thought that he did not immediately see the Turk walking toward him. A sudden shift of wind jarred his senses as it brought a whirl of smoke to lay sodden on the street. Through that smoke he saw the Turk approaching.

Instinctively, Joe turned and walked, pushing through the crowd and down the first street he found, preferring the visibility of an open avenue to the confining crowd in front of Dillard's house. With the Turk following close behind, he again felt like the prey in a lethal game of cat and mouse, but Joe also knew what he was doing. He wanted the confrontation with the Turk to come at a place of his choosing, a street corner not too crowded.

He walked quick-step past businesses with their owners outside sweeping the sidewalk or watching the commotion at the end of the street, a saucer and cup in one hand and cigarette in the other as they leaned against the front of their establishments.

Joe looked over his shoulder. The Turk kept pace with him. Inside the pocket of his overcoat, he kept his hand tight around the small revolver.

Toward the river. He knew that. As though a young boy lost in a wilderness, he knew to walk toward a river. The wilderness he felt lost in was not one of pinions and arroyos, but he was lost and the river would provide an index mark from which he could cipher his way. He walked briskly, confident that the Turk would keep pace.

Joe would choose his place. The hunted becoming the hunter.

As he neared the large boulevards of the city's Left Bank, he encountered more people on the sidewalk. With the din of the growing crowd and the noise of busses and trucks and automobiles, people had to raise their voices to be heard. Joe heard only a distant surge of sound, muffled and loud and far away from him.

When he looked over his shoulder to turn a corner or cross a street, he saw the Turk. The big man was playing with him like a boy plays with a beetle in an ant hill. Except Joe was playing his own game as well. He kept half-expecting Dapper to turn up at the round of a corner, but if the little man were with the Turk he did not show himself. That was not a good thought. He decided that he should make some play before he was herded toward some killing pen.

He stopped after rounding a corner and waited for the Turk. He had been racing around inside the frying pan ever since finding Gresham dead on the sofa. He would just go ahead and jump into the fire and see who got burned.

The Turk rounded the corner, a long and steady stride. His smile dissolved as he came close to Joe, his step slowing. Dressed entirely in black, he could have been the reaper met at the journey's end. Except Joe knew that this reaper preferred to send people on the last journey, not await their arrival. His heavy brows curled. Joe smiled at having done something the Turk had not expected.

The Turk's eyes looked over Joe's head at a pair of uniformed gendarme, close enough to see any action yet far enough to not hear any words.

When the Turk was a dozen feet from him, Joe pulled the short-barreled Smith & Wesson from his pocket and held it to his side. He kept its barrel pointing down so that passersby would not see it against the fold of his overcoat. The Turk, however, did take notice of it and stopped and was pushed from behind by a man carrying a bag filled with long loafs of bread who cursed at the Turk then walked on muttering obscenities about a bread strike in the city.

Joe stepped toward the Turk. He too looked up at the man who stood a good three inches taller than him and outweighed him by twenty hard pounds. But unlike the man with bread loaves in his hand, Joe had a revolver.

The Turk's black eyes stared down at Joe. Joe could not see anything close to fear in them, maybe a recognition or a slight concern over the revolver he held to his side, but not an ounce of fear.

The Turk asked, *"Alors?"* and his breath smelled of garlic.

Joe searched his mind and said in his broken French, *"Je voudrais parler avec* Marcel."

"Pourquoi?" the Turk asked.

"I have something he wants," Joe said. "A manuscript. *Manuscrit.*"

The Turk nodded.

"You know where my hotel is?" Joe asked.

"*L'Hotel Le Couer? Oui.*" The Turk smiled. "I know it," he added in heavy English, the words dropping fulsome from his mouth.

Joe had guessed as much. "At the end of the street is a café called the Gentilhomme. I will be there tonight at the bar. If Marcel wishes to speak with me, he can find me there."

The Turk nodded again, his face tightly set, as though tapped into place by a stone mason. "*Neuf heures. Gentilhomme.*"

He turned and walked away.

The Turk was a soldier, a killing machine. Functional but also thinking. He had followed his orders, but he possessed enough imagination to act on his own. Once the game had turned, the Turk had chosen discretion. Joe would need to remember the man was not an automaton.

Joe watched the big man's back recede into the crowd on the street.

Once he could no longer see the Turk, Joe turned and walked on, crossing and re-crossing streets, entering businesses to buy nothing, sitting on park benches, taking the Metro from Saint-Michel to the Gare Du Nord and back by different lines and waiting outside the exits. He recognized the purpose behind his melodrama, he recognized it from the war.

The isolation of the trenches had forced an unconscious defense upon him. Like others who had lived inside the connecting entrenchments that ran below the ground surface from Switzerland to the North Sea, Joe had formed a nervous obsession with who was watching him, which unseen enemy was readying sniper shots at him. He spent that day's afternoon convincing himself that he was not being followed, so much so that he did almost nothing else.

He did stop at a newspaper stand for another copy of the morning's *Herald Tribune* and a tourist's map of Paris. He took them into a café where he sat near the front window and ordered coffee, eggs, and croissant while he read the newspaper. The single-column article on the American woman who had killed herself did not mention any relationship with Paul Dillard, but it did mention her address. He called over the aproned waiter and pointed to the address in the newspaper. "*Où est, l'adresse?*" he asked.

The man arched an eyebrow, but told Joe how to find the place. Then he bent close to Joe and said that he could sell Joe an illegal entry into the catacombs below Paris where the bones of millions of dead Parisians were piled. He said in a half-whisper, "*C'est ici l'Empire de la Mort,*" and laughed.

"*Merci,*" Joe said, "but no." He placed a couple of French coins on the saucer and left the restaurant. He had witnessed the empire of death at its most epic and did not care to see it at its most bizarre.

Joe found the address on rue Monge. Large chestnut trees, their branches empty in the winter, lined both sides of the street. He stopped across the street from the woman's house, an age-stained brick building. From inside the apartment building behind him he could hear a pianist practicing. While a few errant snow-flakes drifted past, he stood with the pianist running the scales and he studied the front of the woman's building. He crossed the street and walked past it once, turned around at the corner and walked past the residence again. There were no lights shining, no windows open, no drapes even parted, no sign of anyone home, no sounds from inside indicating the police or a neighbor. Joe saw that the heavy carriage doors to the left of the front door were unlatched and left slightly open. Without looking around and as though he belonged there, he walked through the doors and into the court-yard, to the open stairwell at the back of the house and kicked open the rear door. The old wood of the frame held surprisingly hard, but gave way with a splash of wood shards on Joe's third kick. He walked up the back stairs to the kitchen, which was clean other than a few dishes on the counter. Nothing to say a person had died there. He walked to the front room, stopped in the doorway, and looked into where the American woman had been found.

"*L'Empire de la Mort,*" Joe said aloud. In the pale and empty front room, his words echoed.

He looked around, walking between the small but high-ceilinged rooms, not knowing what exactly he was looking for. Not even knowing why he had come to the woman's home, other than coincidences are not supposed to happen. Other than the empty front room, the other rooms were in disorder with drawers emptied and cupboard doors open.

With no fire in the coal stove, the apartment was cold. The only light came in streamers through the windows. The old wood floors groaned and sighed underfoot. The smell of death lingered in the closed apartment. He walked through the rooms with a feeling of imposition, not just that he was walking through the home of someone he did not know and not just that that person had died, but he simply was not supposed to be there. Being in the wrong place at the wrong time had begun the descending spiral he had found himself caught in. There he was, suspected of murdering people in America and on board the *Berengaria* and then to be found sightseeing in a dead woman's apartment. It would be hard to explain it away if he were caught.

He did not at first think about what he saw, the searched rooms, not ransacked, but clearly searched. The newspapers had said nothing about this, nothing to indicate foul play. Someone besides himself had come to the house in search of something, probably the same manuscript he had come for. If they had not found it, he felt he would not and he took his leave by the back stairs.

Joe saw the gendarme as soon as he stepped from the carriage doors. A neighbor, aroused by the sound or the sight of someone entering the courtyard through those large double doors, had probably called the police. The gendarme called to him as he stepped onto the paved road fronting the residence. Joe turned at once, and ran without even a thought. Like a rabbit bolting for cover, he ran for the nearest Metro station, jumped the gate, and took the stairs three at a time to the platform. Then he kept running, dodging frightened people waiting for their ride home, across the platform, and out the exit. He turned in time to see the gendarme just enter the Metro station across the street. He walked on and around the corner and hid himself inside the movement of people along le boulevard Saint-Michel. He did not look back and heard nobody shouting for him. He walked with the crowd, tight like them inside their coats, and turned off Saint Michel and down rue Monsieur-le-Prince, stopping at the Polidor, a crémerie, where he found a table and ordered coffee, which came in a large white bowl of a cup. He watched others eat, men and some women dressed for jobs of labor or of service. They ate plates of simple food piled high like the cafés he remembered in the American West that fed a man full and well. It was a place for the working class and for students to spend time without spending a great deal of money.

He sat and drank his coffee and ordered a second along with a crêpe of butter, eggs, and cheese. With the tourist map laid out on the table, he found Saint-Séverin was not far from where he sat drinking his coffee.

The manuscript Gresham had been working on was awfully important to someone, important enough to have caused the deaths of at least four people. That evening, when he would meet Rene Marcel, he would most likely meet the person who was interested in the manuscript, the person who had continued the carnage from years past. Before then, he wanted to meet Dillard's sister. The Marcel he was to meet seemed to think that Dillard had once owned a copy, otherwise Dillard and his American lover would not be dead. Maybe the sister knew. Maybe he could keep one person from being murdered. He finished his meal and his second bowl of coffee, pulled his collar up tight against the developing Paris cold and left the restaurant.

Joe found and walked down rue de Prêtress-Saint-Séverin, a short, cobblestone street off Saint-Michel, staying close to the buildings and the shadows of the buildings as he walked. Tucked away from the street stood a small cathedral, its name engraved on a plaque near its front doors read Eglise de Saint Séverin, the name of the church the automobile mechanic had said Marie Dillard lived near. He fished the address from his pocket, looked from the piece of paper to the numbers on the brick buildings and found the home on the corner of rue Saint-Séverin and across from the church. Gargoyles reigned with imperious presence along the roofline of the old Gothic church, their hollow eyes watching out across and over the building where Marie Dillard lived. They also watched Joe as he looked across the street. Joe was becoming used to being under someone's stare.

He found a bench outside the entrance to the cathedral's ambulatory and sat facing the street, looking, he hoped, like any other man in need of the church's respite. He checked his pocket watch, four hours until he would meet Marcel. He blew into his cupped hands as he watched each person walk by, waiting for the one who would place a key in the lock of the house across from him.

He looked at the sky, which through the day had become low and heavy with dark clouds, a heaven lacking in color. He wondered whether he remembered how to pray but did not. He sat in the ambulatory on the concrete bench and watched parishioners enter the cathedral, heads already bowed like after-age supplicants, footsteps echoing, and voices empty or lowered in speech. He turned and saw a filigree of light through the stained glass and another stained glass with light that was thick. He imagined people walking across the stone floors, trails worn from centuries of passage, people sitting in their pews, breathing in air heavy in dust and incense as they knelt to the prayers of the penitent. The people hunched on their knees, hands clasped and heads lowered, words muffled, dark forms in the candlelit church. The flames fluttering in reflection in the windows and along the old and stained walls whenever a door was opened and fluttering again when closed. People praying in whispers and some talking in low voices and pigeons flapping outside and people walking across the flagstones to the stone stairs and people on the sidewalk across from Joe as he sat and hoped that she would soon arrive.

He did not know what Dillard's sister looked like nor how he would approach her once he found her. For all he knew she was involved with the killing of Gresham, maybe even her own brother. What could possess someone to murder her own brother was alien to him, but as a newspaperman he had seen a woman who had killed her own children and a man who had killed his father. He had seen an epidemic insanity during the war, an Armageddon. He could not explain the actions of the world's lost citizens. He would not even try.

He was lost as well. He was one of what the automobile repairman had called hopeless, without hope, a lost generation. *Perdu.* That loss had come in the war. It went beyond a loss of hope and it had manifested in Joe's spirit like a plague. The things he had lost in the war, the hope and several layers of innocence and truth and the absolute belief in abstract words and his church, friends, family, the treasure house of his past, had all been replaced by darker monuments. New engravings had been etched upon his soul and memory as though with acid. Joe could not see beyond them, not in daylight nor at night in drunkenness nor in a church's ambulatory under an abandoned sky.

He saw her first from a distance walking on his side of the street, dressed in black. She was tall and quite thin, which, for a reason Joe could not have said, surprised him. Her walk was unsteady and her head was down and shoulders slumped. She walked with her hands in her pockets and her head barely lifted. She wore a cloche hat, but he could see her dark hair cut short.

As she passed within a dozen feet of him, looking toward him with unfocused eyes, she looked like someone who was no longer touched by the sun.

"Marie Dillard?" Joe asked as he slid alongside of her on the sidewalk, placing his hand on her arm. She was as tall as he, and her skin was dark, the almond of a Mediterranean.

She looked at him, startled. Her eyes widened. Her mouth began to open as though to form words.

"Please, don't say anything," Joe said. "I must speak with you. I am an American . . . . My name is Joe Henry. I need to talk with you about Wynton Gresham and your brother."

Her breath drew in quickly from surprise and her eyes widened when she looked at him. She looked around at the street and spit in a low voice and with explicit immediacy, "Assassin," truncating the word as though it were used as a cudgel. Her voice formed almost in a cold whisper that cut quick and raw through Joe.

She pulled her arm from his grasp and swung her other hand up to slap him across the cheek. Joe saw her hand swing in its arc and could have blocked it but did not.

"Assassin," she said louder, more confidently, her head raised as though to announce his condemnation to the world.

People on the street began to slow. Some stopped while others edged around the two of them on the narrow sidewalk. A couple of men who had stopped, leaned against the side of the church, cigarettes held loosely to their sides, deciding whether they wanted to be spectators or participants in that street's drama.

"No," Joe said. "Please listen to me."

She reached into her purse and began to pull something from it. The presence of a crowd surrounding them, however, stopped her, and she drew out her hand empty, pointing her finger at him.

"Assassin," she said once more before breaking away from him and walking quickly across the street to enter the brick town-house. Before entering the house, she turned and said, "*Vous êtes un meurtrier. Vous avez tué mon frère.*"

He took one step in following her although she had already closed her door to him.

A heavy hand landed on his shoulder, and he turned to look into the eyes of a man wearing the clothes of a worker. Unlike the students he had seen elsewhere in Paris, and like those in America as well, his worn clothes had been earned. He had dirt on his cheeks and his skin was dark from the sun, and Joe thought that he could feel the rope scars and callouses and half-heeled blisters of a workingman's hands.

"*Qu'est-ce que vous voulez,*" the man said, his voice raised and his accent something other than any French Joe had ever heard, to the point where Joe struggled at understanding.

"What is it you vant?" The man spat in an accent almost German, Alsatian maybe. His blue eyes alive and hard in the direct-ness of their stare.

Joe looked at the people who had slowed to watch. Their stares of wonder momentarily impaled him.

"Wait," Joe said. He placed his hands up, palms out, as to show his innocence.

"La police!" the man yelled, and another man standing nearby took up the call.

Joe took a step, but the first man reached out to take his shoulder, and Joe swung around and in the close space brought his elbow into the man's nose. Like hitting the hard end of an opened oak door, the man's nose split and he staggered. Joe punched him once more, unnecessarily for the man had been knocked out. The other man, momentarily struck by the change of fortunes, took one step toward Joe but Joe jabbed him in the throat. The man staggered, lost of breath and lost of voice and probably panicking that he might also be lost of life. Joe pushed the man from him. The two men lay sprawled as broken mannequins on the cobblestones of the street.

Joe left, walking quickly but not running and not looking anyone in the eye and within minutes he had found his anonymity within the ever-present crowds of the Left Bank. He continued on and away from her house and away from his hotel and back toward the river. The cold cut through his coat even more than before and he tightened his body against a chill. He walked, head down, following the shadow of his footsteps.

Joe walked along the quai of the Seine, the sidewalk beginning to ice and his breath pluming. He traded his coat and a ten dollar bill—a month's wages for the average Parisian—to a bookseller for the man's old overcoat. He hoped to change his appearance and hoped also not to pick up lice along with the trade. Sitting huddled under blankets, old men on the docked barges fished for barbel as dirty smoke rose from oven pipes on top of the boats. He glanced at the sky and then toward where the sun would be and saw a distant orange glow that might have been the sun setting behind a horizon of buildings, gray against the darkening world. Cold light smeared out behind the borders of the buildings. Empty tree limbs twisted in a slight December wind along the river that carried a beginning of snow. He walked alone with a river of brackish waters, a cold wind, and a diminished and veiled sunset.

He checked his watch and found that he had over four hours before Marcel and his men would arrive at the Gentilhomme.

Even though he planned on arriving early to watch them enter, see where they stood, who they were, how they presented themselves, he still had hours to kill, so he decided to use the time profitably. A visit to the American Library would provide him with something he felt sorely in lack of—knowledge.

He crossed the Seine at Port Royal Bridge and crossed through the Tuileries, the grass wet and the hundreds of chestnut trees empty of leaves. A huddle of men, all dressed heavily against the weather, played *pétanque* in one corner, but Joe didn't slow to watch. He avoided the large boulevards and took to the narrow side streets and stayed in shadows in case he encountered any police.

The library was on rue de l'Elysée in a palatial building once owned by the Papal Nuncio. Above the large double doors was painted in a Roman script, ATRUM POST BELLUM, EX LIBRIS LUX: AFTER THE DARKNESS OF WAR, THE LIGHT OF BOOKS. They were words that Joe had first read in the spring of 1919 when on leave in Paris he stumbled up the stairs to the library in search of a place that did not serve beer or coffee or women. The large and open reading rooms and thousands of American volumes proved a daily escape from his nights.

The scent of old tomes wafted in the building's air and dust motes bounced in the window-light as Joe stepped through the doors and scraped his boots on a rough rug just inside the entryway. He had come to read about the battle and the American Library was the only English-language library that he knew. He asked a young man who sat behind a small reading table with a VOLUNTEER sign facing out.

The young man, not too young to have been in the war, was writing. In front of him was a tablet for writing and he had filled better than half the page, and he was writing furiously and without consideration, as though his mind was moving faster than his brain. Joe had heard of it, automatic writing, and knew that some people were using it as a treatment method for shell shock. Joe had visited a small asylum for the wounded sons of rich men where young doctors were experimenting with it, older doctors disdained it and favored the decades old Rest Cure of Weir Mitchell and wondered why their patients blew their brains out at the first chance. This new method, automatic writing, came from Freud through the Frenchman Andre Breton, and Joe thought that it might work in helping the young vets deal with their trench demons. Maybe not for him, but for others.

The young man suddenly stopped writing, and with a nervous jerk he looked up at Joe and saw that he was being watched. That inchoate sense developed in the trench; those who lived in the trenches of France had grown accustomed to being under watch, under the view of scoped eyes, watched by new officers looking for an improperly buttoned jacket or haggard sergeants looking for a volunteer or a Heine bastard across the distance looking to place a bullet in your brain. You never got used to it. Even when your own eyes closed in sleep, you felt the scrutiny. It was a feeling embedded.

The young man capped his pen, black and heavy, maybe Mont Blanc, and looked up as Joe stepped closer. The young man's eyes were old and sad, a contrast to their clear color, and his left eye twitched a couple of times.

He swallowed and asked, "May I help you?" His fingers, set to either side of the tablet continued to worry against his thumbs as though they needed to catch up with their lost writing.

"*London Times History of the War*," Joe asked and the man's twitch triggered.

Joe had seen it before—other veterans of the war who carried the war with them. Gresham had once told the difference between fact and truth and provided an example. "This is a fact," Gresham had said. "This is incontrovertible. The war ended on the eleventh hour of the eleventh day of the eleventh month in the year of our Lord 1918." Following a moment filled with a drink from his glass of scotch, he added, "This is the truth. The war will never end. You and me and hundreds of thousands of others who fought in that slaughter will carry it with us every single day of our lives."

Joe had seen men who slept underneath their beds or who would not stay in room unless a door was left propped open. He had seen men who walked always hunched to keep their heads from appearing above a trenches lip. He knew one man in Greenwich who refused any job that made him work during the daylight hours and would only work between sunset and sunrise and once the matin sun rose he was safely barred within his shuttered house. Shellshock, some doctor had called it, and Joe felt that he was lucky that he carried only a slight neurosis with him from the war.

The young man, who if one were to see him sitting at a café with his arms crossed and his eyes closed in contemplation of a lovely day one would think nothing of him, blinked several times and his body shuddered and stiffened to control. He swallowed with a jerk and pointed Joe down a row of shelves filled with books and told Joe which shelf to see.

The young man had obviously looked through those books himself, maybe searching for a reason if not hoping for a cure.

Joe pulled the sixth volume from the *Times* history along with other histories. Those by Vast and Hayes, whom he had remembered from Gresham's house, as well one by Alexander Powell and another by Yves Neuville. The story from the first three was much the same—a brave assault and stunning victory. The sort of patriotic jingoism that Joe come to despise.

However, Powell's narrative of the battle was more visceral and Neuville's history contained the questions that Joe had come to hear.

The battle had begun with an extended artillery barrage, over seventy hours of almost constant shelling of the German lines which only increased in ferocity on the morning of 25 September 1915. The French soldiers were told by their officers that nothing could survive such a bombardment and that the worst that they would encounter would be the German wounded who had survived. One major, who was on a general's staff and therefor would not take part in the advance—much to his regret, he had said—had announced that more French soldiers would suffer from sprained ankles crossing through the shelled-out no-man's land than would be shot by Germans.

The Germans, it was supposed, would not have constructed trenches of depth and strength to withstand the barrage. However, the Germans had constructed rooms and tunnels well below the depth of destruction rained down upon them, so that the bombing would have sounded like a strong thunderstorm. They emerged just before sunrise that Friday morning in time to reestablish their positions and knew the trails the French soldiers would follow and where best to place their old Maxim guns and newer MGs. The killing field they produced became filled with the bodies of twenty thousand Frenchmen. Some killed so many men that German soldiers cried as they hoped the French would discontinue the assault, their machine guns overheated and barrels warped, and still the French came.

Neuville theorized that the Germans had known when and where and how the assault would proceed. "A traitorous coward," he theorized, "had undoubtedly sold the honor of France, and one can only hope that that man will have to live a long life with the memory of his perfidy and the blood of his countrymen forever on his hands and forever staining his damned soul."

Joe read them. Unlike Neuville, he hoped the traitor's life would end soon. As he left, he turned to the young man, right hand shaking, and said, "It will get better, brother."

He hated lying, but he felt some need to offer hope.

At the Gentilhomme, most of the tables were surrounded by people eating early dinners of soup and eggs and sausages. Joe saw the broad back of Quire at the bar, the back of a serious worker or the hunch of a serious drinker. Joe took the stool next to him and rubbed the cold from his hands.

He patted Quire on the shoulder as he sat and asked, "How you doing?' He wanted the words to sound jolly.

Quire turned to him. His left eye held the livid mark of a hard knuckle, a play of green and yellow and plum-purple. Quire squinted through the other eye until he recognized Joe. "Hello, Joe," he said and raised his pint. "Want one?"

"What happened?"

The bartender leaned over the bar and stared at Joe. He ordered a pint, Alsatian, and the bartender brought it. Joe fished in his pants pocket for a coin.

Quire took a Franc coin from the pile in front of him and slapped it down. "On me," he said. "Hell, it's only a Franc. That's what? About twelve cents in real money. You can get the next round."

Quire offered his glass for a toast, "To the Lost," and Joe met it. Holding the pint at eye level and looking through it toward the mirror, Quire said, "Down to the sea in ships. Down to life in schooners."

They both drank, with Joe glancing toward the front doors each time they opened and checking the mirror with regularity.

"Tell me," Joe said. "What happened?"

Quire scratched the back of his neck. "One of those damn things that makes no sense. We both been inside those deals."

"Yes." Joe drank, waiting for Quire to explain further.

He watched the mirror as a woman hipped her way across the room and nudged against him to stand at the bar. She had fresh skin and high cheekbones. Her hair was black and cut tight against her face, the favored style from Colleen Moore although even more severe than the film star's cut. The French, Joe thought, did everything a bit more severe. Her eyes, ringed heavily with kohl, were obscured, and she had a small mouth with lips as red as drawn blood.

"Pardon," she said. She waved to the bartender and smiled at Joe, a smile with promises of adventure.

The bartender came and she ordered a Corpse Reviver, which the bartender mixed and served with no reaction beyond a deep breath. She pretended to search for money in pockets that did not exist on her short dress, then drew her mouth into a pout toward Joe and Quire. Quire took another Franc from his pile and handed it to the bartender.

"Merci," she said.

"Pleasure's mine," he said.

"My name is Elle," she said in accented English, extending her hand across Joe to shake with Quire. "It means 'She.'"

"He's Joe. I'm Quire."

"Quire? What does Quire mean?"

"I'm American. In America, names don't mean anything."

She smiled and nodded. "But your eye," she said, her mouth curved down. "That means something."

He shrugged, "The streets can be mean."

"Monsieur, you must be careful." She smiled again but only at Quire. Joe felt as though he had become an audience. "I return now to my friends. Are you here often?"

"Yes," Quire answered, nodding.

"I will see you sometime." Not a question, but a very confident statement. She knew her power. "After Christmas," she said, holding Quire's gaze long enough to pass some message Joe was not privy to.

Quire nodded and smiled. "After Christmas."

She left and the scent of her perfume drifted in a wake behind her. Joe watched her move through the room to her table, her walk a work of art. The room seemed to follow her.

Joe said, "Hell, man, was I even here?"

"Not that I could see . . . nor her apparently."

Joe drank from his beer. "That did a lot for my ego."

"She wasn't thinking no ego, bud." He winked and drank.

"I noticed. Believe me, I noticed even if you two thought I was one of the invisible." Joe turned and looked at the woman and her cloche-hatted friends together at their table. His thoughts grew darker and sadder as he thought of how he sometimes envied people like them, smart set people who seemed to have nothing to think about and nothing to destroy their dreams at night.

She didn't need to buy her own drinks, she didn't need to pay for the things of life.

"Nice," Quire said, turning to look.

"Damn nice," Joe agreed.

"Pretty smart all right. She's got It."

They finished their beers and ordered another as well as a plate of fresh baguette and butter. They talked for a while about women they had known. Joe kept his tone light, not letting a sadness invade just then for he knew the price of morose moments. So he welcomed the next beer gratefully and drank fully.

"You going to tell me?" he asked Quire.

"Tell you what?"

Joe pointed a finger at Quire's face.

Quire touched the swollen area around his eye. "I'm not exactly certain what happened," he said. "I'm walking home and some guys punch me, and one tells me to forget about helping somebody named Gresham. It doesn't mean a shit-load of sense to me. I don't even know anybody named Gresham."

"Son of a bitch," Joe said.

"What?"

"You do know someone named Gresham, in a way."

"What do you mean, Mr. Ford?"

Joe did not even consider how much to withhold from Quire. It was too late to protect him now. Quire deserved to hear everything. That was what Joe told him. He left few details out, concluding as Quire finished his beer and began another, "Someone must have seen us last night, thought there was some connection and decided to convince you to get lost. I'm sorry."

"You didn't know." He shrugged and drank. "If you don't mind, though, I'll be taking the guy's advice. I'm not too keen on dying any earlier than necessary."

Joe nodded. "Don't worry about it," he said. "It's my fight." He drank and waited for the tight silence that followed to end.

When they talked again, they talked about the war. It was a subject that each knew well and neither could easily discard. They talked about the smells of sage and pine that they remembered from their youths but neither had known in many years, and then about the French. Joe told Quire about working on a newspaper. Quire told Joe what the woman at the bar had meant when she said that she would see him after Christmas, "The week following Christmas is St. Catherine's Day. All the beauties wear disguises and go around kissing men they'd like to bounce. It's a helluva' time, no commitments, just a good night's roll." They toasted that. "You just have to be certain you don't end up in bed with a fire ship."

Joe laughed, "How will they ever get us back on the farm once we've seen the sights of Paris?"

"Ah, yes," Quire agreed, glancing again toward the woman with kohl-rimmed eyes. They toasted and laughed and talked some more.

The room then darkened; the night began to turn over.

He first noticed the Turk's presence in the shadows by the rear exit as he had turned for one more glimpse of the beautiful woman and her friends. The Turk walked from the shadows near the rear door and into the canted light of the café. Shadows followed him. His darkness moved with him like a deadly slipstream.

The Turk formed a rear guard, protecting against Joe's escape through the café's rear as well as securing a possible exit for whoever came later through the front. Looming above the seated patrons at tables, he looked even larger than Joe remembered. Below the furrow of his heavy and dark eyebrows, his eyes glared. He smiled at Joe like the eternal footman smiling. With a roll of his shoulders he set himself, a massive standing at the ready.

The café's front doors opened. In walked Dapper. He wore a black overcoat that was buttoned to the collar and extended below the knees. He wore no hat and had dark hair thinning and wet from the wet snow falling outside. He walked slowly into the room, sliding around tables and searching faces until he saw Joe at the bar. When he saw Quire seated next to Joe, he stalled for a second.

"That's him," Quire said and Joe followed Quire's gaze to Dapper. Quire began to rise from his seat. "I'm going to kick that bastard into the last century. Let him know that his big mouth wrote a scrip his little ass can't cash."

Joe placed a hand on Quire's shoulder to steady the block of a man. "Hold on," he said. "You're involving yourself in what you just said you don't want a part of."

"Things change when could-be become what-is."

"In that case, you'll get your chance, but wait a minute and see how things play out."

Hesitating for a moment, Quire's gauged Joe's words, but the man's eyes carried full fire in them. He nodded and sat back down. His low growl, like that of a dog just before its let loose, told Joe that Quire was not willing to wait long. "See, what'd I tell you? A magnet for trouble. Don't even have to go looking for it."

As Dapper ringed around tables filled with drinkers, Joe asked, "You Marcel?"

Dapper looked at him then at the Turk, who nodded, before turning to study Joe's face.

"Non, Monsieur," he said with a careful voice. He breathed and repeated, *"Non."* His voice, like his eyes, was dark and callous. He faced Joe, unblinking.

"Where is he?"

"Marcel sent me." The man's eyes darted between Joe and Quire. "You can do business with me."

"I do business with Marcel."

Dapper gave a French shrug that could have meant okay or fuck you or I don't care.

"I have the manuscript but not here," Joe said in English. He paused to watch the man's reaction. There was very little other than a slight curl of the upper lip, like a mongrel before it bites. "If Marcel wants it, he comes to me."

After a moment of silence between them, the man's eyebrows raised. Joe could see some cogs and gears working overtime as Dapper chewed on that puzzle he had just been tossed.

"I came here with the expectation that we would do business. How you Americans say, 'Talk straight.' I give you something, you give me something." He paused and smiled. "I scratch yours and you scratch mine, huh? I don't like playing games."

"I don't like people killing my friends, but that hasn't stopped you," Joe said, leaning back against the bar. He drank from his beer. He could feel his anger rising, especially following Dapper's attempt to bait him.

"Business," Dapper said, as though people's lives were no more than commodities to be traded.

Sitting on the bar stool, Joe looked into the man's eyes. Just for effect he stood and looked at the man, who was then shorter than him. The Turk stepped closer. Joe saw them as though in a parallax. Both kept one hand inside a coat pocket and both watched him closely.

"Here's business," Joe said. "I have what you want, what do you have for trade?"

Dapper did not look at but nodded toward Quire. "A friend of yours?"

Joe recognized the question as misdirection intended by Dapper to allow himself time to regain his leverage.

Joe looked at Quire. "No," he said. "Just another American to drink with and talk with."

"He and I have met." And he offered Joe a false smile. "If I am really the murderer you say I am, killing your friends, then he is lucky. Wouldn't you agree, Monsieur? If he were your friend and he became a bother as others may have, then I would have to kill him as well."

Quire answered with a steady quickness, "Listen. I've been sailing near the wind for quite a while now and I wouldn't be frightened by some piss-ant like you." He added, "Whatever my friend's in, I'm in."

Dapper did not look at Quire, not while Quire spoke nor when he spoke of Quire. "Your friend has a big mouth, as you Americans say."

"And my butt's big enough to back it up," Quire added as he pushed himself from his stool. He stood eye-to-eye with Dapper, but Dapper could have fit inside Quire's girth with room for a quarter-barrel of stout alongside.

Joe placed a hand on Quire's shoulder. Quire sat back down with his back against the bar. Every muscle in the man's body had tightened. The muscles along his neck and jaw stood out like heavy cords. He looked at Joe, his face hard and a deep maroon red as though just fired in a forge.

Continuing to ignore Quire, Dapper spoke to Joe, "And you, Monsieur Henry?" He waved his fingers. "Everyone in Paris knows your name. If I have killed all of those other men, why will I not kill you as well?"

"Because I have the manuscript, and until your boss gets it, I'm safe."

"You are not safe. Not even now. All Marcel need do is provide the word."

Joe shrugged, not a French shrug but as good as he could offer. He leaned forward. "Tell this to Marcel. I got to his men outside of

Greenwich, and I killed them and took the manuscript from their automobile. I had plenty of time to read it while on the cruise over. You and the Turk over there really should take some lessons in how to toss a room. It was in plain sight, and you missed it. Amateurs. Now Marcel has to play my game. Otherwise, it finds its way to a desk at the Prefecture de Police. Some of them may take an interest in its contents and then an interest in the traitor who sent so many of their comrades to their deaths."

Dapper blinked slowly, the studied movement of a boundless conceit. "Marcel is not concerned with the contents of Gresham's manuscript, at least what he had written before his demise. So sad."

He smiled at Joe. The smile's lack of warmth spread to the man's eyes.

Dapper took a cigarette from its silver case and lit it with a match, waving the match out and watching the smoke that he breathed out dissipate before he continued, "Marcel is not concerned with it. There is nothing in it that causes him concern."

"Obviously," Quire said and rested back into his seat to continue drinking.

Dapper shrugged again and said, almost as an aside, "However, he would prefer to restrain its release."

"Why?"

"That is not my concern; that is not your concern."

"Sounds to me," Quire offered, "like you think a lot of people either are or should be 'unconcerned,' yet somehow people are still killing other people."

Dapper looked from Joe to Quire and back. "You provide me with the manuscript and Marcel pays you handsomely for your efforts."

"And then I die in my sleep."

Dapper shrugged. Head, shoulders, hands, they all shrugged, even his eyebrows shrugged. "*C'est la vie.* Accidents happen, Monsieur. You would be wise to remember that and to help insure that one does not happen to you." He inhaled a breath of his cigarette and let out a cloud of smoke to rise within the din of the café. He looked around and then looked back at Joe. "One thousand United States dollars, Monsieur. That would allow you to live in Paris for at least a year."

"You have it?"

"I do."

Joe nodded. "That's tempting . . . if I thought I would live out the year."

Dapper waved his cigarette-laden hand, a trail of smoke with it. "Swiss Francs, then, at the equivalent amount. They are easier to spend and transfer quite easily if your safety concerns cause you to leave France." He added, as though an afterthought, "Maybe, if the police take an interest in your presence. Maybe someone contacts them about you and you feel the need to leave Paris very quickly— Swiss francs would be helpful."

Joe remembered Gresham lying dead on his sofa with a bullet hole in him and said, "His reach is awfully long."

Dapper smiled. "True, but think of how certain that reach will be if he is not satisfied."

"Point taken," Joe said. "When I figure out exactly what I want for it, I'll be in touch. But next time I talk directly with the man. I want to see what a coward looks like."

Dapper looked at his cigarette and then back at Joe, his dead eyes impaled and devoid of light. "Tomorrow. No later. That is what Marcel told me to instruct you. Following that, you die and he accepts what may come."

He turned and left. The Turk followed and grazed Joe as he walked past. Joe could feel the hardness of a pistol inside the Turk's coat. A reminder. After Marcel's two assistants had left the café, Joe turned to face the bar and found a fresh beer in front of him.

"Thought you might need some assistance in the thought process," Quire said.

"Thanks. A thousand dollars is a good bit of money, but I'm not certain I'd live to spend it all. Anyway, my mind was made up long ago. And," he smiled," I don't have what Marcel thinks I have in the first place."

Quire looked at him, mouth slightly open, then laughed full and deep. "Damn, brother. You do know how to run a bluff. I like that."

He nodded and added, "I think I'll stick around a while to see how it plays out."

Joe smiled. "For someone out of it, you seem to have landed yourself in the middle."

Quire nodded. "It'll give me something to do with my nights besides drink."

"Think about it. In case you weren't listening, people have been dying around me with alarming regularity."

"In case you didn't realize it, cowboy, I've seen enough of death not to be scared off by its prospect. Anyways, with my lungs progressively turning to pudding, I'm not long for this damn world anyways." He drank. "And on top of that, I just do not like that little bastard one bit, the conceited little shit. I'd like to kill him, and I'd like to kill his boss with him."

"You sure?" Joe asked.

Quire held his pint for Joe to meet and said, "Let's wet this bargain. Here's to the blue moons in our lives."

Joe held his pint above the bar. "What the hell's that mean?"

"Beats the hell out of me, but it sounds pretty nice."

They drank.

"This could get tight," Joe said, his tone deeper and more serious.

"It almost just did."

"And you're still with me?" Joe asked

"Within an ace of," Quire said with a wink.

"You have a gun?"

"On me, you mean?"

"No, but can you get one?"

"I do have one, and I do have it on me. Just like you."

"I don't like it, but I need it. I haven't carried a gun since the war."

"Yeah," Quire said, nodding. "I haven't stopped carrying one since the war."

They drank in silence. Through the fog-rimmed windows at the front of the café, Joe could see people walking past bundled against the December night. Once again the night was cold and damp. Despite the large revolving fans in a line on the café's ceiling, however, the room was stifling, hot and humid, as the crunch of people continued to grow. The jazz band began to play in a back corner, a quartet of black men charging the lonely night with music. People began dancing like an apocalypse had or was about to happen, like the world had already ended or was soon to end.

Quire said something, but the restaurant chatter and the jazz and the numbing drinks made it difficult for Joe to hear.

"What?" Joe asked.

"To the Lost."

VIII

Here, during two strenuous years, has taken place some of the fiercest fighting of the great war. Here, too, are some of the finest vineyards of the world; for this was in Roman days the Campania which later gave its name to the province of Champagne.
—Frederick Dean, *Muncey's Magazine*, September 1916, "Champagne and the Great War,"

SOMETIME BETWEEN MIDNIGHT AND MORNING, JOE LEFT THE Gentilhomme with the café's music still strong and Quire still drinking. He walked up the cobblestone street to his hotel, less steady on his feet than he would have preferred. The city was wrapped in a cold night fog that could have been imported from London, brackish and impenetrable. He felt wary as he walked, watching within the shadows and measuring the gait of Parisians walking near him. In the moonlit night, icy puddles shined and curtained windows veiled the few building lights still lit. In the air he could smell the wisps of late-night or early-morning warming fires.

Someone stepped from the recess of a hotel entrance as he passed and touched his arm. He recoiled, reaching for the small revolver in his pocket, but the hammer caught as he tugged.

"Pardon, Monsieur," a woman said, her voice raspy from cigarettes, drink, and age. "*Ont besoin de compagnie ce soir?*"

"What?" Joe said, his mind, startled, did not make the translation. "*Quoi?*" he added.

"Are you in need of company?" she said in broken and heavily accented English.

"*Non,*" was all Joe said, and he walked away.

A block farther, he stopped under a streetlight and leaned against the post to catch his breath. Fear had its own rhythm, and he rested for a moment to regain his composure. He thought of Marcel—why the man relied so on intermediaries. From Huntington's short biography of Marcel, Joe knew the man was something of a recluse, affected like so many others by the war. Joe knew other men, men that he had served with who had retreated in life to some cabin the wilderness of Maine or the Olympic Peninsula of Washington. People had come out of that war changed, irrevocably changed, and their lives were separated like a concrete dam between what once was and what now is. Just like the bodies of water on each side of that dam, they were never the same. So he understood Marcel's inclination toward hiding from a world that had so irrevocably changed him and his world, but there was something more to Marcel's deceit. A greater reason to his desire for anonymity—his cowardice.

If Marcel had wanted Joe dead, then Joe would have been killed on the boat with Huntington or he would have burned in a fire like Dillard. Something in Gresham's manuscript had Marcel nervous enough to want it, even though Dapper claimed otherwise. For the time being, at least, as long as Marcel believed he had the manuscript, the Frenchman might not act. They had searched his room and not found it, and Joe felt that his bluff in the café had worked, convincing enough that Dapper would report that he still had a copy squirreled away. Joe needed Marcel to believe that it was somewhere safe, somewhere from which Joe could have it delivered to the police if anything happened to him. How long that concern would hold Marcel, Joe could not guess. Eventually the man would act, for even cowards did not remain passive forever. Marcel's revulsion at his own cowardice would force him into some movement. By that time, Joe needed some sort of plan of his own.

At the hotel, the old man was again asleep on the front counter but woke with the tinkle of the door's little bell as Joe entered. He raised his head and snorted loudly, put on his spectacles to see Joe walk toward him.

"Monsieur Gresham," the old man said. His hand shook as he waved Joe over. Even when he put his hand on the counter, it continued to shake. His head also shook in a perpetual "No," but his eyes remained kind.

"*Un gendarme*, they visit you this evening," the old man said, his English quite good, but Joe felt a quick panic at the man's choice of tense.

He looked up at the foyer's ceiling. "They're here now?"

The old man laughed, "Oh no no no. I tell them that you are not here and they leave."

Joe sighed with relief and rubbed the stubble of his chin. "Did they say what they wanted?"

The old man waved his hand. "Some suicide, some murder, some fire—*je ne sais pas*—I do not understand. They say much, I listen little, understand less. A fire, I know, they say a fire."

"Thank you. *Merci*." Joe said and started for the stairs thinking that it was time for a night's sleep and then to pack up and leave.

The old man called him back to the counter and looked toward the front door and leaned against the counter to speak. Joe stepped close and leaned over the counter as well, as though they were caught in a conspiracy together.

The old man said, "They ask me to call them after you arrive home, but," he paused and smiled, "they do not say how long after you arrive. I suppose eight this morning is good, no?"

"Nine—*neuf*—would be better."

The old man shrugged, "*Oui. Neuf.* Nine it is. They are suspicious if your trunk is gone, so please use *valise* that I leave in your room. I will store your trunk in our basement for you."

Joe took the old man's hand, thin and bony but still strong in its grasp, and joined with its palsied shake. "You may be taking a risk by helping me."

The old man huffed. "*De rien*," he said, waving a quavering hand as he spoke. "They do not buy me dinner. I owe them nothing. You must take care and come back to us."

Joe thanked him and took from his wallet a five-dollar bill, enough money to have paid for a week's reservation. In his room, he sat in the chair for a moment and looked at the owner's valise, a portmanteau that looked like a doctor's bag, dimpled black leather with leather handles and a brass closure. He would not even need it. He cleaned himself from the washbasin and laid out a new set of Gresham's clothes. He sat on the bed and closed his eyes and took a long, deep breath in order to clear his mind and concentrate, then studied the photograph of Gresham and his comrades in the trenches.

He could not see Gresham's eyes beneath the shadowline of his helmet. His mouth was straight and his jaw fixed, not necessarily confident but certainly resolute. The difference, Joe knew, often came with one's length of time in the trenches. The other men held similar countenances, although one or two were forced to the point of vague obscurity. Something was there that he had missed, but he was a couple of drinks past too drunk to find it that night.

He tossed the photograph on the bed beside him and planned the next day: find the sister, find Quire, find a place to stay alive.

He slid his Smith & Wesson under his pillow and lay down. Had he thought about it, he would have been surprised at how quickly and easily he slid into sleep. With the night cold and calm, he slept soundly for hours until a dream invaded his morning like a strident noise.

In his dream, he saw the face of a man he had killed. Not the first man he had killed in the war, but the first man he had seen close enough to watch as the life drained from his eyes. Short blonde hair, muddy and rough cut. A cowlick waved in the wind from the crest of his head. His eyes were open and at one time blue but had drained to a wan color and unfocused as though caught between distances. A drip of blood had run from his open mouth like spilled ink. His skin ashen. Right at the hollow of his neck, just above the sternum, a hole had blackened and crusted with blood. He was fifteen, maybe, and lived to as old an age as anyone ever could. Joe had spotted the boy peering from the safety of a shell hole not fifty yards from Joe's trench position, caught, probably, by the daylight following a night's recon. Joe waited. He marked the distance and checked the round in his Springfield. The boy raised his head once then twice. Joe shot him. "Damn fine shot, Joe," someone said. Joe had smiled. That night, Joe met his dead man when he left the trench with a scouting party. Many nights since, Joe had again met his dead man.

Joe met him once more that morning. For some who had been in the war, nights were a terrible time. They filled with the anticipation of a morning's advance, either theirs or the enemy's. Nights since filled with the anticipation of nothing. They might drink as Quire did or they might lie alone or with some prostitute. Some dark horror would eventually take them, envelope them like the fog. Joe knew men like that.

Night was certainly bad for Joe. But for Joe, mornings were when his war returned. In the semiconscious moments just before waking, his wounds would rise and he would be left alone as the sun hovered on the opening of day. With those memories held fast as though etched with the featheredge of a lancet, he realized that he had never before returned to Europe because he had never really left.

He rolled over and looked at his pocket watch—8:04. He had to hurry, and he had to travel light. He dressed quickly and made certain that he had his short Smith & Wesson in his pocket. He rolled the photographs and notes inside a pocket of his overcoat. He kept his money in a pants' pocket.

As he crossed the hotel's foyer, the old man raised his palsied hand and said with a smile, "*Bon chance,* Monsieur Gresham."

"*Merci,*" answered Joe.

He walked out into a thick and muddy morning fog. Underneath the fog, however, the city hustled as though shaking its inhabitants from head to foot. He walked to the boulevard Saint-Germain and then along the wide street. A cadence of sounds linked sidewalk cafés—unmuffled automobiles, morning-weary prostitutes, gendarmes in their rain slickers, sleeping drunks, and roaming dogs. Joe stopped once to speak to a one-legged prostitute, turning his back on a pair of uniformed police as they walked past.

His first stop would be the house of Marie Dillard on Saint Séverin. One of two things would result from a second visit. Either he would find out that she was as good as he hoped or as bad as he feared.

The night's fog held into the morning. The city's gas lamps remained lit, casting a yellow haze across the sidewalks. The weather had changed drastically since the sun of the previous day. Joe smiled.

The rain and fog were perfect for a man in exile. People on the street, including the police, kept their heads down against the dampness of the day. It was a weather in which everyone seemed to respect the autonomy and anonymity of others.

He waited again beside the cathedral across from her building, standing under a leafless chestnut tree in the park-like ambulatory. His stomach sounded from morning hunger, but he did not want to find a patisserie and risk the chance of missing her. He knew the French well enough to know that she was not an early riser. She was not of the working class, not from where she lived nor from how she was dressed the previous day. Her day might not begin until noon, but he wanted to meet her whenever it was that she left her home.

He waited over two hours, listening to the church's bells twice ring in the hour as he marched in place for warmth, before he saw her door open. When she emerged from her building near eleven o'clock, Joe remained in the shadows of the ambulatory to watch her. Marie Dillard looked around but he was well back in the shadows and she moved quickly, as though nervous about something. She dropped her keys back into her purse as she fumbled with them before finally taking them out and placing them in the lock.

He followed her as she crossed Saint Michel. She did not look behind as she walked quickly. Joe kept pace from less than a block behind. The crowds of people flowed around her like water parting around a tug and its barge. She turned along boulevard Saint-Germain, busy with people and automobiles and pigeons.

Marie Dillard entered a café. Joe slid behind a clutch of people standing around a bus stop, newspapers raised to signal to others not to enter their little world. He waited for a moment, hands pocketed and collar up as much for anonymity as against the cold, before crossing the wide boulevard, dodging puddles and automobiles and trolleys and deliverymen in the old horse-drawn wagons bringing fresh produce from the countryside around Paris.

The restaurant had a glassed front and long cream-colored awnings, *Café de Flore* scripted in green and gold on the awning. The trees in front of the restaurant were empty of leaves and wet from the fog and rain.

Joe entered Brasserie Lipp across from the Flore, walking through the glassed entry with its tables already taken by straw-hatted Americans bent on the French experience they had heard about in their eating clubs of Princeton or Harvard. He chose a table in the restaurant's front from which he could watch the Flore's door.

A waiter in black suit, white shirt, and bow tie, white apron from waist to the tops of his polished black shoes, took his order of Alsatian beer sausages. He bought a copy of the *Herald Tribune* from a paperboy passing through the brasserie and sat back in the wood and leather chair, watching across the street while scanning the newspaper, and he took advantage of the moment to order a meal. A man at a table opposite him in the small restaurant sat with his back to a mirror eating bread and drinking coffee slowly, as though the acts took forethought. The man, young and not quite gaunt, looked hungry and appeared to Joe to be making his simple meal of bread last as long as possible, as though exacting penance in his meager feast.

Joe sat back and drank his beer and ate his sausage, waiting for Marie across the boulevard to finish her meal. He glanced through the newspaper again, reading a short article on the death of Rose Shaunessy, which according to the Paris coroner was a suicide: "Suicide during temporary insanity brought on by a quarrel with her lover." He folded and dropped the newspaper on the empty chair next to him, thinking about how fiction becomes fact and fact becomes fiction. The man opposite him had wiped his plate clean with bread and sat back with a large coffee and a pad of writing paper and sharpened pencils on the table in front of him. Joe hoped the man's manuscript, whatever it was, would not cause as many problems to as many people as Gresham's had.

Joe finished his lunch and the *Herald* and watched the man, who was dressed as a worker and looked as though he could be a worker but obviously wasn't, for a working man would not be lounging in a café with pencils and paper as the afternoon hours passed. He drank his beer and another and ordered a third just to keep from being asked to leave, but let it sit.

Finally, Marie left the Flore with a man whom Joe did not recognize nor could see well. He wore his trench coat with the collar pulled up and his fedora low over his eyes, and when he spoke, Marie turned toward him.

Joe watched them as they stood in front of the Flore on the wet sidewalk, sparrows jumping around them in search for breadcrumbs. Not far away in the branches of the leafless trees, other sparrows sat puffed against the cold. Joe left a pile of coins on the table and went to stand in the glassed front with the loud Americans, college boys intent on sampling every bit of the Paris expatriate scene they had read about in the pages of *Vanity Fair*.

When they separated to leave, the man turned down a side street while Marie Dillard walked back alone along boulevard Saint-Germain. Joe watched the man walk away, hunched into himself and not looking over his shoulders, before turning in Marie's direction. He let her get ahead before he crossed the street and once more fell in behind.

He needed her to understand what was happening, that he was not a murderer, not the person who had tried to kill her brother. It wasn't out of sentiment that he needed her understanding, however; it was from necessity. If Paul was still alive, Joe needed to talk with him, and he needed her to take him to her brother, to help him get into Paul's hospital room. So he would try once more before finding another way.

After a hundred yards, he slipped up next to her on the sidewalk. He gently entwined his arm with her near arm and slowed her to a stop. A few people grumbled at the pair's sudden and disruptive halt in the sidewalk, but soon the flow of people accommodated their little island.

Before she said anything, Joe said, "I just need to talk with you."

He looked at her and saw nothing other than shock.

He spoke quickly, not giving her a chance to interrupt, "What happened to your brother—I had nothing to do with that. I did not know your brother. Let me talk with you for a few minutes. Here," he lifted an arm, "in the open. You choose a place where you are comfortable. I just need to talk with you for a minute."

She looked at him with her mouth open and her eyes tight and sharp.

"Just give me a few minutes. That's all," he said, hopeful. "Please."

A large truck droned past on the boulevard and in the quiet that followed it, he repeated, "Please."

She opened her mouth as though to speak. She looked around at the people passing them on the sidewalk and at the fronts of stores and then at the sky. Then she looked at him with hard eyes. "Leave me alone. Leave my brother alone. Haven't you done enough harm?"

It was a good question, if Joe had time to consider it. He held out his hand. "Wait. Please," he said.

She looked at him, her body half-turned as she decided whether to wait or to leave. Her face was white, her eyes tight.

Joe sighed and spoke softly, "Your brother has a manuscript—"

She cut him off, turning to face him, "Stop it." She looked at him quickly, a hard glance. "If it did not burn in his house, then it is in Tours."

"Tours?"

"At the monastery there. Paul lived there until three-four weeks ago. He left some of his things behind. He was returning for them this week. Then you. . . ."

"It wasn't me," he said.

"Shut up," she hissed. "I don't care. I don't care about you and I don't care about your book."

"Listen—"

She slapped him across the cheek.

"Leave me alone," she said, her body shaking. "Go to Tours. Tell them I sent you. I will even have a message delivered to them to expect you. Just never approach me again." And then to punctuate her words, she added, "Bastard," and walked away.

He rubbed his cheek and watched her disappear into the sidewalk crowd. An old man caned over to him, a smile on his weathered face. "*Femme*," he said, shaking his head as though passing on information he had learned the long and hard way. "*Ils ne vous laissent jamais les comprendre. C'est comme essayer de décrire la couleur rouge.*" He shrugged and added, "*Elle sera de retour. Après elle sent que vous avez assez souffert, elle sera de retour.*"

He caned off, his head lowered and shaking.

Joe only understood about half of what the man said, but he agreed. It wasn't, however, Marie's gender that he did not understand.

He felt the uncomfortable tethers of being controlled by someone else. Why would she send him to Tours to retrieve the manuscript if she thought he was responsible for the fire? He would go to Tours. He didn't understand if the rules of the game had changed or if he was in a different game altogether. But he would go to Tours the next morning.

He checked his watch—nearly half past two—and took the Metro across to the Right Bank and to the American Express office at 11 rue Scribe where he booked a train passage for the next day to Tours. When asked, Joe gave his name as Diamond Dick Quire. The young man, an American with slicked back hair and wearing Cortland eyeglasses, was efficient and humorless when Joe said that he'd lost his passport the night before in some "café in the Latin Quarter." With a frustrated breath, the young man issued the tickets and warned Joe to visit the embassy as soon as possible. Joe thanked him and told him that it was next on his list.

It was a lie, of course, and right then he had more pressing matters, find Quire and then find a place to stay the night. His hotel would be watched by one or both of the groups he needed to avoid. As afternoon slid into evening, he walked. He strolled past the Hotel-Dieu on Île de la Cite, but was suspicious of too many people loitering. He walked on. The small side streets were dark and empty of people. Joe preferred the night that way. Once, looking back over his shoulder, he saw someone looking at him from a doorway. He stepped into a recess and waited, but nobody came along. Most likely he had seen someone stepping out for a cigarette before dinner. The closer he came to the boulevard Saint-Michel, the louder the street became with taxis and crowds of people, a league of languages from several continents accumulating in concert. He crossed the boulevard and walked to rue de Buci, once again to spend an hour in the shadows of a building watching, this time across from the Gentilhomme.

Quire rounded the corner opposite him, walking along the street with his body hunched and hands tight in his overcoat and looking very much like a roughly chiseled chunk of Vermont granite. Joe stayed in the shadows and watched the street behind Quire, looking for anybody who might have followed him. He saw a handful of people milling along, but could not tell if anyone was seriously behind Quire.

He stepped into the light of a lamppost and motioned to Quire, who raised his head, nodded, and crossed the street. A large automobile, dark in color and dark in the street's half-light, pulled to the curb down the street. Joe watched but nobody left the vehicle and he could not see into the windows.

"Lots of people are looking for me. Possibly for you, too," Joe said when Quire walked up. "Let's find someplace else to talk."

Quire nodded. "Fine by me. There's always a door to walk into in Paris this time of night."

"First, let's find a way to get rid of whoever is in that car back there."

Quire looked over his shoulder. "You sure they're interested in us?"

"I'm not certain of a thing anymore. They just pulled over at the wrong time."

"You sure you don't want to find out?"

"I'm sure."

Quire pinched his lips tight together and nodded. "Okay."

Quire took Joe by the arm and led him toward the large, full boulevard Saint-Germain. "In one door and out another," he said.

It did not take long to leave behind whoever might have been following them. Crossing streets, recrossing them, changing directions, in and out of restaurants, front doors, back doors, side doors, the Metro, and finally a taxi ride across town to Montmartre and Zelli's Jazz Club.

"I know a guy there," Quire said as they crossed the rain-slick roads to the other side of town, "an American Negro in the band. He was at the Champagne with a group of Legionnaires. He can put us up for a night or two."

Joe agreed. A good drink was always welcome, even when caught in a tight spot, for it helped relax the mind. He felt restless, he had no other plan, so he sat back to enjoy the taxi ride for as long as it took. He watched the old buildings pass in the commencing rain and the people on the sidewalks walking quickly between doorways, some dancing on a sidewalk corner to the sounds of a small street band. There was the occasional emptiness of the city, the dark side streets and the empty trees like knife shadows on the street.

Zelli's Jazz Club was crowded, smoky, and noisy. The band's music slapped them as soon as they entered. Quire stopped and breathed in a full lung of air, coughing as he exhaled. He smiled and looked around and waved to someone across the room. People were jammed tight inside the club. Joe and Quire found room at the bar. They ordered beers for dinner and stood back to watch the jam of people dancing in one place and the Negro band at their instruments, sweating and smiling and yelling to the dancers and at each other.

"That's him," Quire said, leaning close to Joe's ear to be heard over the band's music and the noise of the crowd. "On the drums."

Joe nodded, watching the black man go on his drums, hard and carefree and stirring the dancers in front of him to a crescendo of movement. He smiled as he played, watching the dancers, and sometimes he would yell out to them, "Thaaat's riiight. Yeah, thaat's sooo goood." And he would laugh and smile again. Joe smiled at the man's enjoyment of his place, an infectious and unbridled enjoyment.

The music stopped, and Quire said, "Damn fine drummer."

"I agree," Joe said. "You said he was at the Champagne with the Legion?"

"I did. There were lots of Americans, black and white, in the Legion before we actually joined the war, you know. Lots of Americans to begin with. He was one of the few who lived through that morning. The Legionnaires suffered badly, you know."

"Everyone knows," Joe said.

Quire coughed a laugh. "Shit, they probably even know in Helena."

The music began again. Joe and Quire slipped into a silence. Joe watched the dancers, especially a beautiful woman with very short hair who was dancing right in front of the drummer. A tall and thin woman, young, gorgeous enough to know how gorgeous she was and that every man in the room was or had or would spend time watching her that night and thinking about what they would like to do with her. He envied the man dancing with her for what they would do later that night. He also wondered if that was how his life would turn out, watching from the sidelines as other people enjoyed the game. If he lived through the next twenty-four hours, he'd give it some serious thought.

The music stopped again. Again Quire leaned over to speak, "You fight with any of the Negro troops?"

"No," Joe said. "I think most of them were farther north from where I was."

Quire nodded. "Any problems with talking to a black man?"

Joe looked at Quire. He thought for a moment. "I haven't known many, but I knew a lot of Mexicans back in Colorado when I was growing up. People treated them like niggers, but my family taught me to treat a man as a man until he proves himself otherwise."

"That's good," Quire said. "Some Americans can't do that, hell most Americans can't. Over here, a black man is as good as a white man. Took me a little getting used to, I admit. I was raised a tad different."

"Now?"

"Now," he shrugged. "They bleed red just like me."

They drank their beers and another and another while the band played through its set. They did not talk because it was easier not to with the club's noise and people breaking between them trying to find a bartender to serve them. The band rested, each member wiping his head with a towel before stepping from the stage to join one group or another in the crowd.

"Quire-boy, man. Hahre you?" the black drummer said as he clapped Quire on the shoulder.

"Great," Quire said.

"Thaat's good."

"This is a friend of mine," Quire said, reaching out for Joe. "Joe Henry meet Jacques Ballard. Don't let the first name fool you, he may be from Paris, but as in Texas."

They shook hands, the first time Joe had shaken the hand of a black man. Joe was impressed by the size and power in the man's hands. He was not a large man, but his fingers were the size and strength of hickory sticks. He shook Joe's hand and smiled a bright and white smile that made Joe smile in return.

"Got a favor to ask you," Quire said.

"Anything, Quire-boy. You just ask."

Quire gave Ballard an abbreviated explanation. The man listened attentively, asking few questions and nodding, his eyes seldom leaving Quire's and then only to look at Joe. Joe could see Ballard's jaw muscles tighten as Quire talked of the Champagne. Ballard's eyes were seeing images from years earlier, men literally cut to pieces by German 77s, bodies lying across barbed wire and strewn throughout the no-man's land like stepping stones and sometimes used as such when the retreat began. That battle, long over, had left its mark in the lines on Ballard's face as certainly as though he had been hot-iron branded. Joe knew the distanced appearance of a man looking within himself, his soul and his own foul memories, at things he was unable to keep himself from seeing. It was a cauterized look that haunted him, because he also had those lost eyes that peered into the depths of an oblivion, and, rising from his past, he thought of a prayer gone wrong, "As it was then, is now, and ever shall be."

Ballard blinked and ran a hand across the stubble of his short hair. With that action his smile began to return. The sadness in his eyes remained, but only a person intimately related to that sadness could recognize it. "Sure," he said. "Flop in my place. There's a sofa and a chair. The bed's mine. Man, I ain't so nice that I'm giving up my bed." He laughed again.

Joe and Quire thanked him.

"I'll be home in the early hours. We'll talk when I wake up, not too damn early though. I can't tell you anything you don't already know about Champagne, but I want to hear what you have to say. I'd like to know who laid out my *camarades* like that."

The other musicians, all Negros, began to warm up their instruments, and Ballard excused himself. He drank a quick shot of Absinthe without the water chaser, shook his head, and yelled, "Thaat's riight, man. I'm coming."

He shook hands again with Joe and Quire—sealing a deal—and clapped Quire once more on the shoulder before returning to his drums. Picking up the sticks, he said to the crowd, "Damn, let's gooo." The band hit it hard and the floor was again crowded with dancers, crowded so tightly that people basically moved in place.

Joe looked for the beautiful woman and her lucky man but they were not on the floor. He saw them heading for the front door, the woman wearing a green hat and a wrap around her shoulders. The man had on his overcoat and held the door for her. The lucky bastard.

It was an hour past midnight before Joe and Quire, both at least an hour past drunk, left Zelli's. The cold night air with its pretentions of rain slapped Joe hard, but not hard enough to sober him. They walked erratically down the sidewalk to Ballard's apartment, which was not far away. There was little more than a bed, a sofa, and a chair in the single room, a drum set, a coal stove for heat, and a table with chairs. "The man lives Spartan," Joe said after Quire turned on the light, a single bulb hanging bare from the ceiling.

They flipped a coin. Joe won the sofa. He lay down and, surprised at how tired he was, began to drift toward sleep almost as soon as his head hit the sofa's arm. He dreamed of his father's ranch in the hills of Colorado where spring rains cleaned the arroyos and brought color to the fields of grasses and flowers. From them, the grasses and flowers, and also the juniper and sage and pine, the full aroma of spring would wake him to ride all day long in a lengthening sunlit day. He had that dream, a good dream. Later that night and through that night, he had bad dreams that did not wake him only because he was so used to bad dreams.

Even with his exhaustion and his depression and his dreams and his drunkenness, Joe did not sleep long. He woke soon after the sun, still drunk, to find Quire standing backlit and naked in front of an open window.

"I thought the full moon set with the rising sun," Joe said, sitting up on the sofa and stretching his neck, feeling a deep and dark pain in his eye sockets.

Quire turned around. "Damn, man, I couldn't sleep. Not with thinking about that battle. The war was bad enough on its own, but what happened to Ballard and your friend and others at that battle. It worked on me like a canker."

Joe nodded in confirmation. He spoke low and plaintively, "That day seems to have worked under a lot of people." He rubbed his eyes, tight with dried mucus, and his hair, matted. He began to pull on his pants. He had a trip ahead of him which he looked forward to and might find sleep on the train, the lolling movement rocking him like a baby in its buggy. Sleeping like a baby with few concerns was something he had not done in a long time.

Joe added, "And put some clothes on, for Christ's sake."

Quire laughed. "Jealous," he said and walked to a table where there was a water bowl to splash water on his face. "I remember," he said as he combed water through his hair, "when my mother accidentally broke a thermometer and the mercury in the bulb got to her ring. Nothing she could do to stop it from just eating that ring until nothing was left. That's what this reminds me of. Someone broke it open and it's begun to corrode whatever it touches."

"Doesn't bode well for you and me, does it?" Joe sat on the edge of the sofa, working some moisture into his mouth while watching a cockroach move in quick spurts, starts and stops, along the baseboard.

"Then why're you head-long going into this scrape, taking a train today to get yourself even deeper?" Quire asked. He had slipped on some pants but sat with no shirt on and tapped out a thin cigarette from a pack of Gitanes on the table, placed it in his mouth and lit it using a silver lighter. With the first drag he coughed hard and phlegmatic and crushed out the cigarette and said, "Don't know why I even try." He coughed again to clear his throat and spat into his handkerchief.

"Damn, man, can't you boys shut up?" Ballard raised his head from the sheets. There was another form under the sheets as well, but she kept herself hidden, not even unfolding the sheet to expose her face.

Ballard sat up with his back against the wall, the sheet down around his hips. Several scars were apparent on his chest and stomach, knife scars and shrapnel and bullet scars raised like hills and dikes against the dark surface of his skin. His muscles were corded and he was thin. "You say you going somewhere?" he asked Joe.

"Yes," Joe said. "I'm taking the train to Tours."

"Why's that, man?" He took a pack of Gitanes from the table next to him and shook one out. He lit the cigarette and inhaled with his eyes closed then exhaled like a junkie.

"Dillard lived in a monastery there until recently. He might have left some things behind. Maybe a copy of the manuscript."

"You need someone to go along with you?" Quire asked. He sat hunched over the table, looking like he had just ridden in on a rail.

"No," Joe answered.

"Good," Quire said and meant it. For every beer and absinthe that Joe had drunk the night before, Quire had downed two. Joe could see that he was a man of amazing capacities when it came to alcohol, but even Hercules met his match. He sat with his elbows on the table, his hands cupping his head.

"I should be fine. Nobody but you two and Marie Dillard know that I'm going to Tours."

Quire raised his head, his eyebrows cocked. "You're sure about her?"

"Not an inch."

Quire nodded and returned his head to his hands. He raised his head again and winked at Joe, a smile spreading across his face. "I need something," he said. "Either breakfast or a little of the hair of the dog."

"I got me a bottle here," Ballard said. "We should take us a nip to warm our bones. Then there's a bakery down around the corner, not one of the French bakeries with those little *petits fours* and flutes of bread, but a bakery where you can get a real breakfast. Bacon and eggs and bread, and beans, even if you don't want them."

"I'll begin with the bottle," Quire said, and Ballard tossed a pint bottle of amber liquid underhanded to him. Quire uncorked the bottle and took a good drink. "Shit-goddamn," he said. "That's good Scotch."

They shared the bottle. Joe also passed around the photographs and his notes and told them Huntington's story of Marcel. They speculated, each offering his own scenario. When they had finished their conjecturing, Joe again rolled everything into the inside pocket of his overcoat.

They dressed and left the apartment, the lump under Ballard's sheets never raising her head to look at them. The day was cold but the sun was warming the street. The bare linden trees along the street glistened and dripped on the sidewalk. They walked a short distance to the bakery, ordered their food, and took large white bowls of coffee with them to sit at a window table.

Quire took out his pack of Gitanes, and Ballard pulled the fixings to roll his own cigarette. Quire placed his cigarette unlit in the corner of his mouth and left it there and like that. After Ballard had finished rolling his and had lit the cigarette and took a deep drag, he sighed. Joe sat and looked out the window at people beginning their days at work.

"You two weren't there at the Champagne, were you?" Ballard asked and blew out a plume of smoke.

They shook their heads.

Ballard did not wait for Joe to ask about the battle. He began talking like a man telling his single, most abiding secret, low, solemn, in halting starts. "It was lethal," he said. "We thought we had it, though, from the very beginning. Five days of artillery pounding the Germans. The night before, all damn night long it went on. We were sure that whatever Germans had been over there were dead. We were told that there weren't more than a skeleton force in their trenches to begin with, and with the artillery, we figured our worst troubles would be avoiding the mud. Right after sunrise they blew the whistles and we went over the top. I was with the Foreign Legion at the time, damn fine group of men. We begin to trot across the clearing, not going too fast and certainly not a damn bit worried, and then the Germans opened up with their Bergmanns and their oh-eights and then from far away their Whizz Bangs. Shit, man." He shook his head slow and steady before continuing. "It all turned bad. A disaster. How they survived the artillery I don't know, but they did. I knew right then that they knew we were coming, that they had planned the day on top of whatever had been planned by our generals.

The *boches* called in artillery, which they weren't supposed to have, and every shell crater and twig of a dead tree and mound of dirt seemed to be sighted in. There wasn't no place to hide."

Ballard stopped talking for a moment, taking a long, deep breath and then another long drag on his cigarette. He looked at Joe, and Joe could see the pain of memory in the man's eyes, yellowish and blood-shot. There was a distance in the man's eyes that would always be there, a distance between any moment Ballard lived and the time before the war. It was a distance caused by having seen humanity at its worst.

He began again. "Whole sections of our line fell at once, some falling in rows and others on top of one another like cord wood. The machine gun fire was so thick, so constant that the dead, lying there on the field, were hit time and time again, rolling around like target shooting cans. Pieces of their bodies were shot off as they lay dead. Some of the men still charging lost limbs as they ran. I was covered in blood and mud from the shells landing around me. There weren't more than a dozen of us when we reached the wire. It was that way all along the line, and we had to turn around and run back through the same damn firing. There were two hundred men in that company of legionnaires who led the charge, and at roll call that night we had eight. Eight. Shit."

Joe was no longer hungry, but he ate for something to do. None of the men looked at each other as each relived his own terrible violence. Joe had not been at the Champagne, but he had witnessed the carnage at a lesser scale, had seen the bodies immolated and heard the sounds of a world lost to destruction.

After several minutes, Joe said, "That was a bad day."

Ballard said, "There ain't much else you can say about it, brother. It was as bad as they get. One thing, though," he said, pointing at Joe. "You find the man responsible for setting up *les boches* on that morning, and I want in on it. I want to see his eyes when I bleed the life from his body. You promise me that."

Joe nodded. They spent the remainder of their breakfast in silence. After, Joe thanked Ballard for the place to stay and told Quire he would be in contact as soon as he returned from Tours that evening. Joe left, taking the Metro across the city to the Gare Montparnasse.

Police stood in pairs throughout the station, talking between themselves or watching the women walk past. Joe kept his distance as he weaved through the crowd. He walked past a cart of trunks, mostly Vuittons, to the train, found his compartment. Within minutes, the train jerked to life and began its steady climb to speed.

An older couple shared the compartment with him. They also shared their bread, cheese, and wine with Joe. He spoke with the couple in French, as much as he could, before they sank into a private conversation. He was left to himself. They were interrupted once when the porter arrived asking for tickets. Each gave the porter a ticket and then settled back into their seats. Joe sat next to the window and looked out.

He watched as the train passed through an industrial part of Paris and then finally into the country, farms and open landscape, inviting even in its winter gray. The transition was not gradual. Joe could have stood on the boundary had the train stopped and allowed him to. There was a factory with steam and smoke rising from tall chimney pipes and then a set of railroad tracks and then a field and then farms. Joe had seldom seen things as delineated and wished that other things in the world were also so easily distinguished.

People worked their land or rode on carts loaded with a morning's cutting. Later, as the train neared the Loire Valley, Joe wondered at how much more abundant was the landscape there than in Paris. It was December and deep within winter in both places, but Paris held a gray cast within its darkened cityscape while the expanding valley along the Loire River showed its fertile heart just under the barren ground. The soil was dark with humus and rain and lay ready for the next spring's renewal. There was a promise in the land.

The train thrummed along. A recent rain left the landscape glistening and beautiful. Watching France pass outside his window, Joe realized that something had changed in him as well. There was reason for his journey, a quest. He cared about discovering a truth, the reasons for what had happened on a field in France in 1916. Discovering that would lead him to other truths as well. Even though he was not there, it still mattered to him. Nothing had really mattered to him since sometime during the war. Since then he had lived as though anesthetized.

There, with the hum of iron wheel on iron rail, he felt like he might relax for a moment. He was becoming a participant again.

At Tours, he took a cab from the train station to the monastery on the other side of the great walled city, traveling the old roads of cobbled brick and stone that pilgrims hadwalked over for centuries. Even in the middle of the day in the third decade of the twentieth century, the city looked Medieval and old with its small, winding roads, high walls, and stone fortress-like buildings, some still with defensive battlements atop the walls. The walls of the monastery stood two stories high, covered in ivy with mother vines thick as Joe's thigh. Moss clung in the shadows. Small parts of the wall had crumbled, leaving piles of tailings. The large double doors at the front, thick wood and iron bars like a castle's portcullis and with gate-houses to each side like those of a barbican, with square Judas holes at eye level, prevented easy entrance. The wood was old and age-weathered but solid and the iron bars guarding the Judas holes had colored a patina almost black over the years. Above the doors, engraved in the stone and almost faded to nothing, was the abbey's name, Abbey de St. Martin de Tours.

Joe pulled on the leathered handle of a chain. A series of bells rang just inside the door. He could not hear movement from behind the heavy doors but felt that he was being watched. His hair stood on end and he wanted desperately to drop and hug the ground, but stood and waited, looking around and seeing arrow slits through which a person might spy. He looked up at the overhang of the barbican and saw the murder holes above him, and he thought that every century has its own implements of death and the turn from one century to another did not just bring advances in medicine and arts but also advances in the implements of war. And as men at war always had, like dogs they howled.

The square window-door opened, although Joe could not see into the shadows behind. A man spoke softly in French through the barred opening, asking who he was. When Joe answered in English, he heard a shuffling, followed by the voice of another man, this time in English. He asked Joe what he wanted at the Abbey. Like the first man, he remained within the shadows.

"I have come to see Paul Dillard's room," Joe said, adding, "His sister wired you about my coming."

There was no answer, but Joe could hear the muted discussion between two men.

"Mademoiselle Dillard has asked me to retrieve his materials from the abbey."

"Why does she wish to have them?"

He stepped closer to the opening. "Her brother was badly injured in a fire at his home in Paris. He is in the hospital." Joe improvised. "She wants him to have his things with him. He has nothing after the fire, and she hopes these things may help him."

More muttering, one voice raised and then silenced. The small square door was pushed but not entirely closed. Joe could hear the voices of several people in consult, disagreeing but not in heated exchange.

Finally, the small door shut, followed by opening of the large wooden doors. They were pulled back at the center only far enough for Joe to enter, swinging in like irrigation gates and closing immediately behind him as though to allow as minimal an amount of the outside into the sanctuary's courtyard. He entered but was not allowed to walk into the courtyard as three men in cassocks stood with him, not threateningly but still fencing him against the door.

"We have strict rules about attire in the abbey," one of the men said. Like the others, he kept himself hidden within the folds of a hooded cassock. "Please remove your overcoat and hat. Are the soles of your shoes hard?"

Joe nodded, "Yes. Leather."

"Your shoes as well."

Joe did not like the idea of removing his overcoat, his money and passports and revolver all inside its pockets, but if he could not trust a monk who could he trust? He removed his shoes and hat and gave them with his coat to the man at the door. One of the monks gave Joe a brown cassock and soft, moccasin-like shoes to wear while in the abbey. The wool of the cassock rubbed and itched on Joe's neck and wrists. Another reason to not enter the monastic life.

He passed through a corner of the castle's bailey and was led through the old hallways of the abbey, past frescoes and an age-grayed statue of St. Martin offering his robe to the peasant. They passed a reliquary that probably held at least one bone from an arm or a leg of the warrior who had become a saint through his sacrifice and devotion, maybe even a patch from the robe.

They led Joe through a series of dark and damp hallways, the stone walls stained with age and niter. They stopped in front of an oak door, pushed it open, and motioned for Joe to enter.

"His room. His belongings, those that he left, are stacked on the table."

The room, barely ten feet square, was Spartan. A door on one side and a small window near the ceiling opposite. A wooden table and hard chair, also wood, stood against one wall, a bed, little more than a wood frame with sacking on top, in a corner against the other. Plated candles, unlit and inside glass bowls, were on the writing table and the table next to the bed. A single crucifix hung above the head of the bed. Words and dates and names had been carved into the stone walls, but they were all mostly faded even to the touch.

While one of the brothers watched him, Joe went to the table and sorted through the papers and belongings that Dillard had left. It wasn't much, barely enough to have fit into a medium-sized valise. The monk stood nearby, watching but not interfering. Joe found envelopes with letters—some from Gresham, others from Marie and Rose Shaunessy, one from Huntington. On hands and knees, he looked underneath the bed. In a small box was the manuscript.

Joe felt like a kid with buried treasure, even more—something almost religious—as he cradled in his hands the box made of a heavy paperboard which had been taped shut for shipping. The tape had been cut at the seams and on top were Gresham's return address and an address for Dillard that was not the Abbey's.

Joe pointed to the address, a postal box in Tours, and was told that the Abbey received no mail except that sent to either the abbot or the prior.

Joe sat on the bed with the box on his lap, the lid open to reveal its contents—a couple hundred carboned pages of typed paper. That was all, but that was a lot. He looked down on the paper like the knight-errant gazing upon his grail.

"I'll take these to his sister," Joe said, his mouth suddenly dry. He gathered the box in one hand and everything else in a hemp bag provided by the monk—the letters, a single pen and capped ink well, and a couple of old, leather-bound books by Balzac and Zola.

The monk nodded.

Joe was escorted from the abbey by the same three robed monks, one behind and one on either side. They kept their heads in the shadows of their hoods and walked silently through the same halls. From somewhere else in the abbey, Joe could hear the sounds of chanting, maybe a choir practicing.

At the gate, there was no ceremony when he prepared to leave, no farewells. He thanked them for their help, returned the robe, and they nodded and returned his clothes and closed the heavy doors. He heard the latch click tight. He felt returned to the modern world.

He took the same taxi back to the train station, passing back through the ancient walled city, feeling even more anxious than he had felt on the drive to the abbey. He placed the bag of things on the seat next to him and folded his coat over that, but he held the box on his lap as though to relinquish any control of it would cause its disappearance. He wanted to be on the train where he could begin to read.

The train, of course, was late, for trains in France regularly ran late. He had to wait an hour at the train station in Tours and found a wooden bench, worn smooth and dark from the decades of people sitting on it. He sat like a junkie on his way back down, fidgeting and uncomfortable. And before he could make himself too conspicuous, he went into the bar for a drink, the box, now hidden inside the bag under his arm. He drank two Anis del Toro, followed by a beer, and finally felt relaxed enough to sit and wait. He returned to the well-worn bench.

Looking the length of the wood-planked platform, he searched for anyone who might be watching him, either police or Marcel's men who had followed him. He saw none, just as he had seen none while in the depot's small bar. He hoped that maybe he had done something right and at the right time. But he did not have a good feeling. Marie Dillard had as much as invited him to come to Tours, and while he could not see anyone watching him, that did not mean that he was not being watched.

On the bench next to him was a wrinkled copy of the previous day's *Herald-Tribune*. There was nothing of interest other than an article in which the Imperial Wizard of the Ku Klux Klan said they would never unmask—more of the world's violent cowards hiding their true selves. When the train arrived, he boarded with the other passengers and found his compartment, which remained empty of other passengers as the train lurched from the station. A pair of small brown bags rested on the floor against the opposite bench. Joe leaned over to read the names on the tags and smiled.

He did what he needed to do as quickly as possible, opening the cheap locks on one of the bags and dropping the manuscript inside, then placing Dillard's old books inside the box. With pocket knife, he cut the window covering's cord and wrapped it tight around the box, double knotting it.

The train began its heavy tug toward speed and moved through the fogged miasma of its own steam held within the station's wood canopy. He could see birds rise from trees nearby and some birds remain, huddled on the glazed branches of the empty elm trees.

"This is good," he said to himself, as the train pulled from the station. That he could spread out and not be bothered by anyone else was a fortune he had not counted on, at least until the owners of the brown bags returned.

The compartment door opened. In walked Dapper, followed closely by the Turk. Dapper smiled at Joe, a smile with a thousand tiny teeth. He lit a small cigarette with the flick of a silver lighter and inhaled, put back his head and exhaled a long and full plume of smoke toward the ceiling of the moving train. The smoke rose straight up to curl and dissolve in the windless room. He smiled again, a man with oleaginous charm.

Joe sat next to the window with the manuscript box on his lap. His revolver was inside one of the coat pockets which was on the bench beside him. He picked up the coat and covered the box with it. Dapper sat in its place, the smell of fresh garlic heavy with the small man.

"Monsieur, what a pleasure, although not unexpected," Dapper said in patterned English, his voice as affected as his smile. "You do not mind if we join you, do you?"

Joe shrugged, opening his hands as if to say "of course."

Dapper reached a hand across Joe and patted his chest pocket and reached inside the coat to see if Joe had any weapons, then he patted the overcoat, smiled and took Joe's Smith & Wesson from its pocket. He weighed the small revolver in the palm of his hand and smiled at Joe. *"Merci,"* he said and stretched out to place the gun in his own coat pocket.

Joe nodded, *"De rien."*

Dapper moved to the facing bench, leaning forward to be heard over the thrum of the train. Joe could smell a whiff of cigarette breath as Dapper spoke to him, nodding toward Joe's lap, "Right now, I would like to see those papers."

Dapper looked at Joe. He was no longer smiling. The thinness of his lips were dry and cracked. Joe could see that Dapper was younger than he had first thought, not much older than him, maybe thirty.

"Do I meet your boss now?" Joe asked.

Dapper shook his head. "No. You will not have that pleasure."

"My pleasure," Joe said, thinking that his only pleasure would come with Marcel's death.

"We can do this without you dying or with you dying," Dapper said and shrugged. "The decision is entirely your own. However, I have lost my patience, so I will ask you only one more time before I am forced to exert greater measures."

Joe sighed. Dapper was sitting across from him, the Turk standing with folded arms in front of the door. Joe shook his head and handed the bag of papers and letters to Dapper, keeping the boxed manuscript on his lap. He looked outside the window at the landscape becoming cloudy in the evening light. Pastoral farms and farmhouses with red tile roofs, silos, barns passed on the side of another set of railroad tracks occasionally filled with another train headed in the opposite direction. The faces of those train's occupants passed in blurs, black and white petals on broken boughs, and he looked upon the same countryside that he had seen just hours earlier, although now different.

"Please," Dapper said, his mouth tightening into the small and thin line of his lips. "Let's be gentlemen about this. No childish games." He tossed the bag onto the seat next to Joe where the letters spilled out like a pile of autumn leaves.

Joe said nothing.

"Give it to me." Dapper spat. His face drew hard.

Joe shrugged. He lifted the manuscript box, tight within its corded wrap, over to Dapper, who took it with a smile.

Dapper rested the box on his lap.

"And now I have the manuscript," Dapper said, his hands flat on top of the box.

"A copy of it," Joe said.

Dapper uttered, "Ahh," as he smiled and nodded, not a pleasant smile. "A copy. And you have another copy, I suppose?"

"I do," Joe said.

"Why would you want this one?"

"Buying power. I thought I might double my money by selling them both to you. Economics, pure and simple. Your boss should understand that."

Dapper laughed, a laugh even less pleasant than his smile. "You know what I think," he said.

"What?"

"I think you're lying. There is no other copy."

Joe shrugged. "And I once believed in Santa Claus. We're both wrong."

Dapper stayed quiet for a moment.

"Look," Joe said, his back straight and his hands on his knees and facing Dapper. "Either Marcel thinks that I have another copy of the manuscript, maybe even the original, in which case I live, or you think I don't, in which case I die. But if you kill me and guessed wrong, think of who might end up with it. Think of how angry your boss will be when the other copy lands on the prefecture's desk. Of course, I could be just running a bluff. The call is yours to make, and you'll have to make it soon. We'll be in Paris in a couple of hours. I won't be leaving this train with you. Place a gun to my side, I don't care. You won't have me with you."

Before Dapper could respond, there was a knock. The Turk looked at Dapper before moving to the side and opening the compartment door. An old man in a poorly fitting and age-faded blue uniform nodded as he stepped into the doorway and said in a sad, almost apologetic tone, *"Pardon, billets s'il vous plaît."*

"Excus-ah me. Pardon-ah." A large, overdressed woman with as poor a French accent as Joe had ever heard pushed her way past the conductor and the Turk, who looked to Dapper for direction.

Turning to speak past the conductor and out the door, the woman said, "Yes, here they are, Harold. I told you that you left them here."

"Hello, Mrs. McKee," Joe said, standing and lifting his coat from the seat.

The Turk tensed but did nothing.

The large woman turned and for a moment did not seem to recognize Joe. Then she smiled and said, "Why it's Mr. Gresham from the ship," and out the door, "It's Mr. Gresham from the ship, you know that friend of the Blaines, Harold." Turning back to Joe, "How are you, Mr. Gresham?"

"Well, thank you," Joe said.

"Did you ever find the Blaines before disembarkation? I hope you remembered us to them."

Joe smiled. "I did and I did."

She smiled, then added, "We had such a time getting off the ship. Fights and missing luggage and some sort of intrigue. Ghastly."

"Madam," said the conductor.

"Yes?" she said.

"Is this your compartment?" he spoke in frustrated English, and an English heavily accented, pronouncing each syllable with separate emphasis.

"Our bags," she said, pointing to the brown bags on the compartment floor. "My husband left them by mistake. Will you bring them along, boy?"

The conductor straightened, and his face reddened deep purple. He began to speak, but Joe cut him off. "Allow me," he said.

Then, turning to Dapper, he added with a wink, "And then there was one."

Looking down at Dapper, he touched his first two fingers to his brow in mock salute and grinned. "If you will excuse me, gentlemen," he said, "I will vacate this compartment and leave you alone for the trip."

Dapper's face went rigid. The lines on his forehead stood out like cracks in marble, eyes like polished stones. He seemed to snarl, his bared teeth all discolored and sharp. When he spoke, however, his words slid out without any tightness.

"Oh, Monsieur," he said, raising a hand as though to hold Joe for a moment longer. "Be sure to read today's newspaper, any newspaper. There will be something of interest for you."

Joe turned and took his ticket from the pocket of his coat, handed it to the conductor. With the two small bags in hand, he stepped past him into the corridor. Joe winked at the Turk—there would be no easy killing that night. The air in the corridor tasted of sweet and fresh. With Mrs. McKee leading, he carried the bags. Even though they asked him to join them in their compartment for the remainder of the trip to Paris, Joe excused himself. He would visit them later, once he had finished with his business, and he had involved enough people who had later died. He wanted no more blood in his wake. He left for the anonymity and security of a crowded coach car.

In the club car he sat at the first open seat nearly halfway down the right side. With the moment's adrenaline drained, he deflated like a worn tire, head heavy and body depleted. His fingers moved involuntarily from the adrenaline of having lived longer than he would have guessed, but his insides remained hollow and raw. All he could do was sit, looking out the window and barely noticing what the train passed. He sat facing the direction from which he had walked so that he could see if Dapper or the Turk came for him. Twice he saw the Turk's face through the window of the connecting door.

Slowly, his mind began to clear. Whatever was inside that manuscript was too important to Marcel to allow for any possibility of mistake. That was Joe's only weapon, Marcel thinking he still had a copy. At least, maybe, keeping alive the spark of a question. Without that possibility, he knew that he would soon be dead. He might be anyway. He could not trust that his luck would continue. Stretched too thin, he knew, even a run of good luck will snap from its own accumulated weight.

He wondered whether Dapper's cryptic comment about the newspaper would provide that added weight. Whatever it would be, it would not be welcome news. Marcel had been a step ahead of him for a couple of days. It was probably Marcel who had sent the police to his hotel while he was at the Gentilhomme—a message to Joe of how precarious his life had become. Marcel had manipulated Joe into traveling to Tours, using Marie Dillard as a tool. Marcel was calling the shots and turning up the heat. And while Marcel knew his face, Joe did not know Marcel's. Not knowing the face of his enemy made him feel particularly vulnerable.

The weather outside had begun to turn as storms over the Loire Valley dropped rain. Houses and fallow fields and wagons on roads glistened. The rain and the evening cast the approach into Paris in a veiled gray light, a canted shadow on the day. His life had been left in shadows for a long while, sometimes the shadow was long and dark and sometimes light as gossamer. But always there was a shadow.

His trip had been a construction. He saw how it fit together. Twenty-twenty hindsight. If asked, the monks could easily recognize him as the man who went through Paul Dillard's room. Couple that with the suspicion that Joe had once tried to kill Dillard, and right side of that formula read "GUILTY."

Marcel had wanted Paul Dillard's room checked for the manuscript, but he could not do it himself or even send his men. He and Marie—she probably believing that Joe had torched her brother's house with him in it—had manipulated Joe into doing the job for him. If he ever came to trial, now there were dozens more—the monks, the taxi driver, everyone at the station—who could link Joe to Dillard, and through Dillard all the way back to Gresham's murder. He might have just provided a court with motive, depending on what lie was being produced as to his reasons for killing Gresham. He had played the sap so well.

"You idiot," Joe whispered. "Smart as a fucking two-by-four."

He sat in silence, his legs apart and feet flat, his coat, lighter than before, across his lap, his hands empty on his coat. The train hummed and scraped. He felt the train's gentle rocking. Through his feet he felt the staccatoed vibration. He watched the door and watched France pass outside the train and listened to the rain drum on the wooden roof of the train car. At one time, train rides would have put him fast asleep, the deep hum of the engine and iron wheels and the gentle rocking motion of the cars. That ride, however, produced nothing like sleep, despite his exhaustion. He felt once more like he might never sleep well again. It was a feeling he remembered following his return from the war. Everything he had been brought up to believe, the sanctity of life and the importance of honor and the rightness of God and country, had ended up as hollow vessels.

They passed one small village after another as the final bit of daylight faded into dusk. Clouds, pink and black, rested on the bruised ceiling of the sky. Empty fields stretched far away from the railroad line. When the river showed, Joe could see an evening mist rising before it became too dark to see the river or the fields.

As evening brought along its beginning darkness, he saw the villages pass as embers in the distance—larger villages reflecting their light from the night clouds as though casting spectral shadows of their own. With the darkness, Joe could imagine the countryside that they passed. The moon and any stars were hidden. When he leaned his head against the cold window to look above him, he saw a low sky heavy with dark clouds. He pulled his pocket watch out to check the time but replaced it without opening it, deciding it did not really matter.

Soon the sharp outline of Paris rose black against the night. Lines and broken shards of flat-topped roofs and blind windows like patterned quilts.

The train rolled toward a stop into the huge wooden station. People began to gather their belongings, valises and bags and children and bottles of wine. Joe stood. When the train lurched to its stop, he donned his overcoat to follow the other passengers from the train onto the narrow platform. Another train, pointing outbound, steam rising from around the locomotive, waited across the platform, so people mingled as some prepared to leave while others arrived. Joe kept his head up, watching for Marcel's men. He crossed the platform and boarded the other train. He sat in the first unoccupied compartment to watch out the window. Dapper exited, but not the Turk. He was probably walking the length of the train to make sure Joe had gotten off.

A pair of uniformed police stood talking at the end of the platform, not paying much attention to people walking past. Still, that was not good. Joe was a wanted man—the American in Paris wanted for arson and attempted murder, maybe even the murder of Dillard's lover. All Dapper had to do was lay the line, and the station would be shut tight. That Dapper had not walked over to talk with them, however, was good news, for that meant that Dapper was still concerned about Joe's having another copy of the manuscript.

He looked again at the gendarmes guarding his exit and he looked for some way to camouflage himself, blend in with the other passengers walking like insects from here to there.

A small brown valise was in the overhead rack above him, perhaps someone's clothes for a short vacation to the Swiss mountains. Joe pulled up the collar to his overcoat and picked up the valise, now an actor's prop. He left the compartment to walk down the train's hallway. People were busily and noisily readying for the train's departure, businessmen and lovers and old couples and families. He heard a dozen languages from English and French to exotic languages of the Orient. He left the train in the guise of a tired tourist returning from the country, from a liaison maybe or maybe a businessman having returned to life in the city.

He walked in a hunch as though weary-worn. From a distance and with luck, he might appear that way for just long enough to leave Marcel's men behind him. The police seemed to have little

interest in the movements around them, so Joe walked from the platform and into the crowd of Parisians.

Outside of the train station, standing in the rain and the glow of
a streetlamp, he looked around, surprised, if nothing else, that he had
once again dodged a bullet.

He carried the borrowed valise as he walked through the diminishing crowd until there were few people on the street with him,
walking toward the Seine only because Paris leans toward the river.
He walked in long strides, collar up and shoulders hunched, one
hand deep in his pocket and the other with the valise. It provided a
good prop. People who saw him carrying the valise, noticed it. In
that, he hoped that they would form an assumption.

The rain turned to snow. Heavy, wet flakes fell around him. He
walked down the dark street, bleak and silent but for distant and
muffled sounds. Joe could hear the river ahead of them, the churn of
a tug pulling barges, taxis slushing past on the street, the creak of a
shudder closing.

Two gendarme rounded a corner ahead of him and stopped
under a lamp to light their cigarettes. The two policemen, arms
moving and fingers pointing, appeared to debate which way to walk,
maybe what café in which to wait out the snow. They walked toward
Joe. For lack of choices, he walked toward them, passing them with
his face tilted and shoulders hunched as they argued. He was glad
that he kept the valise, for it allowed a certain anonymity. The police
were not looking for a weary traveler.

He stepped into the nearest café, a small and rectangular sign in
gold and maroon against the building's brick, weathered both by rain
and time. The café, dark and small, was quiet and smelled of potatoes,
onions and wine. The door closed behind him with a sigh. Then the
sounds of the café eclipsed those of the street, the din of silverware
and the hum of conversation. He sat and checked his watch, then
ordered fried potatoes when the waiter stepped over.

While he waited for his meal, he opened the valise. It was filled
with papers, some originals and some carbon copies. "Damn," he
muttered and laughed a little at the irony. He had stolen someone
else's manuscript.

"A glass of wine, Monsieur?" asked the waiter when he brought the potatoes, steaming with onions in the oil.

"*Oui,*" Joe said. "Red. And the *Herald-Tribune.*"

The waiter nodded, left, and returned with a glass of red, a table wine, not good but not bad. By the end of the second glass, the table wine tasted much better.

Soon the waiter brought a copy of the newspaper. Someone had already read it and left a coffee stain on the front page. The stain, a hollow circle from the bottom of a coffee cup, was next to an article on the murderer of Wynton Gresham, one Joseph Henry. The article detailed the murders of Gresham and Huntington and Rose Shaunessy. It especially detailed the attempted murder of Paul Dillard. It also mentioned an unnamed accomplice, and that both were then in Paris. He figured Quire was the unnamed accomplice. There were, however, no photos of Joe.

The time to begin taking action was soon. Force Marcel's hand. A winter offensive. The worst kind.

Before he considered the future, however, he tried fitting pieces into his puzzle.

He thought back to the beginning, the night that was supposed to meet Gresham for a drink and some talk about a manuscript that Gresham had written. He traced a step further into the past, why Gresham had not met him—Gresham had been murdered at his house by the two Frenchmen who had then died on the rain-slick road outside Greenwich, Connecticut. Another step: How they had so easily gained entrance to Gresham's house? Not as Greeks bearing gifts but as Frenchmen bearing gifts but still someone to be wary of. And like those Greeks of Homer's tale, the Frenchmen had concealed themselves, even allowed Gresham to drink, before killing him. The gift that they had used for entry was not a giant horse, but a book—Joyce's *Ulysses*—which every literary person wanted to read since its publication in February. Joe had read an installment in a well-worn copy of *The Little Review* a year or so earlier but thought that the author must have been insane. Others, however, looked forward to its publication as a book as though it were a holy writ.

Paul Dillard had taken no vows and would have been free to wander the city when not engaged in his work at the abbey. He could easily have heard about *Ulysses* from someone in Tours, a tourist or at a bookstore or from a traveling writer or an American expatriate while sitting in a café enjoying a morning coffee. He might not have been able to buy a copy or even order a copy from a bookstore in Tours, so he would have written and asked Marie to buy one in Paris at the American bookstore, maybe also arranging for her to send one to Gresham in America. Joe remembered the wrapping and name from Gresham's home. Somehow, Marcel had interrupted that communication and had used the book to get to Gresham. Somehow it connected. If Joe was lucky, someone at the bookstore might remember the sale.

Joe paid his bill and asked the waiter for directions to Shakespeare and Company, then was back on the street walking toward rue de l'Odeon.

A perpendicular signboard with an egg-shaped head of Shakespeare marked the entrance to the bookstore tucked between a shoemaker's shop and that of a maker of nose sprays. Paneled top-to-bottom windows, bright and lit from yellow electric lights inside the store, opened on either side of the front door. On the wooden facades between the windows and the door were written "Lending Library" and the misspelled "Bookhop."

A thin, almost bird-like woman wearing a man's black velvet smoking jacket greeted him as he entered. "May I help you?" she asked, voice both thin and strong at the same time as well as obviously American.

From behind her, a man yelled out, his voice booming and echoing in the bookstore, "By God, Mademoiselle Shakespeare, you help more people than an Italian whore. Or should we call you Mademoiselle Company?" The man, sitting behind a desk and sprawled like a lazy cat on the edge of his chair, laughed out loud at his own joke. His tawny eyes and hair both jumped in the canted and amber light of the store.

"Don't mind him," the woman said, turning to Joe. "He likes to hear himself talk. Browse if you want. I'll be in the back if you need any help." She carried an armload of books with her as she turned toward the store's rear.

"Ain't that a place for to give some help, I reckon," the man said as she walked past him. Joe saw the man wink at the woman. He wore his shirt collar open, even in the store's cold, and one side of it fell outside the lapel of his own smoking jacket. Around his neck, in a careless knot of silken motion, curled a purple cravat. A wide-brimmed Spanish flop hat waited on the table for the man to swoop up in a single devil-may-care motion.

Joe stood like a new arrival in the city, coat buttoned and valise in hand, come to the first place on his list of must-sees. He nodded toward the tawny man and smiled innocently.

He nodded back and read by the light of a table lamp. He looked up from the cloth-bound book in his hands, then toward the rear of the store, then at Joe again, and finally back to his book without saying anything more. He read half aloud but to nobody other than himself, or so it appeared to Joe, for he could barely make out the man's muttered words, "Homing, upstream, silently moving, a silent ship." He slammed shut the book and said aloud, "That's too damn good, if you'd ask me. . . . But you ain't, so's I'll return to me book."

Joe looked at a display of books on a table, a few had been read but most looked new enough as to be uncut. Lining the walls were shelves heaped heavy with books. Those walls not supporting shelves were painted as bright as spring in greens and blues and yellows. Running along the front of one of those walls were racks of small magazines, American magazines with names like *Poetry* and *Exile* and *The Little Review*. Some he was familiar with, some he was not. Above the magazines and on any open space along the walls hung an abundant population of photographs. Black and white woolen rugs covered the hardwood floor. Antique chairs and tables waited in any space not holding books or magazines or racks or shelving or the desk and chair at which the tawny man sat and mumbled to himself.

Joe walked to the back of the store where he found the woman kneeling in front of a shelf of books in a small storage room separated from the front room by a doorway. The door was held open by a red paving brick.

Joe said, "Excuse me, but I am looking for the owner."

"I am she," said the woman. She stopped what she was doing and looked up at Joe. She had piercing eyes, high cheek bones, and a straight, thin mouth, the look of someone intelligent enough to be an intellectual or a professor but smart enough not to be either. "How may I help you?" she asked as she stood. She was taller than he had originally thought, nearly as tall as him, but thin and angular.

"I'm inquiring about a book that was bought here a month or two ago."

"Oh my," the woman said. She touched a finger to her lips. "We sell a good number of books. I don't think that I can remember every sale."

Joe said, "This was a copy of *Ulysses* that was purchased for an American named Wynton Gresham."

"A copy of Joyce?" boomed the tawny man from the front of the store, and even his voice seemed tawny. "Good goddamn show."

The store's owner waved toward the front like a mother waving off her son.

"I do remember that sale," she said, pointing a finger toward Joe. "The customer was very anxious to have the copy and said that he was travelling to America and would deliver it himself. Why do you ask?"

"It's complicated," Joe said. "Was the man who bought it a Frenchman, a dapper fellow about this tall?" He held out his hand to illustrate.

"Maybe," she answered, "but he was not French. He spoke French very well, but this man was not French. English I would guess." She thought for a moment. "Dutch maybe," she mused.

Not Dapper, then.

He placed the valise on the floor. From inside the pocket of his overcoat, Joe pulled the rolled photograph of Gresham and his fellow soldiers in the trench. He flattened it in an empty square on top of a desk cluttered high and full with books, notepads, and other photographs. After pinning the edges of the photograph with the books, he pointed to one of the faces.

"Is this the man?" he asked, his finger impaling the body of one of the two Marcel brothers.

"No," said the woman, taking a pair of reading glasses from her pocket and holding them still folded to her eyes. "That is he," she said, pointing to another man, one in an English uniform. She put her glasses on and looked down her nose at the photograph once again. "Yes, that one." She replaced the glasses in a pocket.

"Are you certain?"

"Absolutely," she said. "And see," she paused to look again at the photograph of five men eating a meal inside the confines of their trench. "And see—English, not French."

"I see," said Joe. And he did. He saw what he had missed the other times he had looked at the photograph. Missing pieces were falling in place.

"Don't judge a manuscript by its cover," he said.

"Pardon?" the woman asked.

"Nothing," Joe said. He paused, then added, "I have a thank you note for him, but lost the address."

The woman frowned, skeptical.

Joe said, "They were in the war together, see, and Wynton had a special message he wanted relayed."

"Oh, yes, I understand," she said, "but he did not give me his address. He picked up the book himself."

Joe kept his smile, although it hid gritted teeth. *Two steps forward,* he thought, *one step backward.* "Thank you, anyway," he said.

As he turned to leave, she said, "But wait."

He turned back. Her mouth was in a slight smile and her finger was pointed to the ceiling. "When he came in to order it, he left his card with telephone number and address. I may have placed it in my book. I send out notices about important readings, so I may have kept it."

When he nodded and thanked her, she walked past Joe and toward the front of the store. Joe took a moment to look closely at the photograph before returning it rolled to his pocket and followed the woman.

He whispered, "I know your face now."

At a desk near the front, the woman pulled a notebook from the center drawer, a blue notebook like students would use at a university. She pulled open the notebook using a silken sash that marked the end of a list of names.

"Marcel," Joe said.

She held out the notebook with her index finger pointing to the address. Below the name, "Rene Marcel" was written in the column next to the title of the book Marcel had purchased for Gresham. "*Ulysses*," she said.

"But no address," she added. "I am sorry."

"Thar she is," said the tawny-eyed man from his perch at the desk behind Joe. "A good man, helping out ol' Joyce. He a friend of yours, this man who buys Joyce?"

"Of my brother's from the war," Joe lied.

"From the war?" asked the man.

"Yes," Joe answered.

"The theater of war," the man said stroking the point of his short goatee beard. "I would not have thought that a theater could cause such harm. I could not have thought how death has undone so many."

The tawny man turned away and put his head in his hands, elbows on the desk in front of him. He sighed, as if a weight were bearing heavily down on him.

Joe did not answer. Though he was not certain what the man had said, he knew absolutely what the man had meant.

He looked again at the notebook, its lack of address. He looked outside through the windows. People walked by with their heads lowered and shoulders hunched. The wind, which had been soft all day, began to strengthen, forcing walkers to bend against it. Inside the bookstore, however, Joe was warm.

The woman closed her notebook. The tawny man slid back in his seat behind the gate-legged table. He once again began his mumbled reading while Joe thanked the woman, picked up his stolen valise, and walked toward the front door. A gust of wind sent a whistle through the seam between the door's opposing sides. The tawny man whistled back and returned to his book. Joe stood, looking out the window and wondering what his next move should be.

He still needed the address, and he knew of only one person who might be able to provide it—Marie Dillard.

IX

J OE WALKED WITH THE WIND TOWARD THE CLOSEST METRO STATION, thinking momentarily of the city of death that lay beneath him in the catacombs, the thousands of bodies reduced to bone. And he thought of the generation of dead that had been ground into the mud of France. And he wondered if the world had learned any lasting lessons from all this death. And he knew that was not so, for humanity would always feel the need to purge its own sins in the blood of another generation. And so he walked on, his breath a disappearing plume in the night. He saw others carrying their valises and suitcases, always more American expatriates looking to leave the wasteland of Prohibition America, refugees from the Volstead Act. He assumed, with his own valise in hand, that he looked like one of those American tourists.

What had at first been a helpful tool, the valise, had become problematic. It had assisted his need for anonymity while in and near the train station, but on the streets of Montparnasse, it drew unwanted attention to him from every Frenchman he passed. It called out that he was an American and to someone paying close attention it might cause alarm, not an American but *the* American, the one who has killed so many.

He thought of just dropping it in a closed doorway and forget-ting it, let someone else have it. But a plan was working somewhere

193

in his mind, deep and beyond his ability to fully articulate. He thought, this valise might come in handy. Not now, but soon.

He stopped in at the first brasserie that he passed, Le Bar Dix, more a cavern than a bar. Young men and women, students they appeared, huddled around tables in the bar's tiny room and Joe saw no place to sit, but that wasn't his purpose. Pulling a single twenty from his roll of money, he asked the first waiter that passed if he could leave his valise behind the bar for a time. Once seeing the double sawbuck, the waiter became quite accommodating. It was nearly his month's wage.

Before handing over the valise and the bill, Joe tore the bill in half, right down between Grover Cleveland's eyes. "The other half when I come back," he said.

The waiter nodded. He may not have fully understood the English words, but he understood the meaning.

"It will be safe?" Joe asked, then pointing to the valise he asked, "*Sécurité?*"

"*Oui, Monsieur. Tout à fait.*"

Trust was not something Joe was finding easy to offer, but he had little choice. He left the valise with the waiter, telling him through words and hand motions that he would return for it either that night or tomorrow, and walked on toward Marie Dillard's home.

He buttoned his collar and thought of what he could have done differently over the past days. The dead, however, would still be dead or hovering in near-death regardless of his actions, but that knowledge did not comfort him. Part of him wanted something like revenge, to put a bullet in one of Marcel's small, black, and red-rimmed eyes. Another part wanted to walk off into the French countryside, escape into a darkness of his own making and his own population. Mostly, he wanted this settled. Closure as Gresham would have said.

He exited the Metro not far from Marie Dillard's house and walked there.

He watched people walking through the declining light from lampposts and welcomed the anonymity of the city's nighttime sidewalk, even felt buoyed by the realization that not having much of a plan meant that at least he would not fail in the plan.

As he approached, he saw her leave the house, locking the front door before stepping quickly down the street. She had looked quickly in his direction before departing, but he was in shadows.

He crossed the street and said, "Miss Dillard. Please."

She turned and looked at him, no recognition. "*Oui?*" she asked.

It wasn't Marie. She was about the same size and had the same close haircut beneath the cloche hat, the same hair color, although a bit darker. She wore her cloche hat and long and heavy coat against the cold. Plumes of her breath wavered in the air as she stopped to face him. Her eyes were a combination of sadness and surprise. She was beautiful. Something, finally, fell into place.

The Marie Dillard who had sent him on the fool's errand to Tours had not been Marie Dillard. Marcel had played that hand well, had known that he would go to Marie Dillard's house that day and had known that Marie Dillard would be at the hospital with her brother. While he had been watching her house, they had been watching him and playing him. They had strung him along, baited a line and set the hook without him even feeling the tug. As the old waddies used to say back home on the ranch in Terceo as they explained the set of a poker game, "If you don't see the fish at the table, then you're the fish." He had not seen the fish and he had been caught by the bad hand Marcel had dealt.

"*J'ai,* uhm, *parler avec vous,*" he said. "*Votre frère.* About your brother."

She tightened her eyes and tilted her head slightly. Moisture glistened in her eyes. Her eyes were brown with amber strikes. She did not say anything for a moment. He wondered if his French was that bad.

"Who are you?" she asked, adding, "I speak English."

"I'm the man the police—"

She cut him off, "You're the American."

"Yes, but I had nothing to do with what happened to your brother."

"I know," she said. "It was Marcel."

"You know." Joe felt an enormous weight lift.

Her eyes welled but did not tear. She spoke in English, her words slow and even. "My brother is. . . . He sleeps most of the time, but he was awake for a short period last night. He told me what happened, that someone sent by Marcel had tried to get his copy of your friend's manuscript. I read in the papers today that you are suspected. I am sorry, assumed guilty. I should have notified the police of what Paul said, but I have had so little time."

Joe lifted his chin and sighed a full breath into the night. As he watched it disperse, he felt like yelling, he felt so good. "It's okay," he said. "Letting the police know will come in time."

She said, "Paul … fell asleep before he could answer my questions."

"Walk with me," he said. "Let me tell you what I know."

"But I do not understand," she said, turning to him. "Why would Marcel want to kill Paul? They were once friends, comrades. My brother was a recluse. He did not offer any harm to anyone. Why would someone wish to kill him?"

Joe spoke evenly and slowly as they walked, "They were in the war together at the Champagne, your brother and Marcel and several other men. Marcel was a traitor and my friend, Wynton Gresham, wrote a manuscript exposing him. Your brother apparently agreed with Gresham. Marcel tried to kill him in order to keep his own treason silent."

He took Paul Dillard's wire from his pocket, which he had carried with him since the ship, and handed it to her.

Marie wiped her eyes and rubbed the tips of her tear-dampened fingers together. She opened the message and read it in silence then looked back at Joe. The automobile mechanic had described her as sad. And she was. She also had lost something in that war.

They left the boulevard Saint-Germain, mingling with the evening crowd and walking the short rue Bonaparte past a string of antique and decorator shops, until Joe found the open door of a small café. They took a table away the front window. Groups of people sat in small clutches around several of the café's other tables, drinking and talking, not taking any notice of the two people near the back wall.

He signaled the waiter, standing nearby with idle condescension written in his slouch against the bar, his round tray under one arm.

The man sighed audibly and almost yawned before walking over. Joe smiled—not even the famed condescension of the Paris waiter could upset him. They each ordered coffee, double espresso for him and café au lait for her, and they waited in silence the few minutes until the waiter brought the coffee and swiftly left to read his newspaper at the bar. The espresso, with its layer of crème the color of caramel, was hot and strong. Joe felt an immediate jolt with his first sip. That was coffee. He closed his eyes and drank again. Good coffee, strong and black and hot, that reminded him of camp coffee back home.

A pair of gendarmes walked past the window. Joe turned his head away in instinct as much as anything, for they were too far from the window to be seen.

After Marie had stirred sugar into her coffee, she said, "My brother returned to Paris just weeks ago. He said he was ready to return to his life before the war. He had thought through some things, he said, and had come to some conclusions. He was going to marry. . . ." Her voice did not tremble but her eyes were uncertain. Her fingers quaked slightly before she placed them around the bowl of her cup and held the coffee under her mouth, allowing the steam to wrap her face in its gossamer column.

She asked, "You have a copy of the manuscript?" Since her English was much better than his French, they spoke in English, and she spoke English with a soft accent.

Joe drank from his cup and thought about it. "Yes," he said. "But I wanted to talk with your brother about his notes, what he wanted to talk with Gresham about."

She nodded. "I do not know." Dillard's notes were probably spread out along a hundred yards of rail line, dispersed by the wind and muddied by the rain. He thought of the other contents of the manuscript box, letters and such, that he had given to Dapper while on the train, that now Marie would never be able to retrieve.

He looked at her. She was in her early twenties, but carried herself as though older. Liquid brown eyes with amber shafts, short bobbed black hair, full mouth set in a synthesis of sadness and uncertainty. The sadness of her eyes was highlighted by the deep rings circling each. She had been crying, and not so long before. She was still pretty, though, and Joe found himself thinking of her beauty as he looked at her. A pretty woman who had not allowed her beauty to spoil her.

Joe sighed, "I don't know all of the whys, the reasons for what has happened."

"But Paul," she said to the air between them, her hands in the air as though clutching for answers. "He only wanted to put the war behind him. Why did this Gresham have to write his manuscript?"

The question was not for Joe to answer, and he did not. He also did not say how difficult it was to leave the war behind like it was an empty box, so instead he told her about Gresham, about becoming Gresham and taking the ship to France, about Huntington. He unfolded the recent drama of his life.

She cut him off, "Why did Marcel not kill you on the ship? Was he on it with you?"

Joe shook his head. "I don't know. Probably only his henchmen were there. He is a coward, and like all cowards what he fears most is his own cowardice. He hides so that others do not see it. Instead of exposing himself, he let his henchmen deal with the problem."

They slid into a silence with Marie thinking her thoughts and Joe thinking how Marcel was the type of man who could not kill another man but could easily sell another man's life or order another man's death. He was a man whose life was not defined by any moral grounding. A man made perfect for the new century.

"What happened there?" she asked, breaking the silence and looking across the table at him with her fluid eyes.

"The Champagne?" He finished his espresso. As the hot coffee warmed him he realized how cold he had been. He ordered a second. The waiter raised an eyebrow but took the order.

"Yes." She leaned toward Joe. "Paul had changed so much. So much. At first I did not think it was any different with him than with so many others who had lost part of their lives to that war. They were all so finished, so ruined when they came home. But there was something else with Paul, something more had happened to him. He wanted to tell me. Several times he tried to tell me, but whenever he began to he would close into himself, as though he hated whatever it was that he needed to say."

She spoke softly, her tone soft with lengthened vowels and lightened consonants, and Joe found himself wanting to wrap up and sleep within the halo of her words.

He forced himself to place a little perspective on the meeting, that he was with and talking to a beautiful woman. He was with her, however, because someone had tried to kill her brother and he had interrupted her on the street. He knew that she may have once thought and possibly still thought that he had something to do with that, and she was right although not how she may have thought. He considered that, sitting in that café and sharing a warm drink on a cold evening, she may also have been playing him. He had, after all, been played before. Still, he thought other things as well, even though no fireworks had exploded overhead, no bells had rung in tall towers, no flashes had been sent along wires.

He breathed deep and said, "Something did happen. All those men died, but men died every day in the war, thousands, like a slaughter yard. But at the Champagne," he paused to think out his words, "someone, one of the group of men that Gresham and your brother belonged to, let the Germans know what was coming off that morning. What and when and where."

"Someone told? Someone—" she stopped. "Are you saying my brother—" She did not finish.

"No," Joe said quickly and firmly, maybe even louder than he had wanted, for people at nearby tables turned to look. He breathed and lowered his volume. "Not your brother and not Gresham either. They would still be alive had they been the one. The only one still alive and not in a hospital is Marcel."

She looked not at him but down at something only she could see, as though she were at grace. She looked back at him with a sudden hardness in her eyes and said, "I do not know him so well, but he has been good to me in recent years. Watching out for me. He gave me a job in one of his businesses—a medical factory, and even loaned me money so that I would not lose my house. I find it difficult to believe that he would do such things."

The waiter came back and interrupted them with their second coffees. They sat in silence after he left. Steam rose from their coffee cups.

Joe finally broke the silence. "Marcel gave you a job that kept you near him and so that he could keep informed of your brother's movements."

His words were heavy with cynicism, and Marie's eyes went wide then shut tight with recognition as she nodded.

She said, "He, Marcel, came to my house three years ago. He said that he was a friend of Paul's from the war who wanted to regain their friendship. I told him that my brother was then living and working in a monastery, that he may return to Paris or may not, I did not know. He said that he was then living in Paris, in Montmartre, and would remain in contact with me about Paul. He offered me a position with his company, but I did not need one then. Soon after, maybe a month, a bank said that they were closing my house. . . ."

"Foreclosing?"

"Yes—foreclosing. I called him and asked for the job. If it was still available. And I went to work for him as a secretary and he loaned me money for the bank."

"Convenient."

"At the time, I thought that it was—what?—providential."

"And you never heard again from the bank?"

"No," she said. "My father had arranged for family business when I was young and then Paul. I did not know."

"He plans things well. And you didn't tell your brother about Marcel?"

"No," she said, still holding her coffee cup in both hands. "Monsieur Marcel asked me not to. He said that he understood the reasons why Paul would want the solitude of a lay brother. He said that reminding Paul of his past might not be beneficial, that I should wait until he, Marcel, could meet with Paul."

Joe nodded. "I can understand that. Your brother may have had suspicions even then, and Marcel would not have wanted to alert him. As long as your brother stayed away, Marcel probably felt safe.

That must have changed with Gresham's manuscript and your brother's return to Paris."

"And you have read this manuscript and know what is in it?"

This time Joe deflected her question. "What's more important is that Marcel knows what's in it and wants it."

"And he killed your friend to get it?"

"Yes." Joe remembered the house in Greenwich where Gresham lay like a man asleep, the tossed rug runner in the hall, the shaft of light from the front room, the empty sounds of the house, a clock ticking and rain in the gutters. Everything pointed toward a meeting of friends, the Scotch and Gresham reclining on his sofa. Only the bullet holes were wrong. Those and the vacant stare of his eyes. Joe had seen enough of death before then to recognize its gaze even before he saw the darkened stain. The look was not like sleep, not sad or peaceful or anything. It was lost, a nothingness, something even beyond nothing.

Joe said, thinking of the scenario that he had formed earlier on the *Berengaria*, "I can't tell you exactly what happened at Gresham's home. There was no fight, but he was shot. What I know of Marcel's men, they probably did not feel the night a complete success without taking at least one life."

A taxi stopped on the road outside their café to pick up a charge before driving on. Both Joe and Marie watched the passing scene on the street. People's lives going on. They looked again at each other and Marie said, "I still do not understand why, if he had killed Gresham, why he did not kill you as well."

"Because he first needs the manuscript, every copy of it. When he had my room searched and couldn't find it, he needed me alive, frightened maybe and a bit beaten, but alive nonetheless. Otherwise the manuscript might be discovered by the wrong people, and he would be in a worse mess. For now he thinks he needs me to find it, so he wants to keep me scared to manipulate me." He paused. "Eventually, though, he'll either tire of that game or get too nervous. That could be good or it could be bad. It comes to a head soon."

"Pardon," she said. "Comes to a head?"

202 • • *Death of a Century*

"An end," he said. "Everything must end, either in his favor or ours." He emphasized the "ours" to include her on his side.

"And you do have a copy of the manuscript?"

"Yes," he said again, though he wasn't sure this was true, but the fewer people who knew the truth, the better: that one copy may or may not reside with an oafish American couple and that he had only guessed at the location of the original. If Marcel found out that neither Dillard nor he still had copies of the manuscript, Marcel would have little reason to keep them alive. That, also, included Marie. Joe could see the chess game being played by Marcel with Marie as one of the pawns. He did not want to see her sacrificed for something Marcel might believe to be a higher purpose.

"He has killed others as well?" she asked.

"Yes," Joe said. "On the ship. Maybe others that we don't even know about. Right now, though, Marcel must feel as though his world is collapsing, so he's trying to circle himself tighter within the lie. His entire life is a lie," Joe said, "and he wants to continue that lie."

"By trying to kill my brother?"

"Yes. Your brother knew what Gresham had written, knew what had taken place in Champagne. That was the reason Gresham planned his trip in the first place, to speak with your brother about the manuscript, his suspicions about what had happened."

She nodded. "Yes, maybe. When Paul returned, he called me on the telephone and said that he was feeling much stronger and that he had some work that needed to be done. I remember him mentioning a friend who was to come to visit."

"Somehow Marcel must have found out, maybe he was watching your brother's house."

"No," she said. "I told him." She paused and in the silence he felt his eyebrows raise. She continued, "I thought he might want to talk with someone from his past, so I told Marcel that Paul was home. He said that he would contact Paul himself once Paul was settled. I also mentioned a friend coming from America. I recall how surprised he was at that."

"Did Marcel and your brother have any meetings?"

"No. I asked, but Paul would not talk about Marcel. I assumed that Marcel was too immediate a reminder of the war."

"Unfortunately, you may have been right."

"But he never tried to kill Paul before, while Paul was in Tours."

"Marcel probably believed that Paul was the only man still alive other than himself. As long as your brother remained in seclusion and as long as Marcel had you, he felt safe. I assume that he would ask about your brother?"

She nodded. "I thought it was out of concern."

"And he probably told you to let him take care of any problems at your family's house, any problems that might arise?"

"Yes," she said. "He helped with the banks, as I said. Paul had secluded himself in so many ways, and Rene Marcel helped me with many things."

"When did you tell him about Gresham?"

"Some months ago, I forget exactly when."

"And you said he seemed surprised?"

She held her coffee cup with both hands. "He became agitated. He said he had to leave. Something to do with his business."

Joe did not say anything.

She nodded and her breath caught in her throat. She blinked several times before looking again at Joe and asking, "What do we do? The Prefecture de Police?"

"The police?" he said and shook his head. "They think I'm a murderer, and by now Marcel may have informed them that he has seen me in Paris. He's going to want to tighten the vise, force me to play his game. No, right now I think the police would be more a burden than a help. I don't think they'd give me much chance to prove my innocence."

"I could tell them," she offered.

He looked at her and wanted to believe her. He remained uncertain. Even if she were telling the truth, however, the police would probably not believe her.

"Not yet," he said. "Not until I can deliver Marcel to them."

He looked at someone entering the café. When he looked at her again, her eyes had dissolved into introspection.

She excused herself to go to the basement restroom. Joe watched her walk away, a strong and feminine and confident walk. A few minutes later he watched her walk back, her eyes downcast and no hint of a smile. He watched her move around tables.

She looked at Joe and smiled, her teeth white and straight and exposed in a line between the fullness of her lips, red with lipstick. When she sat across from Joe, the slight gather of her perfume spun around him like a soft, lavender wind. Like a spring day in the South of France, he thought.

They talked some more, as little as they could about the war or about deaths and mostly about where Joe had grown up in Colorado and her life in France. She told Joe about the monastery in Tours where her brother had lived since the ending of the war. He did not mention that he had already been there. They ordered a meal of sausages and red wine and then they sat and ate in silence. They sat across the round table the diameter of a mere whiskey keg and spoke with growing comfort. Sometimes they stole a glance at each other during their meal, but there were several minutes at a time in which they did not speak.

"How did he meet Rose Shaunessy?" he asked.

"Rose?" Marie echoed the name of Dillard's lover who had been murdered in the fake suicide at her house.

"Yes. If he were secluded in a monastery, how did he meet her?"

She smiled. "She was a nurse in Paris after the war. They met in the American hospital as my brother convalesced from his wounds. So romantic. When he told me that he was returning to Paris, he also said that they were to be married in the spring."

"I am sorry," he said.

She looked at him with great sadness in her eyes and asked, "Are you certain . . . about all this? About all that is happening?"

Her words were meant for answering but she also wanted answers to questions beyond the words. Joe didn't know how he could approach those questions. "Yes," was all he said.

"There are so many lies in this world," she said. "So many. I don't know who to believe."

Joe wanted to tell her to believe him, to believe in him.

Tears formed in her eyes, making her eyes as dark and wet as polished mahogany. He knew sadness. He had been witness to sadness before. But for the first time he felt himself look despair in the eye, and it pierced him.

She wiped her eyes with her napkin. "Paul always wanted to visit America," she said. "When we were young he talked about the Wild West, cowboys and Indians, six-shooters. He loved that idea, that romance. You are from that Wild West?"

"Cowboys and Indians, six-shooters and buffalo," he said. "Last time I was home, Jesse James held up the stagecoach I was on." He looked at her to see her reaction.

"Monsieur," she said with her lips in a pout. "You tell big tales."

"Tall tales," he said. "I'm a writer, a journalist, by trade. I make my living telling tall tales."

"Like Monsieur Gresham, your friend, a journalist?"

"Like him."

She leaned across the table. "Tell me about him."

"Now you're sounding like a journalist."

"Curious," she said.

"So was Mata Hari."

"I saw her perform once," she said, offering the words as an intriguing aside, and she looked at him, her turn to gauge his reaction. "During the war. She danced at the Théâtre des Champs-Élysées. My brother took me with him and some of his friends because he could not leave me alone at home. Our parents were vacationing in Nice and my nurse had left for the night and so Paul took his seventeen-year-old sister to a nightclub. Scandalous had my parents found out, but I loved it. She was very beautiful and I could see, even then as young as I was, why all of the men watched her with such intensity. She captured them. Her eyes and her movements, she captured them. One of Paul's friends talked with her following the show, but Paul took me home and I never got to meet her." She paused. "Later, we found out who she was. Too bad, for she was so beautiful."

"When was that?" Joe asked.

"During the summer, I believe. It was warm."

"Do you remember the year?"

"Maybe 1915. Yes, 1915 in the summer."

"Before Champagne," he mused.

Marie looked very closely at Joe. He watched her eyes and felt them as they traced his face, gentle along the skin of his cheek.

"You were in that war, also," she said. "You have the look in your eyes."

"The look?" he asked.

"Yes. Sometimes, not always, but sometimes you have the eyes of an old man. Paul had that look then even though he was still young, like you. A young man still, but he had seen things that he would not talk about. Not even to me."

Joe felt a bead of sweat trace his spine as he remembered the scarred and bomb-pitted landscapes like postcards from the moon, the drumfire of distant artillery, the smell of sulfur and the Very flares at night, the sing of bullets, the rotting bodies of dogs and horses and men. He had long since ceased to wonder at how easily his memories of the war could be conjured, how fully they developed and came to his mind. He wished them gone but lived every day with their presence, waiting as they did like the sun behind a cloud. Memory had become for him the single most abiding thing he most wished he could discard. He could not, and so he lived within its roil.

"After the war," she said, "he was like a fallen tree. He was so sad. I do not remember him smiling after the war."

They returned to silence, and Joe did not need to tell her that the memories of war were things that prohibited smiles.

He looked at her while she kept her eyes lowered, looking toward her coffee but thinking something else. She was beautiful, a beauty that belonged to a poet. Her face, although somewhat obscured by her downcast, was smooth and rain-freshened. Her hair was black as a crow's wing and cut sharply and diagonally across her cheek. Even with the sadness cast across her face, she was a woman that Joe knew could either inspire a muse or haunt a man for decades.

They finished their meal, and Joe left payment in coins on the table. Before they stood, he asked the question that he needed answered, Marcel's address.

"Yes," Marie said. "I know it. I sometimes was asked to deliver papers to his house."

She took a piece of paper and Joe handed her the fountain pen that Alice Bright had given him so many years ago, a century ago. She wrote and handed paper and pen to Joe.

"Montmartre," he said.

As they left the café, another man and woman entered, the woman wearing a long scarf that flowed from underneath her upturned collar to sweep in the wind. Joe held the door, but the man with the woman failed to take it, and the door closed tight, catching the woman's scarf and causing her head to whiplash, trapping her as certain as if she had been cuffed. She made a feeble noise and threw out her arms to arrest her falling balance, her hands fluttering like wounded doves.

Joe quickly pulled open the door to free the woman.

"Oh, my dear," said the man with her as he held his hand for the door, his hands white and soft, hands of someone whose money was earned off the backs of other men's labor. He gave Joe a hard stare, one intended to show disapproval of a lower class and said in manicured English, "Look what you have done."

"I'm not your servant," Joe said to the man, stepping close and forcing the man backward. He added to the woman, "I am terribly sorry, Madame."

The woman raised her hand and said, soft and cultured as though her words came from a Hellenic heroine, "Don't apologize, my friend. It is the machine again."

Joe nodded with no understanding but apologized once more before he and Marie left the café, joining the people in the streets. The evening remained cold and damp. He could feel the continued cold of winter lurking inside the evening air. They pulled up their collars and buttoned their coats, thrusting their hands deep into the pockets of their overcoats, their shoulders hunched up against the cold. Their eyes watered, their breath clouded in front of their faces, and they walked through those clouds in silence.

They walked into the clearing cold of the evening although the fog had not completely burned off, leaving a dull overcast sky to

ceiling the city. As they walked, their arms touched lightly with
electricity.

Along the boulevard, Joe watched the crowd, searching for either
end of a spectrum, Marcel and his men or the police. From somewhere ahead on the boulevard, Joe could hear the sounds of a protest.
He remembered well how the French loved to protest, especially if it
was something that concerned America, maybe the death of a couple
of Frenchmen along a road in Connecticut. The French, he remembered from the war, were not always good at action but very good at
complaint.

He took her arm. "Let's avoid the ruckus," he said, nodding in the
direction of the protest noise.

She looked and nodded, then turned with Joe down a street that
connected Saint-Germain with the quai along the Seine. As they
neared the river, Joe could hear its sounds over those of the protest
behind them, the mournful horns of the tugs on their slow swim up
the Seine. As they came close to the river, he saw gulls flying over the
liquid black of the river.

They walked on. Their arms continued to touch, like wires
sending sparks, an exhilaration of possibility that Joe had for so long
not experienced that he had forgotten could even exist. Since the
war, maybe even since the death of his father, he had lived in a
series of moments, stepping stone moments that led him deeper
into a dark center of nothing. That moment walking with Marie
near the Seine and with their arms touching more often than if by
accident was different. He had lost a lot, but he also might have
found something.

To others who saw the two walking, they may have looked as
lovers on a winter stroll. The pair and the city and the time might
have composed the fundamental elements of a good thing. The night
and the moon shadows and the glints of reflected light in the water,
the gray fog holding in the lamplight, water puddles shining like
wafers on the wet streets—it was all good. Above them a pallid moon
held in the sky. A man and a woman, both young and bright, with
arms mixed looking more at each other than at anyone who came
near. And Paris, an ocean of life. The cafés, the smell of petrol and

perfume and cooking and the river, and while not springtime in Paris it was nearing Christmas-time in Paris. It all could have suggested love, but Joe knew very well that what one saw suggested from the outside was not always revealed when the truth unfolded.

She turned to him as they walked and spoke in a voice sweet and soft and more than a little melancholy, "I am going to visit my brother. It is late, but I have permission. That was where I was going when we . . . met, and that is where I am now going."

He stopped. She stopped one step further, turned and stepped back to him. The wind was at his back and in her face and blew her short hair back around her cloche hat to show the white skin of her face. He said, his tone deepened and his words spoken slowly so as to be heard over the noise of the river and the street and the people walking past them, "Marcel will be there, you know. If not him, then one of his men. They will be looking for you now as well."

"Regardless," she said. "I will visit Paul."

"Mind if I accompany you?"

She raised an eyebrow. "Do I have a choice?"

"Yes," he said and smiled. "Your choice. I can walk with you or I can follow you."

She sighed and smiled. "Then you might as well walk with me."

She looked at him as they walked, her face drawn and expressive in understanding. They walked on in silence broken only by the sounds of the city at night. A city of light that pulsed its second life once the hint of darkness began.

She said, "He is at the Hotel-Dieu near Notre Dame on the Ile de la Cite. He is a war hero, and he receives the best treatment."

They crossed the Seine on Pont Neuf, passed the statue of Henry IV on horseback, the over-sized arches, the caricatures of ministers and pick-pockets and tooth pullers. The wind blowing the course of the river rattled winter-dried leaves and dead seedpods, sending them to be captured in the moisture along the railing's cement base. The cold air leaked through openings in his coat, and Joe pulled it tighter around him. The full breeze carried with it the scent of the river, a keen blend of diesel and coal and fish and old water. Someone moored close by was frying fish on board their flat-topped barge. The wind at their backs, they descended the stairs from the bridge to the walkway along the Ile de la Cite.

Ahead of them loomed the Palace de Justice with its gloomy façade and its gloomy front. A group of policemen were loitering underneath a lamp along the water wall, sharing a loaf of bread and laughing, paying little attention to the people passing. Even so, Joe pulled his collar higher, as much to hide his face as against the coldness of the evening and the tall building. He kept his head down, his eyes on the walk.

"Madame. Monsieur," someone called from behind them.

Joe turned. A pair of policemen were coming toward them, not walking quickly or even resolutely. They were, however, coming toward them. Joe felt himself caught within a circle of hard places and rocks, police at both ends of the walkway, an overlarge police compound on one side of him and the Seine River on the other. As much as he hated the idea of a winter dip in a cold river, he steeled himself on that possibility.

He looked at Marie. This would be the test. Her eyes did not offer any clue.

The police spoke in French. Joe followed the conversation as best he could, using the inflection of voices as his clue on whether to dive or stand. They pardoned their intrusion and asked what business the two had along that street. There had been difficulties earlier in the day with a protest, and the police feared anarchists would again target the Conciergerie and the Palace de Justice. Marie, looking once at Joe, her eyes clear and her tongue tracing the line of her lips, explained that they were visiting her brother at the hospital. The police nodded, thanked them, and walked on to join the others at the water wall.

"Thank you," Joe said to Marie after the police had left.

She looked at him, words formed in her eyes but she did not speak them. She swallowed then said, "We should hurry."

She turned and walked along the gray walkway with Joe stepping quickly to catch up and walk beside her. The gas street lamps were on, and they walked between shadows. The wind continued, bringing waves of cold and wet air onto Joe's back. They reached the hospital, the Hôtel-Dieu with its stone front standing several stories high, each story having darker stones from the river's wet wind and the diesel and coal emissions of passing automobiles and barges. The words circling the arc above the front door read LIBERTE EGALITE FRATERNITE.

They entered through the large wood doors and walked the tiled halls and stairways to the third floor, their footsteps echoing along with them. Every person Joe saw he studied, looking to see if that person was also studying him, some member of Marcel's soldiers waiting for their arrival. A trap, maybe, ready to be sprung. Dillard as the bait, Marie as the lure, Joe as the prey.

They reached Dillard's room with no trouble, nobody taking any notice of them at all. Two people at a hospital to visit a sick loved one. That was all. Nurses and doctors and patients in wheelchairs and other visiting relatives and friends passing in the wide hallways, walking as close to the opposite walls as possible as though to avoid a contagion. Each person walked with shaded eyes, downcast or unfocused. People both unseen and blind to other people's worries, for they all had enough of their own. Down the hall beyond Dillard's room, a woman sat with her head in her hands, crying silently, her head and shoulders bouncing with her sobs. A teenage boy stood next her, his one hand on her shoulder, his other hand wiping the tears in his own eyes.

They entered Dillard's room, walking into the rectangle of light cast from the hallway into the room, dimly lit from the single bulb of a table lamp. She looked at her brother in his bed and asked Joe to turn on the room's ceiling light. Dillard lay on his back, one arm outside of the blanket. A bandage covered the arm from fingers to shoulder, open only where an intravenous tube was needled under the skin of his forearm. His head was also bandaged although his face was not. An antiseptic lotion, however, had been spread across his cheeks and nose and forehead like a glossy layer of film on his skin. His eyes were closed. He breathed with difficulty through his mouth, his breath barely passing through the gauntlet of his swollen throat.

Joe recognized Dillard's labored wheezing, having heard similar from men caught in the mustard gas. Dillard's lungs and throat had been damaged from heat and smoke, and now each breath became a battle. He had seen men who had lived through a gassing, like Diamond Dick Quire, but he knew also that for most men whose breath became such a difficulty they did not survive. Eventually Dillard's lungs might fill with fluid or his throat might constrict or some infection might take hold elsewhere on his burned body, and he would not be strong enough to fight it off.

Joe could see the man dying without ever regaining consciousness, without him being able to tell Joe why exactly Marcel had killed Gresham, without telling the history of those treasons. He could see Dillard dying without ever telling the police who had killed him, leaving them to continue their assumption that Joe was responsible, regardless of what Marie might say. He could see Marie's brother dying without ever again telling her that he loved her. He could see all that because he had seen all that before.

He watched her bend close to the bed and whisper words lightly into Dillard's ear. He could not make out the words, but as she spoke softly to her brother, a tear ran from her eye and dropped onto the bed sheet. Dillard's eyelids fluttered, but did not open. When Marie knelt to bended knee beside her brother's bed, pressed her hands together and began to pray, Joe felt a lump grow in his throat.

He had not prayed since the war. When he had then it was more out of fear than belief. Watching her silently pray, her lips moving and her head bobbing with her words and silent crying, he considered offering his own prayer. For her and for Dillard, for Gresham and Huntington, for himself, for the thousands of men who had died at Champagne, for his mother and father who had died long ago. But he had quit believing. He had quit believing in so many things that he couldn't bring himself to offer any words. He opened his eyes and watched Marie continue her own prayer, her hands now holding her brother's hand.

Joe felt that he was a voyeur looking into someone's very private sanctum. As quietly as he could, he opened the door behind him and slipped from the room. The same people were in the hallway, their eyes still averted as they walked along the hallway. The same woman was sitting, now with her head lain back against the wall, and the same boy remained standing next to her, his hand still on her shoulder. They had been joined by three others, an old man and woman and another woman. Joe met the eyes of the old man. He saw how the old and the young and the women carry the world's grief.

He stood to the side of Dillard's door, leaning back against the wall, his feet together and his eyes watching the shadows of passing people on the floor in front of him. It was not long before Marie left the room and joined Joe in the hallway, her eyes wiped clear of tears but left puffy and red. She looked at him. They left without speaking.

Outside the hospital, street lamps were bright and wedges of light came from building windows. The sky above, where he could see it through the boundaries of buildings, was black and hollow, empty and immense.

Joe took Marie by the arm, turning her gently toward him. "I'm sorry for your brother," he said.

Marie nodded and swallowed hard. "I prayed for him to not suffer. I can see that he will die, and I prayed that he die soon." He could see tears begin to well and he took his handkerchief and gave it to her. She took it and dabbed softly at her eyes.

Joe pressed his lips to her forehead and laid her head against his shoulder. He could feel her staggered breathing. "Where do we go now?" he asked.

She pushed away from him and looked around as though she did not know where she was. "Home," she said. "I think I will go home."

"Marcel was not here," Joe said. "He's certain to be waiting at your home."

"I do not care about Marcel."

"You should."

"I do not care about anything."

Joe felt like saying that he knew that was not true, for he had seen how deeply she cared about her brother.

He said, "You should not go home tonight."

She looked at him.

"Is there somewhere you can stay, someone you can stay with for at least the night?" He added, "I'll come see you tomorrow, to make sure everything is all right."

She considered it for a moment.

Her breath caught in her throat as she spoke, "Yes. I have a friend nearby I can stay with. On rue Dante not far from where I live. She will let me stay."

He walked with her to her friend's apartment. They walked in silence with their hands in their pockets, their coats buttoned tight, their collars up against the wind and gathering cold. The short bridge on which they crossed the Seine was cold and wet. Bare trees on the quai stood in stark relief against the night sky. The lamps were alive, but the night was still dark and darker still when they turned off onto the unlit side street that led them to rue Dante.

A woman answered the door following the second knock. Marie talked to her in French. The woman nodded, looked at Joe with suspicion. She said something and Marie agreed.

Turning to Joe, Marie said, "She is wary of you."

"That's okay," Joe said. "I probably don't look like the most trustworthy Yank," and told her that he would talk with her the next day. He took her hand, cold and dry but strong, and told her to sleep well. Not too far away, the bells in Saint Sèverin rang on the hour. He heard them count the strikes but tried to not think of them, whether the bells were tolling for him.

As he walked away, he heard the door close and latch shut behind him and felt their eyes watching him through the slightly parted curtains of a window.

X

Aᴛᴛᴇʀ ʀᴇᴛʀɪᴇᴠɪɴɢ ʜɪs ᴠᴀʟɪsᴇ ꜰʀᴏᴍ Lᴇ Bᴀʀ Dɪx ᴀɴᴅ ɢɪᴠɪɴɢ ᴛʜᴇ waiter the other hemisphere to the bill, he walked to a Metro station. The ride was quick, with only two stops to slow the run, and as it was hours past midnight, few people were aboard and those who were appeared closer to sleep than wakefulness. He found Quire's address near the La Villette area of Paris easier than he thought, a second floor studio off a narrow and dark cobblestone street in a building with a crumbling brick exterior. With its wide wooden doors fronting the street, the building's first floor appeared to be some sort of garage or warehouse. As he mounted the stairs, however, he swore he could smell cattle, the familiar saccharine musk of their breath and their deposits.

Quire answered soon after Joe knocked, stepping aside and inviting Joe inside the small apartment. He held a pistol in one hand, a drink in the other.

"If I'm ever shot again," Quire said, holding up the glass of amber liquid, "I'm damn sure going to have some anesthesia nearby. That last time near Saint Mihiel I had to sit in the goddamn mud for two frigging days with a German slug in my leg before anyone found me. That won't happen again."

Joe grunted in agreement, stepping past Quire.

"The being shot ain't as bad as the fact that my hip flask ran out of Trench Lightning after the first day. That's sorrowful, not having a whiskey to finish your evensong with."

Quire's was a small, square room with an old carpet over pine planks worn brown and smooth from use, a brass bedstead with an unmade bed of wool army blankets, brown and green. A large window opened to the street with a wardrobe on one side, table and chairs on the other. Thick curtains hung together on tarnished discs from a brass rod. Another table, a sideboard more like, was against another wall with a washbasin on top and towels folded neatly next to it. The washbasin was brown and shiny from use. An expatriate's apartment, a flop for a bohemian bum.

Quire nodded toward the valise in Joe's hand. "How was the trip?"

"Not good." He smiled.

"Why not?"

"Give me a minute. Let me catch my breath."

Quire tilted his head motioning for Joe to sit on one of the bent-wood chairs next to the round table and he sat in the other. He squinted at Joe through his bruise-colored eye that had turned more yellow ochre than any other color. His feet were bare and his hair uncombed, while he sipped at the amber drink held in his glass. "Want one?" he asked Joe, extending the glass for Joe to see its contents.

"I do," Joe said, "but not right now."

"Suit yourself." Quire smiled and drank the last of his whiskey in one quick gulp. He winked at Joe. "A ruddy cup of luscious liquor. Fills you with the Dutch on dark nights."

"You still carrying your pistol?"

Quire winked at Joe. The wink was more of an attempt as Quire's eye was still colored and swollen. "Fool me once, shame on you. Fool me twice, prepare to die."

"And you think someone's out to shoot you?"

"None 'cept that little piss-ant that said he'd do exactly that if I helped you. And after you told me about all your friends turning up deceased, I figure the odds are good. While my life may not have much direction, I'm not quite ready to cash it in."

"That's good," Joe said. "You have that blonde chippy to think about come St. Catherine's Day"

"Ah, yes, and she's a good thought to think about." Quire poured himself another couple of fingers from his bottle of Bushmills. "To modern women," he offered and drank half the glass and nodded. "Good stuff." He put the glass on his table and crossed to the unmade bed, sat to remove his shoes, and begin undressing. "You like my humble abode?" he asked.

Joe looked again at Quire's small apartment. The ceiling of the tiny apartment was high, but the walls stood so close and tight that the room had the feeling of a coffin. It was warm even though Joe could not see any stove. And he still smelled cows.

"Is that cattle that I'm getting a whiff of?" he asked.

"Yes . . . shit," Quire said. "Cow shit. It's part of my gas treatment."

"Your gas treatment?"

"Yes, the fucking gas treatment." With pants unbuttoned and shirt untucked, he walked back over to the table for his glass and drank most of his whiskey. "I signed on with some crazy Russian bastard who took six months' rent on this place and told me that smelling cow's breath will heal me. It's healed all right. I don't want to smell another damn bovine beast again in my short damned life."

Joe shook his head. "That's a new one. Smelling cow's breath as a treatment for a gassing."

"And cow shit."

"And cow shit."

"I met some expat Russians who had taken a few gas attacks on the Eastern Front before Lenin took over and rent hell. These Russians told me about this guy—looks like flogging Rasputin, all dressed in black and all. He looked like the black angel of death the first time I saw him. He damn well may be. But I guess he's no crazier than the last treatment I tried. Some frog doctor in Auteuil who forced a balsamic gas into my lungs with a tire pump about five, six times a week."

"A bit of the hair of the dog that bit you?" Joe asked.

"I suppose. Felt more like a back-assward enema. I left that French quack and signed on with this Russian quack, and I imagine I'll still die before I see thirty." He drank a little more and nodded toward the wall. "The woman in the next room, some English writer dame with tuberculosis, a pretty little thing but not much for fun, she feels like she's taken a new lease. Me, I've decided to go down drinking." He lifted his glass and drained the last of the whiskey in a loud gulp.

He shook the alcohol down and asked, "And so what's with you, *mon ami?*"

Joe told him about the day's events—the trip to Tours, Dillard's room, the newspaper article, the real Marie.

"Always a dame, ain't it," Quire said once Joe had finished. He shook his head and slumped his shoulders. "And no photos in the newspaper?"

"No, but I'd expect one of me soon."

"I suppose that means that we have to act soon or you should plan a trip to the German frontier and lose yourself with some fräulein."

"No," Joe said, shaking his head. "I don't want this dogging me the rest of my life, however short it may be."

"So, then, what's the present plan?"

"I'm not sure. I need some sleep first. Tomorrow it may all come to a head, and I'd like a little backup with me when I do it. I'll be going to Marcel's house."

"You know where he lives?"

Joe waved the paper.

Quire cocked an eyebrow and asked with more than a hint of anticipation, "You're set on killing him then?"

"No. Not unless I have to."

Quire again walked to the bed that lay out unmade and sat in a slump on the mattress. He placed the revolver beside him. "What the hell," he said. "We'll take it to him. His men give us shit, we shoot their asses."

"You looking to die young?"

"The young, they do die good . . . don't they?" He tried again to wink at Joe.

"I hope not to find out."

It was past sunrise when Joe finally laid down on a pallet of coats, towels, and blankets. He had been awake and active for a long time, nearly twenty-four hours, and he fell asleep quickly. While his sleep was not restive, it was at least long. His dreams visited him again and his mind whirled on thoughts he could not fully conjure, the one thought nagging at his mind as a splinter works under the skin. He came full awake in late afternoon and realized what had been bothering him since the previous night.

Why had Marcel not killed Paul Dillard in the hospital? If Dillard talked with the police, then Marcel was ruined. He washed in the sink and even shaved off a couple of days of growth, for looking like a bum did not help his desire for anonymity. He dressed quickly, making as little noise as possible. He could hear the sounds of Paris fully alive outside the window, but he also heard the lowing of cattle from the first floor of the large building.

"Is it time?" Quire asked from his bed. He was up on one elbow, eyes slitted. He reached for his bottle and took a pull before pouring a couple of fingers into his glass. He held out the bottle, "Breakfast?"

"No to both," Joe said. "I've got something to take care of. I'll be back before too long."

The Metro was filled with the shuffling silence of a workday. Most people kept their eyes to the ground, not wanting to acknowledge another day behind a counter or under a thumb. The air was humid from the day's moisture as well as the breath of a crowd of people. Joe stood to the side, collar up and hat down.

He boarded the train with the crowd and rode it from Gare de l'Est to Châtelet, one stop before his destination. Marcel's men could easily be waiting at the next stop, Cité, for Joe to visit the

Hôtel-Dieu. He wanted air and space and options that might not be available to him in the Metro station, so he walked across the bridge to the city's main island. He kept pace with the crowds of government workers crossing to the island, watching for anyone who might be watching for him.

The day was cold and a Paris drizzle was making it colder. However, that made it easier for him to hide within the crowd of winter-dressed men around him. It also made it more difficult to spot anyone waiting for him. He spotted the man anyway. He was the only one who looked to have been standing at the building's corner for hours. He looked like a wet rat smoking a soggy cigarette.

Joe kept his head down and let the crowd's current move him safely past the rat. The halls of the hospital were busier, more visitors, more doctors, more patients. Some of the patients were young men, legless and wheeling themselves along the corridors. The hospital was a good place to keep them—the populace did not want to remember the cost of war, not in Paris or London or New York. Out of sight, out of mind. Joe wished he could parade everyone, especially the politicians and the generals and the old men who ran draft boards, into the halls of every hospital to see what those leaders had wrought upon his generation.

Joe slipped into the room across from Dillard's before removing his hat and coat, laying them on a chair beside the room's bed. An unconscious man, sleeping or drugged, lay in the bed. Joe looked at him. Old, gaunt, cavernous eyes, breathing through his mouth. Not long for the world.

He stood so that he could watch Dillard's door. When it opened, a doctor and nurse left, leaving the door wide. Joe saw the crossed feet of someone sitting in a chair along the opposite wall of Dillard's room. He waited. Carrying his overcoat and fedora, he crossed into Dillard's room. He had no plan.

A young gendarme, a *flic*, looked lazily up at Joe as he entered. A Paris newspaper lay folded on his lap. No recognition in the man's eyes. Joe knocked the door shut with his heel and flung his coat on the *flic*, who raised his hands out of surprise. Joe pushed his head back with one forearm and unsnapped and pulled out the man's pistol. It was a French Ruby pistol from the war, light weight and plenty potent.

Joe placed its barrel against the man's forehead and said, *"Taisez-vous."*

Joe pushed him back down into his seat.

The *flic* raised his hands and looked with wide eyes first at Joe then at the closed door then back at Joe.

Joe picked up the newspaper and stepped behind Dillard's bed, keeping the pistol centered on the *flic*. Dillard was still comatose, still breathing with shallow, constricted breaths, still hooked up to tubes. Joe opened the newspaper until he found a photograph of himself alongside an article about the American murderer in Paris.

"Look," Joe said to the *flic*, holding the paper up for him to see. He looked but was too afraid to understand.

"Look," Joe said, pointing to his face. He looked at Joe.

Joe held the newspaper next to his face. *"Regardez."*

The man's eyes finally showed recognition.

Joe dropped the paper, leveled the pistol, and said in broken French, *"Je reviens,* when I return, if you're sleeping, *dormez,* I will kill you, *vous tuer."*

The *flic* swallowed at the threat of his own murder. Joe could see that he fully expected to die right then. Joe told him to lie face down on the floor beneath the bed and not get up for two minutes, which he did. Joe left the Ruby on the bed sheets—he thought of keeping it, but didn't want the *flic* unarmed should Marcel's men arrive—and walked quickly across the hall to retrieve his hat and overcoat. Marcel's man watching the front door would be expecting him to approach the hospital and not leave it, so he felt secure.

He knew what the *flic* would do. He would call his superiors and report that Joe Henry had tried entering the room, but he had prevented it. The police would double their guards around Dillard. That was what Joe wanted anyway—more protection for Dillard from Marcel.

He took another circuitous route back to Quire's. It had become habit to not go places in straight lines, to look over his shoulder, to listen to footsteps behind him. The weather continued to turn colder; Joe's mood was turning as well. He was angry; he was ready.

Quire met him at the door, once again holding a pistol in his hand.

"You finished with your errand?"

Joe told him.

"So now?"

Joe shrugged. "Now we begin."

Quire smiled. Without speaking, he sat and slipped on his work boots, lacing them quickly and tight around his ankles—a man ready for the fields or the mines—before walking to the wardrobe. He pulled a long coat from its hangar. With one arm in its sleeve, he said, "We're wasting daylight, cowboy. Let's get this road on the show."

"There isn't much more daylight to waste, but you're right. Let's do this."

"You packing?" Quire asked.

"I'm without."

"The hell's wrong with you?"

"I keep losing them."

"We'll fix that. His soldiers will have something that we can take."

"Most likely."

"You know where he lives, right?"

"I do."

"All right, then. Enough talking," Quire said. "Let's get going. If it's to be done, better it be done quickly, or some shit like that."

"Over the top," Joe said and stood.

"Don't say that. My blood chills just hearing those damn words." Quire finished putting on his coat and walked to the wardrobe. He opened a drawer and moved things around until he found what he wanted, a YMCA-issue Bible from the war that he placed in the left-hand breast pocket of his shirt.

"I wouldn't have taken you for religious," Joe said, watching Quire pull on his overcoat and tuck his pistol neatly inside the pocket.

"I'm not," Quire said. "My first sergeant wore one. I saw him take a hit right there in Genesis and live to tell about it. I figured right then, a little religion can't hurt."

Quire put a box of shells into the other pocket of his overcoat.

Joe watched him and asked, "You looking to do a lot of shooting?"

Quire said, "You can never have too many bullets. You might be able to have too much fun and you can certainly have too many women, but you can never have too many bullets."

Joe shook his head and muttered, "I feel like the straight man in a vaudeville show."

"And so it goes." Quire put a pint bottle of whiskey in his pocket with the loose shells. "Ready for anything now," he said.

He faced Joe, arms down at his sides and feet steady and shoulder-width apart like some sort of cowboy gunfighter.

Joe arched one eyebrow and asked, "You set, Diamond Dick?"

"You're my Huckleberry, Joe."

They left the building that smelled like cows and walked out into the evening darkness like a pair of duelists. Joe carried the valise in his left hand, his right hand ready. The street was narrow and dark. They walked with overcoats unbuttoned and flapping in the wind.

Sometime during the war, like so many men he had known, Joe had quit becoming. He had quit evolving. It was not that he had suddenly felt complete. He had stopped forward movement and lay bobbing in still water. Walking with Quire down the dark and narrow cobblestone street of the Marais District of Paris made him feel existent again. A flame that had burned out was once again lighted.

The contradiction of actions did not, however, escape him. He had lost a vitality in his life during the slaughters of the Great War and was now reenergizing himself through the prospect of a new battle. In the former he had been a pawn. In this new game he was a player. From object to subject. That had made all the difference.

As they approached the large Metro station at Gare de l'Est, Joe saw Dapper and the Turk emerge from the block-long building. A third man walked with them, a man whom Joe did not recognize. He pulled Quire by the arm into the closest station door. The station was crowded, the air pungent with the powerful smells of a large number of people heavily clothed. They watched through the condensation on the cold-fogged windows as Marcel's men approached, their fogged breath partly obscuring their faces as they walked. The three walked a little hunched over against the cold night, watching their feet instead of their way and taking no note of their surroundings nor of the two Americans watching from behind the window.

Once, just before reaching the window from which Joe and Quire stood watching them, the three men stopped and turned and looked behind them, speaking once to each other before turning again and continuing their walk. In ways that made Joe uncomfortable, Marcel's men reminded him of himself and Quire. Men with reason and purpose and violence.

As Dapper and the Turk and the third man passed the front of their window, Joe and Quire stepped back into the shadows of a wall, then stepped close again and leaned over a wood bench to watch.

"Their confidence makes them lazy," Quire said.

"That's good for us," Joe answered.

Quire nudged Joe and winked at him. "Let's you and me fall in behind them. When we get close to my apartment, the dark street just outside, we'll take them from behind. Hopefully that little dandy will fight, and I can kill him."

"No," Joe said.

"No? No what, man?" Quire's eyes raked Joe, a violence in them that showed how badly Quire wanted this battle to begin. Two nights earlier when they first met at the Gentilhomme, Joe had recognized in Quire a man with whom he could become friends. A good man, which was the highest compliment he had ever heard his father afford another man. Joe also knew that while Quire was a good man, he was also a short fuse that had already been lit. Joe hoped that he could hold off the violence of explosion long enough for the fuse to ignite its charge when he most needed it.

Joe said, "If they're here, then that's fewer we have to worry about at Marcel's place when we get there."

As Dapper and the Turk disappeared from sight into the darkness, Quire turned to Joe and asked with some little derision, "And you don't think they'll be at Marcel's place soon enough? Where do you think they'll go after they find nobody home at my apartment? They won't head around the corner to take some loose skirt into a hotel."

Joe shrugged his shoulders, "You're probably right, but if we hurry maybe we can beat them there with enough time to take care of things before they even arrive."

"Pipe dreams," Quire said. He shook his head, took one step away, then turned and faced his partner. "You've been letting other people control your actions for so long that you're afraid to take control. You have to decide whether you're the man with the hammer or the man being nailed to the cross."

Joe gave him a dull, hard look. He shook his head as though he was thinking through a wad of cotton. He knew what Quire meant. He could not deny it. He rubbed his eyes with the palms of his fists.

"Well, damn," he said. "You think they're too far away to catch?"

"Now you're talking Mr. DeMille."

"Let's take 'em."

They left the station, a cold draft of night air hitting them as the doors opened. They walked as two desperados. They walked with heads up and hands to their sides, watching the dim figures of their opponents in the night fog ahead of them, walking with long strides in order to close quickly on the other three. That was their mistake, for their own confidence had also made them careless.

Marcel's men stopped in the night shadows of the street where Quire lived. Quire took Joe's arm and the two slid next to a building, away from any lights cast from the moon or windows or lampposts. They watched Dapper and the Turk walk on while the third man stepped back into an entry to a building.

"You see him?" Quire whispered to Joe. "He's lighting a cigarette," he added, nodding toward the darkness.

A short flame illuminated the man's face. Then the flame fell to the street and was snuffed out underneath a shoe. Then the small, red glow of a burning cigarette dotted the darkness like a fallen star. The glow moved in a slow, reciprocating arc as its owner dragged on his cigarette.

"The guy's bored," Joe said.

"You think so?"

"He isn't concerned or interested, otherwise he wouldn't be smoking in the first place. He isn't nervous because he takes too long between each hit. He probably thinks we're in your apartment and is just trying to pass the time until the other two return to tell him that they have killed us. He's just a lookout."

"Well, shit, Sherlock, I hope you're right. It'll make our next move that much easier."

"And what is our next move?" He looked at Quire. In the darkness he could not see the look on Quire's face, could not even see the difference between the man's good and bruised eye. He could, however, trace the menace carried in Quire's words.

"I'll just walk on up and introduce myself."

"I don't know."

"What? You want to wait until morning light before you bound over the top. Sometimes, my friend, you've just got to scream shit and let loose the dogs of war."

"What if—"

"If-shit. It begins now." Quire unbuttoned his overcoat and walked from the shadow, not waiting for any response from Joe. It was to begin, and Quire had begun it. Joe watched his friend's steady gait, his shoulders roll, his fists clench and unclench. He watched Quire take the Colt from his pocket and hold it within the fold of his coat against his hip. A cold wind blew and folded Quire's coat around his arms to conceal the pistol as he walked.

Joe studied the street, looking for signs of another person, of possibly Dapper or the Turk returning already. He watched for others who might also be Marcel's men but saw none. Yellow squares of light tossed from a window spread across the sidewalk in front of Quire, and Quire walked through them. Marcel's man must also have seen Quire, for he dropped his cigarette, snuffing it dead beneath his shoe. He stepped forward from his shadow.

A dog barked from somewhere down the street, a cat hissed, a metal can clanged against the cobblestone street behind him. Joe turned to see who was approaching. He saw nobody but heard the sounds of two cats engaged in a hissing battle. He looked again toward Quire and Marcel's man. They were closer together.

Quire stopped in front of the man, who had stepped to block Quire, holding his arms out like a cop directing traffic. Quire's Colt remained within the folds of the coat and against his hip as Quire looked to say something to the man, who abruptly pushed Quire backward and took one step toward the street in the direction Dapper and the Turk had walked.

Quire swung around and hit the man hard on the crown of his head with the thirty-nine ounces of metal in his right hand. The man went down immediately. From his place in the shadows, Joe heard the swollen sound of skin opening. He ran the distance to where Quire stood over his quarry, breathing hard. Two small pools of blood had begun to form. One from the man's wound to his head as well as another from his nose, which was the first thing to meet the concrete sidewalk when he fell.

Quire lifted the man by his armpits and pulled him back into the building's entry. He pulled the collar up to hide his ruined face. Quire also lit another cigarette and placed it between the man's lips, letting it dangle as though the man had simply fallen asleep. He opened his flask and emptied an amount of whiskey on the man's clothes before taking a good brace of it himself and returning the bottle to his coat pocket. He bent over the man, lifting his wallet, keys, Webley pistol, and black jack. He took three steps away with Joe before returning to the man and tying his shoelaces together.

"Insult to injury," he said.

They walked into a square of soft light from a window. "Damn," Quire said, trying to wipe blood from his shirt. "That son–of–a–bitch bled on me."

As they walked toward Quire's apartment, Quire discarded the fallen man's keys and wallet, after removing any paper money. He said to Joe, "He can't drive without keys, and he can't ride the Metro without money."

Joe nodded.

Quire passed the Webley to him.

Joe took it and checked the clip and chambered a round.

As they walked farther from the lights, Quire's street became darker, like a catacombs. They unconsciously slowed their pace, walking deliberately, like blind men without canes. Joe could not see what might be along either side of the street, who or what might be hiding within the shadowed recesses. Any small sound made him hold more tightly to the revolver, which he held at his side.

A rush of cold, wet wind blew over him as he passed into a glade of light, followed on its wings by the strident crack of a pistol firing and the sound of wood splintering.

Standing near that rectangle of light, Joe felt momentarily spot-lighted until Quire pulled him into a side alley, pitching the world into a palpable darkness. There were no stars nor moon nor lights from windows nor streetlamps to open the blindness that Joe felt as he lay prone on the alley's cold and wet surface. He lay facing the direction from which the first bullet had come, his legs spread wide and the Webley held in both hands in front of him and steadied on the valise. He kept his sight down the barrel toward the gray end of the alley.

Another shot fired from around the side of a building at the end of the alley. Joe answered twice with quick, snapping rounds at where he had seen the small muzzle flare. He heard scampering sounds of a man moving from cover to cover and then the sounds of another man further away running toward them.

"Let's go," Quire said. They were both up and running, running as though hell was on their heels and not looking back over their shoulders to see if anyone were following, letting their ears tell them what was behind them.

Joe heard Quire trip then regain his balance and then the sounds of Quire running flat-footed close behind him. Shots followed, ricocheting from the stone surface of the alley and the sides of the buildings. A man yelled, *"Arrêtez!"* but Joe did not know if it was the police or someone else nor whether the man was yelling at him or the shooter. He did not stop to ask. They ran through the streets back toward Gare de l'Est, weaving around startled people. From behind them, they heard other people running as well as the shouts and whistles of the gendarme. Joe felt the same automatic nature he had slipped into so many days during the war before his wound placed him in a hospital bed until the armistice. It was a mechanical impulse that moved his body, his hands and feet.

Joe hurdled the entrance gate and took the steps two and three at a time. By the way people recoiled from his advance as he reached the landing, he must have appeared like a shriek in the night. White and drawn faces receded to opposite ends of the platform, leaving Joe and Quire standing alone in the middle.

Joe's chest hurt from the running. He bent to rest his fists on his knees, keeping the pistol tight in his grip and the valise on the concrete floor between his feet. He breathed hard and felt the sweat beading on his forehead.

Quire leaned an arm over Joe's back and between coughs spoke in convulsions, "A little … trigger talk … huh, Joe?"

Quire stepped away from Joe and bent over in a tubercular cough, then spit bloodied sputum into the Metro's railway. When he turned back to Joe, he was wheezing heavily.

The sounds of yelling near the station's entrance stopped both Joe and Quire. They stepped behind a pillar, pistols against their hips, fingers white on the triggers. Those first sounds of men yelling and running were eclipsed by a railcar as it pulled to a stop, rosettes of electricity sparking from the overhead wires.

The doors of the subway car opened. Joe and Quire stepped from behind the pillar and into the last car, walking quickly to the rear. There they could watch the entrance to the landing through a dirty window as well as use a dividing wooden wall for some protection. Nobody else stepped on to the train, either in that car or the other two that opened doors at that station. The commuters already on the autorail, seeing two sweating and ruffled and heavily

breathing men enter their train carrying sidearms at the ready, gathered their belongings and left to stand apparitious on the platform
while the doors closed and the train jerked with a pneumatic hiss
to motion.

Through the flaws, condensation, and dust on the windows, Joe
watched as two men ran onto the platform, yelling and gesturing at
the leaving railcars. Dapper and the Turk. The Turk spit as he yelled.

"Someone should give a saliva test to that dog," Quire said and
laughed between coughs.

Joe leaned against the wicker back of a seat and sighed, "Almost
too damn close," he said, his voice gravelly. He wiped his brow, which
ached from tension.

Quire coughed, then hunched into himself as though to stifle his
hacking through a physical challenge. "No almost about it," he
coughed. "But, damn, wasn't it fun?"

Joe hung his head and had to agree that having at least done
something, having at least instigated something had felt good. The
results were not so positive, but at least not negative. He felt how
bound tight his body had become from the small battle and the race
afterward. Every muscle seemed as though it had cinched. The tightest
and last to loosen were his jaw and shoulders. He rested a hand against
the seatback in front of him to exhale fully. He felt something like an
old man whose clock had begun to wind down.

Quire offered a weary smile and said, "Things are rolling now.
Now we all know. No secrets about tonight. Marcel knows we're
coming for him." He checked his revolver and replaced the spent
shells with new ones he pulled from the box in his pocket. He loaded
three for his own revolver's cylinder and put the rest loose in his
pants pocket, dropping the empty box to the floor of the railcar.

"Yes. He knows," Joe said.

Quire added, "And he knows we're coming to kill him."

"I don't know if that's in his plan. His plan has him killing me.
He's drawing me to his house like a lighted lamp calling a moth."

Quire coughed and held his head as though he had a migraine.

"Think we were foolish?" A glint of amusement passed through
Quire's eyes. "Like I always say—"

"Yes I know. Cry shit and let loose the dogs of war."

Quire winked. "That's right. We'll have plenty of time when we're dead to rethink it all."

Joe coughed an unconvincing laugh even to himself. "Sounds like a fool's plan to me."

"That's all it takes to start a war, and, pardner, that's what we're in right now."

"It takes a lot of fools to start a war," Joe said.

"No. It takes a lot of goddamned fools to start a war."

"So what does that make us?"

"No Solomons, that's for damn sure."

XI

In short, the Champagne offensive was a trial of strength which was in
some ways comparable with the victories of Austerlitz and Jena, although
it did not achieve so victorious a result.
— *The [London] Times History of the War,* vol. 6

THE METRO ALTERNATED IN A SYNCOPATED RHYTHM, LIKE A NECK-
lace made of sparks held together by a strand of darkness. Joe felt
as if his blinking eyes were operating backward, the dark tunnels
closing his sight for longer periods than they seemed opened.

Inside the darkness between stations, Joe remembered one of
his first nights in a trench when German 240-millimeter mortars
had shelled a section not fifty yards from where he tried to sleep. He
listened to the whine as the shells descended and felt the reverbera-
tions of the ground with the exploding shells, but the dog legs in
the trench had kept the shrapnel from reaching him. He had covered
himself through the attack's duration and prayed words he had
thought were lost from his memory. The ground heaved and rolled,
bounced with a fury of sudden thunder. In ten minutes, a silence
filled the trench followed by the low moans and calls for help from
wounded men. Then the calls that an attack had been mounted. Joe
had run with others through the mud and viscera to where the
shelling had been. He slipped, fell to one knee in the slime and
bloody spume. Next to Joe, scatter-lit by a half-moon that had
begun to give way to false dawn and shrouded in fog like a grave-
cloth, lay a man's body without any head or right arm, his blood
dark and abundant where it flowed from the truncations. The smell
of shit and burned skin and entrails gagged Joe. He vomited
violently, as did others. Then someone yelled that the Huns had

come through the wire. He stood, his Springfield rifle dripping from the excrements of war. The pinholed glow of flashlights bounced tight together as the Germans huddled in close compact to make their way through an opening in the barbed-wire entanglement. A man near Joe took a gas lantern, lit it and threw it flaming toward the Germans. It broke and burst into flame on one man, his body a sudden torch. Each man in the trench began firing their five-round magazines and Joe fired with them, stopping only to reload until he, like others, ran out of ammunition. One man cradled a heavy Lewis machine gun and fired indiscriminately until the weapon jammed and seized up. He dropped it into the muck at his feet and pulled a Colt from his belt and continued to fire. They exhausted their ammunition in minutes, rifles and revolvers and pistols alike. They threw hand grenades or wielded their Springfields by the barrels as clubs like ancient warriors. Still the Germans spilled over, crossing the edge of the blown-out trench and joining the Americans in their muck. One man lost his hand when he picked up a German stick grenade that exploded in his grasp before he could throw it back at the Germans. The man sat down in the mud and cried, holding the stump at his wrist. Joe reached down and took a trench club from the waist belt of a dead man and ran for the closest German. He swung the wooden shaft with a round of scrap lead tied onto the end by a barbed-wire binding, and he split the German's cheek, dislodging the jaw and opening a wound that exposed the entirety of the man's mouth. The German stopped short and dropped his weapon, his eyes wide with fright and surprise as he tried in vain to return his face to how it should have been. Joe swung again and killed the man with a blow to his temple. The fighting went on with clubs and knives and hands and teeth for another hour until the Germans retreated with the full sunrise. The morning became lost in the echoed sounds of struggle and death. The surrounding death became academic and men became numbers. Finally, the sounds of battle slackened and were replaced by the sounds of men who did not know they were as yet dead. None of the Americans standing said anything or looked another man in the eyes. They had each found the darkest and most primal foundation of their souls. None would face another man in quite the same way again.

Eventually the bodies were gathered and carted to the rear, born on other men's backs. Later, after a rain had washed the stench and remains of battle back into the mud of the trench, an American colonel came forward to congratulate Joe's unit for a job well done, for their courage and bravery in the face of the enemy, for upholding the honor and the name of their battalion. The colonel did not venture to where the fighting had taken place and instead talked to them as they rested in a wide spot of the second trench.

"Damn, man. You all right?" asked Quire as the Metro pulled into the turbid light of another station.

Joe felt a feverish sweat rise on his brow and back. He shivered against it. "I'll be fine," he said. "I just need some air."

"This is our station then."

"You sure?"

"No, but it's the station we'll be getting off at."

"Why?"

"We should make sure of where we're going before we end up in Versailles."

The platform was empty of people as they stepped from the train with a few other people from other cars. The other exiting people left quickly, looking furtively and fearfully at the two Americans they had watched enter the train's last car, leaving Joe and Quire alone in the sepulchral underground of Paris. The train echoed as it receded into the tunnel. They looked into that dark union as the train disappeared, dust swirling within its void.

They walked to a map and found their place, Etienne, neither close nor in line with Marie's house in the Latin Quarter or with Marcel's house in Montmartre. They debated what they would do next and decided that Joe would go to Marie's friend's house while Quire would find Ballard at Zelli's. A coughing fit sent Quire to a nearby pillar, bent over like a beggar retching. While he was there the next train pulled into the station.

From the train stepped an acne-scarred man whose close-set eyes focused narrowly on Joe. He held a pistol in his hand and lifted it, pointing it toward Joe and sighting down the length of the barrel. He said in broken and heavily accented English, "Where is your friend?"

"Behind you, sport," answered Quire.

The man turned quickly. Quire fired twice into the man's body. He stumbled backward like a drunk before crumpling to the ground. Blood stained the cement platform of the station.

Quire spit bloody sputum to the side then looked down at the dead man. He said, "Help me move him to the bench."

Joe took hold of the man's ankles while Quire lifted the head. They placed him face down on the bench, wrapping the man's coat around him to help soak up some of the spilling blood. They wiped their hands on the tail of the man's coat.

"I'm taking a taxi to Zelli's. Ballard'll want to know that things are coming to a head." Quire coughed. "You?" He turned and looked at the platform as though he were searching for someplace to spit.

"A crossing train," said Joe.

"You think that's a good idea?" Quire asked, eyebrow cocked.

"Maybe not, but I should make sure she's okay before I go any further with this."

Quire shrugged. "You want me to follow you after I find Ballard?"

"If you can, yes. We'll set the rest of the night's plan from there," Joe said.

Quire said, "Tell me where Marcel lives. I'll send Ballard on ahead."

"Near the Barbe depot." Joe showed Quire the piece of paper with Marcel's address written on it.

"Not far from me, huh? A neighbor? I had noticed a rather fetid stench in the last couple of months."

"That was your gas cure, the cow shit under your flat."

"Besides that. A certain damn compound of villainous smells."

Joe looked doubtfully at Quire, who smiled back at Joe like the little boy who knows what nobody else knows. *Here was a man*, Joe thought, *who mixes killing and profanity and Shakespeare with ease.*

"Take the valise," Joe said, handing it to Quire.

"Why?" Quire asked.

Joe told him and Quire nodded. "Besides," he said, "I don't know what I'll find at her place. I may need both hands free."

Another train was slowing to its stop. Joe nodded at Quire, and Quire left through the dark hallway of an exit. Joe walked to the edge of the platform, leaving the dead man to rest on his own, alone as any dead man must inevitably be. He walked past a couple of gendarmes as they exited a train, his head down within the collar of his coat. He reached to pull down his fedora, but he had lost it someplace and sometime during the short fight. The police were too busy talking to notice the overcoated man trying his best to hide his face.

As the train pulled from the station, the policemen saw the smear on the platform, a blood-red mark like a pock on the gray of the concrete. One stepped toward the man on the bench and the other turned quickly to look Joe in the eye as the train began its release from the station. He pointed and said something to his partner as the partner touched the dead man, who rolled onto the platform like the unraveling end of a mortal coil. The train was gone inside the darkness of the tunnel. Joe saw nothing more.

He rode in the echoing silence of the Metro through the next few stops. Parisians, bundled heavily against the night's increasing cold and carrying bags of groceries and presents, pushed into the car at each opening. At the Gare du Nord, most of the travelers left the train with a mechanical proficiency. Those who exited were quickly replaced by as many more, all looking the same and carrying the same bags.

Joe watched the people come and go and thought of how easily any single person is replaced. Without a name or even a face, a person becomes the same as the person who stood in that spot ten minutes earlier, and the other person could be dead or a shadow of another. He remembered new recruits coming into the trenches, who after a single day of mud and fear looked like the casualty men they had replaced. The officers never knew, calling men by names that had been dead for weeks. One morning a man was a best friend and the next barely a memory.

When the train stopped at the Saint Michel station, Joe exited into the noise of the platform. He did not look at anyone else and took the steps up and out into the cold wind and commencing rain.

The sky had lowered and a little wind had risen to carry a new rain still so slight to barely cause moisture. The wind caught Joe's overcoat and flapped it open, so he re-buttoned the front and pulled up the collar. Within a block of leaving the station, the rain filled into a full rain. Large drops slapped into puddles already formed in the seams, cracks, and dips of the cobblestoned street.

He passed prostitutes who stood behind glass doors or windows, offering a view of their wares. He skirted around men with old wooden handcarts laden with fish or vegetables or carts closed tight against the rain to protect a supply of books. He crossed the opening of an alley from which he heard the sounds of a man and a woman engaged.

He walked on in the darkness, his shadow nonexistent until he reached the halo of lambent light underneath lampposts. Then he passed into and through and away from his cast image, then on, then toward and through again as if chasing a lost thought.

At the friend's house, he was told that Marie had left that afternoon for her own house. She had wanted some papers and had wanted a change of clothes and thought that she would be okay at home during the day and would return by nightfall. "She has not," the friend said.

Joe left, walking quickly, his head down in that constructed silence of the city's night until he stood across from Marie Dillard's home.

He stood and watched the light and dark of different windows, trying to read what lay inside that house, but he could see its soul no more than a disciple could see the soul of Judas. He could see nothing but the light and dark of windows and crossed the street to knock on the door, glad that the bells of Saint-Séverin were not tolling.

She answered the door. Her eyes went wide. She leaned forward and whispered, "Leave. Please." Her hand pressed flat against his chest, pushing, her eyes pleading.

"No." A voice called from behind her. The door opened farther. "Please," a man said. "Come inside. Join us." His smile was as cold as his words. "It is, I think, time that we meet, formally."

She stood to the side. Joe stepped in. The front room was dark, lit only by a candle in its glass, the flame waving from the breeze of the opened door. He stopped and turned to her.

She did not look at him as Marcel closed the door, fingering the dead bolt. "Go inside," he repeated, his words sounding like gravel. "Please. *Entre* "

Joe stepped inside the parlor and looked around the room. The fire in the fireplace had banked, orange glows soft within the diminishing embers of its last heat. The marble mantel held photographs of children, men and women with children, and soldiers strong and proud in their French uniforms. A rug boundaried the wood floor. Electric wall sconces and floor lamps lit the room, which was empty except for a sofa and chair countering the fireplace like entrance pillars. A fat man stood behind the sofa with a small pistol at his hip aimed at Joe.

"But first," he added, his hand outstretched as Joe stepped past him.

Joe looked at him.

"Your weapon," Marcel said. "I'm certain that you did not come without one. You are not that stupid of an American."

Joe began to reach into his pocket and the fat man coughed to let Joe remember his presence. Joe handed over his Webley and Marcel underhanded it to the fat man.

The fat man with the pistol had a fat, sallow, unshaven face. He had a small mouth and a recessed chin. His small mouth tightened into a taut smile.

Joe turned to face Marcel, the last of the five men who had been with Gresham at the Champagne. The man who had sold out his friends to the Germans and helped seal the deaths of 20,000 men in one haze-filled morning. Joe's hatred of the man was intense and immediate and complete, fueled from many sources—the death of his friend, the recent deaths of others he had only met or even did not know, the distant deaths of thousands, the deaths of honor and courage and belief.

Joe wanted to put a bullet into one of the man's eyes. He liked the idea enough to hold that thought until further notice, some pleasure to retain for later in the rainy night when he had retrieved his gun.

Marcel stood no taller than Joe but was thinner. His skin was a pallor, the color of over-cooked pasta; his eyes were gray and lifeless and the underlids were red; his hair was thin and cut short. He looked as though his life had been bled from him, as though his own cowardice had begun the process of rot from the inside, like a maple tree rots from its heart out until the shell is left withered.

"Frederick Gadwa," Joe said.

Marcel, Frederick Gadwa, bowed his head slightly. "You guessed," he said in perfect British English.

"It took some time, but eventually it all fell in place."

"What do you mean?" Marie asked.

"He's not Marcel," Joe said. He looked from Gadwa to Marie and back.

Gadwa nodded and gestured with his hands, saying, "Go ahead. I'd like to hear what you know as well."

"They were all members of an advance reconnaissance unit— Gresham, your brother, Gadwa, the Marcel brothers, and Thomas Wilde. In 1914 as the war was beginning and before the English had much practice in trench warfare, Gresham and Gadwa and Wilde had been assigned to join a French unit, to learn from them. They were to gather information and scout routes and wire holes before an attack. The day of an attack, they were to precede the troops and record the action. This photograph had everything I needed."

He began to reach inside his coat for the photograph.

The fat man levelled his pistol, and Gadwa cautioned, "Be careful, my friend."

Joe bristled at the moniker but let it slide. He opened the over-coat to show the inside of its flap and slowly pulled the rolled photo-graph from inside the pocket. He handed it to Gadwa, who unrolled it and looked, then handed it to Marie.

"I have always hated that photograph," Gadwa said.

"For good reason," Joe said. "Like Ephialtes viewing a photograph of Leonidas."

Gadwa reacted as though bee-stung, but recovered and spat, "Don't be dramatic." He waved. "Go on with your little story. I find it entertaining."

"In the photo, I knew who Gresham was from the beginning. From their uniforms, I could tell the French from the English, and I knew who had died and who had lived. Huntington, the man you had killed on the ship, told me how you had prospered following the war. Since I had not met you, I assumed that you were Marcel, but the woman at a bookstore showed me differently. "Once she pointed you out, it all came clear. How long had you been selling information to the Germans?"

"Since before the war," he answered. "I had been a military liaison in Berlin for a few years and began then. That, actually, was how I ended up where I was. Through others, I was transferred to the Champagne following the first battle there because everyone knew a second would eventually come. Joffre was so predictable."

He looked to Joe almost expectantly, his fingers worrying against his thumbs. The man had probably not ever been able to tell his story to anyone, had held only his own council. Joe understood that being able to hear it and to tell it must have felt somehow liberating for the traitor.

"Every night that you went out, you sold something to the Germans—where holes were in the concertina wire, when troop movements were scheduled and advances planned, where the approach roads were. You volunteered to go out alone. Everyone thought you courageous for taking their spots in the rotation. Your superiors probably talked about medals. After that morning, though, with the slaughter that took place, you must have known that you needed to disappear. You were in advance when the day began, out front with Rene Marcel. After the battle, or during it more likely, you kill Marcel and change uniforms, wound yourself enough to be removed from the front. You slide into hiding."

"Very good," Gadwa said.

"I wonder, though," Joe said.

"Yes?"

"How did you pull it off since then?"

"It was so much easier than you might think, so much easier than I imagined that it would be. I thought that I would have to disappear into Germany and begin again. That would not have been so bad, for I had accumulated millions in Swiss francs over the many years that I worked for the Germans.

"But once I became Marcel and spent my time convalescing as him, I had the opportunity to go through his business papers and realized that I had a fortune waiting to be picked, like low-hanging fruit. Especially with Wilde dead in the battle, and, I thought, everyone else. Imagine my surprise when I found out that Dillard had lived . . . and then Gresham. By then, though, I had already taken over that business and built it into what it now is."

"And nobody questioned it?"

"Why would they. The facts supported the story, even if the facts were wrong. That is what truth is—whatever you can support with facts. People wanted to believe, so they did. And once I became Rene Marcel, one of the richest men in France, I could tell my story as I wanted it to be. Politicians and businessmen kissed my toes because I had what they wanted—money and power."

"And why rock that boat?"

"Pardon?"

"The politics of pragmatism. Goddamn you."

"Yes," Gadwa said. "He probably already has," then added, "I suppose we will both see if Nietzsche is right or not. But, please, sit." He waved toward chair.

For emphasis, the fat man pointed the barrel of his pistol toward the chair.

Joe sat, his hands in his coat pockets. He watched Marie, her eyes steady and black, but not looking at him even though she stood facing him, backlit by a floor lamp. Gadwa walked up behind her then stepped to the side to stand to her right and turned to say something to the fat man.

For a moment, Joe felt as though he was looking at Vermeer's "Soldier and Young Girl Smiling." Marie, beautiful as he now knew her, faced him with her hands drawn together in front of her and her fingertips dusting lightly together as though she was holding a small cup, the expression on her face more lost than warm. Gadwa, standing tall and with his back to Joe as in Vermeer's painting, was shown in the orange glow of a lamp. Except the young girl was not smiling and the nearly faceless soldier was a coward.

Gadwa turned to look at Joe, his small, red-rimmed and gray eyes searching and steady. He crossed his arms, but he did not smile as he looked at Joe. His mouth slowly tightened into the small, thin line of his lips. "You are a fool," he said.

Joe had to agree, and it wasn't the first time that notion had crossed Joe's mind. He just hoped it wasn't the last time as well. When Joe did not answer, Gadwa walked to a side table to pour himself a brandy. Before drinking, however, he held the bottle up and read the label. Then he took a mouthful, moving it around in his mouth to test it on his palate. A mantel clock chimed the hour.

Gadwa nodded and turned to Joe. "For you?" he asked.

"Whiskey."

Gadwa nodded, "Of course." He tined ice into a small glass then splashed in whiskey. He handed Joe the whiskey and Marie a brandy and raised his glass, "*A votre sante.*"

Joe paused. "To the Lost," he said, then he drained his glass. He held the glass to the light and examined it, amber liquid clinging to the sides.

"Why did you come here?" Gadwa asked, licking his lips, thin and pale.

"Seemed like the thing to do at the time," Joe said. "I'd be happy to leave if I'm interrupting anything."

Gadwa laughed. "The famous American sense of humor. . . . I hate it."

"It's gotten us through some tough times," Joe said.

"Yes, I suppose it has. You don't always realize when you're beaten."

"Maybe that's why we never are." He looked at Marie standing with her back to the fireplace, her glass full and placed on the marble mantel. She avoided his eyes with studious labor.

He looked at the fat man with the small pistol. "Boss not let you imbibe?" he asked.

The man smiled his sallow smile but did not answer.

Joe shrugged. "You have a large number of people working for you."

Gadwa shrugged. "I do," he said. "And in many places across Europe."

"It must cost a bit of money to pay such an army."

"It does, but, then, the peace has been very good for me."

"You did all right from the war."

Gadwa took three long, slow strides to stand in front of Joe. He backhanded Joe in the mouth, a feline blow that bloodied the corner of his mouth but one that nearly sent him to the floor. His first reaction was to strike back, but there was the large man with the sallow face smiling at him and that little pistol readied. He looked at Marie. In her eyes he saw fear. Her eyes told him to do nothing, to say nothing.

Gadwa looked at Marie. "We have to leave."

"You bastard," she said. "Why have you done all this?"

Gadwa cupped her chin in his hand. "You are so beautiful," he said. "So naïve and so stupid."

He squeezed, she jerked away, he slapped her.

Joe lunged for Gadwa, but the fat man was there. He clubbed Joe with the pistol and sent Joe back to the floor.

Gadwa smiled at Joe. "The cowboy to save his damsel in distress. How noble. But, thank you for coming here tonight, Monsieur. It helped immensely."

He took Marie by the arm, "We will leave now." She tried fighting loose but Gadwa held tight.

Gadwa said to Joe, "My man here will stay with you. Please listen carefully to what he tells you."

"And Mademoiselle Dillard?"

"She will come with me." Gadwa looked from Joe to Marie, a thin smile on his lips. He took Marie by the arm and led her out, stopping to whisper in the large man's ears.

"*Mort?*" Joe asked after Gadwa and Marie had left the room.

"No," the man answered, shaking his head. He waited as a door closed in the back of the house. Silence interrupted the room. All Joe could hear was the popping of the coals in the fireplace. The large man stepped around the sofa and to the mantel where he took Marie's glass of brandy. He drank a little, swirled it in his mouth as Gadwa had and tasted it, shrugged at Joe, and drank the rest in a single gulp.

He looked toward the back of the house before pouring himself another glass of brandy. He kept the pistol on Joe and placed the glass on an end table, using one hand to pour. His eyes darted between the flow of brandy waving in red circles in the glass and Joe sitting. The man leaned against the mantel, a look of sullen content as he sipped from the glass and licked his lips as he finished.

He placed the glass on the end table. Again he lifted the stopper from the bottle and began to pour the brandy.

"What then?" Joe asked.

"I will let you go," the man said.

"What?"

The man shrugged, indicating that it was not his decision. "I am to tell you that Gadwa is leaving France tonight. He will be at his house in Montmartre for a couple of hours. If you bring the manuscript, he will let the woman go. If you do not bring the manuscript, he will take her." He laughed. "I suppose that means that he will kill her, eventually he will kill her."

His eyes returned to the pouring brandy. Joe leapt at him, taking hold of the gun hand in his own and circling his arm around the man's side with his other, lifting the man onto his shoulder and driving the large man back against the brick of the wall.

The fat man dropped his gun but did not fall. Instead, he hit Joe in the back using his joined fists as a club, battering them together on Joe's neck. His grip loosened. The fat man pulled Joe away and head butted him. Then his legs went rubber, and he fell like a sack of cement. The fight had not gone well. He was getting his ass kicked.

The fat man stood over him, huffing. The pistol was back in his hand and pointed again at Joe.

"*Arrêtez.*" The word came from the back door where Quire stood, his own pistol leveled straight arm at the fat man.

The fat man looked from Quire to Joe and back at Quire.

"Don't," Quire said, then in French: "*Je vais vous tuer.*" He added in English, "Sure as shit, Mr. Arbuckle, I will kill your ass."

The fat man sighed and dropped his pistol. He shrugged his shoulders.

"Bon," said Quire. "Sit against the wall. There. Legs straight out in front of you." He quickly pointed with his pistol.

The man did as he was told. His large legs stuck out from his large body.

"The Webley," Joe said.

The man shrugged and slid the Webley across the floor.

"Impeccable timing," Joe said to Quire. He wiped blood from a cut on his forehead.

"Like I told you. I have luck with trouble." He added, "And I said that I'd meet you here. After I got to Ballard, I came straight here."

"Many thanks, brother," Joe said.

Quire nodded. "You going to kill him?" he asked.

"It's a thought."

""*Mort?*" the large man asked. His hand moved slowly toward the fireplace tools racked near him.

Joe lifted the pistol from the floor and aimed, cocking it and sighting down his arm and the short barrel into the man's large chest. Shoot for the middle, he had been told by his sergeant, and you won't miss. His finger tensed.

"Wait," Quire said, stepping forward and bending on one knee next to the large man. He held a small pillow in one hand and a Webley pistol in the other. He bent close and asked a question in French. When the man did not answer, he asked again, louder.

He did not answer and Quire placed the pillow against the man's foot and sank the Webley into the down of the pillow and shot. Feathers and blood and bone meal exploded from the man's foot. The man cried out. He went to grab his foot, but Quire took the man's head by the hair and drew it back so that the man looked Quire in the face, sweat and tears running down his cheeks.

Quire repeated his question. He still did not answer. Quire let go of the man, who slid into a fetal position with his hands holding tight to his bloody and now useless foot. Quire stepped to the sofa and chose another pillow. Down from the first pillow was stuck to his hand by the man's blood. Quire knelt again and pulled the man to a sitting position and placed the pillow to his crotch and sank the Webley into the pillow.

""*Non,*" he cried, pitiful and bestial. "Please," he said in English, the single syllable broken.

Quire asked again, "How many men are with Marcel?"

The large man, sweat rolling from his forehead, his shirt beginning to darken. He swallowed and said, *"Deux, trois."*

Quire said, *"Merci,"* then patted his shoulder. He hit the man in the face so hard that his head bounced from the bricks and he slumped to the floor.

"If you want to kill him, we can, but I don't think there's a need." Quire stood and wiped his hands free of down on the back of the sofa.

"Shall we tie him up?" Joe asked.

Quire shook his head. "If he leaves, it won't be to follow us or even to warn Marcel. He has failed. I imagine Marcel is getting tired of the sloppy work of his people and will probably kill him. No, he'll be visiting a doctor to fix up that foot of his. Us, though, we should be going." He stood and winked at Joe as he walked past to the front of the house.

They walked out into the increasing cold of the night, down toward Saint-Germain to find a cab, and while they walked, quickly but not so quickly as to draw attention, Joe told Quire the story and that the man's name was Gadwa and not Marcel.

"Damn," Quire said.

They found a taxi and Joe gave him a ten spot to hurry across the city.

The driver, a bellicose man with a short, stubby cigar attached to his lower lip, nodded when Joe told him the address. He then offered to sell Joe and Quire cigars from a box he kept on the seat next to him. "They are not Algerian," he said in French.

"Just what you need, a bad five-cent cigar," Quire said. He reached a hand over the back of the driver's seat, exchanging a couple of franc for a cigar and pulled the cigar under his nose, inhaling the aroma. "Might even be Caribbean."

Joe sighed and looked through the front windshield. "What I need," he said, "is not going to be found in something that looks like a dried dog turd."

Quire smiled. In a moment, his smile dissolved. He looked at Joe. For the first time in the couple of days that Joe had known Quire, Joe detected an introspection in the man's voice. "Yes," Quire said. "What you'd like, what we'd all like again, is to be right. In this world, brother, that is the most difficult thing to be."

Joe did not answer. Quire sat back in the shadows of the seat, looking out his side window and thinking his own lost thoughts.

The street's tarred pavement ahead bounced in shimmering lines in the headlights of the passing automobiles. The buildings on either side of the rue Saint-Martin disappeared into the gray, acidic smoke and the haze of the blue-black sky. As they crossed the Seine, Joe looked down along the lighted quai alongside the river, black and empty except for a series of tugs and barges tied to the pilings along the concrete pier. Fog pooled in wraithlike vapors alongside the banks of the river which ran slow and opaque and controlled within the city's charter. He looked back at the river as they passed over the bridge. The river curled and flowed black through the city, sparkling with bounced reflective light but welling heavy and dark as it approached and underran the bridge's supports. The river disappeared behind them. Joe turned to look again at the city cast in shades of gray under the black sky. The night fog shone in the streetlights of the city. Like the night and the river, the fog floated as though it might lay dark and mazy on the city.

A few minutes after passing over the river, Joe directed the cabbie to let them off at the end of the street down from Marcel's house. They stood fifty yards from the house, often the width of the no-man's land between the trenches during the last war.

"That it?" Quire asked.

"It is."

Joe could feel Quire's tension rise, like someone turning on the heat from pilot to full.

"Ballard should be nearby." Quire's tone was as hard as pounded steel.

"That would be good."

"I told him to wait for us here."

"He have the valise?" Joe asked.

"He does," Quire said.

Joe nodded. "I hope he hasn't begun without us."

"I hope he hasn't finished without us." Quire laughed a little, the temper in his tone loosening.

"I suppose we should wait a moment and see if we see him."

Quire looked around him and smiled. "You know," he said, placing the unlit cigar in the corner of his mouth and chewing. "The first hotel I stayed in was around here somewhere. A real ritzy place that I had decided to put up in for a while. I figured that I was dying fast enough, so there was no reason to save my money. It had a damn drinking fountain in the bathroom, it was so damn ritzy. The goddamn thing must have been made for midgets, though, 'cause it was down near the floor and I had to get on my hands and knees to get a drink from it." He looked blank faced at Joe, then winked.

Joe looked at Quire open-mouthed. It was as though Quire had no notion of the errand they were on, like they were drunken comrades intent only on the easy promises due young men on a Paris evening.

"What?" Quire asked, looking at Joe, his hands open-palmed and away from his body.

"This is too much," Joe said.

"What is?"

"Your talking, your joking. You're acting like we're hiking Mont Blanc. Man, don't you understand what this night holds? We are killing people."

Quire lowered his eyes for a moment and removed the cigar from between his lips. When he again looked at Joe, his eyes were glassed and hard. He stepped forward to stand close to Joe and spoke, his voice deep and collusive, "Would you rather I talk about how many men I have killed in my past or who I have seen die and how and how long it took? Should I tell you how sickened and frightened I am at how much I am looking forward to this killing I know will take place? Would it be better to tell you that my hands are shaking and my legs feel weak as gimcrack? That my stomach is turning? Would that be better?"

"No," Joe breathed. "I suppose not." He knew then something that he had long wished, that the world was not as empty as he had supposed, that it was not a world constructed of no known or moral paradigm. Good men lived, even though their goodness was covered in veneers of past evils, not necessarily all of their own making.

They stood shadowless in the dark night across from the building, stark and obscure and cast within numberless shadows. They waited and stood and waited across from the house and watched and listened. Their eyes adjusted, the form of a house became a house, its frontal visage taking shape and appearance.

"Dark as a wolf's mouth," Ballard said from a shadow nearby.

"Ballard," Quire said. "Glad you're here."

"Man, I was there before the curtain raised on this drama, and, Quire-boy, I'll be damned if I miss the last act." His dark eyes were calm and appraising as he spoke. The eyes of a man who had seen too much, and, since those interrupting sights, had slept too little.

Joe swallowed what little moisture he had. A coldness cut raw to his bones as he anticipated the violence cast within the oncoming moments. He studied the exterior of Gadwa's building, his stomach tightening cold and hard as a shot of lead. People were about to die.

Tall behind a waist-high iron fence, four bare elm trees sentried the building's front. The front stoop and brick exterior rose three stories from the level of the street. Two curtained windows were to either side of the ground-floor entrance like blindered eyes. The two floors above each had four windows spaced evenly across the front and which were outlined in light sandstone. Gadwa's was a house of the rich, not quite a centuries-old aristocrat's *palaise* but maybe once a wealthy merchant's home. Set off from surrounding houses, ostentatiously removed from the fronting sidewalk as though to say that the owners cared not for the added taxes on wasted space, probably with a back entrance and a delivery entrance all its own. Ironworked bars laced the windows of the top two floors, and the front doors were a dark wood with square Judas holes in each.

"This man's afraid of something," Joe said.

"Evidently," Ballard agreed. "I been around back. The place is surrounded by a wall—eight foot. It's like its own Medieval fortress, fully enclosed. There's a delivery door back there but it's set pretty tight."

"Rich people, especially rich French people, don't trust poor people, especially poor foreign people," Quire said.

"But like I said," Joe said, "he isn't French."

"No. He isn't, but he tries to be."

Joe leaned against the brick of the building behind him. He took a deep breath and looked around at the street and the quilted sky above and the light rain still falling and the front of Marcel's home. He looked for something he could not find.

He said, "What would make a man sell out the lives of so many of his countrymen? His friends? I get the money part, but I still don't understand."

Ballard answered, "What would make a man produce defective ammunition for you and me to use in that war? Like you said—money. Just money."

"Men do things for only two reasons, love or money. Money is all this man loves," Quire added.

"How can it be worth it?"

"You're asking the wrong guy, brother," Quire said. "All of my money came from my old man, and that son of a bitch didn't care where his came from."

"Shit." It could have been any one of three voices that said it.

There was a long silence during which Joe again looked around. A hidden moon, no lampposts, no people walking, no automobiles, no lights in nearby house windows. Only a dark and leprous night, cold and wet and tactile.

Ballard broke the silence, "We should do something, and we should begin doing it."

"All right," Joe said. "What do you think?"

"Ballard goes around back and finds his way in or stops whoever tries leaving."

"And us?"

"We have two choices."

"They are?"

"Either you follow me or I follow you."

"Goddamn but you're a strategist."

"I do my best."

"Shit," said Ballard. "Let's do it."

Quire rolled his shoulders like a boxer between early rounds and took the first step into the street. As they crossed to Gadwa's house, he said, "Remember. Start tight, stay tight."

"Shut up with that shit," Ballard said. He picked up the valise and carried it with him.

Each step toward Gadwa's house opened another cleft in Joe's reservoir of remembered deaths and losses. Even with the night air a palpable cold, he could feel a ball of sweat run his spine.

Ballard separated from them and made his way into the shadows that lined the houses and around to the back. Of the two windows on the building's lower floor, one had light behind the heavy curtains and the other darkness. They went first to the dark. The window was double-hung, and the bottom of the windowsill was even with Joe's chin. He pushed up on the lower half but no movement. The window was latched shut.

"Give me your knee," Joe said.

Quire bended to one knee and braced his other leg behind him, his shoulder against the building. Joe stood on Quire's elevated knee and held the window's frame to look in at the lock, a simple brass rotating latch fastened where the double-hung windows overlapped.

Joe dropped to the ground and bent next to Quire.

"We'll have to break the glass," he said.

"First," Quire said, placing a levelling hand on Joe's shoulder. "Let's have a look inside that lit window and see what we may be up against."

Joe smiled. "Since when did you stop to think before jumping into action?"

"It doesn't happen very often, so you should take heed of it when it does."

Joe nodded.

They crossed the front walk. Once again Quire boosted Joe up so that he could peer through a finger opening in the drapes.

Gadwa and Dapper stood in front of a fire in the brick fireplace. Dapper was buttoning the front of his overcoat while Gadwa held a glass of brandy. He held the glass as if he were offering it for view, the way a man does when he wants to remind others of their relative position to him.

The floor was hardwood and shined in reflection of the fire. Gadwa and Dapper, however, stood on an Oriental rug, rust-colored and worn only slightly from use.

Marie sat cross-legged on a sofa and her hands in her lap. She looked at the fire. Joe saw only her portrait in profile but could see that she had recently been crying. The skin around her eyes was maroon. A smudge of black mascara remained on her cheek. Joe watched her chest move with unsettled breaths. The Turk hovered near her.

The sofa Marie sat on was antique and elaborate in its design and construction, something from some Louis who had spent the lives of his countrymen on his own comfort. The mantel held small statues ready for observation. Sepia portraits and small paintings, neither modern nor Impressionist but much older, ringed the walls. It looked like the type of room some people might call home, but Joe saw sterility and falsity and pretense.

In the fireplace behind Gadwa and Dapper, a full fire popped and hissed. Joe smelled the sweet smell of burning wood, a smell that would usually remind him of his boyhood home.

Gadwa looked like a man entertaining guests in a pre-yule time fete—brandy and a warming fire and conversation.

Joe saw all that in a short time, just long enough to have peeked through the narrow opening in the curtains and scan the room. Then he dropped beside Quire and whispered, "Just the four." He held up four fingers. "Marie, Gadwa, Dapper, and the Turk. That guy at Marie's was right."

"Dapper the dandy who gave me my shiner?"

Joe smiled and Quire smiled back. His blue eyes shined significantly in the darkness, and he started for the front door.

Joe placed a hand to Quire's shoulder then a finger over his own mouth. He held out his hand, palm downward, to signal that Quire slow down and wait for a moment. He whispered to Quire, "Listen to that little voice that wants you to think before acting."

The time had come. Joe knew that he could not hold it back any longer, but he needed Quire's assistance first. "Help me through the window," he said.

"Let's make it quick."

They re-crossed to the darkened window. Joe took off his overcoat and wrapped the Webley inside. He tapped his hand to gauge the strength of this softened mallet, unwrapped and rewrapped with less insulation around the butt of the pistol, and winked at Quire. "Ready?"

"Just don't swing for the fence, Babe."

"A tap should do it."

Quire bended his knee again and Joe stood. His first swing bounced from the glass with little more than a dull thud. The second swing hit more fully and more forcefully, streaking a crack from the bottom center of the glass where Joe had hit it to the top right corner. Another, softer blow sent the glass into a spider web of cracks.

Joe dropped his gun and overcoat to the ground and began poking at the broken glass until he had loosened a few pieces enough to push them into the room. They hit the wood floor with more sound than Joe was prepared for. He fixed himself to jump and run had the noise been heard from the other room. Nothing. He pulled another couple of pieces loose and dropped them in the bushes until he could reach through with his hand and unlatch the window. He felt a shard cut a single line along his forearm.

Jumping back down to the ground, he said, "I'll go through the window. When you hear things going down, you come in. Break it down if you have to."

"A little gunplay, Wyatt."

"Just don't shoot one of the good guys."

Quire pushed open the window then cupped his hands for Joe to use as a prop. "You watch your back," Quire said.

"You do the same," said Joe.

"Ain't no thing for me. I'll be in there soon."

Joe stepped onto the brace of hands and pulled himself up and over the sill. He stood for a moment looking into the dark precinct of the room until his eyes adjusted and he could make out the outline of furniture, electric floor lamps, the outlines on the walls where pictures hung, and the cord of light at the bottom of the door to his left.

One last look out the window at Quire padding to the front room window to watch as things began. Joe listened to the sounds of muffled voices, but could hear little more than his heart beating in his ears. From a long ways off, he heard the thrum of thunder sounding like artillery rounds. Standing in that dark room with a sliver of yellow light at the bottom of a door he was set to open, he drew a deep breath and felt the muscles of his body pulled as tight as a bow string.

XII

*After a bombardment which continued for seventy-five hours, the French
human wave started forward by irresistible bounds.*
—Henri Vast, *Little History of the Great War*

JOE TURNED THE GLASS DOORKNOB IN SLOW TEMPO. WHEN HE HAD
pushed the door less than an inch, he looked through the sliced
opening. He saw nobody and continued opening the door to expand
his field of vision. Against the wall opposite from Joe, a girandole
holding four tapered candles sat on a wood hall table like a chancel
lamp. The feathered flames of the candles lit the entranceway, and the
flames of the candles bent then righted themselves as Joe stepped
through the doorway then closed the door behind him.

Feeling like the thief in the night, he walked to the open doorway
from behind which came the sounds of voices. He felt a little tremble
in his free hand and clenched it into a fist, the other hand held the
Webley. He breathed deep and silently, then stepped close to
the corner and listened. The voices were of two men and a woman,
Marie.

He looked quickly, peering around the door frame and looking
only through his left eye. A fire bounced from the hardwood mantel
behind Marcel and the Turk. Marie sat on the sofa near the fireplace.
The two men stood together at the mantel, ignoring Marie.

He could not see Dapper. If Dapper had left the room, Joe
wondered whether Quire would stick to the original plan, as nebu-
lous as it was. Quire wanted Dapper. That might take precedence in
Quire's mind.

He leaned close to the edge of the doorway, eavesdropping again
on the conversation in the other room.

Gadwa and the Turk spoke in French. Joe could understand most of what they were saying—driving that night for Lausanne. In Switzerland, nobody cared where one's money came from and the Swiss had a myopic view of the world that extended only as far as their own borders. With his riches secure in Swiss banks, Gadwa would be rich and free, regardless of the blood on his hands.

"The train would be faster," the Turk said.

"True," said Gadwa. "However, the trains establish our itinerary. With an automobile, we have the freedom to change our plans if necessary. We also have more control over our baggage."

"*Oui*," said the Turk.

Marie said, "You lied to me."

"*Oui*." In the way Gadwa dropped the word, Joe could imagine it being accompanied by a dismissive huff and wave of the hand. "We have been through this," he said.

"You lied to me," she repeated. "For years, you lied. Everything you do and say is a lie."

Joe heard her stand and walk. "You tried to kill my brother." He heard her slap Gadwa, a flat sound like raw meat dropped on wood.

He heard another slap and then someone fall back. That sound almost began the violence. "Your brother will be dead soon. And the American will either be here to save your life . . . or not."

No answer.

Gadwa said, "We should leave soon, within the half hour. If he does not arrive, then I must deal with whatever happens."

"Shall I bring around the automobile?" asked the Turk.

"Yes. Send Bert. The bags are stowed in the back?"

"*Oui*."

"We should pack some wine for the trip and make sure we have blankets. The ride is long and cold."

"And her?"

"Later."

"And if he comes?"

"All the better." In his mind, Joe could see the words spoken with a smirk and received with a smile.

A silence beneath a shuffling of feet.

A couple of fuses in Joe's brain burst in anger. He saw a kaleido-scope of reds and blacks. Only one thought focused in his mind. That thought was darkness.

He took a second to breathe then stood and felt the familiar adrenaline kick of fear and excitement. This had all begun years before on a single haze-laden morning in central France. This had all begun that long-ago day with the sun rising to greet the deaths of 20,000 young men. Men whose lives were ended like candle flames in the wind. But it had all come to that night and that room in that house on a cobblestone street near the Sacré Coeur in Paris. Where, when, and how it had all begun belonged in other men's histories. Its ending, however, was Joe's.

He felt balanced. He was wanted for killing people in America, on the Atlantic crossing, and in France, as well as for attacking the sheriff in Greenwich and any number of other crimes both high and small. He felt set to face down a man who had sold out his country as well as the lives of thousands of his own comrades. He was outnumbered. If that were not enough, he had no home, no job, an enormous henchman ready to murder him in a shake. All-in-all, a shifting world in which he stood. Still, his pulse beat slow and steady. He stood resolved that his world had spiraled to that place and that moment in time, and in that place and time he was resolved to end the spiral.

"It ends now," he heard his voice echo within his mind. He stepped into the room. In a moment slowed to its increments, Joe saw Gadwa turn as though with an inchoate sense that the room's dynamics had changed, saw the Turk begin his draw and Marie's surprise, and he saw two other men standing in the far corner of the room. They backed through the door behind them, flipping off the electric ceiling light as they left and leaving the room lit only from the flames in the fireplace.

Joe was surprised at how quickly Gadwa saw and reacted, raising the revolver he had taken from Joe on the train as Joe aimed the Webley. The Turk, however, was faster than either Gadwa or Joe and fired first, grazing Joe's arm and knocking him off balance. A quick and short volley of rounds erupted between the triad of shooters. A crash of pottery glass and a single slow moan of pain followed.

Joe fell behind a padded chair, the thickness of which offered no protection. His left arm ached from the bullet's grazing, a burning pain as though stabbed by hot pokers. The bullet had opened a small trough on his arm, more bloody than harmful. He flexed to test his strength. It remained, more or less.

From his place behind a single chair, Joe looked and saw Gadwa sitting in a crumpled heap on the floor, holding his arm. A vase lay in shards on the mantel and on the bricks in front of the burning fire. Water ran in corded streams inside the mortar amid the broken vase and the loose pipettes of flowers.

Joe heard a shuffling from behind some chairs across from him followed by two undirected and errant shots, one of which splintered the wood on the wall behind him and the other sent the window into an eruption of glass. He fired four quick shots from the Webley toward the Turk, and retrieved his Smith & Wesson from where Gadwa had dropped it, moving to behind another insufficient chair for cover. The room danced only in the amber shadows of the fireplace. He hid in silence in the darkness of a corner away from the fire's fingers of light.

"Cabrion?" he heard Gadwa call to the Turk.

Joe waited for the response, but the Turk was too smart to acknowledge.

He waited some more. The sight of Marie's eyes entered his mind, her eyes as he had stepped into the room, eyes surfeit with terror and confusion. He held the impulse to call to her as he held the impulse to shoot. In the dancing darkness of the room, he felt the familiar architecture of his past, one of fear and violence. Except, in that room's battle he knew who he wanted to kill and why he wanted to kill that man. The knowledge neither comforted him nor troubled him. His hand did not shake, nor did his desire to kill slacken.

He checked the Webley and found it empty. He checked his Smith & Wesson, a single chamber hollow, and others filled with 325-grain roundtip bullets. He heard the whispered French of another man as that man stepped into the doorway from which he had entered. The man was small. His eyes, lit in the fire's glow were like a weasel's. He wore a coat and hat too large for him and would have looked comical in his desire to be a big man if not for the large pistol he held.

Joe registered the information in a blink. Without consideration, he flipped the cylinder shut and swung the revolver in a slow curve, light running along its barrel. The little man saw the reflection and began his own reaction. Completing his arc of action, however, Joe fired once into the middle of the little man's body. The little man fell backward into a pile with his over-large clothes and did not move beyond a final convulsion followed by a high, liquid gurgle.

After another series of shots that sailed above Joe's head, the room fell back into a silence in which Joe felt himself trapped. He was backed into a corner with a thin chair for cover. Gadwa hid behind a sofa. The Turk lay behind some overturned chairs. Quire was nowhere, as was Ballard, who was probably unlucky enough to have been ambushed around back of the house.

Marie was lost inside the room's field of fire.

"You are trapped, Monsieur Henry," called Gadwa. "Mademoiselle Dillard is here . . . with me. You do not wish to injure her. Give up your weapon and possibly we can come to some sort of accommodation."

Joe looked from behind his chair. In the dark room, he could not find Marie. He hoped that Gadwa was lying, but even if he were, Joe knew that Marie was caught somewhere within the lines of fire.

"Damn," Joe whispered.

"*Quoi?*" Gadwa asked.

"No damn way." A silence followed.

That short silence was broken by the Turk, who fired again at Joe. A bullet passed over Joe's head, its wind and whistle close enough to cast shadows.

"Shit," Joe screamed and let loose, firing quickly and tightly toward where he had seen the muzzle flashes. The revolver bucked like it wanted to jump from his hand and make its own separate peace. He heard a grunt like an animal. He kept firing until he heard the hollow click of an empty chamber.

Tired from the pain and the loss of blood from his wound, he stood and listened and watched for the Turk or Marie or Gadwa.

Although his wound was not deep, it bled readily. His mouth was dry. The breath he drew in had the texture of red sand and lodged in his throat dry and barren.

"Cabrion?" Gadwa called again, and again there was no answer. Joe felt certain that the reason had changed, that the Turk could not answer now because he was dead.

Joe's concern then was with Dapper and the other man who had left the room when he had first entered. He hoped that the little man in the large coat was one of those original two, but that still left Dapper unaccounted for. Then that last soldier became accounted for as Joe heard the sound of a car coming to life and then the opening of large carriage doors and then the surety of shots fired and the automobile left to run in the absence of its driver.

"*Décès*," Joe said to no answer. "It looks like it's just you and me, Gadwa."

"We can make a deal, Mr. Henry. You, yourself, commented on my wealth."

"No deal, Mr. Gadwa."

He decided to chance that Frederick Gadwa was the coward he had proven himself to be, that the man who had taken Rene Marcel's name and surrounded himself with henchmen could only kill through others. He stood and crossed the room to turn on the electric ceiling light.

Near him lay the Turk. In front of the fireplace stood Gadwa, blood showing through the sleeve covering his left arm which wrapped around Marie. In Gadwa's right hand was another small Webley pistol.

"Dammit," Joe said, shaking his head. "Webleys grow on trees around here?"

He looked down at the Turk, who lay motionless on his side, one arm bent under his head as though he were cradling himself to sleep and the other reaching impossibly for the pistol that lay several inches from his curled fingers. He lay on his side with his neck twisted so that he looked with dead eyes at the ceiling. Blood percolated from a hole in his chest, and another hole opened most of his cheek and exposed the dark and bloodied cavern of his mouth.

Looking down on the Turk, Joe recalled something his major had said one frosted morning in the Argonne, that more death does not mean anything other than just more death.

As dark stains formed in the lines of the dead man's neck, Joe bent and touched the pistol, its barrel still warm and placed his emptied revolver on the floor next to it. His entire body ached and he was beyond tired, a weariness deep within his bones and a weariness that had been building within him for years.

"It seems that once again I hold the trump card," Gadwa said and smiled.

Joe looked at Marie, tears in her brown eyes and lines of tears down the sides of her nose. Her eyes wide, dark, and undone against the pale of her skin. She stood in that hushed moment of uncertainty.

"I wouldn't be so certain," said Quire from the entryway, holding the small brown valise in one hand and a pistol in the other. Beads of sweat had formed on his brow, and blood had dried from a cut on his cheek. Blood also stained the fronts of his shirt and coat as he entered the room like a combatant stepping from the tableau of a bloodied field. While his breathing was unsteady and emphysemic, the aim of his revolver was as steady as his stare.

They formed a triangle with each watching the movements of the others. Gadwa held the barrel of his pistol against the side of Marie's head, Quire had his revolver aimed toward Gadwa's good shoulder, and Joe stood without a gun in his hand. Gadwa's wounded arm wrapped around Marie's shoulder, holding tight to her upper body. The blood in the wound to his shoulder remained red and sharp and glistening in the room's light and dripped onto her side. Blood also ran from his nose, staining Marie's shoulder and dripping to the wood floor.

Gadwa said, "Since I have Miss Dillard as a shield, I believe that I remain in control. Drop your weapon."

"Think again. You won't shoot her because then I'd kill you deader than shit, and if you use her as that shield, she'll die and then so will you. And the longer we stand here talking, the better chance of the police arriving for you. Not something you want, I'm sure," said Quire. "So think about this. A trade. The girl for this suitcase. That's what you wanted."

"The manuscript?"

"The manuscript," Joe said. "We came here to make the trade, just like you planned. Your men were too fast on the draw, so we didn't have time to talk. Now we do. I give you the manuscript, you give me Marie."

"Open it," Gadwa spat.

Quire coughed a single laugh and handed the brown valise to Joe. "Open it, Joe," he said. "I don't especially want to drop my pistol." He did not look at Joe nor did he wipe away a runnel of blood that had started down his cheek from the cut there. Joe cradled the valise in his good arm and opened it. He picked up a sheaf of pages wrapped in string and held it up for Gadwa to see, then returned the pages to the valise.

"So?" Joe asked as he closed the valise.

"Well, shit," said Ballard as he entered the room from the door behind Joe. "There's been a lot of killing here tonight. Two in here and the two we shot dead out back by the automobile. Just one more killing," he said as he raised his pistol to aim straight at Gadwa. "One more killing and this thing's done."

Quire smiled and said, "What we have here is a Mexican stand-off inside a French house between expatriate Americans and a false Brit. There's got to be something like irony in there, don't you think, Mr. Gadwa?"

"I don't even know what you're saying," Gadwa said. His voice cracked from frustration at trying to decipher Quire's words and maybe even at the growing realization that his night had turned over on him.

"What he's saying," offered Joe, "is that we each have something the other wants, and we have more guns. You can't have this manuscript until you let her go, and you won't let her go until you have the manuscript."

"How long does this last?" Marie asked. Her voice did not crack although Joe heard something like her own frustration. He looked at Quire, who smiled but did not avert his eyes or his aim from Gadwa.

"Up to him, sweetheart," Quire said.

Joe saw concern in Gadwa's eyes. The longer the game played out, the worse for Gadwa. That, Joe knew. He could see from the sweat on Gadwa's forehead that Gadwa had also come to realize it. This would not end well for the traitor.

"Oh, *mon dieux*," Marie said. She grabbed Gadwa's gun hand with her right hand and she pushed the thumb of her left hand into Gadwa's shoulder wound.

Gadwa screamed and shot, but Marie had pulled the pistoled hand from her direction. The bullet struck Quire in the chest. He bounced back on drunken legs and went down with a groan.

Marie fell to the floor. Joe ran to her. Gadwa aimed again at Joe. Joe looked up into the barrel hole at the end of the Webley, at how damn large that cavern was from which a heavy-grain bullet would exit.

A single shot exploded and Gadwa fell backward, both arms now useless and bloodied from gunshot wounds. He stood, eyes wide like a frightened and cornered animal, but Ballard shot again, taking out one of Gadwa's legs. The traitor went down and could not stand again. He sat ruined on the floor like an old marionette, his feet splayed in front of him and blood running from wounds to three places on his body.

Ballard stepped closer to stand over Gadwa, who lay on the floor trying to stop the bleeding and the pain in his arms and leg. Sweat ran down the side of Ballard's face. His eyes had lost meaning, black coals deep and burning and seeing the deaths of his friends so many bloodred mornings earlier on that terrible and misted field of great death.

"You still with us, Quire-man?"

Quire moaned, "Shit but that hurt."

Ballard laughed. "Better'n being dead."

He leveled his pistol against Gadwa's temple. He said as his finger tensed on the trigger, "You're lucky my friends need you, else you'd be dead right now."

He dropped the aim of his pistol, then said, "Oh, what the hell." He casually placed the pistol back against Gadwa's temple and pulled the trigger. The firing pin hit on an empty chamber. He laughed a full and deep laugh.

Gadwa wet himself, a pool of liquid expanding around his body to join with the blood spilling from his wounds.

"Piss-ant," said Quire, sitting with his hand against his chest and with blood showing bright and red through his fingers. "Don't let the ball play you, son, you play the ball."

"Hell's that mean?" Joe asked.

"Don't know," said Quire. "But my sergeant used to say it every morning before we went over the top, just before he put his Bible in his chest pocket." Quire held the small Bible up for Joe to see, a bloody hole through it.

"The preachments saved you?"

"Hell, no," said Quire. "Bullet went right through the good book, Genesis through Revelations, and into my damn chest. One more thing I can't trust."

"Who is he?" asked Marie.

"A friend of mine."

"You have funny friends."

"Good friends."

"It is over now?" Marie asked, her eyes soft, and Joe recognized what had first drawn him to her. He nodded, and she said, "*Oui*," with a softness, and Joe knew that maybe, after all, the right person and the right time had met.

Marie pulled the valise to her. "It was all over this," she said. "A book."

"No," said Joe. "It was all over a lie."

"Lies and money," Marie said.

"You don't know the half," said Ballard. "In that auto he was planning on driving away in, I found two suitcases filled with Swiss francs." He whistled. "Legal tender for all debts public and private."

"And there's our payment for a job well done," Quire said.

"*Batard*," Marie spat. A tear rolled from her eye and she repeated in English, "Bastard. And for this?" She held a sheaf of papers from the valise. "All for this?"

"No, not for that," Joe said. "That manuscript exists, and I'll see it published, but that's not it."

"What's this then?"

"Look."

"What are you saying?" asked Gadwa.

"Insult to injury," said Quire, as he stuffed a pocket handkerchief underneath his shirt and over the wound.

Marie slid the valise to Gadwa, who opened it and read the name on the pages of papers. His bloody hands shook, from pain or rage. "Who is this Hemingway? This is not it."

Quire laughed.

He bent over, coughed and spit, and said, "Damn, but this hurts. I'd forgot how much pain a little piece of lead can cause."

Gadwa threw the papers into the fire, pulled another handful from the valise, inspected them and tossed them into the flames as well. His hands had been dyed red from his wounds and the blood stained the pages as he grasped them and the valise where he touched it.

Gadwa then smiled. "Without the manuscript, how will you prove anything that you are saying?" He looked at Joe with a slick smile.

Quire shrugged. "We'll think of something."

Marie said, "My brother is still alive. When I visited him this afternoon, he talked. The doctors told me that they are optimistic." She looked at Gadwa, "Paul will be able to explain."

Gadwa snorted. "I sent one of my men to his room tonight to kill him. So you see, it is your word against mine. The police will accept mine long enough for me to leave the country."

Quire said, "If that fellow you sent is that short, little, dapper dressing fellow, he's got a third eye in his forehead. He'll be making his bed with a shovel tonight."

Gadwa sat back against a leg of the sofa, his body hunched even further into itself.

"And," said Joe. "I sat across from Gresham long enough to see his routine when he wrote—everything in triplicate. One copy of the manuscript ended up in the mud in Greenwich when your men ran off the road. The other copy I placed in a small case on the train. If the owners don't take it to the police, I can trace them through an American Express office."

"But you don't. . . ." Gadwa said with a hint of confidence.

"No. I don't, but I have a good idea where they are. I know them from the ship, but even if they tossed out the copy I placed in their baggage, I know where the final copy is. In a safe deposit box in Greenwich. He had one copy to take with him to France—the copy your men stole from the house after shooting him. He sent one to Paul. The other copy would have been stored for his safe return. It's there and waiting to be read by the right set of eyes."

Ballard added, "It appears to me, you traitorous son of a bitch, that your pancake butt has been handed to you."

The distanced sounds of sirens came closer, and Ballard said, "I'll be driving that car away now. Stop by my apartment in a couple of days, and we'll have a money dividing party."

"Will do, brother," said Quire. "And you two might as well leave. I'll either have me a room at the hospital, hopefully the American Hospital on Victor Hugo, or else in some dank penal institution. I'd appreciate it if you could, and make it quick. I got me a date with that French dame from the Gentilhomme next week for St. Cathrine's Day. Get me a lawyer because I can foresee this mess getting deep. Get one for yourself before you come in. Lawyer that is."

Joe nodded.

"Go," Quire said. "Don't worry about this old bastard. Remember, I have luck with trouble."

"I thought you had luck for trouble."

"Luck for, luck with. Same thing. Now go." He smiled, then added with a wave of his hand, "I need a surgeon and both of you need something the night don't hold."

"Yes," Marie said. "We could use some rest."

"What's the night have to do with rest?" Quire laughed. "Now go."

The city's fog had not lifted although it had lessened. The rain had eased and then ceased as they walked away from the house and had left dark liquid pools shimmering in the rain darkened street. A few morning stars shown through the clouds, distant as diamonds. In his youth, Joe had imagined a world rich in possibilities. He could almost imagine that again as he walked down the street next to the woman he wanted very much to be in love with.

They passed the pantheonic structure of the white-stoned Sacré Coeur, and Marie said, "How beautiful it is in the night." Her voice cracked as brittle as her tears.

She reached her hand for his. He took hers in his. Joe rolled his fingers around her hand, cool and fragile and strong at once.

"Come," she repeated. "Walk with me."

Joe stepped close to her. They walked together, their arms touching electric in the dark night. He took his hand from hers and put his arm around her and she moved into the circle of his arm. The lights of the Sacré Coeur cast a warm yellow glow around them, and they walked a long time without speaking.